The Legend of the Blade

T. James Reese

Veritas et Virtute
Media Production

For Liam, Samantha, & Garrett – I love you with all of my heart.

"A single dream is more powerful than a thousand realities."

J.R.R. Tolkein

CONTENTS

14th Century Japan

The year 1303 of the Kamakura Period

1

DAYS OF OLD

Snow crunched beneath his feet with each labored step. He'd traveled on foot for days, climbing to the crest of the tallest peak in the treacherous range of mountains that surrounded the quiet valley below. The air grew thin and he found himself short of breath, exhausted by the arduous terrain.

He stopped momentarily to rest, turning to look back down the snowy mountainside, the fading trail of his solitary footprints a reminder of the lonely burden only he could bear. Slowly, he pulled back the hood on his thick, leather-hide wrap, revealing his young, tired face. He looked but a boy, his cheeks still round with youth, but his body was strong, lean, and tall. A long black braid fell from his shoulder and hung at his waste. His dark, piercing eyes squinting in the bright sunlight.

His journey was far from complete. The young man turned his attention to the unmarked snow that laid ahead, the top of the mountain still a half-day's climb away. The twinge of hunger haunted him as the cold wind bit at his face and he knew he could not linger. Amidst his pain, his desire for warmth, for food; he pressed on.

With another heavy step, he continued onward towards the summit.

His own village had once rested at the foot of this mountain, but that was a decade ago, before the rise of Takeshi Hasegawa, usurper, self-proclaimed emperor. The old village – his childhood home – was now nothing more than a faint memory. Hasegawa had seen to that, a secret until only recently too well guarded. He did his best to stave off the unwelcome thoughts, but the slope of the mountain grew steeper with every step and all too soon he felt his legs go numb, falling headlong into the snow, his eyes slowly closing as his body gave in to the elements.

His unguarded mind flooded with memories, some never before recalled. They flickered quickly: his home, his family, the other children he grew up with; all orphaned in the same attacks that spread across the entire valley. No village was spared.

I must not fail, he warned himself, managing to open his eyes.

With great difficulty, he tried to raise himself up, but his weakened arms gave way and he collapsed back down once again. This time, he did not struggle. The lonely young man passed out, surrendering to his thoughts, traveling back to his childhood in his forgotten memories.

"Sheng? Sheng? Sheng-bō!" a woman's soft voice called out, startling the young boy awake.

I know that voice, he smiled, his eyes twinkling as he rubbed the sleep from them.

"Breakfast," she announced.

The boy stood from his mat on the floor and pulled on his robe, his shaggy black hair sticking up in places. Hurriedly, he raced down the hand-hewn wooden stairs of his family's home.

Warm summer air breezed through the open front doorframe as he stumbled into the large room that held both the kitchen and sitting quarters. Only ten, Sheng was a spitting image of his father, his hero, who he quickly scanned the room for.

"Where's father?" he asked, finding his mother alone, her eyes sad.

Slowly, she answered, her voice soft and full of concern, "The *daimyō* has called your father to battle, as well as the rest of the men in the village, beyond the mountains."

She pointed out the window at a tall mountain rising high into the clouds above, using the moment to look away as an opportunity to hide her tears.

"When will he come back?" Sheng wondered.

"He will return when those that threaten us are gone," she said with hope. "Now, eat and go play with your friends. Don't worry for your father. He is a *samurai*, and very brave."

With those words, she disappeared out the back door, her bare feet slapping against the hard planks of the wooden floor. Sheng thought he heard her cry. Leaving his bowl on the table, he stood and peered out the door. The porch was empty. His mother was gone.

Sheng thought nothing more of it as he ran back upstairs and changed into his worn, pale gray play clothes. The men of the village had gone to war many times, always returning home to their families. Why would this be any different? His father, same as his fellow samurai, was strong, fierce. Sheng truly believed there was nothing to fear.

Properly dressed, he quickly raced back down to the lower floor and hurried out the front door, slipping his toes into his sandals as he stepped out into the sunshine. His family's residence stood at the end of many winding pathways lined with small, well-built wooden huts with thatched roofs. Their house was nothing grand, but much bigger than the others surrounding it. In all, ten samurai families claimed ownership of the land, each of their large homes surrounded by the smaller dwellings of loyal villagers who tended the crops and helped to maintain the properties. All this was granted by the daimyō who they served.

Sheng's father was the un-appointed leader. His great grandfather had been one of the founders of the village nearly a century earlier, swearing his allegiance to the daimyō and the *shogunate*, so his family had always held a place of respect, though never demanding it. They humbly lived their lives like everyone else. His mother worked side by side with the other women in the fields and his father raised cattle and chickens. The village itself was guarded by a heavy timbered wall built around the perimeter. The housing was set to the rear of the compound, a town square was found at the center of the community with space for the market and traveling vendors to offer their wares. Battlements watched the gated entrance. This was also the area where the men trained their bodies and minds for combat, practicing daily in the martial arts and both close quarter and ranged weapons – the sword and bow.

On this day, the village was unusually quiet. The normally busy paths typically packed with merchants and conversing old men were strangely, almost morbidly, bare. As he walked past the small huts, he searched for his friends, but all the windows were empty. Here and there, women walked to and from the market or the gardens, minding their daily work, trying to push away the fear of war.

"*AAAAAHHHHHEEEE YAAAAHHHH!*" a scream came from up ahead.

Sheng froze. His fingers instinctively clenched into fists.

Did the fighting come to the village? he thought, his mind racing.

He hurried around the corner of an abandoned cart of goods but stopped quickly, kicking up dust from the cobbled path. Nearly thirty children were standing in a circle, the bald head of the town elder barely visible in the crowd. A shaky voice rose from among the children.

"And then the terrible dragon flew back up into the sky, once more circling the encampment!" the elder exclaimed.

Sheng realized it wasn't an attack. He was missing one of Old Shou's stories. The old man shouted out once again, his face red and exasperated as he exaggerated the flapping of the dragon's wings, flailing his arms dramatically as he roared hoarsely. The children burst into laughter at Shou's wildly comical theatrics. Finally, Sheng spotted his best friend leaning against a short stone wall that encircled the square, an ancient water well just beyond, marking the center of the village.

"Suke-chan…" he whispered, sneaking around the crowd to approach the rather portly boy from behind.

With a very mischievous grin, he turned, shrugging his thick black hair out of his eyes. His round face, cheeks rosy and bright, greeted Sheng without a word.

Sheng stepped alongside Daisuke, overshadowed by his friend's large frame. *Suke-chan*, as the children called him, was one of the biggest boys in the village, a fact of which Daisuke himself was very proud. One would assume he was a bully by looking at him, but he had a kind heart and only raised his voice when he came to one of his companions' aid.

Daisuke's arm thudded around Sheng's shoulders in a friendly embrace, his chubby hand looking like a giant cured ham. Sheng looked up at him smiling, feeling his knees weaken under Daisuke's weight.

They happily listened as Old Shou continued on, speaking in different voices. His stories were always incredible: tales of jade-green dragons and caves bursting with hidden treasures, of sword fights and glorious battles, and of samurai and their honorable way of life. The adventures were never ending. His boney arms waived high in the air, his old skin hanging loosely and flapping with each movement. With every word, Shou's eyes widened more and more with the anticipation of each expressive word, the masterful spinning of a tale.

By some of the villagers' accounts, they believed Old Shou to be at least one hundred years old, give or take a few harvests. He was so old in fact that even he could not remember his own age; but his stories, those he never forgot. He was delirious and delusional, but most importantly, loved by all. The hot sun reflected off his gleaming, sweaty head, a long, scraggly, white beard covering most of his face. Stumbling around on his large, old feet, he looked out of place surrounded by so many youthful dreamers.

With one last, triumphant yell, Shou finished his story, the overjoyed group laughing and clapping their hands loudly in thanks. The only-moments-ago nimble Old Shou bowed, then hobbled towards the tea house, his trusty cane in hand. His tale complete, the children all headed off to play, separating into smaller groups of friends and going their separate ways. Sheng and Daisuke headed for the front gate.

There, just beyond the protective walls, they saw the silhouette of a young girl standing atop a grassy hill. Her name was Kimiko. Her soft hair was pulled back into a tight ponytail and she wore a pretty silver chain around her neck, the chain adorned with a small stone charm: a birthday gift from Sheng, handcrafted from an oddly shaped rock he'd found while they'd explored a shallow riverbed nearby. As usual, her mother had dressed her in a fine *kimono*, this one made of beautifully embroidered red and gold silk. She was standing in her bare feet, alone as she looked up at the mountain that loomed ominously over the whole valley.

Sheng tugged on Daisuke's sleeve and they headed up the hill. Kimiko heard the heavy footsteps of Suke-chan coming up behind her and turned, a half-smile on her pale face.

"Our fathers have gone," she said matter-of-factly. "They're chasing bandits on horseback."

Despite her show, Sheng noticed her eyes welling with tears.

"They'll be alright," Sheng declared. "Our village has strong men and our fathers have never lost in battle. They will come home, Kimi-chan."

His confidence was reassuring.

"I want to be a warrior just like them." Suke-chan said, breaking the sad silence, loudly slamming his clenched fist into his open palm.

"Me too!" Sheng grinned excitedly.

"Really?! You two? Brave warriors?!" Kimiko challenged, as she turned and ran away, giggling down the hill. "You can't even catch me!"

The boys looked at each other, then watched as she disappeared into the village. Their mischievous grins faded as they realized she was getting away.

"Come on!" Suke-chan shouted eagerly.

They raced after her as fast as they could, but she was quicker than either of them. Sheng swiftly passed his large friend and headed into the village, Suke-chan wheezing along behind him. They followed the path they thought she'd taken, but she was nowhere to be seen. After pausing to catch their breath, they looked in and behind barrels, around shrubs, anywhere Kimiko could be hiding; but she was gone – disappearing seemingly into thin air.

The boys continued searching every hiding place they could think of when they soon heard her laughing. After all that, she'd been hiding by the well in the center of the village all along and they'd ran right past her! Sheng and Suke-chan headed toward the sound of her laughter, Daisuke clutching his chest wincing, still trying to breathe.

"Too slow!" she yelled, jumping up and racing out of the square, then back up the hill that faced the mountain.

The friends followed, trying desperately to catch up. But Kimiko was tireless and managed an ever-growing distance between herself and the exasperated boys. She was nearly out of sight when suddenly she stopped and they found her once again standing at the top of the hill, though this time she wasn't smiling. Standing at her side, they followed the fearful glower on her tear streaked face. Four dozen horses were galloping towards the village, their riders adorned in battle-scarred red and black armor. The man in the lead was flanked by another samurai who carried a green canvas banner that flapped in the wind, a circled-cross embroidered on its face: the *mon* of the *Shimazu* clan.

"Father!" Sheng cried out.

2

THUNDER

Faint groans echoed down the dim hallway. Sheng peeked around the sliding door into his parent's bedroom. Shadows slowly moved in the candle light, visible through the thin paper walls

His mother's voice spoke softly, comforting his father. Sheng could see him resting on the floor, sitting with his legs crossed, as she carefully removed pieces of his marred and bloodied armor.

"Taekori, you're hurt!" she whispered. "I'll get bandages right away."

"Thank you, Amikori," he heard his father say.

Thick scars covered his father's arms, chest, and back: mementos from the many battles he'd fought. His body was a living record of the life his village was forced to endure, both the pro and con of service to the daimyō. She pulled his chest plate over his head and tended anxiously to the large purple bruises on his ribs. A bandage soaked in blood was wrapped around his father's shoulder. Sheng glanced at the armor and saw still-wet blood shining in the flickering light. Looking back, he felt the cold stare of his father's gray eyes piercing into him.

"Son…" was all Sheng heard, the rest was muffled in a deep cough.

Amikori quickly stood and came to the screen, "Please, Sheng, go to bed. Sleep. I will tend to your father."

"But," he protested.

"Goodnight," she replied softly, cutting him off before he could continue his argument.

She slid the screen shut and Sheng was alone. He watched her shadow through the thin wall as she hurried back to Taekori's wounds. Slowly, Sheng turned and shuffled back down the narrow, dark corridor before climbing the stairs and heading for his corner of the room where he laid down on his mat. Pulling his blanket up around him, he stared out the window at the stars, the painful moaning of his father still in his ears. Some of the other children in the village weren't so lucky – at least Sheng's father had returned home.

The next morning, Sheng excitedly woke before the roosters could announce the arrival of dawn. He ran downstairs as usual, nearly tripping over the last step as he stumbled into the large room at the bottom of the stairs. His mother was already up, steaming rice. Without a word, she glanced at Sheng, a warm smile on her beautiful face.

Amikori was quite young. She had married his father just after she had finished her schooling and Sheng was born within a year. He thought his mother didn't look much older than some of the girls in the village, but he knew that was not possible.

He smiled back at her and followed the nodding of her head out onto the back porch. His father was sitting on the steps. His robe was only half-worn, hanging loose from his shoulders and tied around his waist, covering his legs. His strong chest was bare, bandages caked with dried blood hiding the fresh wounds beneath.

As Sheng quietly approached him, he studied the intricately detailed and brightly colored *horimono* of a tiger that marked his father's back. The design was done in such a way that it appeared to be leaping off of him, the claws unleashed, the tiger's teeth bared as it snarled. Around the tattoo were thick, pink scars, each one a vivid memory of blood shed on the battlefield. The scars were intense, but Sheng's eyes moved back to the tattoo.

"I hope I did not scare you last night," his father said. "My injuries were not as severe as they appeared and your mother is a wonderful nurse. I'll be fine."

Sheng nodded, still looking at the tattoo.

"What is it, son?"

"The tiger," Sheng replied, touching the tattoo carefully, tracing the lines of the tiger's face with his finger, "what does it mean?"

Taekori smiled. "The tiger symbolizes strength and courage," he explained. "It is also protection against evil spirits."

"So you're like the tiger?" Sheng reasoned.

"I am the tiger," his father smiled, standing up and taking his son into his bruised, muscular arms with a warm, proud embrace.

"Do not worry for me, my boy," he said, holding him tightly. "I will always return to you!"

"Yes, father."

"Now go," Taekori chuckled, loosening his grasp, smiling at Amikori as he did. "Get yourself ready for breakfast. Hurry!"

Sheng ran back into the house as his mother grabbed him around his torso and kissed him on his forehead. He laughed, breaking loose from her. He stumbled back up the stairs and changed from his bed robes.

The midday sun rose high in the sky, warm and bright. All the people of the village headed for the square. A gathering had been called by the elders to discuss the details of the previous day's battle. Several of the men, including Sheng's father, stood by the well in front of the crowd. The children were all sent off to play in the fields as they began. An older man in green robes spoke eagerly, thanking the men for their quick action. As always, the men had fought valiantly, bringing honor to their families and the whole village in the eyes of the shogunate.

"It has been several seasons since raiders last threatened our valley. We owe a debt of gratitude to our brave warriors."

The crowd nodded silently in agreement.

"But I warn you," he continued, "the bandits who attacked us yesterday were well organized, not like the sort we've dealt with before. Please, Taekori, share what you know."

Sheng's father stood from where he'd been leaning against the well, his sword at his side. His ribs were obviously causing him pain, but he disguised it well.

"Thank you, Elder Hui," he began. "I am proud of all my fellow samurai. You fought more bravely than I could have asked. And, we must not forget the men who did not return from battle, but met a glorious death and have been reunited with our ancestors. We will continue on and honor them in their deaths. As Elder Hui said, these attackers were no mere raiders. I believe the bandits were not looting, but searching for something."

The villagers listened. A soft murmur spread from person to person like ripples on a pond.

"When we chased them from the village, we followed them up the foot of the great mountain," he said raising his arm to point with some difficulty, "We attacked before they could reach the temple."

Whispers now hissed loudly from the crowd that filled the square. Old Master Hui raised his hands to calm them but it had little effect.

"What would they want at the temple?" a farmer in the crowd yelled out. "It is not made of gold or jewels. There is no treasure there!"

Taekori gathered his thoughts and answered, slowly. "You are correct, my friend. The wealth in the temple is not precious jewels or gold. It is something that is beyond worth, something my family has guarded for centuries. I believe these men are followers of Takeshi Hasegawa, a man who has bought the loyalty of many daimyō in the North. He has rallied an army of assassins which he uses to scour the countryside searching for this *artifact*."

With those words, many in the group bowed low, covering their faces in humility. The artifact, by all appearances was a modest sword, a deeply held secret, a myth; but if it were true, the bearer would wield a power more imaginable than any in all of Japan. The sword held special powers: power to lead, power to fight. In the hands of a tyrant, it meant great suffering for all, at least that is what Taekori's progenitors believed. And so, the legend was born.

"Hasegawa's eyes are fixed on Kyoto and I believe he thinks the sword will grant him victory. When the blade was made, or how it came to be in my family's charge is unknown. But my forefathers kept it hidden from the many emperors, both good and evil, who have ruled and died. My ancestors were afraid of its power, knowing that absolute power can corrupt even those who led our people honorably. My family has been the guardians of this blade for many generations. And though only I know the location of the blade, the bandits must have believed it to be there in the temple for it is a secret place, the location breathed only as a rumor. Traversing the mountain is difficult, few could manage. Hundreds of men have died, seduced by the aspirations of glory that the blade promises to its master. Still…I promise it is safe," Taekori finished confidently, running his hand across the hilt of his sword.

Hui closed the meeting and everyone returned to their daily tasks. The village elders walked towards the tea house, whispering amongst themselves, their voices low and hushed. Could Taekori be correct? Was the great warrior, Takeshi Hasegawa, in search of the blade?

"I wonder why they sent us away?" Kimiko asked as she lay next to Sheng and Daisuke on the soft summer grass, the three of them staring up at the beautiful blue sky. "I think it's important for us to know what goes on in our village. I mean…we won't be kids forever."

Suke-chan shrugged, silently thinking about the cloud he spotted shaped like a leg of lamb. Sheng's mind was on his father.

"I'm sure the elders were discussing the battle and didn't want us to worry," Sheng replied. "They only want what's best for us."

"Could be? Or maybe they didn't want to bore us to death?!" Suke-chan joked, snapping out of his daze as the cloud blew past in the wind. "I hope Old Shou has a story for us after dinner!"

"Really, Suke-chan? That man tells too many stories!" Kimiko interjected, "I don't even think he knows what's real anymore. Don't tell me you think his stories are true?"

"Of course!" Suke-chan argued in the old man's defense. He wouldn't tell them if they were made up!"

"Shou *is* a great story teller," Sheng added.

"A good exaggerator...*maybe*," she snapped back.

Sheng began laughing, "A good exaggerator for sure!"

"Do you think there will ever be a battle from which our fathers do not return?" Kimi-chan asked, growing suddenly serious as their laughter faded, her thoughts far from legends of fierce dragons and mysterious swords.

"If that day ever comes, I know our fathers will fight honorably to the very end, unafraid, knowing that the loss of their lives would be to save ours," Sheng replied.

"My father would never give up," Daisuke grunted, his ham-fist once again slamming into his open palm in a defiant gesture of unparalleled strength. "He would crush any man who crossed him!"

Again, Sheng laughed. They all did.

Minutes passed, then hours, the warm sun shining down as the sun labored across the sky. Dinner bells would soon ring, calling the children home. They wished they could lay there forever, basking in their friendship. But, like all moments of absolute calm, it was not meant to last. Sheng quickly sat up, a curious expression in his eyes.

"Do you hear that?" he asked, breaking the peaceful silence, startling Suke-chan who had dozed off.

"*Uhhhmmm*...is it dinner time?" Daisuke asked groggily, rubbing his eyes as he sat up.

"What?" Kimiko wondered, turning to face her best friend.

"That sound," Sheng whispered curiously. "Listen!"

Suke-chan strained to hear, but could only make out the sound of his stomach growling. Kimiko heard his stomach too. She grinned at their chubby friend.

"I'm being serious," Sheng said fearfully and the two stopped laughing. "There it is again, rumbling in the distance, low, steady...it sounds like thunder. Can you hear it?"

"I can," Kimiko shuddered, suddenly leaping to her feet, her eyes focused on the horizon.

3

THE DREAMS THAT FOLLOW

Bells rang in the distance, coming from the direction of the village. But what they heard was not the welcoming call to their evening meals. This was the warning bells that hung in the watchtower. From there, a lookout could see the entire valley.

Sheng and Suke-chan jumped to their feet, standing alongside Kimiko, as all three stared towards the smaller mountains to the east. The ground was hilly, hiding what must have been making the thundering sound. Sheng stared intently, watching for any glimpse of movement. The sound was getting louder, almost like it was echoing across the mountains in direct opposition to the warning that rang out to alert the villagers of coming danger.

Suddenly, Daisuke began pointing at the sun-washed ridge. A black cloud was racing across the waiving green fields of grass. The blur drew closer and they began to make out individual shapes in the mass: black shrouded riders on jet black horses, nearly one hundred warriors strong, the glint of their swords the only distinct color.

"We have to get behind the wall!" Kimiko cried. "Come on, before the guards close the gate!"

They ran as fast as they could. Suke-chan thought his lungs were going to burst from within his chest, but he pushed himself harder, convincing himself that a warrior would go on. Sheng tried to match Kimiko's stride, but she was too quick to keep up with. The closer they got to the village, the louder their hearts pounded in their ears, blocking out all sound. They could just see the tops of some of the houses over the hill. Soon they would be able to take shelter with their families. They were almost there. Hopefully, the gate was still open!

Kimiko stopped at the top of the hill that overlooked the village. The sound of her beating heart replaced by the screams of people running in panic. Sheng and Suke-chan hurried to her side, horrified by what they saw. The village was already engulfed in flames. The approaching riders were not the coming storm, they were reinforcements! Black horses darted in and out of the pathways, their riders striking down anyone they came upon. Plumes of smoke filled the darkening sky as the trio stared on in disbelief. The men of the village were nowhere to be seen. The agonizing cries rang in their young ears. They felt so helpless, but there was nothing they could do except watch in horror as everything they knew was destroyed.

A blur dashed past them, quickly followed by another, and another. The cloud of riders they had seen had closed the gap and joined the attack. Caught by surprise, Kimi-chan was lifted right off the ground, a rider grabbing her around her waist. She screamed, reaching out towards Sheng and Suke-chan who reached back, but just as their fingertips touched, the boys were taken from behind as well and the three friends were pulled in different directions.

Sheng struggled to get free, scanning the battlefield for a glimpse of Kimiko or Daisuke, but there was too much chaos and he couldn't see them in the midst of the raging sea of black shrouded riders. For an agonizing moment, he was sure that he could still hear Kimi-chan's screams fading out under the thundering of the horses' monstrous hooves.

Sheng found himself sitting on the wooden floor of a large horse-drawn cart, enclosed on all sides, watching as a heavy iron door slammed shut with a deafening clank. He looked around him, tears wet on his cheeks.

Six other boys from the village were there with him, confined within the makeshift cell.

Daisuke was gone, likely forced into another cart, that is if he'd survived. Sheng tried to push the thought from his mind, but his head pounded with the idea that his best friend was dead.

The cart bounced across the uneven ground as the driver paraded the boys down through the village square. Too shocked to speak, the prisoners watched their smoldering homes crumble in the heat of the flames. Bodies lay here and there. Mothers, fathers, grandparents, aunts, uncles: none were spared.

Sheng clutched the iron bars that imprisoned the boys, hoping to see his father riding fearlessly toward them, his sword raised high ready to strike, to cut down the attackers and rescue him. But the village was empty, quiet – except for the crackling of burning wood.

With every second that passed, the fear that started as an ache in the pit of his stomach grew into a panic-induced lump in his throat. The cart was passing his house. He could already see that the roof was in flames. Sheng's eyes darted about as he helplessly took it all in. His home was gone, a fractured skeleton once fleshed with happy memories was all that remained. And then, his world ground to a halt. His eyes stopped on a lifeless body that lay slumped over on the wood-planked porch. Sheng tried to scream, to yell with every fiber of his being, but his mouth barely moved. His heart felt like it was going to beat out of his chest, his tears uncontrollable as he stared at his mother, her beautiful face a comfort amongst all the evil about him. He wanted so desperately to see her smile one more time, hoping that she would take another breath and tell him he would be alright. Her eyes were still open. Sheng stared into them as long as he could until she had passed from view, the cart rounding the path. The driver steered them eastward returning up the hill from where the raiders had come. Sheng scrambled to the rear of the cart, pushing the other boys aside as he did, a fleeting remnant of hope still flickering in his heart. But it was for naught and soon, the village was out of his view. Only the lingering cloud of black smoke could be seen meandering across the darkening sky. Grief had yet to set in, only shock. How could this have happened? The thudding of the horses' hooves against the ground finally pulled Sheng's attention back to reality. His mother was dead. His father must have been killed too as he defended their people one last time.

Sheng's eyes stung from the smoke. He felt like crying but couldn't manage another tear. His face was red, just like the other boys around him, the sobs now reluctant sighs. In silence, they road on. Through the bars, they could see riders in black armor escorting the wagon, hideous masks hiding their faces. Sheng thought the men looked like demons. Their masks were grotesquely human with disfigured dragon-like snouts and razor-toothed mouths. *Oni*, Sheng remembered: Old Shou's name for the demons in his stories.

Turning his attention away from their *demon-like* captors, he moved to the front of the cart. Beyond the horse that pulled them along were more cages, at least four that he was sure of as the coming of night shrouded the landscape. Scattered balls of light glowed from the torches carried by the samurai. Perhaps more were even further ahead? His heart sank just before he noticed that a hand was carefully waiving out the back of the cart they followed. Sheng looked hard in disbelief. It was Daisuke. He was alive!

Sheng waved back discreetly, wanting nothing more than to burst free from his cage and hug his friend. But in the midst of that sudden hope, his thoughts turned to Kimiko. He wondered if she was in another cart? She was certainly not with Suke-chan. His cart, like the one Sheng rode in was filled with boys. What had happened to all the girls?

"Do not lose hope, my son," Taekori smiled warmly.

"Yes, Sheng" Amikori added. "We love you very much."

Sheng laughed, sitting with his parents on the porch of their home. The sun shone brightly for it was a perfect day. Birds sang cheerfully and the flowers on the trees were in full blossom. And as he stared into his parents eyes, he wondered at the marvelous aura of light that seemed to radiate from their faces.

"I love you both so much," he replied

With a sudden jolt, Sheng woke. He'd been dreaming. The air had grown cold and he sat up with a shiver, his teeth chattering. He couldn't believe that he had fallen asleep and was unsure of how much time had passed. The night sky was pitch black and they'd already crossed through the mountains.

Sheng rubbed his head. His neck was stiff from sleeping on the hard floor of the cart. The boys around him were huddled into one of the corners, all asleep, trying to stay warm. The moon glowed brilliantly above, the stars dancing in place, twinkling and flashing, but it was as if the world around them was swallowing the light, keeping it from reaching down to them.

As his eyes adjusted to the night, he remembered the dream he had been having just as he'd been startled awake. If only it were true. He already missed them more than he could imagine. But with that thought, the dream slipped away from him. Oddly, he felt better. Even if his parents were dead, they would live on in his memories. This comforted Sheng. He would be brave for them.

The night lingered on. Dawn would soon come. Sheng clung to the memory of his dream and began anticipating the future. And even though he was uncertain of his destination, adventure surely awaited. Excitement grew as he watched his surroundings change. Gone were the soft grassy meadows. The ground was rocky and trees were sparse.

He had never left the village, never ventured into the mountains. His father had gone to the temple almost weekly and must have climbed the mountains many times. But this was all new to Sheng.

Looking at the cart ahead, he saw that they too were all clumped together, mostly around Daisuke; he blocked the strong wind from the east. Sheng laughed to himself. With all the boys huddled into the corner, the cart leaned dangerously to that side, especially under the weight of his stout friend.

Feeling an impossible peace, Sheng leaned against the pile of boys. Perhaps he could once again drift away into sleep and dream of his parents. But his eyes didn't want to close. He stared off into the fleeting night, the darkness all around him broken only by the occasional glint of torch light across one of the armored guards on horseback.

The sway of the cart finally lulled Sheng back to sleep and his heavy, exhausted eyes slowly closed, his thoughts turning once more into dreams. The cart bounced along the travel-worn path, the large wooden wheels crunching over stones, the narrow mountain pass now far behind them. The boys slept silently, not knowing what would await when morning came.

4

NEW BEGINNINGS

Sunlight broke over the peaks of the eastern mountains as the carts pulled to a stop in front of a tall gate made of heavy wood and iron, spikes protruding from its surface. As the wheels stopped, the boys were all jolted awake.

Rubbing their eyes, they squinted in the bright light as they marveled at their surroundings. The boys all stared in awe at the giant stone wall ahead of them, the structure rising up from the earth like a man-made mountain. Slowly, the towering gate opened, its hinges creaking under the immense weight of the solid wood doors. More armor-clad men stepped out from behind the wall and motioned the carts to enter .

Sheng thought of another of Shou's old stories, a tale of a curious boy who wandered into a cave only to later discover it was the open mouth of a dragon. The boy was never seen again.

Will that be my fate as well? he wondered.

The drivers whipped the horses and the carts lurched forward. As they crossed the gate's threshold, the boys all clambered to the sides of the cages to gawk. Beyond the wall were buildings larger than they had ever seen, towering and, in the least, intimidating.

What was this place? Sheng had never heard anyone speak of it before. Sheng knew of the imperial city – Kyoto -- that was home to the Emperor, but this couldn't be it. The imperial city, as he understood it, was much too far away to reach in a day's travel from his village.

The carts wound past shops and tea houses, blacksmiths and geishas. Approaching the center of the city, Sheng's mobile-prison stopped next to the cage that held Suke-chan. His eyes, like everyone else's, were wide with scared-yet-awe-filled expressions, matching the wonder on their faces. They realized that their wagons were in a crowd of twenty or so, each one identical, filled with children. Sheng spotted girls' faces peering out from behind some of the bars and hoped that Kimiko was somewhere among them. He recognized a few faces, but hers was nowhere to be seen.

Still searching for his lost friend, Sheng came to a startling realization: there were many more children here than there were in his village, of that he was sure. These unfamiliar boys and girls must have been taken from other villages as well. He was deeply saddened at the thought that all of them, himself included, had been violently orphaned.

Who could do such a thing?

A whimper caught his attention. Sheng turned to the boy next to him, the son of another samurai from his village. He was terrified, shaking where he sat.

"Don't worry," Sheng said, scooting closer and placing his arm around the boy's shoulders, "there is great purpose in our arrival at this mysterious city. We will be fine if we stick together!"

The boy was too scared to speak. Sheng's hopeful words didn't seem to help.

Soon, a bald man in black robes approached the guards and mumbled something quietly, pointing somewhere in the distance. The sound of cracking whips filled the air and all the carts that carried girls headed off in the direction to which the man had gestured. He then pointed once again, this time in the opposite direction. The wheels creaked to life as the horses were driven forward and the carts filled with boys headed off, away from the girls and Sheng's hope of finding Kimi-chan. There was nothing he could do and Sheng decided the worst thing possible was to feel sorry for himself or his friends.

Certainly no one would harm innocent children, he assured himself.

Now determined to make the best of his situation, Sheng returned to watching the people in the city. Strangely, there was not a smile to be seen. In fact, everyone he saw looked incredibly unhappy. They all wore black or gray, no bright and vibrant colors as the women had dressed in his village. Many were completely shrouded, their faces hidden, their eyes looking to the ground as they lumbered along. No one seemed to pay the captives any mind as they were driven glumly down the streets.

This can't be a common sight, Sheng wondered, *children locked in horse-drawn cages?*

They continued down another street until finally the horses clomped to a stop in front of a tall house with narrow windows. An old man stepped from the shadows of the porch, a cane in one hand as he stroked his long beard with the other.

"Welcome," he happily said to the boys who all stared up at him from behind the iron bars. "You are all guests of our gracious master, *Master Takeshi Hasegawa the Great.*"

The old man managed a meager bow as the guards unlocked the doors to the cages and began unceremoniously pulling the boys down from the back of the carts. They were given no time to rest after their long, uncomfortable journey, but were all quickly pushed into neat lines and ushered up the steps, then through the large double-wide front doorway.

Sheng stretched. It felt good to walk after their cramped trip. The boys around him looked on uneasily as they were led through the building. Jade and opal carvings decorated the wide open space. Beautifully colored, intricately woven rugs covered the wooden floors.

The old man stopped at a modest stairwell and pointed up with a toothy grin, "Your rooms are ready for you. Please, get familiar with each other and the house. This is your new home. I'm sure you are all hungry. Food has been prepared for you. You will not go hungry here, I promise you that!"

The old man disappeared through a hidden door and the guards left as well, taking posts just outside the front doors. After all that had happened, the boys were finally alone.

Eagerly, they all stared at one another. Daisuke ran to Sheng, hugging him so hard that he lifted him right off the ground. The other boys from their village followed Suke-chan and they all clustered together off in one corner of the great room. The rest of the boys did the same, gathering into groups that represented each village, four in all. Soon, the room was buzzing with all the different stories of how they all came to be in this wondrous place.

"I saw my mother on the porch as we left the village." Sheng said sadly to Suke-chan, his voice hushed.

"I figured you had," he replied, "I saw her too. I'm sorry, Sheng."

Sheng thankfully nodded as he looked about the room. Some cried while others embraced. Apparently, none were injured in the attacks. Fortunately all seemed well in spite of their circumstances.

"And what about your parents," Sheng asked. "Are they gone as well?"

Suke-chan looked down at the floor, his head hung low, "I didn't see them, but they must be dead too. I'm pretty sure those monsters left no one alive."

The same sentiment was shared by the other boys. All their parents seemed to be gone.

Disgust filled Daisuke's eyes. His fists clenched tightly, his eyes welling up as a tear ran down his ruddy cheek. "Why did they have to do this?" he cried. "What did our village ever do to anyone?"

"Nothing," Sheng answered. "But we are alive for a reason. Just remember your parents as they were – good people. They will survive in your heart."

Suke-chan smiled, wiping the tears from his cheeks. Sheng was certainly a great friend. They hugged once more and then tried to encourage all the other boys from their village.

Slowly, as they all grew more comfortable, the braver boys began introducing one another to the other groups, sharing which village they'd come from and what they'd seen. This was a welcome help for many of them, if only to serve as a distraction from the awkwardness that had been thrust upon them. And though the groups seemed to be warming up to one another, some of the boys still remained in their small groups, speaking only to their friends.

A small boy, tiny compared to the rest, was standing amongst six burly looking boys, glaring around the room with contempt. His eyes weren't red from tears, in fact, other than the scowl on his face, he looked like he couldn't be happier. The boys surrounding him looked more like body guards than friends, as they all wore the same angry expression.

He was dressed in expensive robes, far from the tattered clothes the other boys wore. Even his shoes were in perfect condition, like he'd never wore them out to play. His eyes danced about the room, stopping on each boy, like he was evaluating each one, sizing them up. His gaze fell on a much younger boy sitting on a footstool crying.

"You there," the short boy scoffed as he parted his large friends with his hands and headed through the crowd.

"Me?" the young boy asked from where he sat slumped over with his head in his hands.

"Yes, you! Don't be such a baby," he teased, his friends towering over him, making mocking, tearful faces, pretending to rub their eyes. "It's not like you're the only one whose parents are dead."

Looking up from his tear-soaked hands, the young boy stopped crying, now appearing much more angry than sad as his lips curled into a snarl and he glared at the boy. The mean group of boys laughed at what they reasoned to be his feigned attempt to intimidate them.

"Leave me alone!" he shouted over the many voices in the room.

The tall gang leaned in over the young boy, their shadows covering him. Again they laughed mockingly.

"No, I don't think I want to," the leader chided. "You're a pathetic little…"

But before he could finish his insult, the young boy dove from the stool, shoulder first into the bully's stomach, knocking the wind out of him as the two tumbled to the floor with a thud. A dozen hands grabbed at the young boy's robes, lifting him right off the ground.

"Hey!" he screamed, his feet dangling beneath him.

The loud drone of talking stopped. The room's attention was stolen away, the focus now on the scuffle that erupted right in front of them. Everyone stood silent, staring on as the small boy struggled to get free.

Sheng finally had enough. He leapt into the crowd of attacking boys, Daisuke followed, plowing his way through behind him as the bodies scattered quickly.

In a heartbeat, Suke-chan tackled the cluster of older boys as Sheng pulled their victim away, stepping in front of him and facing the antagonist who was just climbing back to his feet.

"And who do you think you are?!" he yelled at Sheng as he straightened his clothes.

There was a moment of silence while the two stared each other down. No one dared even breath.

"Nobody," Sheng finally answered. "I'm nobody. Just leave him alone, okay?"

"And if I choose to go after you instead?" the short boy arrogantly questioned, the sound of his personal army cracking their knuckles making a smile flash across Suke-chan's eager-to-fight face.

"Gentlemen!" a voice called out from behind the crowd of boys that had encircled the brawl. "I'm glad to see we finally have some fighters. The last couple sets of recruits were too terrified to raise a sword."

A slender man with short black hair walked into sight, a thin straight mustache he obviously paid too much time grooming proudly displayed on his pale face. He was dressed in a red and silver set of silk robes that hung all the way to the floor, hiding his feet, giving the appearance that he was gliding across the room as he moved.

"I am Master Wong, one of your new sensei. You will train under me as well as others, each who can teach you a great deal about many things," he said smirking, apparently very pleased with himself.

Sheng and Daisuke looked at each other with shared confusion. Turning back to the mean boy, they found he was gone. He and his gang had moved to the opposite end of the room.

Master Wong spun around quickly, his robes swishing as he motioned for them to follow. He then slid open two large panels in the wall that led out onto a porch facing a beautifully maintained courtyard filled with lush trees and pebbled pathways. Brightly colored peacocks strutted about as other birds swooped in and out of the branches. Several monks meditated on a grassy clearing, their orange robes glowing in the warm sunlight.

The boys followed through the courtyard. Just beyond the first cluster of trees, they saw a training session just off to the right, two dozen students dressed in white robes all moved in unison, their actions exactly matching those of their sensei.

"That is Master Haiku," Wong said, assuming the boys were all looking in that direction. "He will teach you the art of balance and control."

They continued on into the next clearing. On the left, boys in all black robes were sparring: one blocking while their partner practiced strikes.

"Master Kinshi..." Wong called out as he smiled at the old man sitting on a bench facing his students.

The old master waved, a toothless smile on his face. He, just like many of the other masters, had a long white beard which seemed to hang all the way to his knees.

"He is a master of unarmed fighting," Master Wong added in a happy voice.

Suki-chan and Sheng walked together. Their friends from their village kept close, as did some other boys who had watched them bravely intervene against the bullies. But not all were as impressed. Apparently some of the boys from other villages hadn't taken a liking to Sheng and Daisuke sticking their noses into someone else's fight, so they hung around the gang that had attacked, showing either their support or fear. But Sheng couldn't care less. He had other things than rivalry on his mind.

After passing a rock garden, Sheng stepped close to Suke-chan and quietly spoke. He hoped Wong wouldn't overhear. "Why do you think they are being so nice to us?" he wondered.

"I don't know…" Suke-chan trailed off, distracted by a caged tiger to their right.

"I can't figure them out?" he questioned, his words attracting the ears of the surrounding boys. "They killed our families, destroyed our villages, and now they're treating us like *guests*? All I know is that the first chance we have to get out of here, we should take it!"

Wong's voice interrupted their hushed conversation. They stopped to listen.

"Over there," he pointed smugly, "you can see the entrance to the *dungeons*."

His eyes fell upon Daisuke and Sheng as he finished his sentence. They looked back expressionless, trying not to appear guilty, like they hadn't been talking through the entirety of his grand tour across the grounds.

The short bully who had started the fight back in the first house smiled creepily at the thought of seeing the new hero in chains on his first day away from home. He cast a wicked glance at the two of them, but turned just as they looked his way.

"I'm going to hurt him," Suke-chan scowled, "badly."

Sheng grinned as some of the other boys around them laughed. They all continued on, voluntarily divided into two very separate groups. Wong noted the segregation and smirked, pleased to see a blooming tension.

Before long, Sheng felt a small tug on his sleeve and he turned, looking to see who wanted his attention. It was the boy he'd helped earlier.

"Sir," the boy began, "I just want to thank you, Sir."

"Please don't call me that," he blushed. "My name is Yamashita Sheng."

"Oh…alright…*Sheng*," the boy smiled, nervous as he spoke, "my name is Mori Masaki."

"It's nice to meet you, Masaki." Sheng said, hoping to sound sincere. He wasn't trying to make friends. All he and Suke-chan wanted to do was find out why they'd been brought to this strange place and how they could escape.

Masaki stared up at Sheng with a tear in his eye as he suddenly reached around his waist and squeezed tightly. Sheng tried to pry himself loose, but the boy had an astounding grip. Daisuke grabbed the boy by the collar of his robe, trying to pull him off of Sheng, but all he did was successfully transfer the boy onto himself. It didn't seem to matter who Masaki hugged, as long as he was showing someone his gratitude.

"Thank you for saving me," the boy said, finally letting go, embarrassed that he didn't know his co-rescuer's name.

"He's Daisuke," Sheng helped.

"Thank you, Daisuke," Masaki grinned, finally letting go.

Suke-chan pushed the boy out of his way gruffly mumbling something about it being no trouble. Little Masaki happily bound back to his friends, telling them how great his champions were.

The large group of boys continued on, closely following Master Wong. He led them around the last group of students studying. These boys were much older. All wore gray robes and hoods and wielded razor sharp katana as they practiced slashing strikes on wood and straw dummies with their lethal blades. Oddly there appeared to be no sensei present.

Thankfully, the tour seemed to come to an end and they headed up a long flight of stairs into what looked like a palace. Their eyes hardly blinked as they tried to take it all in.

"This is where the honorable Master Takeshi Hasegawa lives when he is not visiting the Imperial City. Upstairs are his personal chambers. They are very much private and he is never to be disturbed. Straight ahead is the great hall where we eat our meals. When we enter, take a seat wherever you like. I am going to check that the food is ready. I trust you are all quite hungry after your trip," he said slipping away before their eyes, as if he vanished into thin air.

As they entered, Sheng heard his name called out over the crowd. It was the mean, short boy.

"Where are you sitting, *Chinese boy*?" he spat at Sheng.

"Anywhere you're not," Sheng grinned, ignoring the attempted insult. "What's your name anyway?"

"I don't want my name disgraced by your immigrant lips," he said, his eyebrows furled in disgust.

"Fine! The less I know of you the better," Sheng shot back as he turned away from the short boy and looked at Daisuke.

The next thing he felt was a hand on his shoulder. Sheng spun around quickly and grabbed the hand ready to throw the boy to the floor. But he froze, his expression matching the faces of all the other boys in the room.

It was Master Wong. Sheng was still gripping his wrist.

"Very good, boy!" Wong exclaimed, breaking the deafening silence and tugging his hand free. "My ancestors hail from China as well, young – *Sheng* – is it? You will do well here."

Wong patted him irritatingly on the head and motioned the boys through two hidden doors that servants slowly opened for them. Suke-chan smiled, but Sheng didn't appreciate it.

The next room was enormous, the ceiling reaching high above them. They had never seen anything like this before. Sheng thought it was what *Takama-ga-hara*, the Plain of High Heaven, might look like. Gold and sapphire could be seen glimmering everywhere they turned. He half expected to see *kami*, or divine spirits, hiding amongst the elaborate architecture.

"It's like Shambhala!" Daisuke said in awe.

"Yeah, but this is real," Sheng reminded his best friend.

"Shambhala *is* real," he replied sincerely. "Old Shou told us many stories about it, remember?"

"It reminds me of home," they heard the mean boy smugly gloating to his adoring friends.

"Listen to him go on!" Suke-chan muttered.

"Forget about him," Sheng urged "He's just trying to get attention."

"Sheng, Daisuke...over here!" they heard Masaki's squeaky voice cry out at them. "I saved you two seats!"

Reluctantly, Sheng and Suke-chan joined him at the table. At least their backs were turned to the short boy who had been causing all the trouble.

Servants began to file in, each one carrying a large serving plate in their hands. Steam rose from the hot food as it was placed in front of them on the tables. Suke's eyes swelled at the sight of all the food. Sheng hated to admit it, but he was very hungry and as he began to eat, he was quite thankful that his captors had provided them with such delicious food.

There were bowls of rice and thinly sliced fish covered in different sauces, another plate held a duck prepared with brightly colored vegetables, beak and all. A roast pig stared at them, peanuts scattered around its body. It was glorious. They had never eaten anything like this. It was a far cry from the rice and fire charred chicken or beef they were used to. As they ate, a guilty thought bothered Sheng.

"What do you suppose happened to Kimiko-chan?" he wondered.

Daisuke finished shelling a shrimp he was about to eat, but stopped short of gobbling it down. He now shared Sheng's concern.

"I don't know...I haven't really thought about her," he admitted, sadly dropping the uneaten shrimp on the table. "You don't think they killed all the girls do you?"

"I can't imagine so," Sheng said, drinking water from the gold cup in front of him. "Why bring them all this way just to kill them? That wouldn't make sense."

"I wonder if they brought her here as well," Suke-chan mumbled hopefully, picking up his shrimp and shoving it into his mouth.

"Not likely..." Sheng said, recalling the fact that he hadn't seen a girl anywhere on the grounds.

His words were interrupted by a loud shuffling of benches at the front of the room. The mean boy and his gang had jumped from their seats and were bowing respectfully, their heads nearly at their knees. The rest of the boys at their table did the same.

"What's going on?" Sheng wondered, looking around and seeing that the plates around him were growing empty.

"The feast must be over," Suke-chan said solemnly, stuffing some wafer-like cakes into the pockets of his robe.

Sheng gave him an amused look, "Seriously?"

"They're for later," Suke-chan quickly explained, "in case I get hungry!

Sheng smiled. Daisuke grabbed another cake, the last one on the tray and stuffed it in his face, grinning as he did.

Master Wong could now be seen standing at the head of the two very long tables they had been eating at. Four large guards dressed in finely detailed samurai armor stood just behind him.

"Please," he said looking at Sheng's table and then glancing at the opposite table all bowing.

Sheng and Daisuke realized what Wong was implying and dropped their heads in a low bow. Masaki and the rest of the boys caught on and did the same.

"I introduce to you all the great Master Takeshi Hasegawa," Wong declared in all his glory.

The guards divided and a very handsome man dressed in blue and yellow silk stepped between them. He was not very tall, but his muscular arms showed his strength. His hair was pulled back in a tight bun and his pale, hard face was emotionless. Hasegawa was just as impressive as this house. He looked wise beyond his years and as powerful as an ox. A beautifully detailed sword hung at his side in an ornately engraved sheath, his hand resting on the handle of the blade.

"I welcome you to our dojo. This will be your new home. Here, you will train, you will learn, you will become *great* warriors," Hasegawa declared, his arms crossing proudly across his chest as he spoke.

Listening to the man, watching his every movement, Sheng was reminded of his father, especially when he noticed the scars that covered Hasegawa's arms. Sheng nudged Suke-chan and pointed out the healed wounds

"My father had scars like that on his arms," Sheng whispered. "They were from his many battles."

"Well it looks like Hasegawa has seen his fair share as well," Daisuke whispered back.

Hasegawa stood examining the group of boys, studying each one, sizing them up. His eyes met Sheng's stare. For a moment, they were locked in a piercing gaze. Sheng felt like he was going to be sick. Hasegawa didn't blink.

"I'm sure you all have great potential," he said as closing words, still fixed on Sheng. "I look forward to watching you all grow as you master your abilities."

Silently, Hasegawa's guards followed after him as he promptly and unceremoniously left the grand room. Master Wong once again stood in his place.

"Now that you have eaten, I have arranged for the older students to meet in the courtyard and escort you to your rooms," he smiled in closing, pointing at the table to his right, the table where the gang sat.

Wong then gestured to the door from where they had come before the feast. They stood and exited as commanded. Sheng's table was now alone. Wong waited a moment, staring awkwardly over their heads – nowhere in particular – then finally pointed toward the same door. Apparently it was their turn to leave. They filed away from their empty plates and out of the room, the guards closing the ornate doors behind the last boy to leave.

They found themselves once again looking out at the beautiful garden. Stone dragons peered out through neatly trimmed bushes. A screech filled the air above them as they all looked to see where it came from. A falcon swooped down and snatched a mouse in its giant talons. The bird flew away as fast as it had appeared. Several monks were walking along the path quietly discussing something the boys were most likely too young to grasp.

Standing at the end of the path was an older looking boy in gray robes. Another boy, younger and in black robes, stood just behind him, slightly hidden in the shadows. The two mumbled something to each other and then walked towards the group of boys.

"You there, come with me," the boy in gray said, dividing the group in half and heading off towards the west end of the garden.

The boys all looked at each other, not sure which ones he meant. Sheng and Daisuke stepped as far from the main group as possible without looking obvious. Silently, half of them volunteered to follow. Masaki was pulled along with little choice, finding himself pushed forward by the solemn wave of boys.

He looked back at them sadly as he disappeared behind a wall of tall shrubs. Sheng was actually relieved. Fortune it seemed had smiled on them: they wouldn't have to share a room with young Masaki, not that he figured they would be there that long. In fact he hoped to talk to Suke-chan that night about a plan for escape.

The boy in black smiled at those who were left and headed off to the east. The boys followed. Hasegawa's grand hall was built on the north end of the property. Sheng was working it all out in his head. He remembered that both the gate to the city and entrance to the dojo faced the same direction. And knowing from which direction their carts had delivered them, he knew approximately where they were.

"Southwest," Sheng thought aloud nudging his friend and gesturing off into the distance. "Home is that way."

5

AN UNLIKELY FRIEND

The old wood-planked stairs creaked under their feet as they walked up to the third floor where they were told they'd find their beds. This wing of the sprawling building was just as beautiful as the others that they had seen, but had fewer gems decorating the walls. All around them were older boys, some smiling, others even stopping and bowing in welcome.

"We've got to think about how we can get out of here!" Sheng whispered as they were led into a communal room of sorts.

Daisuke nodded, stepping through the doorway. Inside were four padded mats, much thicker than the ones they had in their village. They looked quite comfortable. Next to each mat, tucked into the four corners of the room were large, heavy wooden chests for them to store any personal items in.

"Can we look around the grounds some more?" Sheng asked their escort, trying to sound only innocently curious. "This is my new home, I'd like to know more about it."

"If you like," the older boy smiled. "Just wait for your roommates to get here before you head out. And be careful! There are many ways that trouble can find you here."

The door slid closed and Daisuke slumped down onto his mat. Sheng dropped down next to him.

"As soon as we can get into the courtyard, we need to try and find a way over that wall," Sheng plotted.

"Do you think we'll look suspicious?"

"No…" Sheng stopped mid-sentence as the door slowly opened.

Two boys timidly entered. One was very tall and thin, the other was small, mousy in appearance. They both carried large sacks.

"Hello," Sheng greeted, standing to bow.

The boys stood silent for a moment, looking nervous. The tall boy dropped his sack to the ground and untied the top.

"Hi…" the small boy squeaked, offering a meager bow of his own, "I'm Jin. This is my best friend, Naoki."

"Hello," the tall boy said, mustering some confidence, a weak smile on his face.

Immediately, he started rummaging through the bag, his hands somewhere near the bottom. The social stress of meeting new people was clearly too much for him.

"I'm Sheng," he smiled in return, "and this is Daisuke."

"It's an honor to room with you," Jin bowed once more, this time much more properly, "especially after watching you stand up for that young boy earlier today."

"Are you really Chinese like that bully said?" Jin asked.

"Would it matter if I was?" Sheng asked smartly.

"Well, no," Jin replied. "I just wondered. I meant no offense."

"That's okay, Jin. And *no*, I am not Chinese. I'm named after one of my distant ancestors. For many generations, my family has worked the land and proudly served the emperor and our daimyō," Sheng explained.

"Well I'm sorry you were treated that way. You're certainly a hero."

Sheng was growing uncomfortable. He knew his name was traditionally foreign, but he'd never been treated as different before, all simply because of his name.

"It was nothing. I'm no hero. What's in the sacks?" Sheng asked taking the attention off of himself.

"Oh, yeah," Jin blushed, "Master Wong gave us these as he saw us heading into the house. Here."

Sheng took a small white bundle from Jin's outstretched hand and unfolded it. Daisuke did the same. They each held very clean, new *karategi*, or *gi*; their training robes.

"There are enough sets in these sacks for us each to have five as they become worn from sparring," Naoki added, pulling more out and piling them on his mat.

Sheng and Daisuke gave each other huge toothy grins as they proudly held their new clothes. Neither of them had ever had anything new, especially like this. The material was thick and smooth, a cotton canvas, rigid yet soft. The robes must have been made in the city, very expensive they figured.

Pulling off his old tattered robes, Sheng tried on his gi. It fit perfectly.

The next moment, laughter filled the room. Naoki and Sheng were doubled over. Jin and Daisuke stared at each other, confused and embarrassed.

"I must have gotten the sacks switched," Jin whimpered. "This bag must have been for you two and Naoki's bag for us."

Standing in pants nearly six inches too short and the top of his gi pulled tightly across his large stomach and broad shoulders, Daisuke joined in the laughing as he looked at Jin whose robes where draped around him like blankets on a snowy day. Finally, Jin erupted in glee with a happy snort, their laughter echoing down the hall. Suke-chan looked as if he was about to split the pants in half.

The door to the room slid open suddenly.

"What are you four going on about?" the older boy who had showed them to their room asked.

Then, without needing an answer, he spotted the two in mismatched clothing. His serious scowl cracked into a smile he desperately tried to hide.

"Switch clothes and settle down. You'll get all the other boys riled up and it's only your first day here."

"Of course," Sheng bowed respectfully, still smiling.

Finally in their proper gi, Suke and Sheng told their roommates that they were going to walk through the gardens before dinner and promptly headed out and down the stairs into the main room of the house. Several boys were standing near the window, all in the same matching white robes.

Sunlight poured through the doorway as the two walked onto the porch, but they knew it wouldn't last long. Their house faced the west and the sun was low in the sky, burning bright in its last remaining hours. Quickly, they headed down a path in the garden and into a cluster of trees, hiding amongst the low branches. They looked back up at the house, hoping to see a way to the roof and over the wall.

A sign they hadn't noticed before hung over the entryway on the porch. *Tiger Clan*, it read. Beside it was an engraving of a tiger's snarling face.

"That reminds me of the tattoo on my father's back," Sheng said excitedly.

"Yeah...I remember!" Suke-chan agreed grinning.

"Tiger Clan," Sheng wondered aloud, "who are they?"

"No clue."

"Come on, let's find a way out." Sheng said, stalking off through the trees, still looking up at the rooftops.

His friend followed along pushing branches out of his way, some snapping off with little cracks. Stealth was not Suke-chan's strongpoint.

"*SSSHHHH!*" Sheng scolded over his shoulder, "Try to keep quiet."

"Sorry," Daisuke whispered.

They walked the length of the garden, dodging between trees and jumping across paths. As of yet, they'd remained unseen.

"There!" Sheng said, coming to a stop on the edge of a crystal clear pond filled with huge, gold fish.

He pointing up at a water spout that hung from the top of the wall all the way to the ground below. Daisuke nodded.

"Keep your eyes open," Sheng warned. "I'm going to go take a look."

Daisuke pretended to watch the fish darting about in the pond as Sheng climbed all the way up the spout, hand over hand as his feet pushed against the wall, and pulled himself up onto the ledge. He could see over the top!

The city streets were packed with merchants calling out their prices and goods to passersby. Sheng could hardly believe his eyes. Beautiful women in elegant silk robes walked along the tables drawing stares from the surrounding men.

"What can you see?" Daisuke hollered still gazing at the pond.

Sheng remembered what he was doing at the top of the wall and tried to find a way down. He was out of luck.

"It's a straight drop," Sheng said regretfully, "too far down to jump."

"There's nothing to climb down?" Suke-chan asked, turning away from the fish and looking up at Sheng.

"Nothing," came a dark voice from the path behind Daisuke.

A tall and burly man in brown robes stepped into view. Shading his eyes with his hand, he looked up the wall at Sheng. Daisuke looked like he was about to pass out.

"You there," the man bellowed. "What are you doing up there?"

Sheng thought quickly, his mind racing. What could he say? His stomach was churning. They were in big trouble!

"Just hoping to learn about the city," he admitted, trying to see the man's expression, but he couldn't with the bright sun in his eyes.

"Well come down from there before someone sees you," he called up.

Daisuke watched on, a horrified look on his round face, as Sheng carefully scrambled back down the spout. He wanted to run, but he couldn't leave his best friend behind. Sheng's feet hit the ground and the man lowered his hand from his eyes. The boys stepped back, their faces twisted.

The man's face was disfigured, covered in scars, most of them small, but the largest ran from his brow, over his eye, and all the way to his chin. His lips were discolored and the rest of his face grew pale as he saw their reaction.

"Sorry," he said, pulling his hood over his head, hiding his face in the shadows. "Sometimes I forget how I look. People call me Scar, for *obviously* apparent reasons."

"Master Scar, I wasn't..."

"Not Master," he interrupted, "*gardener.*"

"Oh..." Daisuke mumbled, still looking like he was holding his breath.

"You should be more careful. Hasegawa's men might spot you and then you'll be sent to the dungeon for sure. The outside world is forbidden, at least till you're old enough," Scar grinned, trying to look less deformed and turning away from the boys. "I'll see you around."

Quickly, he headed off into the trees as he pulled a small, shiny garden spade from his pocket and disappeared. The boys were left standing alone next to the pond.

"That was...*weird*," Suke-chan chuckled. "I thought we were done for!"

"Yeah," Sheng answered thoughtfully. "We'll have to be more careful."

A hollow gong rang out across the garden from Hasegawa's house. Sheng and Daisuke headed in that direction to investigate, hopes of escape still in mind.

Passing into a clearing and turning up the path to the main house, they came upon a group of boys wearing robes like theirs. Naoki's head stuck out above the rest by nearly a foot. He saw them coming and gave a meager wave. Jin spotted them as well and motioned for them to come over. Sharing a look of reluctance, they joined the group.

"What's going on?" Sheng asked from over Jin's shoulder.

"Master Wong announced dinner. We're heading into the great hall." Jin explained.

"So the gong means dinner?" Daisuke wondered.

"And breakfast and lunch," Naoki added.

"I'm still full from earlier," Sheng grumbled, wishing he could skip dinner altogether.

But he knew he had no choice. He followed along as they filtered into the great hall, all taking seats with their roommates. There were more boys there this time. The older students had joined them and now the room was full.

"Welcome, let's all eat," Master Wong declared with a clap of his hands.

Servant girls flooded in through the side doors carrying plate after plate. The girls were all of different ages and were looking down at their feet as they served each table, clearly avoiding eye contact.

"Thank you," Sheng said kindly to a girl who set a tray of sushi between Daisuke and him.

She ignored Sheng's gesture, her eyes fixed on the floor. Sheng couldn't understand. The girls in his village didn't act like that.

"I wonder why they won't look at us?" he asked Daisuke.

An older boy leaned closer and explained, "They're told not to look at us, or speak to us, or anything. Hasegawa thinks it's disrespectful for a woman or girl to speak to a man in public."

"Oh," Sheng sighed as he watched Suke-chan shoveling food in his mouth.

"Subaru Tatsuo," the older boy said, introducing himself with a smile.

"I'm Sheng and this is Daisuke," he said pointing first at himself and then at his red faced friend.

"*Plead ta meechya*," Suke-chan grinned, his mouth jammed full of grilled octopus.

Tatsuo looked confused as he watched him continue stuffing yet even more food into his already bursting cheeks, "Sorry, but I didn't catch that."

"Pleased to meet you!" came the reply as he finally swallowed the mouthful and grabbed for his cup to wash it down.

"Listen. I know now is not a good time to talk," Tatsuo said turning to Sheng, "but it was hard for me to adjust when I was first brought here too."

"What happened when they brought you here?" Sheng asked, reluctantly beginning to eat.

"Several years ago, Hasegawa's men raided my village, way up in the north. Anyway, he took my parents as slaves and brought me here to his dojo to train. I've never seen my parents since. That was five years ago," he explained as he crossed his muscular arms.

"I'm sorry to hear that," Sheng said hesitating. "But, haven't you ever thought of escaping so that you can try to set them free?"

"I've thought about it, but I don't know where he sent them," Tatsuo said before pausing thoughtfully. "I've searched all over the city and they are definitely not here."

Wait...so you've been in the city?" Sheng questioned, looking over at Daisuke.

"Yeah. I used to sneak out all the time. There's a hidden passageway under the temple. After my fifteenth birthday, they let me go freely. Master Hasegawa gives us an allowance of copper coins every few weeks so that we can buy ourselves new clothes or anything else we need. Anyway, what about your parents. Do you know where they were taken?" Tatsuo asked, taking a sip of water.

"My parents?" Sheng asked.

"Of course," Tatsuo answered sincerely.

"They're dead," Sheng said as he dropped his head in anger, not wanting anyone to see the tears in his eyes. "Hasegawa's men killed them."

"Are you sure?" he asked. "To my knowledge Hasegawa rarely kills the villagers. He makes them servants. They work in the different villages he governs. He pays them too and gives them a place to live. Why would he kill your parents?"

"Not just our parents," Daisuke interjected, "but the whole village – every adult, even the elders. They took the girls, but they could be dead as well for all we know."

Tatsuo looked shocked. "Hasegawa wouldn't kill children. Did the men of your village fight?"

Sheng was no longer in the mood to eat. He pushed his plate away and rested his head on his arms at the table.

"Of course they did. Especially Sheng's father. He was a brave warrior. Hasegawa killed our people." Daisuke answered.

"Well, I'm sorry. I did not mean to offend you. I had no idea what happened to your families. Look, if either of you ever need to talk to someone, just find me. I know it will be hard, but we are taken great care of here. In time, you'll see that Hasegawa is a great man." Tatsuo concluded, standing and heading back to his seat among the older boys.

6

ALMOST LIKE HOME

The next three weeks passed quickly. Sheng and Daisuke found themselves settling in. The homesick pain in the pit of their stomachs was fading. Occasionally, they bumped into the strange and mysterious Scar as he quietly tended the gardens. They'd come to understand that he was less scary and more lonely in the few moments they'd spent with him. In fact, it seemed like they were the only ones who even paid him any notice.

Though the memories of their destroyed village were still fresh wounds, the time spent at the dojo brought healing. The grounds were serene and there was no lack of comforts. But what helped them most, more than absolutely anything, was that they had started their training, finding it to be quite a welcome distraction as they adjusted to their new lives within Hasegawa's walls. By far, their favorite lessons came from the old Master Kinshi: the art of unarmed fighting.

Sheng's hands were lightning quick. The other students his age were no match for him and martial arts came naturally. Suke-chan on the other hand wasn't nearly as coordinated. But what he lacked in speed, he made up for tenfold with his immense strength. Blocked or not, his strikes still sent his sparring partner to the ground, which Master Kinshi found to his pleasure, cackling happily with a toothless grin each time Daisuke mercilessly dropped someone on their backside.

The art of balance and control, taught by Master Haiku, was much more structured and much less fun. Haiku emphasized the importance of concentration to a degree that no ten year old could manage, especially considering that the garden they trained in was filled with squawking peacocks and roaring tigers. Still, Sheng thought it would eventually be useful no matter how boring it was now, no doubt a wisdom gleaned from his father and his old life in the village.

They'd also been studying the art of concealment and stealth with Master Ken and spiritualism in battle taught by a Buddhist monk named, Hirohito. But what they really wanted to learn was fighting techniques with real weapons. As of yet, in any class where they would need a sword, they were given *kendo sticks* instead: swords made of bamboo rather than steel, non-lethal, but still quite painful when struck.

At the moment however, they were lost in their thoughts, daydreaming through Master Gaiden's history class and reading from scrolls that highlighted the *Yayoi Period*. Their sensei was rambling on about differing forms of pottery production and the emergence of bronze-made tools and weapons in post-Paleolithic Japan.

"That is all for today!" Master Gaiden shouted suddenly, clapping his hands together loudly as he finished his lecture, jolting the boys back to reality.

Daisuke wiped a little streak of drool from his chin as they were dismissed. Sheng rolled up his scroll and waited for his best friend to do the same.

It was nearly noon. The mid-day sun was warm on their backs as they headed towards the great hall for lunch. The room was packed, not a single place to sit.

"Everyone must be between lessons," Sheng observed, a grumbling Daisuke following him towards the table of white clad boys.

They decided not to wait for seats to open and began grabbing handfuls of food and stuffing it into their pockets. They would eat in the garden.

A small clearing seemed nice and they plopped down on the soft grass, looking around at the surrounding houses as they hungrily ate. The buildings were all connected and accessed through hallways and corridors, some hidden, as Sheng had discovered by roaming the halls on sleepless nights.

Each house was supervised by a *hogosha*, or guardian, an older student who was now a sort of overseer for the different groupings of younger boys. The students were divided into three clans, each with animals that represented them, though the reasons weren't made clear. Over the past several weeks, Sheng had tried to figure out the symbolism behind each of the three animals, his own clan being represented by a roaring tiger.

The house on the west side of the grounds bore an engraving of a dragon, twisting in a fierce and beautiful spiral. The eastern house was engraved with the image of a monkey, its sharp teeth bared. As of yet, nothing had come to mind. So they sat, eating quietly, ever contemplating the clan animals.

Shortly, the rustling of leaves in the trees behind them announced the arrival of Scar, pruning away in the garden, his hood covering his deformed face. His appearance had become more common and the boys were no longer startled by his shadowy movements among the cherry blossoms.

"Good afternoon, boys," he said, without giving them a glance.

"Hello," they replied in unison, Daisuke's words muffled behind a mouth full of bread.

"Don't mind me, just doing a bit of eavesdropping," he said in a sing song voice and turning his head slightly, just enough for them to catch a glimpse of his mangled grin.

At that moment, Master Ken and Master Gaiden came strolling around the corner on the path that came nearest to the clearing. They were deep in a discussion that promptly stopped upon seeing the boys. The masters bowed as they passed, but said nothing till they were out of earshot. Sheng was sure his sensei hadn't wanted them hearing whatever it was they were talking about. There seemed to be many secrets at Hasegawa's dojo.

Daisuke looked less interested in the teachers than he was in the gardener, especially after watching his reaction to the passing instructors. He had turned quickly back to his pruning and acted as if he was unaware that anyone else was present.

"*Psst*...Scar..." Suke-chan hissed, trying to get his attention, "What's wrong? Why'd you turn away from us when our teachers passed? Don't you like them?"

Carefully looking around to make sure that no other masters were close, Scar lowered his voice and spoke softly. "I don't mind the teachers at all. It's Hasegawa." Scar explained in a hushed voice, very matter-of-factly. "He doesn't want me talking to any of his students."

"But why?" Sheng asked.

"Never you mind. It's better you don't know." Scar answered, disappearing into the trees.

"Do you think he's so mysterious on purpose?" Suke-chan joked, finishing off the last of his food.

"I don't know," Sheng wondered aloud. "But I think he told us more than he figured he should."

"Why do you say that?"

"Because if he's not supposed to talk to students in the first place, then why did he talk to us at all?" Sheng explained as the post-lunch gong rang out, announcing the start of afternoon classes.

Daisuke stood, a confused expression on his face, and followed Sheng towards the north end of the garden. They were off to Master Ken's class.

Scar's cryptic words lingered in Sheng's head, haunting him all through the lesson that followed. Master Ken was explaining how to move silently. There test was to aptly traverse the crudely booby-trapped room, the floor covered in small pebbles – pebbles that dramatically crunched under the student's feet as each one took his turn. The idea of moving across a floor covered in insignificant stones seemed simple enough, yet the challenge was oddly real – and frustrating!

"No, no, no," Master Ken exclaimed as Masaki clumsily stumbled over the tiny pebbles as if they were boulders, the grinding sound anything but stealthy. "You must concentrate. Think of silence and you will be silent."

Pushing Masaki to the side, Master Ken closed his eyes and walked over the pebbles as smoothly as if he had simply glided across. A scurrying mouse would have been louder.

Finally it was Sheng's turn. He was so lost in Scar's words that he never heard Master Ken call his name. After several nudges from his classmates, the startled Sheng hurried across the pebbles absentmindedly, walking right over them without giving it another thought. After he had his go at the challenge, he turned to head back to Daisuke. Sheng couldn't have cared less whether or not he succeeded, but he was very surprised to see his peers' reactions. Everyone was staring at him like he was inhuman. Their jaws were dropped as if trying to speak, but couldn't. Master Ken was ecstatic.

"Quite remarkable, boy!" he said rushing over to Sheng and clapping his hands down onto his shoulders.

"What?" Sheng wondered, looking at all the still-shocked faces.

The afternoon gong sounded the end of classes for the day and the students quickly headed out into the sunshine. The day had passed too slowly for Sheng and he was ready to roam the dojo grounds.

"Remarkable!" Master Ken exclaimed once more as he left the room, looking back once more at Sheng.

"What's the big deal?" Sheng asked, a hint of anger in his voice as he and Daisuke followed everyone into the garden.

"How'd you do that?" Suki-chan asked excitedly, nearly jumping up and down on the spot.

"Do what?!" Sheng said, his frustration more evident.

"You walked across the pebbles."

"So? Everyone else did too," Sheng muttered.

"But you didn't make a sound!" Daisuke praised.

"I didn't make sound?"

"No...you were as quiet as Master Ken."

"But I didn't do anything *special*," Sheng pleaded.

"Well then you'll have to teach me how to *not do* anything *special* as well," Suke-chan replied with a wink.

Sheng didn't say anymore as they wandered back to their house. He didn't care if he walked silently across a bunch of stupid little pebbles. All he could think about was Scar and the tiger over the door to their house.

Sheng's head was spinning as he went about his evening. He hardly touched his dinner and didn't help Daisuke with any of their chores around the house. As they headed up to their room for bed, he walked right past Naoki and Jin as they said goodnight. Flopping down on his mat, he grabbed his blanket and pulled it up over his shoulders and turned so that his back was to his roommates. Suke-chan mumbled goodnight and blew out the candles that rested on a small table in the center of the room.

Forcing his eyes to close, Sheng hoped he would quickly fall deep into sleep. But soon, between Suke-chan's ghastly snoring and the sound of crickets outside the window, he found himself wide awake: another sleepless night. He could hardly stand lying there in the dark so he quietly pulled on his robes and crept out of the room. The last thing Sheng wanted was to wake the guardian, who would most definitely tell him to go back to bed. Glancing out the window as he tip-toed into the dimly lit hall, Sheng could see the garden bathed in moonlight. It was beautiful. He wanted to stop and just take it in, but he knew if he stood there too long, someone was bound to find him.

Sheng headed downstairs and across the entrance hall, the centuries old wooden floor boards creaking loudly as he passed. He was sure that each step was bringing him closer to waking the whole house. Thinking hard, he remembered what Daisuki had told him he'd done in Master Ken's class that day. In concentration, Sheng closed his eyes and stepped forward, slowly placing his foot on the floor in front of him. He anticipated the sound of his own footfall, but there was no noise at all, not a single creek of the floor. Sheng couldn't believe it as he opened his eyes and looked at his feet. He felt as if he were floating, but he was still firmly on the ground. Continuing on silently towards the next hall, Sheng felt his hope surge. He could go anywhere like this and no one would be the wiser. It was an incredible feeling of absolute liberation.

Turning down the hall that led into the house of the monkey, he found that it was decorated very much the same as his clan's house; except, instead of tigers everywhere, their house was filled with playful monkey statues and scrolls that hung on the wall depicting different types of monkeys and explaining their attributes.

Sheng stopped and read one of the scrolls. His mother and father thought it was of great importance that he could read and write *kanji* so he had studied the art of calligraphy from an early age and he was now very thankful for the lessons he'd endured back home in his village.

"Exceptionally quick and stronger than they appear, these tree dwellers thrive in familial societies, sharing with each other and living peaceably, showing general concern for the other animals which coexist in the forest. However, do not let their playful nature fool you, when provoked, they can strike with ferocity and accuracy. A monkey can be your best friend or greatest enemy."

Sheng considered the words, trying to fit them into the puzzle he had shaped in his mind. He wondered if this was a clue to the monkey which symbolized this house. He had met many of the students in this clan and they seemed nice enough; though, Sheng did remember seeing one of their students throw an angry wad of food across the dinner hall at the mean boy from the dragon clan only a few days earlier.

These thoughts were quickly pushed from his mind by the sound of someone approaching. Squinting hard in the darkness, Sheng could make out the tall shape of an older student: the monkeys' hogosha.

Sheng wished he could disappear, but they had only just started learning sneaking skills in their *Art of Concealment and Stealth* class with Master Ken. Desperately, he looked for a place to hide.

There, he thought to himself, ducking under a low table and withdrawing as far into the shadows as he could.

The guardian walked past slowly and turned through an open doorway just beyond the table. Sheng held his breath as he waited for the sound of the door sliding closed. It seemed like forever, but finally, the door shut. Having come so close to being caught, he decided not to take any more risks and hurried off, figuring he would be much safer in his own house. If he couldn't sleep, at least he could study.

Peeking outside, Sheng saw that the coast was clear and headed out into the cool night. It would be faster to cut across the garden than to sneak back through the halls.

The tigers were sleeping peacefully in their cages as Sheng passed. He stopped for a moment. They were his favorite animals in the garden menagerie. Often, he thought of himself as a tiger, ready to pounce. His mother had said it herself when he was younger, the way he would stalk his friends as they played hide and seek. One of the tigers stirred, Sheng moved on quickly. The last thing he needed was a roaring tiger bringing attention to his midnight exploration.

Ducking under branches, Sheng could see the steps that led into the temple. He was getting closer to his house.

Something caught Sheng's attention as he snuck around the side of the temple. Out of the corner of his eye he saw a figure emerge from behind a thick shrub just beside the temple stairs. It was Subaru Tatsuo.

Sheng watched as he hurried off toward the Tiger Clan house. What was he doing under there at this time of night? Tatsuo disappeared into the trees. Sheng took off after him in full stride, hoping to catch up.

Running noisily through the branches, he was having trouble seeing. The dense trees blocked the moon's glow, leaving the wooded area pitch black. All Sheng could hear was the thumping of his heart in his ears and his feet thudding against the grassy earth. He figured he was gaining ground. Tatsuo couldn't be that far ahead now.

Sheng thought he must be closing in when suddenly, *SLAM!* He tumbled to the ground, his head pounding. A hand reached down and pulled him to his feet. Sheng went to speak, but a finger shot up, silencing him.

Tatsuo was staring into the clearing ahead. Sheng followed his gaze.

Scar was arguing heatedly with a figure shrouded behind a long, hooded black cloak. Sheng strained to hear Scar's angry voice. "I don't care what you say. I'm telling him. And if you don't like it, you'll just have to kill me." Scar said, wagging a finger in the face of the stranger.

"I nearly killed you before," an oddly familiar voice spat back calmly. "It wouldn't take much for me to do it now."

Scar raised his finger again, ready to retort, but apparently the hooded man had had enough of their conversation. He turned, his cloak sweeping around his feet as he headed off towards the wall. The dark figure effortlessly scaled the barrier and disappeared over its top, slipping away into the night.

"Who was that?" Sheng asked, rubbing the knot on his forehead.

"I don't know." Tatsuo replied, "but we'd better get moving. Here comes Scar. If he catches us, we're done for."

"What are you talking about? Scar won't turn us in," Sheng argued.

"I've been here a lot longer than you, Sheng," Tatsuo told him, leading the way back to their clan's house. "Scar isn't someone you want to mess with. He's dangerous. It's a wonder Hasegawa has even allowed him to stay on as gardener."

"What?!" Sheng exclaimed as they bolted up the stairs to their bedrooms.

"Never mind," Tatsuo said, tiptoeing into his room "pretend you didn't see a thing. Now get some sleep and we'll talk about this tomorrow at lunch."

Tatsuo slid the door closed before Sheng could protest, leaving him standing by himself in the hallway. Small rays of light were beginning to filter in through the eastern windows. It was nearly dawn. He crept into his own room, trying not to wake his roommates as he dressed in his training clothes and headed back down stairs to the great room. Sitting down on the floor, he read through a scroll from Master Gaiden's history class.

Soon the other students would be up and about. He tried to

concentrate, but Tatsuo's words repeated over and over again in his mind. What did he mean when he said to stay away from Scar, that he's *dangerous*? Sheng couldn't wait to tell Suke-chan.

7

SAMURAI & SECRETS

A loud yawn echoed through the halls. Sheng looked up from his scrolls just in time to watch Daisuke trudge sleepily down the stairs.

"Morning," Daisuke managed between still more yawns, his mouth gaping like a cavern.

"Sure is," Sheng answered sarcastically.

There was a brief pause. Suke-chan must not yet have woken up enough to catch on to Sheng's joking, but he grinned all the same and sat down on the floor next to his best friend. He looked over at the scrolls scattered about their feet and was glad he wasn't the one reading them all.

"Where'd you go last night?" Suke-chan questioned finally, his grogginess beginning to diminish. "I got up to go to the bathroom and you were gone."

"You're never going to believe what I saw!" Sheng said excitedly. "Last night, I was sneaking through the house of the monkey…"

"Stupid chimps…" Suke-chan muttered with a wink.

"And I was almost caught by their guardian."

"Wow, really exciting," Daisuke yawned, this time mockingly rather than sleepily.

"Seriously, listen! That's not what's important," Sheng replied as he gathered his thoughts. "I snuck out into the garden to avoid their keeper and I saw Tatsuo sneaking out from under the temple. I chased after him to find out what he was doing when he stopped me."

Sheng pulled his shaggy hair from his brow, showing Daisuke the purple bruise on his forehead where Tatsauo had accidentally hit him. Daisuke winced, then yawned again, this time for real.

"So what happened?" Suke-chan asked.

"I'm getting to that…"

Their conversation was discouraged by the sound of nearly two dozen feet on the old wooden steps clumping their way down. Naoki and Jin were towards the front of the crowd.

"Are you guys coming to breakfast?" Jin squeaked.

"Do I look like I would miss breakfast?" Daisuki said as he stood and helped Sheng to his feet. "Definitely not!"

They mingled their way into the middle of the crowd and continued talking quietly on their way to the great hall. It was an unusually breezy morning and the sound of the wind whipping through the branches of the trees helped hide their words from curious ears. Finally sitting at their table Daisuke recounted in between bites what Sheng had told him, wanting to make sure he had all the details right.

"So then you saw Scar arguing with somebody?" Suke-chan questioned, scooping more rice into a bowl.

"Exactly," Sheng answered through a mouthful of food.

"And what were they arguing about?" he wondered as he poured water from a tall pitcher into his cup.

"That's what I've been trying to figure out," Tatsuo interrupted, squeezing in between Sheng and Naoki. "I couldn't sleep at all last night so I decided to take a walk in the courtyard. While I was near the temple, I saw a man shrouded in black robes, a hood hiding his face, sneak out into the city through that secret passage I mentioned to you, the one under the temple..."

"Was it the same man we saw with Scar?," Sheng interjected. "Was it him?"

"Yeah, at least...I think," Tatsuo answered thoughtfully.

"So what happened next?" Sheng pushed.

"Okay. So I waited to be certain the hooded figure would be far enough ahead that he wouldn't notice me behind him. I followed the man into the city and found him talking with four samurai."

"Samurai?! Are you sure?" Daisuke asked, dropping his food on the table. "Did you recognize any of them? Maybe they were from our village and they were looking for us?"

"Were they marked with the Shimazu clan symbol?"

"No, not that I saw," Tatsuo answered. "Their faces were hidden by oni-like masks. I couldn't identify them. And their armor was black and simple, not as ornate as any of the clans I have seen."

Sheng and Daisuke cast each other angry looks. Tatsuo wore the same expression as well.

"So then who was the man under the hood last night?" Sheng asked. "Was he a samurai as well?"

"No...I think...well...it sounded like...*Master Hasegawa*," Tatsuo explained cautiously.

"WHAT?!" Sheng and Suke-chan replied in unison.

"But it couldn't have been," Tatsuo reasoned. "He's here to train and protect us."

"You honestly believe that?" Sheng challenged. "Have you forgotten that he takes children from their villages and then separates them from their families? How is that protecting anyone?"

"I can't say I understand Hasegawa's methods, but I believe he means well and in the end, our training turns us into great warriors. Remember, not every boy here came from a well-to-do samurai village. For some of these boys, this is an improvement and a much more promising life!"

"That's not what I was trying to say," Sheng backpedaled.

"I know. But all this is speculation anyway. So don't say anything to anybody till I've had a chance to look into it more," Tatsuo said firmly. "Words spread like fire here!"

Tatsuo stood and headed off through a door in the back of the room. As he left, servant girls streamed in to collect their empty plates. A gong rang out across the garden.

"Come on, Suke-chan," Sheng said standing up as did all the other boys in the room. "It's time for class."

Master Gaiden unrolled his scroll and stood in front of his students. His thin gray *fu manchu* mustache hung long past his chin, as did his sparse, matching beard. He smiled at them as they unrolled their scrolls as well. Finally he sat down facing them, his bony fingers pointing out students to read to the class.

Daisuke hated reading aloud. He always felt so anxious when it was his turn. Inevitably, he always ended up with a word that he did not know and would, to his embarrassment, pronounce it improperly. And worse, he would then be corrected by the teacher. As Gaiden's finger stopped on Suke-chan, his face turned bright red but he did his best. Sheng didn't understand why reading in front of everyone bothered Suke-chan so much. For as much as Sheng could tell, Daisuke was a much better reader than he was and had no reason to be nervous.

The morning lessons passed quickly. Master Gaiden wrapped up his teaching and thanked the students for listening. Sheng lingered, wanting to stay after class and ask Master Gaiden what he had been discussing with Master Ken. He was curious about the details of the conversation that he and Daisuke had nearly overheard while they'd been eating lunch outside.

"What are you doing?" Daisuke asked Sheng, watching as the last boy left the classroom.

"Hold on, Suke-chan, I want to ask Master Gaiden a question."

"There's not enough time," Daisuke pleaded. "If we don't go now, we'll be late for Master Haiku's lesson. And you know he won't like that!"

"I know, but…"

"Come on, Sheng! Don't forget that Tatsuo explicitly warned us not to ask any unnecessary questions or talk to anyone about Scar and Hasegawa!"

"What's that about Master Hasegawa?" Master Gaiden asked them suddenly interrupting their argument from over Daisuke's shoulder.

"*AHHH!*" Daisuke exclaimed fearfully as Master Gaiden laughed.

"Nothing, Master," Sheng said with a hurried bow as Suke-chan grabbed him by the sleeve of his karate gi and drug him out of the classroom.

"For all we know they *were* talking about Hasegawa and Scar," Daisuke whispered as they left Master Gaiden alone in his classroom, an amusingly confused expression on his face.

Grudgingly, Sheng followed Suke-chan towards the training grounds on the opposite side of the garden from the classrooms. He certainly wasn't looking forward to Master Haiku's class. There was simply too much on his mind to care about sneaking techniques. Still, he decided it would be for the best if he cheered up and thought of his mother's advice: smile even when you don't want to. So he did. His mother was right and he found himself feeling better, if only a little.

The two friends walked on, laughing as they clowned about how boring the next lesson would be, imitating Master Haiku's stance and flamboyant movements. Daisuke was always happier when Sheng was in a good mood as well. They continued on gleefully, but before either friend could crack another joke, they were startled by the soft sound of crying that came from within a cluster of trees in a nearby grove.

"Hold on," Sheng said cautiously as he crept towards the sounds of whimpers and sighs.

Pushing through the branches, Sheng found little Masaki, the boy from the monkey clan who Daisuke and Sheng had saved on their first day at Hasegawa's dojo. He was lying on his stomach, tears streaming down his small red face.

"Masaki?" Sheng tried to console him. "What's wrong? Are you alright?"

The crying slowed as he raised his face slightly off the ground. His eye was red and swollen and a trickle of blood ran from his lower lip.

"I was just going to Master Kinshi's class…" Masaki warbled.

"And?" Sheng asked, noticing that the small boy's eyes were once again flooding with tears.

"I was attacked," he sniffled.

"By who?!" Daisuke shouted angrily.

"Yoruichi Rin and his friends," Masaki cried dropping his head back to the ground.

Suke-chan reached down and grabbed Masaki by the neck of his robe, lifting him to his feet.

"Who's Yoruichi Rin?" he asked as he straightened out the boys robes he had just crumpled.

"The mean boy from the dragon clan," Sheng answered, "It has to be. Only he and his gang would do something like this."

Masaki nodded. Another tear ran down his cheek.

"This isn't the first time they've attacked me, Yoruichi Rin and his friends," he managed to wheeze through yet more tears.

"Why didn't you come let us know?" Daisuke asked. "We'd have taken care of them for you."

Little Mori Masaki didn't answer, he just hugged Suke-chan, drying his eyes on Daisuke's sleeve. Sheng snickered at the look of disgust upon his large friend's big round face as he sneered at the tear-wet, snot-spotted mark on his once-clean sleeve now marked with snot.

The gong rang and they all realized the time. They raced off to their classes, Masaki going one way, Sheng and Suke-chan heading in the other. Sheng knew that Master Haiku didn't tolerate tardiness, but there was nothing they could do: they were late as they stepped into the sparring square.

"Nice of you to join us, boys," Master Haiku taunted.

They took their places and stared at their feet avoiding eye contact. Master Haiku was Sheng's least favorite sensei and apparently, after several difficult lessons, Sheng wasn't on the top of Master Haiku's list either.

"Concentrate on nothingness. Believe you are weightless," their sensei droned in a mysteriously calm voice. "Follow me and do as I do. Now, my students."

Master Haiku stood effortlessly on one leg, his other leg cocked out to the side and bent at the knee, the heel placed tightly against the knee of the leg that supported him. Slowly, he began sweeping his arms in what seemed like some sort of exercise or strange interpretive dance Whichever it was, Sheng thought it looked quite silly. Master Haiku's eyes were closed as well and he sounded as if he were humming monotonously to himself. The class watched in awe at his balance. Fighting the urge to laugh, Sheng nodded at Daisuke and they joined the other boys in following the instructions of their sensei. They each raised one leg and tried standing on the other.

Sheng tried very hard to maintain his balance, but no matter what he tried, he ended up leaning forward till he had to put his suspended foot down to keep from falling. He looked around apprehensively. Some of the boys were doing much better than him, most of the boys in fact. This irritated Sheng, but he reasoned that they didn't have as many thoughts running through their heads as he did.

Even so, Master Haiku was unshakeable. He didn't even appear to breathing as he maintained the rock-steady pose.

Maybe this isn't as easy as it looks?, Sheng admitted to himself as he looked on in silence, an odd and sudden appreciation for his least-liked sensei.

The hour and a half long class passed agonizingly slow. Each minute felt like a lifetime. They were more than halfway through the lesson and Master Haiku was still standing strong, unflinching, his eyes remaining tightly shut in meditation.

The harder Sheng tried, the quicker he seemed to topple. He thought that if he concentrated any harder, his head might explode. But still, he carried on, hoping to stand for at least thirty seconds.

Three boys yelled out as they tumbled to the ground, Suke-chan falling on top of them. Master Haiku finally blinked.

"Are you even trying, my round, little pupil?" he challenged without a bit of empathy.

"Sorry, Master," Daisuke mumbled climbing back to his feet and helping the boys he knocked down to do the same.

Sheng held back his laughter just long enough to hear the afternoon gong announce the end of classes for the day. Master Haiku finally placed both feet back on the ground and dismissed them, casting a disdainful look in Daisuke's and Sheng's direction.

Their muscles ached from Master Haiku's exercise. They were certain the pain would be worse the following day. Two hours remained before dinner would be served in the great hall, so they headed off to the menagerie to pass the time. It had been weeks since they last visited the animals there and they found it to be a great place to relax after a tough lesson. Perhaps they could sit and watch the tigers? That seemed like a perfectly good idea to the exhausted Sheng.

Following the path, they again came upon young Masaki, this time; his face was bright and cheery, except for his swollen lip. He raced up to them with an excited gallop.

"What are you so happy about?" Daisuke asked as Masaki skidded to a stop on the gravel path.

"Master Kinshi just told me how good I was doing," little Masaki

61

beamed.

"Um...that's great!" Sheng said, trying to sound encouraging as he glanced at Suke-chan who shared the same look of doubt.

"I didn't know you were doing so well in Kinshi's class...you know, unarmed fighting and all," Suke-chan said easing his way into the conversation. "You are a lot smaller than most of the other students – except for Yoruichi Rin."

"Well now I know I can handle myself. Yoruichi shouldn't be a problem now," Masaki concluded confidently.

"You can handle yourself?" Sheng questioned, looking at the cut on his lip.

"Yeah? Didn't Yoruichi just rough you up?" Daisuke added.

Masaki thought for a moment, as if Yoruichi Rin's recent attack was a long forgotten memory, and grinned. "Uh huh!" he exclaimed. "But that was before I thought I could do anything on my own. I was always bullied at home too, but Master Kinshi told me I should believe in myself. So I did. Next thing I know, I'm sparring with Jin, you know, the big guy from the dragon clan? Anyway, I knocked him out cold with one move. I didn't even know what happened. He tried to strike, but I ducked out of the way and hit him as hard as I could. It was a blur!"

Sheng and Suke-chan were speechless. They looked at each other with surprised expressions, silently sharing a moment of disbelief. Small, little, whiney Mori Masaki was talking about dropping a big, strong, experienced student who had been training at the dojo for five years, nearly as long as Tatsuo.

"So, do you want to come with us to the menagerie?" Daisuke offered. "I heard they've gotten some new animals, even a panda all the way from China!"

"Sorry," Masaki answered, "I promised to help some of the other students practice the move I used against Jin. I'll see you later."

They watched him run off down the path, dust kicking up behind his feet. It was hard to believe, but certainly must have been true.

"That was incredible, good for Masaki...but poor Jin will never hear then end of it: laid out by the scrawniest boy in the dojo!" Sheng noted as they rounded the corner leading into the menagerie.

The doorway was tall. Echoing bird calls bounced off the walls as they entered. Various bamboo cages of all different sizes stood on each side of the room. Daisuke took a seat on a bench facing a cage of monkeys all chattering away. Sheng bent down and stuck his hand between the bamboo bars of a rather large cage. Two small pink tongues licked at his fingers, then a meager growl. The snow leopard cubs were Sheng's favorites. They played with him, jumping at his hand as he moved it quickly above their heads. A loud grunt scared the cubs away from Sheng. A pair of glowing yellow eyes stared at him from just behind the two little balls of white and black spotted fur.

"Hey boy, watch yourself! They haven't eaten yet," a voice bellowed from the maintenance entrance that was purposefully hidden behind four small potted trees.

Sheng jerked his arm from the cage as the mother leopard nipped at his hand, only narrowly missing. He turned to see who it was as Daisuke jumped to his feet, a look of fear spread across his round face.

"Calm down," the voice said as Scar emerged from behind a cage, a basket full of fresh meat for the carnivores. "Sorry to startle you. I just didn't want to see you lose any limbs. I'm certain you'll need them."

Scar tossed a slab of bloody meat onto the floor of the leopard cage and the mother quickly forgot about Sheng, happily gnawing on the food, snarling as her cubs pulled at the meat too.

"Scar! I've been hoping to see you for days," Sheng said excitedly, almost sounding like Masaki. "Where've you been?"

"That's none of your business," Scar answered, winking with his good eye as he moved onto the next cage. "Why?"

"Well, I *sort of* saw you *arguing* with a man in the garden," Sheng said sheepishly. "Do you remember that night?"

"What were you doing up that late?" Scar demanded, not denying an argument had taken place, a small grin on his deformed face.

"I couldn't sleep," Sheng answered simply. "You said you wanted to tell someone something, something that they ought to know?"

"There are people here who have hidden intentions," Scar said ominously, his voice deepening and growing quieter. "I can't tell you. And if I did, you wouldn't understand."

"I can try," Sheng grinned.

"Well…" Scar paused, choosing how to begin carefully, "what do you know of this place?"

"The menagerie?" Suke-chan asked thoughtfully.

"No, the dojo, you dolt," Scar spat back impatiently.

Daisuke stared at his feet and sat back down on the bench. Scar gave him a little grin and then turned back to Sheng.

"Well, I know there are three clans, each with a different animal symbol: dragon, monkey, and tiger. We are all trained in many different arts and the techniques we learn seem to be unique to each clan," Sheng said.

"Why do you think there are three clans?" Scar prodded.

Sheng cast a glance at Daisuke for help, but Suke-chan stared back blankly.

"I don't know," Sheng admitted.

Scar pulled Sheng over to the bench were Suke-chan was seated and pushed him down onto its hard stone top. He knelt in front of them and whispered, looking quickly over his shoulders for anyone who might overhear. When he was quite sure that no one was around, Scar spoke softly.

"I'll start from the beginning – and remember these words I tell you because undoubtedly Master Gaiden will not speak of this in his history lessons. This place was not originally a dojo, but a secret palace. More than three hundred years ago, the Fujiwara clan, through political strategy and the marrying of their daughters to emperors, seized control of Japan. Emperor Murakami was left as a figurehead, but little else. In 960, the Imperial Palace burned to the ground. Emperor Murakami had a very large family and he chose to build this palace here in Kamakura as a secret refuge at the same time that the official palace was being rebuilt in Kyoto. It wasn't till much later, nineteen years ago, in fact, that this place was designated a dojo. Following the first attack by Kublai Kahn in 1274, three samurai requested to use this old palace as a training ground and were given permission by the *Hōjō* regency to take possession of the property. It was then converted to what you see today."

"Who were the three samurai?!" Sheng immediately questioned with great excitement, barely giving Scar time to breath after telling the history.

"I knew you would ask that. These men sacrificed everything following the Mongol invasions. They left behind their land, their property, that had been gifted by the daimyō . They became master-less samurai, wandering *ronin*. Hasegawa Takeshi, of course, was one of these ronin, another was perhaps the greatest warrior I have ever known…" Scar paused, a sad expression across his face.

"And the third, who was he?" Sheng asked.

With much thought, Scar finally answered, his voice echoing with pain and regret, "It was me."

"You!?" Sheng blurted. "Then why aren't you in charge too, or at least a master?"

"Honestly, I am very fortunate that I have even been allowed to stay here as the gardener. I'm not so certain I would have shown the same mercy that was afforded to me."

Scar was hiding something, of that Sheng was certain. But why? Fear of Hasegawa? Fear of his memories? Sheng felt sorry for this withering man who used to hold such power.

"So if you were here in the beginning, then why does Master Hasegawa get to run this place with you as only the gardener?" Daisuke wondered. "That doesn't seem fair to me."

"It's more than fair, I assure you. Hasegawa allowed me to stay after he…*took over*," Scar explained.

"Alright. And so you said there were three founders. You, Master Hasegawa, and a third samurai, where is he then?" Suke-chan asked.

Scar looked over his shoulders again as if expecting someone to be spying on them as he spoke, "Master Hasegawa thinks he's dead, I think that's for the best."

"So is he?!" Sheng pleaded to know.

"No, not physically at least, but he had what he treasured most taken from him and that is a fate worse than death. You see, after our falling out, he left this place and disappeared into the south. It was rumored that he settled in a village. There, he took a young wife and shortly thereafter they had a child. Hasegawa ruthlessly hunted him down and destroyed his family, leaving him all but dead. But against all odds, he survived. Now his unquenchable thirst for revenge has consumed him."

"And where is he now?" Sheng asked.

"You can never tell anyone what I'm about to tell you. Hasegawa would certainly torture me for this information. The man, the lost samurai, he's…"

Voices echoed just outside the front entrance to the menagerie. Then shouts! Someone was fighting. A loud karate yell filled the air, then, silence. Sheng and Daisuke turned towards the door and then back to Scar, wanting to hear the rest of his story, but he was gone.

8

A FAMILIAR VOICE

There were suddenly more shouts and then the unexpected sound of cheering: Daisuke and Sheng jumped up from the hard stone bench and raced outside of the dark menagerie, quickly shielding their faces as they were blinded by the brilliant afternoon sunlight.

Rubbing the spots from their eyes, they saw the most unusual sight. Mori Masaki was being hoisted onto the shoulders of two students. About fifteen more boys followed closely behind, celebrating louder with every step. Yoruichi Rin was lying flat on his back, his gang fussing over him, one of them in tears. Master Wong stood off to the right vigorously clapping his hands together and grinning from ear to ear. Apparently he witnessed the whole ordeal.

"Sensei, what's going on?" Daisuke asked Master Wong as they looked down at the unconscious bully.

"Oh…" Wong beamed, sounding thrilled to relive the event that had only just unfolded, "young Yoruichi here was teasing that little boy, I think his name is Masami…"

"Masaki," Sheng corrected.

"Yes...Masaki...I knew that of course," he said in his most eccentric way, "why would a boy have a girl's name? Anyway, it was wonderful. As Yoruichi and his gang encircled the boy, I thought I would need to intervene, but to my surprise, that little Masami..."

"Masaki!" Suke-chan interrupted.

"Yes, you know the boy? Anyway, where was I? Oh yes, he countered Yoruichi, throwing him to the ground with a most excellent flip and then turned to face the rest of them; but before he could fight them, the surrounding students hoisted him up and carried him off in celebration," Wong said, still smiling gleefully.

By now, Yoruichi Rin's gang had picked him up and headed off to their house, the unconscious bully slumped over the biggest boy's shoulder. Several turned and glared at Sheng and Daisuke, almost daring them to laugh.

Master Wong turned and strolled off to his quarters still mumbling about the events to himself, every once in a while exclaiming, "Wonderful!" as he finally disappeared around the corner.

Sheng and Suke-chan hurried back through the entrance of the menagerie, startling all the animals in their cages as they rushed by, and out the rear of the building through the maintenance door. The thick trees made it hard to see if anyone was hiding in the woods. Scar was nowhere to be seen.

A gong echoed across the grounds. Dinnertime.

"Come on!" Daisuke said, grabbing Sheng's sleeve and pulling him out of the trees, "We'll talk to Scar later. Let's go eat."

The room was peculiarly quiet. The dragon clan kept to themselves rather than throw food as they usually did and the monkey clan, though still celebrating Mori Masaki's victory, sat in silence, happily eating and casting occasional glances of admiration at their new hero, Masaki.

Suke-chan sat across from Sheng as always. Naoki and Jin were discussing their training from that day as they ate. There was an empty spot just beside Sheng, apparently saved for someone. Each person who attempted to sit there was kindly asked to find another seat.

Silently, Daisuke stuffed food into his mouth. Sheng hardly touched what was on his plate. He simply poked at it, his mind on the conversation that he'd had with Scar that afternoon. Eating was the last thing he wanted to be doing right now.

Someone slipped into the seat next to Sheng, startling him from his trance. He was about to turn and tell the person that he couldn't sit there, but then happily realized this was precisely who the seat had been intended for: Tatsuo.

"Sheng," Tatsuo said sounding short of breath like he'd just been running, "I saw the shrouded man a little while ago. He was flanked with samurai. They found Scar in the woods and carried him off to the city."

"What?! Why?!" Sheng demanded excitedly jumping up from his seat.

Tatsuo grabbed him by his shoulder and pulled him back down, "I don't know why, especially while Master Hasegawa is here, but I'm sure I know where they took him."

"Then let's go!" Sheng said, trying to fight free from Tatsuo's strong grip.

"Not now," the older boy urged, quieting his voice, "tonight. Meet me in the woods near the temple. Come alone."

The evening slipped by quickly. Suke-chan argued the whole time, hoping to convince Sheng to let him come along, but it was useless. Sheng was going to do just as Tatsuo had ordered.

"I'll tell you all about it when I get back," Sheng said pulling his robe from the back of a chair as he watched Daisuke grumpily flop down on his bed mat and pull his blanket around him.

"Have fun..." Suke-chan mumbled, rolling on to his side and forcing his eyes closed tight.

Sheng slipped out the door without waking Naoki or Jin and sped off down the empty corridor towards the stairs that led to the garden. As he ran, he pulled his robe on over his night clothes.

He skidded to a stop. The robe was huge. He must have grabbed Suke-chan's by mistake! Sheng stuck his hand down into the pocket and sure enough, he pulled out a fistful of leftover bread from dinner. With a grin, he dropped the bread back into the pocket and headed outside. He figured he didn't have time to head back for his own robe. Tatsuo hadn't said exactly when to meet, but Sheng figured he would wait if he had to. All he could think about was Scar.

Running across the grass and disappearing into the trees, Sheng headed towards the temple, his heartbeat the only sound he could make out. It was very dark, just like the night he witnessed Scar and the stranger arguing. He wondered if that was why Scar had been taken away.

Approaching a clearing, he saw a shadow slink off the path and into the trees that surrounded the temple. It must have been Tatsuo. Sheng hurried across the path, fully exposed in the moonlight. He didn't care. Soon he was going to see Tatsuo, they would sneak into the city and find Scar.

Hope rose in Sheng's heart as he crunched through the branches and into the dense trees. And just as quickly, his hope was slammed back to the pit of his stomach as fear spread through him. An arm reached out from the shadows and knocked Sheng to the ground. A man stood towering over him, a small laugh muffled by the fearsome samurai mask that shrouded his face. The oni mask snarled in a frightful smile, taunting Sheng as his head thudded against the earth.

A familiar voice spoke, "What business do you have out here when you should be sleeping?"

Sheng tried to stand, but the man's foot was pressed down on his chest, pinning him to the ground. He had to get up, get away. Rustling branches to their left distracted them both. The man peered into the darkness. Sheng had his opportunity.

With the stranger's defenses lowered, Sheng forced himself free.

Though only half the man's size, Sheng struck out, his flurry of strikes lightning quick. He moved unintentionally, almost as if by reflex. The shrouded man fought back, blocking Sheng's blows. But Sheng persisted, pushing the man out of the trees and into the clearing at the base of the temple. The stranger who had been caught off guard gathered himself and laughed.

"Very good, boy. You are learning well," he sneered ducking low to the ground and then leaping straight into the air and disappearing in a cloud of gray smoke.

Sheng stood in shocked disbelief, staring at the dense, gray cloud that was now dissipating. He almost didn't notice Tatsuo who was now standing at his side, looking not at the lingering smoke, but at the steps into the temple.

"Let's go!" he said grabbing Sheng's arm at the elbow and pulling him towards the secret tunnel.

Tatsuo held aside the branches of an overgrown bush at the edge of the stairs, revealing a small dirt pathway leading into the darkness. Sheng felt an encouraging nudge and he and Tatsuo disappeared under the temple. The path wasn't very long, but crawling in the dark seemed to take forever. Every few feet, Sheng felt his back graze the framework of the temple above and he tried to slink lower, closer to the rats scurrying about. Soon the ground began to slope, giving him almost enough room to stand as he stepped from the path into a stone tunnel lit by flickering torches that hung on the walls.

"Follow me," Tatsuo said, stepping around Sheng to lead the way.

The flaming lights glowed warm and bright, casting dancing shadows on the walls, ceiling, and floor. The tunnel was just as Sheng had imagined. Stale air filled the space, an eerie haze seemed to hover like mist. The stone walls arched above them into a rounded ceiling and the floor was covered in a thin layer of cool water, run off from the pond that surrounded the temple as well as the storm drains that were fed from above.

After about ten minutes of walking, they came to a fork in the tunnel. Sheng peered down each end, wondering which they would take. Tatsuo paused, obviously thinking, and then confidently set off to the left without a word. Sheng gazed back to the right tunnel, hoping his friend had made the right choice and then followed him down the left tunnel. He felt like they were going the wrong way, but he had to trust him. After all, Tatsuo had said he'd been sneaking through these tunnels for years.

Finally, Sheng caught the welcome smell of fresh air. Their feet splashed as they hurried towards the exit. Tatsuo leaned out of the opening and glanced to each side. The coast was clear. Sheng followed behind. It seemed colder outside of the safety of the dojo's walls. The streets were empty, the city asleep. This night was exceptionally gloomy. The moon seemed to hide just as they too were hiding, thankful for the darkness that concealed their movements.

Ducking behind a vendor's cart, Tatsuo and Sheng crept along the stone wall of the dojo, moving further from the safety of the tunnel that led them home. Sheng felt a bubble of despair rising inside him as they tip-toed along. How were they ever going to catch up to Scar's captors if they had to move this slowly? And then, both of them froze, holding their breath. As if on cue, a grunt followed by the sound of rustling came from the other side of the cart they were just about to use for cover. Sheng's heart was pounding. Tatsuo dropped to the ground and peered underneath. He could barely make out the shape of a raggedly clothed body and two bare feet.

In silence, Tatsuo motioned orders to Sheng and they snuck around the cart, their backs pressed against the wall. Sheng was sure the sound of their robes scraping against the cold bricks would alert the man. Stoked by his fear, Sheng imagined the man was most surely a guard taking a break from his patrol. But, as they rounded the cart, he was relieved to see it was no guard after all, but simply a man sleeping in the street, a cat sniffing at his ratty hair. His clothes were pulled about him tightly for warmth, but they couldn't have been of much comfort. His old robes had been heavily worn, having large holes that had been patched and torn again.

"The city is filled with men like him," Tatsuo whispered. "Look, do you see that crest sewn on his robes, just there, on the sleeve."

Sheng looked closely. His eyes finally focused in the dark. A dirty, faded emblem was stitched onto the man's filthy robes. He could barely make out the shape of a yellow chrysanthemum flower.

"He used to be a member of the royal guard for the emperor in Kyoto, the Imperial city, probably a member of the rebellion led by samurai," Tatsuo explained, his voice low and soft. "They believed that the emperor had failed the people and was allowing a sect of secretive men to direct the fate of all Japan. Which I think is most certainly true even today. Anyway, many of the emperor's own guard abandoned him and followed the rebellion here. Not long after, the dojo was founded."

"So the founders of the dojo were in rebellion against the emperor?" Sheng asked trying to make a connection.

"Not necessarily against the emperor, but certainly the questionable politics, Sheng. We don't discuss it in our history classes," Tatsuo mused. "It might be the only thing I've never learned at Master Hasegawa's dojo."

"But you thought the stranger sounded like Hasegawa. So obviously, if he rebelled against the emperor, he wouldn't want it taught in class. Rebellion against the emperor would bring great dishonor to a samurai," Sheng pointed out.

"No! As I've said before, Master Hasegawa is looking out for us. I did my research. He is a wise and honest man. He founded the school for us to learn and grow, to become great warriors."

"He took us from our homes and killed my parents!" Sheng blurted, causing the sleeping man to stir.

Tatsuo contemplated Sheng's words and tried to quiet his voice, hoping Sheng would do the same. But, for some reason, he felt like he couldn't look Sheng in the eyes.

"Look, I'm sorry you lost your parents…"

"Lost? They're not lost! It's not like tomorrow I'm going to wake up and find them under my bed mat! They're dead, Tatsuo," Sheng said, anger bubbling deep inside him, ready to boil over, "DEAD!"

"My parents may as well be dead too," Tatsuo replied calmly. "For all I know, they are. True, Hasegawa brought us to the dojo against our will. But I've been here longer than you. Master Hasegawa has given us an opportunity for a greater life. I'm sure that in the end, when we are finished with our training, our parents would be proud to see what we've become."

Sheng stared at his feet and then at the poor man sleeping on the dirty stone-paved street. His heart softened and his anger was replaced with sorrow. The man was sickly; thin and pale. Placing his hands in his pockets, he felt the lumps of bread. Carefully, Sheng slipped out of Daisuke's oversized robes and gently covered the homeless man, knowing that come morning, there would be food for him as well.

Tatsuo watched sadly. He was arguing with this boy who cared so much for everyone around him, giving no thought for himself. "I think your parents would already be proud of who you are," he told Sheng as he stood up, still looking down at the man on the ground.

Sheng turned to Tatsuo, the cold feeling he had just a moment ago now changing to a soothing warmth, "I just wish I had more to give him. He's lucky Suke-chan hoards food in his robes."

"He certainly is."

"And I'm sorry I got so upset," Sheng continued. "I'll give Master Hasegawa another chance."

Tatsuo smiled and put his arm around the much shorter Sheng as they headed back down the street. Behind them, the man snored loudly, sound asleep, warmly wrapped in Daisuke's robe.

The streets stretched into the darkness and the boys felt like they had been walking all night. With every turn, they were holding their breath, hoping to see Scar, or the stranger. Sheng wondered what the rest of the city must look like during the day, when people would be about their business, as he remembered that day that he climbed up the wall of the dojo and peered down on the world outside. However; tonight, not a single window flickered with candlelight. It was as if the city had been abandoned.

Finally, they neared the towering city gate and peeked around the corner, a guard stood post at the entrance. His head hung to one side. He must have been sleeping on his feet, looking quite comical. Approaching hoof-falls thudded against the ground just outside, startling Sheng and Tatsuo as well as the guard, who jumped and straightened his uniform. The gate creaked open. Four riders covered from head to toe in dull black armor trotted into the city. The guard gave a very low bow followed by proud laughter from the men on horseback.

"Samurai," Tatsuo whispered as if Sheng couldn't see them himself.

In a cloud of dust, the riders set off through the streets. Sheng and Tatsuo ran back the way they came, following the echo of the thundering hooves. Out of breath, they found themselves in the North West corner of the city. The buildings were nicer here. Oil lamps lit the stone streets and alleyways.

"Do you supposes this is where they have taken Scar?" Sheng asked leaning against the outer wall of a house.

"This is one of the places I figured he could be," Tatsuo answered confidently.

"What is it?" Sheng said sizing up the opposing building as his eyes followed the samurai through the tall iron gate.

The structure that stood across the street from where they hid in the shadows had thick, imposing walls, much like the dojo. However, this place did not have the appearance of a house of learning. The walls were unkempt and dense ivy grew, sprawling all over.

"It's a prison," Tatsuo replied. "The city guard is housed and trained within its walls. Supposedly it was built as a mansion for a very wealthy person, but that was long ago."

The iron gate clanked shut. Soon, they watched light from a lantern glowing through windows as the samurai marched down the halls on what the boys figured to be the third floor. Without the riders thundering down the streets, a creepy silence filled the air. Sheng suddenly wished he still had Daisuke's oversized cloak to wrap around himself and fight away the cold.

Tatsuo noticed Sheng shivering and put his arm around him again, "It will be winter before you know it. You'll need some proper robes."

Sheng looked up at Tatsuo appreciatively. If anything, he finally felt like he was with family, someone who cared.

The same familiar voice they'd hoped to hear floated out of a window to their left. The lantern stopped just past another window in the direction they heard the man speak.

"Come on!" Tatsuo said, pulling Sheng along towards the ivy covered wall.

Carefully, he tugged at the vine, making sure it was strong before he began climbing. Sheng followed right behind him and they ascended the wall. As they reached the window, they found that the third floor was accented by a narrow ledge that was hidden beneath the ivy. There was just enough room to kneel.

Above them, their heads nearly level with the bottom of the window frame, the boys could hear the man welcoming the samurai as honored guests. Cautiously, they peeked into the room. The samurai were seated with their backs to the window and the stranger paced near the door. The room glowed with the light from the lantern they had seen through the windows, but just barely. It was very dark. They could hear the floor creak under the pressure of each of his slow, steady footsteps.

"I'm glad you've been able join me tonight." the man said from under his hood, "but I am sad to say that we have a problem."

He pointed into a dark corner and the four men turned, as did Sheng and Tatsuo. They followed the stranger's finger, but it was almost too dark to see where he meant for their attention to be directed. Sheng finally made out the shape of a man tied in a chair. He wasn't struggling, just sitting – fearless.

"It seems that our old friend, Scar, as we have come to call him" – at this the samurai all chuckled – "believes our intentions are wrong. Seeing how he used to be one of us, I can't believe we are at odds on this issue. And, I'm afraid that his ramblings may draw interest. At this time, I can't afford for him to share all my secrets, even if he believes it's the right thing to do!"

A soft knock on the door broke the stares at the corner of the room. The stranger opened the door. A young girl walked in, her head hung low, a tray with glasses and a bottle of *sake*, as well as some bread and meat, in her hands. Carefully, she set it down on the table and stepped away, taking a place just out of Sheng's line of sight. The hooded stranger pulled the top off the bottle of rice wine and poured it into the glasses. This was it, Sheng was sure of it, the moment they had been hoping they would witness: they had found Scar and the man with the familiar voice, the one hiding beneath the mask was finally going to show himself when he drank from his cup.

The man raised his drink and pulled his mask away. They were going to see his face just as soon as he withdrew his hand. His chin was now visible. Was it Master Hasegawa? Sheng felt every muscle in his body go tense, and then…*CRASH!* The man pulled his mask back over his face and rushed to the corner where the servant girl had retreated. A half dozen ornamental swords clanked against the wooden floor. She must have upset the display and sent them tumbling down.

The man disappeared from view. Sheng craned his neck trying to see what was going on. The stranger must have been furious.

"Are you alright, girl?" they heard the man ask sternly.

There was no reply. Sheng was no longer kneeling on the ledge. He was standing in full view, staring through the window, a horrified look on his face, afraid the girl was about to face the mysterious stranger's wrath.

She weakly raised her head as the lantern lit her tear-streaked cheeks. She tried to raise herself up, but collapsed back onto the floor under the weight of the heavy swords. Sheng only caught a brief glimpse of her face, but she seemed familiar to him.

"Kimiko-chan?" Sheng cried out, no longer thinking about the samurai or the shrouded man.

Before he could react, he saw that all four of the samurai were now on their feet, swords drawn as they rushed towards the window. Suddenly, he felt a tug on his robes. Tatsuo was already climbing down the ivy covered wall. Quickly, Sheng did the same.

He had only just begun the descent when a brawny hand lunged out of the window and grabbed the collar of his nightshirt. Sheng was caught in a tug of war: Tatsuo was below him, pulling at his leg with all of his might, above, the man in the mask was trying to drag Sheng back through the window. For a brief moment, Sheng's eyes met the man's, deep and green, just barely visible through the slits of his samurai mask. With no other choice, Sheng quickly untied his belt and raised his arms, slipping free from his clothes. Stunned, he found himself shirtless and freezing, sprawled out on the ground next to Tatsuo.

Without thinking, they raced back to the secret tunnel and ran down the passageway. Water splashed high, covering them. Emerging from beneath the temple, soaked and freezing, Tatsuo decided they should split up as they hurried through the garden and into their house. Sheng was relieved to see the tiger crest as he ran under it and up the stairs to his room.

Daisuke, Jin, and Naoki were still sound asleep. Exhausted and chilled to the bone, Sheng collapsed down onto his mat and wrapped up tightly in his warm blanket. He was ready to explode, wanting to share all of his thoughts with Suke-chan. His head was spinning and he could still feel his heart pounding in his chest like it was trying to get out, but it would have to wait till morning.

Soon, Sheng was asleep. Amongst the snores, he dreamt about what he had witnessed: Scar in trouble, samurai meeting under the veil of night, and Kimiko...was that really her? Was she alive?

The hooded man stood over Scar where he sat bound in the chair, Sheng's shirt clutched tightly in his left hand. With his right, he quickly pulled a *tanto* from his belt and lunged forward with the razor sharp blade. The moonlit glint of the short sword's steel reflected in Scar's wide eyes. Neatly sliced chords of rope fell to the floor as Scar stood, freed from his bonds. The four samurai handed the girl a small cinched bag full of copper coins.

"Do you think he bought it?" Scar asked the masked stranger as he rubbed the spots on his wrists where the ropes had rubbed him raw.

"You did an excellent job finding her," the man said in amusement. "She looks almost identical to Sheng's old friend."

"So what of Sheng, then? Do you suppose he suspects you?"

"He saw exactly what he needed to see. Let the mystery drive him onward and he will become a great warrior."

9

LOST & FOUND

Thunder boomed across the imperial city of Kyoto, the hour late, its residents fast asleep as torrential rains poured down on their rooftops. What began as a light drizzle had grown violent, wind and lightning terrorizing the night.

Silently, a young girl sat curled in the corner of a cold and vacant vendor stall in the city's central market. She had no blankets, no robes. Her peasant clothing was worn with holes in the knees, a tear in the left sleeve at her elbow. Her bare toes curled under as she shivered.

She watched as a steady flow of runoff plummeted through a hole in the tiled overhang that covered the stall. Sporadic bursts of lightning illuminated the stream of water in brief flashes that seemed to freeze it in time, crystal clear, almost beautiful. Another loud rumble of thunder crashed and she shuddered, the water only a temporary distraction from her plight. For weeks, she'd been just like this, alone, forgotten…hungry. A mouse scurried about, a small crumb of *something* locked tightly in its jaws. She envied the rodent, whishing she had even that small speck of food. But through all this, she did not cry. Her tears were reserved for tragedy, as she'd learned only recently just how fragile and fleeting life really was.

Her eyelids grew heavy as her thoughts lingered on harsh memories, memories colder than the night itself. She envisioned her capture, separation from her friends, her village burning before her eyes...death. That was her past. This was her life now as she drifted off to sleep.

"You there, urchin, get up!" an old man shouted as he tried to position his cart of wares in the stall. "This is no place for a child to be sleeping. Move along!"

The girl sat up, her neck stiff from the awkward position in which she woke. Her eyes were red, heavy: she wished she could sleep longer. But the storm had passed and the rising sun marked the arrival of a new day. The market would soon be packed with people.

"Come now, girl," the man pleaded, resting his cane on the back wall of the stall as he fussed with the knotted ropes that secured his cart, "stand aside."

She hurried to her feet and watched as he folded down the side panels on his cart. The sweet smells of honey and vanilla filled the crisp morning air. The old man was a baker of sorts and he'd brought freshly made cakes and bread to the market.

"I don't have time for this, girl. The market will soon be full and I must be ready!"

"I'm so sorry, sir," she replied timidly, her head bowed, her long black hair falling in front of her face.

He nodded at her and then turned his attention once more to the cart. Quickly, the girl knocked over his cane and then stepped aside as he grumbled after it cursing her as he did. With his back turned and great effort made in bending down to retrieve his walking aid, the girl made the most of the opportunity and grabbed two honey cakes off of the cart, one in each hand. As the man returned to the cart, she was gone. Empty spots where the goods had been proved he'd been duped.

The girl sprinted away from the baker through the forming crowd and ducked under a display of oriental rugs hanging from a line drawn across the front of another stall. She greedily ate up both cakes, careful not to waste a single crumb. She never knew when she might eat again, and though she greatly regretted stealing, she believed it was all she could do to survive. Finishing the last bite, she licked the sweet frosting off her dirty fingers and smiled, knowing that, at least for a little while, she wouldn't go hungry.

Satisfied, she slipped back into the crowd. Since she'd been on her own, she'd discovered she had an uncanny knack for sneaking along behind shoppers, appearing at a glance to be a child out on a day at the market with her mother or father. Often, this afforded her opportunities to snatch fruits and vegetables from carts as they walked past the many vendors. Occasionally, her small, deft hands found their way into unsuspecting pockets, small round, copper coins a reward for her risk. The smarter city folk, she found after observing their behavior, carried their coins on a rope that was threaded through the open centers of the currency. But not all did this and she assured herself that this was about survival.

For weeks, she watched and waited, learning faces and patterns. Who knew who, who shopped where, which vendors were friendly, which were ruthless: she saw it all and she remembered. Her patience had clearly paid off and now she had become quite the skilled little pickpocket.

Her observations had become so keen, that she was aware that she was not the only thief in the market. Certainly she recognized when a person had been marked as a target and watched to see how professionals did the job. There was one person in particular that the girl had noticed several times over the passing weeks. She was certain this young woman was also a thief, and a very good one at that!

The girl was happy to see that, as fate would have it, the young woman was indeed at the market on this very day, stalking the oblivious crowd for a handsome score. She followed the woman as she would have followed her own target, slipping gracefully between people, never making a sound, blending into the bustling surroundings. Slowly, the girl crept up behind the woman; then, for whatever unknown reason, was no longer compelled to simply watch. The girl wanted to meet this thief., Perhaps they could be friends, maybe even benefit in some way from one another?

She reached out to touch the young woman's arm, but as she did, another hand reached out from the crowd on her right side and instead took hold of her. It was another young woman.

"Don't be afraid," she insisted, seeing the panic in the young girl's eyes. "You need to be more careful. *You* are one, but *we* are many."

The girl struggled, trying to pull away from the young woman. Her effort was beginning to draw attention.

"Please do not struggle, for both our sakes. What is your name, girl?"

She thought long before answering, her mind racing with questions. What should she do? She'd been alone for what felt like so long now, was it worth the risk? What if this was her only chance?

"Not here," she replied. "I'll tell you my name, but not here. Take me with you. Please, take me with you!"

The young woman looked around cautiously. Had she missed something? Was this a trap by the authorities?

"How do I know I can trust you?" the woman asked.

"And how do I know that I can trust you?" the girl answered back wisely. "But I am willing to try. Please, I beg you: take me with you!"

Tears began to streak down her young, round cheeks. The woman felt sorry for the girl and decided that helping her might perhaps be for the best. She quickly took her by the hand and led her through the dense crowd. As they passed the stall where the girl had stolen the cakes that morning, they saw the vendor arguing his case with imperial guards. Apparently he was reporting the crime and they were less than concerned over his emergency. The girl smiled as she kept her face turned away from the old man, not wanting to be picked out from the mass of people. But she was safe: the old man was far too distraught to notice her.

Soon, they dodged down a narrow alleyway, squeezing between two stone buildings. The tight passage dead ended into a third building, this one sided with wood planks. The girl was unsure of where they could go, seeing no doors or ladders. She began to fear a trap.

The woman stopped at the end of the alley and rapped a distinct pattern of knocks with pauses in between on the wooden building. The sound of wood grating against wood came from the other side of the wall and the girl looked on, wide-eyed, as the wall itself swung inward: it was a secret door!

She followed the woman into another tight space that turned immediately left and down a very steep wooden stairway. There was nowhere else to go but down. A lantern sat on a small table at the bottom of the stairs, illuminating where their feet should follow. As the secret door closed to the outside world, the girl became aware that yet another young woman was present, this one had opened the door for them and was apparently a guard. She remained on the shallow landing, a dagger sheathed on her side. The room opened up once they reached the bottom of the steps. More lanterns, these ones hanging from the ceiling, provided ample light. An assortment of girls and young woman sat in awkward silence at the arrival of a new person.

"This way," the woman who guided her smiled, directing the girl past the leery onlookers.

Without argument she followed and was greeted with a towel and wash basin in a small, private room in the back of the narrow, long space. They sat down on the wood-planked floor and the young woman began gently wiping the dirt from the girl's face.

"Where are we?" the girl asked.

"First, your name. I trusted you, now you must trust me."

"Fair enough," she smiled. "My name is Kimiko."

"Very pleased to meet you, Kimiko. I'm *Asami*," the young woman replied, pulling Kimiko's hair back to get a good look at her face. "You are new to Kyoto?"

Kimiko paused, wondering whether or not she should tell Asami everything or only reveal small bits about herself at a time. The young woman was kind to her, helping her bathe. But perhaps, she decided, she would save some details for later.

"Yes, but also no," Kimiko finally replied.

"How's that?"

"Well, I haven't been here long, but long enough to have learned a few things along the way. Some of those things have kept me alive."

"So you're on your own?" Asami questioned as she continued the bathing process.

"Yes."

"What about your parents? Are they not here in Kyoto as well?"

"No, they're dead," Kimiko revealed.

"I'm sorry to hear that," Asami said with certain empathy. "We are all orphans here, Kimiko. We have all seen darkness, tragedy, but we have survived. And even now, we survive – together."

Kimiko listened in silence, thinking about Asami's words. *All orphans,* she thought to herself.

"Here," Asami continued, handing Kimiko the towel. "Undress and finish washing. I'll return shortly with some proper clothes."

She watched as Asami quickly stood and left the room, sliding the panel door closed for privacy. Kimiko got up from the floor and looked down at her ragged clothes. They were dirty, torn, but they were hers and she felt very much in the same condition as the clothes: neglected. She undressed and neatly folded and stacked the old garments next to where she stood, then continued bathing. She closed her eyes and remembered washing in the hot springs near her old village, imagining she was there once more; a wonderful escape! But Asami's gentle knock at the door brought her right back to her present circumstances. Kimiko quickly covered herself with the towel as the door slid open.

"I have your new clothes," Asami beamed, entering and once more closing the door.

In her hands were comfortable looking pants, two traditionally styled shirts for layering, and sandals that looked to be just the right size. Kimiko glanced down at her blistered, raw feet, thankful that she'd no longer have to go barefoot in the city.

"Let me help you," Asami said handing her the pants.

Kimiko dressed and Asami helped her with the robe-like shirts which required tying like a kimono. Lastly, she slipped her feet into the sandals. Asami stood back and inspected the fit of the clothing. Kimiko smiled as she examined the simple, but pretty pattern woven into the cloth. As she did, her long, black hair once more fell in her face.

"That won't do," Asami said, pulling a silk ribbon from her own hair and using it to tie back Kimiko's. "There. Keep your hair out of your face. Let people see your eyes. After all, you're a very pretty girl."

Kimiko blushed. She was so used to playing with Sheng and Daisuke that being in the company of a girl was a very nice change, like having a big sister. With Kimiko's hair pulled back, Asami noticed the small stone charm that hung around her neck.

"I like your necklace," Asami said, gently taking the stone between her fingers as she admired it.

"Thank you. It was given to me by a friend. But…"

"But *what?*"

"I doubt I'll ever see him again."

"Do not lose hope, young Kimiko. Perhaps fate will one day bring the two of you back together. Now come with me. It's time to meet Shiroi Usagi."

"*Shiroi Usagi?*" Kimiko asked.

"That's right. She's our leader. I think you'll like her."

"She calls herself *white rabbit?* That can't be her given name."

"Our names do not define us, Kimiko. We make our own destiny."

Kimiko followed Asami out to the main room. All eyes were on her, it was both awkward and thrilling. The girls she'd seen before, when they'd entered, had moved to opposite sides of the space. Now, standing in the very center of the room was the young woman who Kimiko had followed, attempted to contact. She must have been Shiroi Usagi.

"Hello, Kimiko," Usagi greeted, her head tipped in a bow, "and welcome to our home.

"You all live here?" Kimiko wondered.

"We do. We sleep here, eat here – this is the center of our world."

"I was watching you today, in the market," Kimiko admitted.

"And we were watching you, my friend," Usagi smiled. "We've *been* watching you, for weeks now in fact."

Kimiko suddenly looked worried. Was she in trouble?

"You are skilled, but you lack finesse," Usagi explained. "You were not so obvious to those around you. You blended into the crowd, used people as your cover. A casual onlooker might have given you no more thought other than that you were simply a child drug along with your mother to market. Very good. But to us, well…let's just say a thief recognizes her own."

"What is this place?" Kimiko asked cautiously. "It's not an orphanage, not a school…you're the leader and, pardon me, but you are what, eighteen? Nineteen?"

Usagi smiled. Asami put her arm reassuringly around Kimiko's shoulder.

"You are a very smart girl," Usagi continued. "You are right. This is no orphanage, no school. What it *is* is a guild, alive for many years – the skills passed on from one generation to the next. And you are right, I am nineteen, in many ways still just a girl, yet I have been trained well and am a master in my art, a sensei in the truest meaning of the word. In Kyoto, girls are looked down upon, treated as a second in society. We are laborers or entertainers, or worse. Our destiny, if we did not so act, would have us be *saburuko* girls or rice farmers. Certainly, you could serve tea the rest of your life, or slave away in fields that may or may not yield a crop, or dance for and entertain old, wealthy men…but would you want to? Here, we make our own destiny. Here, we do what we want to do. You are one of us now. Welcome, young Kimiko, to the thieves guild."

10

HOPE & UNCERTAINTY

The next three months passed quickly. The leaves had changed and fallen. Snow now covered the mountain tops and hillsides. What had previously seemed like cold nights in the city were now longed for warm memories.

Night after night, Sheng and Suke-chan snuck out of the dojo through the secret tunnel and roamed the streets of Kamakura, hoping to catch a glimpse of their lost friend Kimiko-chan. As of yet, they had not found her. They did however discover another group of houses, like the dojo. But the young girls held there were not trained as warriors. They were taught skills needed as servants and entertainers.

Scar was also nowhere to be found. The boys searched every inch of the gardens including a forbidden section in the northwest corner that was reserved as Master Hasegawa's personal grounds. They assumed that the samurai must have killed Scar. A new gardener now tended the grounds. They feared that Kimiko met the same fate at the hands of merciless samurai: something of which they tried not to speak.

Their lessons were going well. Daisuke had become one of Master Kinshi's best students in unarmed fighting, second only to little Mori

Masaki, unsurprising after his stand against Yoruichi Rin. Sheng was taking to the art of stealth and concealment as a natural, leaving Master Ken astounded at his progress after each and every lesson. Tatsuo was now studying advanced swordsmanship taught by Master Hasegawa himself. In fact, Hasegawa had begun taking a much more active role in the day to day operations of the dojo. He had started eating his meals in the great hall with the boys and was present to watch many of them spar.

As far as Sheng could remember, their first several months at the dojo, Master Hasegawa kept himself locked up in his wing of the houses, only appearing for brief meetings with teachers and troubled students or making some lackluster announcement during dinner. Daisuke and Sheng felt their distrust for Hasegawa slip away with each day that passed. Maybe Tatsuo was right.? Master Hasegawa seemed kind enough, especially now that he was even teaching lessons.

Tatsuo raved about Hasegawa, saying that he was the best fighter he had ever seen with a sword, a boast which peaked Daisuke's and Sheng's interest. They started watching Hasegawa's lessons. He was an artist with a blade – fluid – every movement linked to the next like a beautifully dangerous dance. Tatsuo wasn't bad himself, nearly as quick. He was the only one of the students who could hold his own against Master Hasegawa in a duel.

They were making great progress and, against their first impressions of the dojo, were beginning to actually enjoy themselves. Their only complaint was Yoruichi Rin who believed that Sheng must have put Masaki up to attacking him and was quite angry about the black eye he acquired as a reminder of his foolishness. Yoruichi and his thugs had taken to cornering Sheng and Daisuke at every perceived opportunity, hoping to catch them off guard. As of yet they had been very unsuccessful, much to the chagrin of Master Wong who always seemed to witness their fights. He was getting more elated after each narrow escape the two boys managed, never once trying to intervene and stop the battles.

Sheng's focus turned to becoming the best fighter he could, wanting to be just like his father. He still hated the art of balance and control, almost as much as he thought that Master Haiku must have hated him. But, as Daisuke pointed out after their last lesson, Haiku seemed to hate everyone, even the other sensei. He muttered under his breath, even when a student succeeded. This aggravated Sheng all the more and pushed him to try harder and harder, if only out of spite for his sensei.

They hadn't even given another thought to the meanings behind the symbols of the three houses at the dojo or to any of the words Scar had spoken that day long-since-gone in the menagerie. Their only thought of the outside world was of Kimiko, hoping that, wherever she was, she was safe. For whatever reason they simply felt at peace. They had made a new home.

Sunlight beamed in through the window. It was a snowy, cold winter morning.

"Hey Sheng, wake up!"

Slowly, his eyes opened. Two hands were shaking him, trying to bring him out of the dream he much wished to continue. Rubbing the sleep from his tired, blurry eyes, Sheng found Suke-chan sitting beside him on the floor, grinning a very toothy grin, his round face looking quite happy, if not a bit exaggerated.

"Happy Birthday, Sheng!" Daisuke spouted so loudly he now woke both Naoki and Jin as well.

"I hadn't even thought about it," Sheng mumbled through a yawn as he stretched his arms over his head.

"How old are you?" Naoki asked, looking just as tired.

"Twelve," Sheng answered grinning.

"Congratulations," Jin grunted, rolling over and pulling his blanket up to hide his eyes from the bright sun.

"Let's go get breakfast, Sheng," Suke-chan said, grabbing his robe and heading through the door.

The day was beautiful. A fresh dusting of snow covered the lawns of the garden. They must have been the first ones up as they headed towards the great hall. As they trudged across the grounds, their footprints were the only ones to be found.

Quickly climbing the stairs into the hall, the boys came across a tall man who stood in the corner of the entrance, talking to Master Wong in a hushed voice. He casually glanced over his shoulder with a slight smile. It was Master Hasegawa. Sheng and Suke-chan smiled back as they passed through the doorway, never giving the secretive conversation another thought as they had become so used to seeing Hasegawa about the grounds.

Within the next few minutes, the great hall was flooded with boys, followed shortly by servant girls bringing in plate after plate of food. As usual, the girls kept their heads down. Against all their hopes, Kimiko was still yet to be seen, further evidence that she had met an unfortunate end. They ate their food happily, though Sheng wore a glum look on his usually bright face, especially solemn for his birthday. Daisuke filled his mouth with bite after bite so quickly, it looked as if he were about to choke at any moment.

"It's your birthday…*smile!*" Suke-chan grinned, after finally swallowing the mammoth wad of food.

Sheng shrugged. The left corner of his mouth raised slightly in a meager attempt at a happy expression.

"This is my first birthday without…*them*," he said regretfully, "without my parents."

"I know, but your parents would be happy to see where you are, what you're learning. It wasn't their choice for this to happen the way it has, but it's what we have to live with. We can either go on sulking or do our best to honor them. Our parents are dead, but we're not," Daisuke finished resolutely.

He wasn't sure what to say. Instead, Sheng stared at his food.

"You're right," Sheng finally admitted after a long, uncomfortable silence. "Our parents would want us to make the best of this. My father would tell me that it's time to move on."

They finished breakfast without another word. Soon, the girls came along to clear the tables. Sheng and Suke-chan waited till nearly everyone else had left. They had hoped to catch up with Tatsuo, but they hadn't seen him all morning. Apparently he hadn't been to breakfast at all. Sheng went to stand, but felt a strong hand guide him back to his seat. Daisuke looked stunned, his jaw gapping widely.

"Master?!" Sheng wondered, hoping he didn't sound disrespectful.

Takeshi Hasegawa sat down next to him and crossed his arms. His shallow cheeks were gaunt, yet strong. Piercing eyes stared deep into Sheng's.

"I have heard it is your birthday," he said calmly, matter-of-factly.

"Yes, Master…" Sheng hesitated, "how did you know?"

"I overheard two boys leaving your house this morning, one sounded quite grumpy, like he was woken up earlier than he would have liked on his day away from class," Hasegawa answered. "I was wondering if you had some time for us to talk?"

Daisuke looked disappointed. First he missed out on Sheng and Tatsuo's first adventure into the city, now he would surely be asked to give them a moment to speak alone.

"Of course, you are more than welcome to stay. It involves you as well," Master Hasegawa explained, noticing the saddened look on Suke-chan's face.

Sheng and Daisuke tried to look casual, but inside, they were bubbling with excitement. They sat, eagerly awaiting the words their Master had to share with them. Suke-chan's sad expression transformed into a mischievous and anxious smirk.

"I want to first say how proud I am of the both of you. It is a joy and honor to have you train here at my dojo. You have begun an incredible journey and are both well on your way. Second," Master Hasegawa continued sweetly, "I would like to take this opportunity to ask the two of you to join in my swordsmanship lessons. Normally, I would not offer such a prospect to students of your age, but I have watched your progress closely and I believe your skills deserve greater cultivating. Continuing at the pace of the less capable students would only be a detriment to your learning. Of course you would train with the older students. In fact I believe you are already friends with one of them, a student named Subaru Tatsuo – one of my best."

The boys sat ever-silent, soaking in what they were hearing. They wanted to stand and bow, graciously thanking him for the opportunity.

"But, I also have a special charge for just the two of you," he said, lowering his voice and leaning towards them in a cautious manner. "I know that the two of you spent some time with our gardener, Scar. I wondered if you have seen him recently. You see, he has...*disappeared*. I would like to know if you have heard from him. He is...*sorely missed*."

"No, Master," Sheng said, thinking back to the night that he and Tatsuo saw Scar bound and captured by the samurai and the masked stranger. "We haven't seen him since before the first snow."

"Yeah," Daisuke added, "we've searched the gardens and he's nowhere to be found, not even in the menagerie."

"So you *have* looked for him?" Hasegawa asked.

"Well, yes. He was giving us advice..."

Master Hasegawa interrupted Sheng, seeming quite interested in this news, "I see. And what was he...*advising*?"

"Just extra help with some of our lessons," Suke-chan thought up quickly, seeing that Sheng looked reluctant to share with Hasegawa what Scar had told them, especially about the founding of the dojo. "He helped us with balance and control, mostly."

"That's a laugh," Hasegawa grinned. "What does a gardener know of fighting?"

"Not much!" Sheng feigned to laugh along.

"So he was helping you with balance and control? Well, very good. Enough about the gardener. You won't have to worry about that class anymore. Balance and control is at the same time as my training sessions, so I am sure that Master Haiku will not be offended if I dismiss you from his lessons," Hasegawa smiled cunningly, "unless you enjoy Master Haiku's instruction?"

"Of course we'll train with you!," Sheng exclaimed, relieved to hear that he could skip Haiku's class.

Daisuke was relieved as well, seeing that balance wasn't his best subject. Fighting with swords would certainly be much more enjoyable.

"Then it's settled," Hasegawa announced as he stood and readied to head out of the great hall. "You will finish your lessons with Master Haiku this week and then you will begin attending my training. Tatsuo will mentor you."

Master Hasegawa turned slightly pail, as if he forgot to mention something that grieved him deeply, as if this was the whole reason he had spoken with them in the first place, "By the way, I was wondering if you boys might be able to do me a simple favor."

Sheng and Daisuke looked on eagerly. They nodded their agreement in unison.

"Since you have already been looking for Scar and since he has taken a liking to both of you, I was hoping that you may be able to help...*search* for him. There is a secret tunnel that leads out of the dojo. It's underneath the eastern steps of the temple. You are more than welcome to leave the dojo by that passage anytime you do not have lessons, even though I have always reserved that as a privilege for my older, more deserving students. If you happen to find him, please do your best to convince him to return. His work here is essential and this dojo is not the same without him. I trust you will honor me in this task."

With that, Master Hasegawa turned away from them, his beautifully ornate robes fluttering around him as he did, and headed out through the main entrance into the snow flurry that had begun outside. Sheng and Suke-chan couldn't believe it: Hasegawa actually gave them permission to explore beyond the dojo's walls, no more sneaking around!

The next week was a blur. Between the dirty glances Master Haiku gave them every time they crossed paths on the grounds and the thought of never hearing him correct them again, they were wanting to skip their last lesson in the Art of Balance and Control simply because they would never have to study with him again. Thankfully, the week was coming to a close and their last class with Haiku was over quickly. He paid them little attention, mostly casting sarcastic mutterings and judgments under his breath, but nothing that made Sheng and Suke-chan do anything but laugh to themselves.

Later that day, they ate lunch just as the usually did and then headed straight out through the secret tunnel and into the city. Now that they were allowed to venture out, they didn't have to duck behind carts for fear of being seen, something in itself which was absolutely wonderful.

The city was so different than the dojo. Though the gardens were beautiful and bright, the city was vibrant in its own, very distinct way. Having come from a small village, the things Sheng and Suke-chan had now become accustomed to seeing made them feel like they were from a strange and distant world. Merchants and vendors lined the streets in and around the market district, shouting out their daily specials and bargains, each one battling for the attention of the potential customers who passed them by, the customers in turn ignoring the boisterous sellers, walking on as if they couldn't hear the dichotic symphony of chaos all around them.

After passing a row of fish mongers, they came across one of the local trade shops: a blacksmith. Here, several men all worked together to produce fine metal-goods. Daisuke and Sheng tried to stop by this shop on every trip they made from the dojo. But it wasn't the farming tools or cooking pots they came to see. One of the men in particular, much older and life-worn was an exceptional craftsman in the art of sword-making. Each blade he forged was unique, strong…and razor sharp. But with his quality came a steep price. His least expensive blades cost much more than a commoner earned in a whole year. Most of his swords were afforded only by nobility. Samurai often requested custom blades, traditionally made and marked with their clan mon.

The master smith's current forging was no exception. For the last month, he'd been working on a brilliant katana made of smooth, blackened steel, folded over and over for strength. The blade's matte finish hardly reflected any light, making it very difficult to see in battle, especially at night. Rumor amongst the city folk was that the sword was ordered for Master Takeshi Hasegawa himself. But the blacksmith preferred theatrics and denied the rumors, instead telling a twisted tale of a dark samurai who demanded the blade and as payment, this evil samurai allowed the sword maker to live.

Sheng was convinced that the story, no matter how exaggerated for dramatic effect, must be true seeing that the black sword perfectly matched the black armor that the samurai who had taken Scar and killed their parents wore. After every trip to the blacksmith's shop, Suke-chan danced around as they walked on, as if he was locked in a heated fight with an invisible swordsman. The old, gray blacksmith only chuckled to himself, as always, loving the enthusiasm that young Daisuke emanated.

They continued on, wandering the city for hours searching in vain. And now, after another afternoon spent without a glimpse of Scar, the two decided it was time to head back to the dojo. The sun was setting and they had missed dinner. Hopefully Tatsuo saved them some scraps off the table, even a crust of bread would do.

Daisuke was moaning with hunger pains as they passed back through the market. He held his hands on his stomach as they passed cart after cart filled with fruits and vegetables, rice and fish. Nearby, a woman was chopping the heads off of squawking chickens, her cleaver thumping sickeningly against her wooden chopping block. They stopped for a moment to watch her wrestle with a rather large and understandably flustered chicken, feathers going everywhere as she tried to hold it down.

"Good evening," a hushed voice whispered behind them.

Sheng and Suke-chan whipped around not knowing who they would see. They hoped for Scar, but didn't expect it to be him.

"You boys should be careful," the man spoke, "wandering the city streets at sunset. This is not a safe place for boys your age, especially when night falls. There are...*dangerous* people here."

The man was tall with broad shoulders. He looked strong, very strong – warrior strong. His cheekbones were pronounced and his eyes were dark and deeply set, but there was still an unusual softness in his face. He smiled, catching the boys' questioning expressions. His face was covered in a thick beard, so thick that it hid the outline of his jaw and cheekbones, and his hair hung down across his brow.

"It's alright. I used to be a member of Master Hasegawa's guard. I have seen you in the dojo. In fact I've seen you in the streets many times. Tell me, are you looking for someone?" he asked slyly.

Sheng thought for a moment. There was something oddly familiar about this man, yet as far as he could remember he had never seen him before. It wasn't his voice, or his smile, and it certainly wasn't his face! Sheng just couldn't put a finger on it.

Daisuke muttered something about being too hungry to eat and the man turned to look at Suke-chan with a grin. As he did, the last light of day glinted in the man's eyes, his bright green eyes. The sun was at the man's back when they had first met. Sheng couldn't see his eyes very well. But now he knew for certain. That's what was familiar about him. He had eyes just like the masked stranger who had held Scar captive.

"Um. Yes. You're right," Sheng said, bumbling through his words. "Boys our age should not be outside of the dojo after sunset. We'll be going now."

Sheng tried to smile innocently as he grabbed Suke-chan's sleeve and raced off towards the entrance that led back through the tunnel. The man said nothing, just watched them run away.

They hurried in the opposite direction of the man, their lungs aching and their hearts pounding, their legs growing weak as they splashed through the stagnant runoff in the tunnel. No caution was warranted for fear the stranger had followed them back. They galloped through the gardens and across the grounds, not caring if they were seen by any students or masters. They wanted to hide till daybreak, safe and sound under their blankets.

As soon as they made it to their room, they were happy to find themselves alone. Naoki and Jin must have been somewhere out on the grounds. For the time being, they could speak candidly. Sheng re-imagined all the small details about the night he saw Kimiko and Scar with the stranger in that room, trying to recall anything of importance.

"How could I be so stupid?" Sheng exclaimed at last. "This whole time I've suspected it was Master Hasegawa who was doing these horrible things, but Tatsuo was right. Hasegawa *is* on our side. That man we saw tonight had green eyes and the stranger, his face was covered by a mask, but his eyes: I saw them clearly. He had the same eyes, I'm sure of it! He must be the leader of the samurai and..."

"Wait," Daisuke interjected, "the samurai that you saw were wearing black armor right? And the samurai that took us from our village wore the same black armor right? And those samurai brought us here, to learn under Master Hasegawa. So how could they take orders from two different leaders? Wouldn't they end up loving one and hating the other? They could never be loyal to both at the same time."

Sheng thought about what Suke-chan had just very wisely said before answering. He did make an excellent point. How could a person honorably serve two masters?

"Maybe the samurai answer to Master Hasegawa for show? Maybe they secretly only answer to the man with green eyes? Maybe Master Hasegawa thinks they follow him and that they are still faithful to the emperor, but what if that man is trying to take over the dojo, to kill Master Hasegawa, than maybe the samurai are in league with him." Sheng reasoned.

"I don't know?" Suke-chan said somewhat doubtful, sitting down on his mat and crossing his legs. "But that's a lot of *maybes*, Sheng. Too many."

Hungry and exhausted, they drifted off to sleep, never stirring when Naoki and Jin came to bed. Daisuke was right: there were too many maybes. Sheng was determined to uncover the truth.

11

HAUNTED

The following morning, Sheng and Daisuke woke with such an intense hunger, they could hardly wait for breakfast. They dressed and hurried out into the blustery winter weather. As they neared the great hall, Suke-chan sniffed at the air like a wild dog, certain he could smell the delicious food that awaited them.

"I could eat a horse!" Daisuke laughed, brushing heavy, wet flakes of snow from his uncovered head.

"I'm sure you could," Sheng agreed.

As they hurried along, they watched as the footprints of the students ahead of them quickly disappeared, covered over by fresh blankets of white.

"Can you believe all this snow?" Sheng grinned. "It just keeps coming!"

Daisuke reached down and scooped up a big handful, then shoved it in his mouth, "Delightful!"

"You're crazy," Sheng replied, his nose wrinkled with friendly disapproval. "We'll have all you can eat in a moment. Can't you wait?"

Daisuke didn't answer. His meaty hand was slapped against his forehead and his mouth hung agape from the pain of brain-freeze after hastily gobbling down the ice cold snow.

"That's what you get," Sheng chortled, punching his big friend in the arm. "You deserve every bi…"

Sheng's sentence was violently cutoff. Breakfast would have to wait. Without warning, Sheng let out a yelp as someone reached out from the trees, firmly grabbing him by the arm and dragging him from the path. Suke-chan desperately chased after him; his fists clenched and his teeth bared, ready for a fight.

Daisuke had only caught a glimpse of the attacker. He did his best to catch up, his feet plunging deep into the snow with every labored stride. When he finally did, he was surprised to find Sheng and Tatsuo talking in hushed voices.

"You…scared…me…I thought…that…you were…the *stranger*," Suke-chan panted as he slumped against a tree to rest, accidentally shaking the branches and covering himself in snow.

Tatsuo paid no attention to Daisuke. He gave a little smirk and went back to his conversation with Sheng. "As I was saying, I know this grove is forbidden because it is part of Master Hasegawa's private gardens, but since the leaves have fallen, I discovered something I've never noticed before. Follow me."

Tatsuo took off swiftly into the woods leaving Sheng and Daisuke listening to the now-distant sound of snow crunching beneath Tatsuo's feet. They looked at each other; their faces screwed up with curiosity and followed after the sound of his feet.

Soon they found Tatsuo. He stood in front of a building, much smaller than the menagerie, that was hidden deep in the trees. There was no path leading to it and it was made of a much darker wood than the rest of the dojo. It also bore no distinct markings.

"What is it?" Suke-chan asked, packing a snowball and rolling it from hand to hand.

"I'm not sure," Tatsuo replied. "The door is locked and it has no windows. I haven't found another way in yet."

The three boys walked around the curious structure till they found what appeared to be the front. Two short planks stepped up to a small porch and pair of weatherworn pillars supported a small overhang that shaded the lone, wooden door. They stood staring, unsure of what they might find. A strange fear began to overtake them. Daisuke tried the door, just to make sure it was locked, even leaning into it, putting his full weight behind his effort. For as old as the wood appeared, the door held fast and didn't budge. The walls too, Suke-chan observed, were solid as well.

Next, Sheng took his turn. He ran his hand across the wooden door. His fingers hit a shallow groove hidden by snow. Quickly, he began wiping away the snow, tracing the lines of the channel and stepped back to get a better look. It was a *kamon*, or family crest, carved right into the door itself. The lines were straight and well cut: a large triangle made up of three smaller triangles, connected at their points and creating in the center a fourth upside down triangle, all in equal scale.

"I've seen that mon before," Sheng thought aloud.

"Yeah, it's the *Mitsu-uroku*: the mark of the Hōjō clan," Tatsuo said ominously. "They rule as regent and possess more power than the *shogun* or even the imperial court in Kyoto.

"So what do you suppose is inside?" Daisuke asked.

"I'm not sure, could be a lot of different things," Tatsuo reasoned.

Without warning, the familiar sound of feet trudging through the crunching snow made their hearts jump. They raced from the building and headed back into the trees. The ground all around the small structure was clearly disturbed and they realized that their hasty footfalls had a created a path that led straight back to them. But there was nothing they could do now about their obvious prints in the snow: someone was emerging from the leafless, bare trees.

Laying low to the ground, their bodies pressing into the deep snow as their only cover, the boys watched as the hooded stranger, shrouded in black, approached the door with an old, rusty key. He paused as he did, recognizing that he was not alone, his eyes falling on the heavily disturbed snow at the base of the door. The stranger turned and peered into the trees, intensity in his eyes as they darted about, searching for whoever had trespassed in this secret place and dared to spy on him. If he did see the boys, he didn't act as if he had.

As soon as they heard the door clank shut, they jumped up from the cold snow and ran as fast as they could towards the great hall. Heading up the stairs and in to breakfast, each one of them looked dazed. They were trying to understand what they had just seen. The masked stranger was there, on the dojo grounds, right under Master Hasegawa's nose! They tried to eat, but Suke-chan seemed to be the only one with the stomach for food at the moment. Sheng and Tatsuo couldn't stop wondering what was in that building hidden on the forbidden grounds. Even worse was the thought that whoever that shadowy figure was, he was able to move freely about the dojo without drawing any attention.

"We should tell Master Hasegawa," Sheng finally said.

"I agree," Tatsuo nodded. "Today is your first class with him. We should all tell him together."

Daisuke shrugged, his mouth too stuffed to speak. They considered that his show of support for their plan.

Sheng and Daisuke attended their morning classes, but were only present in body. Their minds were already at Master Hasegawa's afternoon lesson. They couldn't wait to tell him about what they had seen. Sheng imagined the proud look on Hasegawa's face when he would find out that his students had discovered someone plotting against him, and in his own dojo no less!

The morning drug on painfully slow. The ringing of the lunch bell was a relief, knowing that they were allotted an hour to eat. Sheng's grumbling stomach continuously reminded and scolded him for neglecting to eat breakfast. He ate his fill as the anticipation of impending glory loomed closer with every passing minute.

They'd finished eating before the bell was rung that would announce the end of lunch and the beginning of the afternoon lessons. Excitedly, they trudged out through the billowing white bursts of snow, figuring a head start was warranted. They were glad they had because as they fought their way through the wind, the lunch bell rang. Soon, there would be a rush of students out into the snow and the trek across the grounds would take much longer as they'd be at the mercy of the group's pace. Although it was one of the coldest days since the first snow, the crisp air didn't feel as bitter as it had the day before.

The training square was empty when they arrived, not that that was a surprise, knowing that the rest of the students were only just out from lunch. But after several very long minutes of standing alone in the cold, they thought that they must have gone to the wrong place, that Master Hasegawa must be teaching indoors today. Afraid of being late to their first lesson, and feeling a bit more of the cold biting at their toes, Suke-chan and Sheng turned round and started towards the classrooms.

"Hey...where do you two think you're going?" a voice cried out, almost inaudible in the whistling of the bone chilling wind.

"Did you hear that?" Sheng asked, stopping as if someone had just whispered in his ear.

They paused, listening intently, but there was nothing but the sound of the howling winter wind. They started off again when all of a sudden, *THWAP!*

Daisuke threw up his hands, protecting his now red, throbbing ear and ducked, just as another snowball went zooming over his head. Sheng dropped down as well. He grabbed a handful of snow from the ground and packed it tightly. Looking for the best target, Sheng took aim at the blur of a boy ducking in and out of the trees. He was about to launch the snow ball when he saw three, then four, finally five more students racing around the outskirts of the training square, each one hurling snowballs at the them.

Sheng waited for the right moment, he zeroed in, timed his throw. He followed the boy with his eyes as he circled the two friends. At the last possible moment, Sheng turned and chucked the snowball as hard as he could.

Time stopped from the second the wet, snowy clump left his fingers. He immediately regretted throwing the snowball. Standing within fifteen feet and walking into the line of the perfectly aimed winter-weapon was Master Hasegawa. In utter morbid embarrassment, Sheng realized what was sure to happen and tried to react, grasping out at the snow ball that had only just left his hand. He felt nothing but air – no snowball – it was too late! All the students who had been running around the square stopped in their tracks. Daisuke climbed to his feet, still holding his stinging ear.

In one fluid movement, Takeshi Hasegawa flung back his heavy winter robes and pulled his sword from its sheath on his belt. With a brilliant flick of his wrist and the *whoosh* of his blade cutting the air, the snowball shattered, small chunks flying in every direction.

Holding his breath, Sheng watched as he lowered his sword. Hasegawa stared back at Sheng, his eyes boring into him. Slowly, Hasegawa inched towards Sheng. The sound of his sword sliding back into its sheath was muffled only slightly by the gasps of everyone around them. Sheng's head dropped sadly as his master neared. He couldn't see the smile stretching across Hasegawa's face as he reached out and raised Sheng's head by his chin.

"I see you are fitting right in," Hasegawa laughed.

"Yes, Master, I guess so," Sheng replied, relief warming him once again.

Now joined by more students, they all followed Master Hasegawa into the center of the snow covered square. Two large men dressed like city guards appeared at the entrance of the square and stood on each end of a large chest they carried into the training grounds. The men set it down next to a long stone bench which they then dusted off and sat on. As Hasegawa waived his hand towards the chest, one of the men promptly lifted the lid.

The boys who had already been initiated into Hasegawa's class approached the wooden container and reached in, each one pulling out something long, wrapped in black silk. Sheng and Daisuke looked into the chest after the other students moved back to the center of the square. There were two left. They each took one and found their places amongst their fellow students.

Master Hasegawa stood before them and they all instinctively moved into two straight lines of seven. Sheng stood across from an unhappy looking boy he couldn't recall having ever seen before. Suke-chan was pleased to look over and see Tatsuo smiling back. Without a word, Hasegawa drew his sword. In a matter of seconds, twelve sheets of fine black silk floated elegantly to the ground as if impervious to the biting wind.

Sheng and Daisuke unwrapped the objects they held, expecting kendo sticks but happily surprised to find lightly rusted, but not dull katana swords. Smiles quickly flooded their faces.

Hasegawa, imitated closely by the older students, began artfully swinging his katana through the air. They moved in perfect unison, each movement matching one another as if it were a well practiced dance.

Suke-chan's smile quickly faded as he tried to move like the rest of them, his tongue peeking out the corner of his mouth as he desperately concentrated. Sheng was much more natural with his sword, but still a step behind the rest. Although the swords were light and well balanced, the slow, precise movements of the exercise wore down their constitutions quickly, their endurance greatly tested as they strained with the blades.

The class passed in silence. Sheng felt his fingers going numb from the cold. Daisuke's face was red and chapped, his nose running heavily as he squinted against the bitter harshness of the wind. By the time their lesson was over, both boys' muscles ached from head to toe. Though they hadn't moved from their spots, it was by far the most physical class they'd ever been through, even more so than Master Haiku's instruction. They were relieved as the class drew to a close.

Remembering their excitement to speak of the day's discovery with their master, Sheng and Suke-chan hurried to place their swords back into the chest. They were certain that Hasegawa would be appreciative when he heard their warning about the man with the green eyes and the shrouded stranger they watched sneak into the hidden shack, but as they turned to face him, he was gone.

Feeling dejected, they decided that all they wanted to do was get inside and away from the cold. So they headed back to their house to change out of their wet training robes, soaked with a mix of sweat and snow.

Later that evening and happy to be warm and dry once more, Sheng and Suke-chan sat in the noisy great room in the House of the Tiger. All around them, boys played games. Naoki chased after a freckled boy who had playfully stolen his history scroll. Jin laughed hysterically, his eyes watering.

It was too early to sleep and they weren't tired anyway. Still, they were exhausted none the less. Sheng glanced about the room, the warm glow of the fire washing over the walls with a soft orange light. A shadow outside on the porch caught his attention as he looked past the window.

Suke-chan was busy arm wrestling with an older student, so Sheng slipped away unnoticed. Cautiously, he slid the door open and leaned out into the crisp night air. The snow had finally stopped. A bright round moon illuminated the sparkling white grounds. Tatsuo stood at the top of the steps, his back to the house, staring off in the direction of the tree-hidden shack.

"Still thinking about the stranger we saw today?" Sheng asked, trying to start a conversation as he approached.

Over the last week, Tatsuo had seemed distant. He had separated himself during meals, usually eating after everyone else had gone.

"Huh? Oh, it's you," Tatsuo mumbled as he turned and watched Sheng step up alongside him before continuing his half hearted answer. "Yeah, but…it's more than just that. Do you ever still think about the village were your family lived?"

"Of course!" Sheng answered. "Sometimes I feel like I can still hear my mother's voice in my sleep, like she's calling me from afar, trying to wake me up from a dream."

Tatsuo thought for a moment and then turned to face Sheng, "See, I've been thinking a lot about when I first met you and you told me that your parents were…"

"Dead…" Sheng said very matter-of-factly.

"Right…" Tatsuo paused, "I couldn't help wondering why my village was spared. But, it's more than just that. The other day, I was in the city and I could have sworn I saw my father heading into the tea house. I tried to follow him."

Sheng was intrigued, "Go on."

"Well, he disappeared around a corner off the main room.," Tatsuo explained. "When I found the door he went through, a city guard pushed me back out before I could see in. He said that I wasn't of age and I belonged outside with the other boys, but I was taller than he was. I hate it when people treat me like a child."

Sheng understood the feeling. He nodded silently in agreement.

"Anyway, since then, I can't get my parents out of my head."

"I wondered if you were alright, when we saw each other this morning," Sheng said, "and not just today, but for a while now you've seemed distracted. I know this sounds funny, seeing as how you already said the same thing to me, but if you ever need to talk about anything, just let me know."

Tatsuo, though sadness showed in his eyes, smiled as he grabbed Sheng around the shoulders. By the sound of laughter and cheering echoing from inside the house, the arm wrestling match must have ended and, apparent by the loud whooping of his voice, Daisuke was the winner.

Since Tatsuo was the house's guardian, he shooed the youngest boys off to bed and joined Sheng and Suke-chan by the fire. They talked long into the night, mostly about their families and childhoods. And though Daisuke and Sheng had accepted some time ago that the dojo was their new home, they now, for the first time, felt the calming warmth of family, something they had yet to find.

That night, while the rest of the dojo slept, quietly awaiting the next day's lessons, Sheng tossed and turned, his dreams haunted by the memories of his village and fallen parents. He found himself walking down the fading hazy paths of his old home. Reliving each moment in his sleep, he wanted to wake up. But, he couldn't fight the curiosity pulling him closer and closer to the porch of the house in which he grew up, knowing all the while that he would find his mother lying dead on the cold, wooden floor – just as he had last seen her.

The way leading to his mother seemed to stretch on and on. With every step he took, he felt like he was further away. Every fiber of his being hoped that he would see her smiling, the way he wanted to remember her. Soon he would get his chance to find out.

The silhouette of the house's steeply pitched roof emerged from behind the fog that filled his dream. Within moments, the burning frame of the house came into view and he remembered it wasn't fog...it was smoke.

Slowly, he approached the steps leading up to the porch. He closed his eyes and blinked, but he couldn't wake up. The smoke was so thick it was hard to see through. Maybe he wouldn't even be able to find his mother on the porch. He held his breath with a nervous gulp. The porch had become so shrouded in smoke that he could no longer see his hands in front of him.

Sheng dropped to the floor, feeling around in the cloudy darkness. He crawled on all fours, now desperately calling out to her as if she were hiding and was about to pull him into her arms when he finally found her. He moved along faster: he must be close now. Sheng was no longer blinded by the smoke, but by the solemn tears that raced down his cheeks. He swept his hands first to the right and then to the left as he crawled, searching the floor.

Suddenly, Sheng froze. In the darkness, his hand touched something soft, familiar. He continued feeling for whatever it was when the thought struck him: it was his mother's hand. He reached out and clutched a hold of it, pulling as hard as he could, trying to draw her out of the smoke. Maybe she would still be alive?!

The harder he tried to save her, the heavier she became. He realized, though, that her skin was strangely cold and he was growing tired. Finally, in anguish, he gave one last desperate tug and collapsed to the floor next to her lifeless body.

"I'm so sorry," Sheng cried. "I wish I could have saved you."

He closed his eyes tightly, wanting nothing more than to wake up. He still couldn't see her through the smoke.

"You must come home, Sheng," a soft voice spoke in the disorienting darkness.

Sheng squinted, but still couldn't see his mother. He stood, searching for the voice. Carefully, he stepped over where he believed his mother's body rested, but he could no longer feel her on the ground.

"You must come home, Sheng," the voice called again.

He hurried his pace as he stumbled through the dense smoke, his arms waiving straight out in front of him feeling for a wall, but it was like he was in the middle of an endless black void. He heard the voice again, but now it was growing louder. Something brushed his face, then his back. Sheng spun around, hoping to find what lurked just beyond his reach. Still, he couldn't see a thing. The voice called even louder now, and with a whistling rush, the black cloud of smoke that engulfed him in terrifying darkness parted, and there, standing right in front of him, eye to eye, was his mother.

Sheng collapsed to the ground and scooted backwards till he slammed into the outer wall of the flaming house. Gracefully, she glided through the smoke and, in his shock, she grabbed his hand and effortlessly raised him to his feet.

She looked like his mother though there was a faint translucence to her and a curious blue glow radiated about her figure. Her eyes burned bright blue but still held the same love that Sheng always remembered. He knew she wasn't real, *couldn't* be real; but still, after getting over the pains of fear that battered his insides, he felt a warmth wash over him and the fear that had just filled him eased away like a receding wave on a sullen shore. Her spectral mouth showed her happiness, displaying the smile he longed to see. Sheng fought back tears as he looked at her standing as if she were still alive.

"Sheng…you must come home," she said one last time with her soft, loving voice.

Before he could answer, she drifted away into the smoke, pulled away by an unseen force. He reached out and called to her, but he couldn't find his voice. It was as if the whole world had gone silent. And in the next moment, Sheng found himself spinning back through the clouds of black, choking plumes till he sat up on the floor in his bedroom, Suke-chan sleeping calmly just next to him.

Sheng pulled his sweaty, matted hair from his face and stood up, walking to the window filled with the moons soft glow. The snow covered gardens glistened below, each flake sparkling like a diamond, and the cold night air felt refreshing on his hot face.

The next morning, Sheng tried to explain the dream to Daisuke, but he felt foolish saying he was afraid of his own mother, even if she was ghostly. Suke-chan happily ate his breakfast *plus* the food that Sheng didn't touch.

Throughout the rest of the day, and for some time after, Sheng couldn't shake the dream from his thoughts. In fact, the dream began to haunt his sleep. Night after night, he relived the dream, each time finding his mother calling him home.

12

MORE QUESTIONS, NO ANSWERS

Within a few short weeks, the last remnants of snow melted away and the fresh smell of spring filled the air. The lotus trees that filled much of the gardens began blooming with beautifully colored flowers and the happy chirping of birds building new nests invigorated the dojo, chasing away the cold memories of winter. Happily, all the students at the dojo stowed away their heavy winter robes in their bedroom storage chests and now wore much lighter clothes, all the better to practice fighting.

Sheng and Daisuke had taken to their sword training very quickly, now rivaling many of the older students. Tatsuo still remained at the top of Master Hasegawa's class, but he was especially proud of the two young boys' progression as he had made their development a sort of personal interest. Their friendship was mutually beneficial.

One afternoon, after a long history lesson, Sheng and Suke-chan, joined by Tatsuo, returned to the city for the first time in weeks. Tatsuo was hoping for another glimpse of the man he thought could be his father, Sheng and Daisuke were still searching for Scar on Hasegawa's orders. They had tried in vain to tell Master Hasegawa about the man with the green eyes who they believed to be the mysterious shrouded stranger, but as of yet, they were unable to find a way to talk with Hasegawa in private. He always disappeared immediately following their lessons and was seldom seen outside of class without Master Wong at his side.

As they wandered through the packed city streets, the setting sun peeked its last over the top of the city wall, covering some of the streets in shadowy darkness but leaving the western side of the village still bathed in warm spring light. They had nearly given up hope of seeing anything exciting when the smell of smoke reached them. Tatsuo looked up, pointing out the dark plumes rising up into the early evening sky. Racing around the corner and down they next street, they found a crowd gathered at the steps of a burning house, but oddly, they were staring at the ground and not the flames that licked through the windows. The boys pushed their way through the mass of people till they found what everyone else was already taking in.

Masato Katsumi, the old sword maker, laid dead; face down in a pool of blood. Off in the distance, the echo of hooves galloping down the stone streets cast a heavy and unknown fear into Sheng's heart.

"What happened here?" Tatsuo demanded of a woman standing just beside him.

"It was a man, a *man* in *black armor...*" she stammered," we saw the flames through the windows and we came to help the swordsmith, but..."

"But what!" Tatsuo yelled angrily.

"As we approached the house, the door burst open and old Katsumi tumbled to the ground." Tears filled her eyes as she continued, "When he climbed to his knees, he had a look of such horrible fear across his face, a look like I have never seen. We all followed his eyes towards the doorway, and there, amidst the smoke and flames, stood the samurai."

"Samurai?!" Daisuke exclaimed as he took a step back.

The woman's face was soaked in tears now, like many of the others around her, even some of the men. They had been neighbors of Masato Katsumi for decades.

"The black-garbed samurai ignored the sword maker's pleas for mercy and struck him down with the very blade Katsumi had just finished. He then wiped the edge clean on Katsumi's robe and ducked down the alley where he emerged in full stride on the back of a great black horse," she finished, her grief finally overcoming her.

Without hesitation, Sheng pushed through the other side of the crowd, stepping right over the swordsmith's lifeless body. Daisuke followed close behind to the dismay of the mourning crowd who muttered remarks of youthful disrespect for the dead. Tatsuo dropped down next to Masato Katsumi and witnessed a slowly drawn, labored breath.

"Wait!" Tatsuo shouted at Sheng. "He's still alive!"

Sheng stopped and turned, rushing back to Katsumi's body. Tatsuo cradled the dying man's head in his lap. A weak and nearly inaudible whisper escaped his quivering lips.

"What did he say?" Daisuke asked.

"I'm not sure," Sheng replied, leaning closer.

Again, Katsumi exhaled a phrase, his eyes growing dim as the light of life began to fade. Sheng leaned in even more, trying desperately to make out the man's dying words when all of a sudden, Katsumi reached up, violently taking hold of Sheng's face, the blood that covered the old man's hands smearing on his round cheeks.

"Climb the mountain!" Masato Katsumi gasped before falling limp.

Sheng leapt up from the lifeless body, staring down at his blood-soaked robes. Tatsuo closed Katsumi's eyes out of respect.

"What does that mean, *climb the mountain*?" Daisuke wondered.

"There's no time to worry about that right now," Sheng said, wiping the blood off of his face with his sleeves. "Let's go!"

"Where are we going?" Suke-chan huffed between breaths as the three boys left Katsumi lying in the street.

"To find that samurai," Sheng said confidently.

Tatsuo, also covered in the old man's blood, sprinted to the lead, "Follow me. I think I know where he's going."

"The jail?" Sheng questioned as they ran down a narrow alley, climbed over a fence, and raced down the next street.

"No…just keep up!" Tatsuo told them.

Master Hasegawa paced in his study. Books and scrolls were scattered about his large wooden desk. A messenger had just left word saying that Master Masato Katsumi, the swordsmith, was murdered and the unequaled blade that Hasegawa had ordered to be made, the blade that Katsumi had placed all his last efforts into forging perfectly, had been stolen, and worse, used to kill its maker.

"Do you have any idea who did this?" Hasegawa asked the messenger who had delivered the terrible news.

"No, Master. But the city guard will investigate the matter thoroughly," came the reply. "We'll get to the bottom of this, for Master Katsumi's sake."

"Thank you," Hasegawa answered with a royal wave of his hand. "That will be all."

He slumped angrily into a chair that sat in a shadowed corner of the room as he sent the messenger away. There, alone in the darkness, the flickering candle light cast an odd glow across his face. It almost appeared as if he was smiling.

The boys skidded to a stop in front of the tea house. Two large men stood guard at the front door, long blades held at their sides.

"Well, looks like we can't get in," Suke-chan said, trying to sound disappointed. "I bet dinner is about ready back at the dojo. What do you say we…"

But before he could finish, Tatsuo and Sheng disappeared around the side of the adjoining building. Daisuke was not looking forward to this. Reluctantly, he followed them up a pile of crates, through an open window, and into a small room filled with barrels full of dirty robes ready to be washed.

"What is this place?" Suke-chan asked as he removed his leg from a barrel he had clumsily stepped into as he looked around the space, his nose wrinkling at the foul smell of long-worn clothing.

"It looks like a laundry room," Sheng teased, watching Tatsuo carefully peek from the doorway and into the bright hall.

"I figured that out," Suke-chan smiled, casting a glance at the steaming tubs filled with hot water that lined the inner wall. "I *MEAN*...what *IS* this..."

"It's an inn that's attached to the tea house, Suke-chan," Tatsuo whispered, putting a hand up to silence him. "Now, Sheng, why don't you sneak down the hall, and see if there are any workers around who might see us and turn us in. If not, we'll try to find a way into the tea house."

Sheng, being particularly good in the art of stealth, snuck off down the hallway without a single creak of a floor board to announce his coming. He peered around the corner. Everything was clear. Daisuke and Tatsuo tiptoed behind him, though not nearly as quiet.

They found their path unobstructed. A door at the end of the hallway led to the kitchens, which the boys discovered were shared between the inn and the tea house. The kitchen, like the hallways was empty as well. At the far end of the room, several pots stood boiling rice and the smell of fresh bread was in the air.

Tatsuo peeked under the door that led into the tea house. A man stood just beyond, his back to the door. They could see his shadow moving across the threshold.

"We can't go this way," he whispered.

Sheng crept up a flight of stairs and looked out carefully. It seemed their only chance. "This way," he called quietly, "It leads to a balcony overlooking the main room of the tea house."

Tatsuo carefully climbed the stairs. Suke-chan filled his pockets – and his mouth – with small, fist-sized loaves of bread and followed his friends to the balcony.

They stayed low to the floor and peered over the railing cautiously, trying not to draw any attention. The obnoxiousness of Daisuke chewing carried over Sheng's shoulder irritatingly, but it was drowned out quickly by the sound of the men drinking and talking below. All around the room stood guards, swords at their sides, a cup in their hands, toasting to some unseen victory. Some men laughed, others played drinking games, trying to match each other cup for cup. But, in one corner, three men sat quietly, grave looks upon their faces.

A door in the rear of the room flung open. Twelve men, all clothed in black armor, haughtily entered, followed quickly by a thirteenth. In his hands, he held a long object wrapped tightly in black silk. The three men in the corner still shared uneasy expressions, but joined in what now looked like the celebration that everyone else had begun prematurely. The black-clad samurai stopped in the middle of the room and the one holding the curious package raised it high above his head. The men quickly fell silent. He uttered something muffled through his armored mask, and the men all cheered.

In the uproar, Sheng and Tatsuo whispered back and forth, each wondering if the other was able to make out what was said. They shared a similar confusion while Suke-chan was finally pulled from his bread and now fixed, as was everyone else, on the object the samurai carried.

When the cheers finally subsided, the man slowly unwrapped the silk and held, quite triumphantly, the blade that was Masato Katsumi's last and greatest work. Then, the thirteen samurai removed their helmets and were met with more cheers and praise from the rest of the men.

Tatsuo gasped. His face turned a light pale that matched his white robes almost perfectly.

"What's wrong?" Sheng worried, taking his eyes off of the samurai for just a moment, just long enough to see Tatsuo's sickly reaction.

Tatsuo didn't answer. He only looked back at the group of samurai.

"This, my brothers, is the time we have waited for," the man holding the sword of Master Masato Katsumi said proudly. "For years, we have hidden ourselves away in this city, behind its walls searching for those strong enough to join us. Indeed, many of us began not as samurai but as poor farmers and beggars and even slaves. Our Master has given us purpose. Soon we will see those plans come to fruition, for now is our time. Now, we are ready to move out and no longer search for allies, but bring those who would oppose us to their destruction. Let us follow our Master now without fear, for he will hold in his hand this sword, worthy of an emperor!"

The gathering of men cheered uncontrollably. Smiles were shared and backs were slapped among all of them as more rice wine was passed around and the clinking of cups emboldened their triumphant merriment.

Night was upon them. The long walk back to the dojo was solemn. Sheng, Daisuke, and Tatsuo had managed to slip away from the tea house without being seen. Still, the unmasking of the samurai and the following celebration weighed heavily on their thoughts.

They made certain to pass by the burnt shell of Masato Katsumi's house and blacksmith shop. The fire had long since gone out. Wisps of smoke haunted the charred frame. Katsumi's body had been taken away, but dried blood still marked the street where the old master had fallen.

The three boys trudged through the gloomy darkness of the tunnel and made their way across the silent dojo grounds. An overcast night added to the grimness, the bright moon hidden by bleak clouds that threatened rain.

In silence, they reached the house of the tiger clan. The boys stood for a moment, each one wishing to end the tension, yet not knowing what to say. Sheng looked off towards the temple and Master Hasegawa's private quarters.

"The samurai spoke of a *master*," Sheng wondered, "do you suppose he meant Hasegawa?"

"Perhaps," Tatsuo said thoughtfully. "But maybe we should refrain from telling Master Hasegawa all that we know? For the time being, it might be best to keep our secret between us."

Sheng weighed Tatsuo's words. What if he was right? What would than mean for their future at the dojo? Knowing all that they did could ultimately put them at great risk.

Lightning suddenly flashed, illuminating the dojo grounds. Thunder followed in a long, rumbling peel. Small droplets of rain splashed at the boys' feet.

"I think it's time to call it a night," Tatsuo said, turning away from Sheng and Daisuke before they could agree.

They heard him say goodnight as he headed through the door to the house. Sheng and Suke-chan followed, but neither seemed eager for sleep.

They had again missed dinner, something that was becoming a regular occurrence, but Sheng didn't care. Daisuke didn't care this time either as he sat alongside the fireplace in the house's great room, contently chewing on the delicious bread he'd pilfered and brought back in his pockets. Sheng stared into the flames, sparks crackling from the cinders in the bottom of the hearth. They spent the rest of the night talking there by the fire, going over what had happened just a few short hours before. Reliving each moment in detail, the two best friends marveled at their bravery and exaggerated the parts that lacked pertinence till they too were just as exciting as the rest of the story. Finally, they felt their heads begin to nod and soon they were fast asleep, dreaming of samurai and dark conspiracies.

They woke early the next morning to find the fire smoldering, shivering after sleeping on the cold planks of the great room's floor. Tatsuo sat just behind them, a sack resting against the leg of his chair. He was already dressed, but not in his white robes. He wore clothing that looked like light armor, the kind one would where when heading off on an adventure into the unknown.

"You never made it to bed I see?" Tatsuo teased. "If I cared about doing my job as guardian, you two would be in big trouble for breaking curfew."

"Going somewhere?" Sheng replied, ignoring the attempt at humor and putting the focus on Tatsuo's clothing.

"Away," Tatsuo answered bluntly. "I would have been gone already if I hadn't felt that I must say goodbye to the two of you."

"What?" Sheng nearly shouted, leaping up from the floor in protest.

"I can't stay here any longer. I've learned all that I can from this dojo...including some *unintentional* lessons. I just have to move on." With those sad words, Tatsuo stood and slung his sword across his shoulder and onto his back, securing the worn leather straps by its pitted steel buckles. He tried to smile as he picked up his sack and headed towards the door.

"And what should we tell people when they notice you've gone missing?" Daisuke asked groggily.

"Tell them you don't know where I am," Tatsuo answered, his back turned to his young friends as if looking at them would make it harder for him to go. "Or better yet, tell anyone who asks that I'm dead! At least then your story would match the pain in my heart."

Sheng sprinted after him as Tatsuo reached the door. He tried to block his way, but Tatsuo was so much stronger than Sheng and he was simply pushed aside.

"Was it last night, at the tea house?" Sheng asked as Tatsuo placed one foot out the front door.

Tatsuo stopped and slowly turned to face him. "It has everything to do with last night. When you think of your parents, be glad they are dead. Be proud that the good things they started in life were never spoiled by selfishness like my parents."

"What are you talking about?" Sheng questioned in utter shock. "Your parents are slaves. What is selfish about that?"

"I never knew what really happened to my parents. I only assumed they were made slaves," Tatsuo said bitterly, turning back towards the door.

"Then what does this have to do with last night?" Suke-chan chimed in.

"Because," Tatsuo said slowly, "last night, the black-clad samurai, one of the men who had helped retrieve that horrible blade, the blade that killed Masato Katsumi: I recognized him. He was there celebrating the downfall of the rightful emperor and the raising of an usurper – celebrating that *he* would help lead the conquest of this new empire."

"Who?" Sheng demanded. "Who did you see last night?"

Tatsuo stared out at the world beyond the dojo, his voice full of hate as he replied. "My father," he spat. "Last night I saw my father. His is no slave, Sheng. He's a traitor."

Tatsuo's words echoed in the boys' heads as they watched him step out the front door and close it behind him. Their friend, the only person who had made them feel at home in Hasegawa's dojo, was gone.

13

YOUNG MASTERS

Days turned to weeks. Weeks turned to months. Months turned to years. Leaves changed, snow fell, and flowers blossomed; over and over without regard for the fleeting whims of man. With every passing season, Sheng and Daisuke grew taller, stronger. They studied hard and fought harder, surpassing any and all other students at Master Takeshi Hasegawa's esteemed dojo in Kamakura. They were now young men, twenty-two years old and masters in their own right.

Ten years had passed since Tatsuo fled the company of his fellow students. Not long after, the man who Sheng and Daisuke had understood to be their lost friend's father was found dead. Rumors abounded, but Sheng knew the truth. Certainly Tatsuo had exacted revenge for his father's treachery. A few short years later, the remaining twelve samurai who had assisted in the murder of Masato Katsumi had also been alleged dead – targeted, hunted down like animals. Sheng believed this was the work of Tatsuo as well. That was the last hint of his whereabouts and their mentor slipped away, now nothing more than another piece in the puzzle that was their fractured past.

Master Hasegawa was seen much less frequently on the dojo grounds.

Master Wong had effectively taken over all administrative aspects of the facility and Sheng was honored when he had been asked to replace Hasegawa as instructor in the bladed arts. As for what the founder of the dojo was doing with his time, no one could speculate. Candle light flickered throughout the windows of his private quarters at all hours of the night and his days were spent travelling beyond the dojo's walls, not just into the city, but outside of Kamakura, even to the imperial court in Kyoto. Hasegawa's movements, his very nature, had become incredibly calculated. He'd formed alliances within the shogunate and had begun offering his graduated students to the local daimyō as warriors for hire. Aptly trained samurai had become ruthless mercenaries.

Most telling was Master Hasegawa's regard for the emperor, *Go-Nijo*, and his father, the former emperor, *Go-Uda*. Hasegawa refrained very little from his critique of the *Daikaku-ji* family and had grown openly political in the short years that the *Jimyō-in* family ruled with Emperor *Go-Fushimi* in power. The transition from the thirteenth to fourteenth century impacted Hasegawa greatly as the shogunate settled the dispute between the two imperial families by forcing them to alternate the lines on the throne. Proud of his Hōjō clan lineage, Takeshi Hasegawa made it no secret that he believed military and political power should remain in the more than capable hands of the shogunate for the sake of all of Japan.

And perhaps Hasegawa was right. Sheng had found himself privy to many conversations that other students – past and present – would have never been invited. After Tatsuo left, Sheng decided to follow Master Hasegawa, almost blindly. In reality, what other choice did he have? Hasegawa was a brilliant tactician and had a great understanding of warfare. The stories he told of the Mongol invasions and the coming together of warriors from clans all over Japan to fight this great threat were more enticing to Sheng than any of Old Shou's tales for he knew without certainty that *Kublai Khan* wanted to expand his territories beyond China. And almost as fantastic as Shou's stories of dragons and treasure was the defeat of the Mongols, not by swords and arrows, but by a supernatural power: a *kamikaze* wind that crushed Khan's forces and stopped his advance. This was observed and documented truth, not the fictitious ramblings of a senile town elder.

In this, Sheng came to understand a greater truth: pride. Often times Master Hasegawa referred to himself as a similar force, a supernatural, divine wind – unstoppable and merciless. Sheng saw this as Hasegawa's weakness, but wisely kept this to himself, knowing his place at Hasegawa's table, and at his young age, was an honor not to be taken for granted.

Under Takeshi Hasegawa's leadership, Sheng and Daisuke had become battle-hardened samurai, tested and scarred. They had spilled blood and witnessed friends fall. Both Jin and Naoki were lost in battle. Little Mori Masaki had died as well, but not in vain as his ferocity more than made up for what he lacked in size. Hasegawa was merciless and his samurai followed his example. Hasegawa taught that prisoners were only instruments of death waiting for a chance to exact revenge, so all adversaries were slaughtered, reducing chances for assassination from within.

Sheng witnessed secret dealings with daimyō; money, goods, and favors changing hands for allegiance. Loyal samurai from Hasegawa's dojo had been infiltrating the power system of the local lords for over two decades and held a power second to only the regent, or *shikken*. And as the shikken was Hōjō Clan, he confided often in secret council with Hasegawa, unaware of the dealings and opposing power amassed right before his very eyes.

Takeshi Hasegawa's thirst for power, fueled by his belief that his actions perfectly displayed his own twisted interpretation of the writings of *Hōjō Shigetoki* – respected author of documents that illustrate the core principle of an honorable samurai's code and a warrior's way of life – emboldened his distrust for the imperial families and even the role of the shogunate in an ever-warring Japan. He would often quote Shigetoki in his meetings, saying "If one will fix his heart in such a way and assist the world and its people, he will have the devotion of the men who see and hear him."

In the end, peace was his goal. As he understood it to be, if a leader managed to unify all of Japan under one banner, then all the death, all the underhanded agreements would be worth it. To lead would be an honor, and in his pride, Master Takeshi Hasegawa believed *that* honor was his and his alone.

The men at the table burst into laughter, their bowls and cups rattling as Daisuke slammed his enormous fist down on the table. His theatrics were meant to illustrate a recent battle for his friends in what had become his typical, over-the-top-if-not-abrasive comedic fashion. Sober, he was indeed funny. Add a jug of rice wine and he was the life of the party, his deep voice thundering over everyone else's. On this night, the tea house was alive with samurai blowing off steam, many of them with fresh wounds from their last battle: a battle they won and were celebrating now. And there was Daisuke, the center of attention.

Sheng tried to focus on the party, but his mind was elsewhere. Courtesans and entertainers mingled among the samurai. A young woman offered him more sake. His cup was still full, having not even taken a sip of his first drink, and he politely turned her away.

"You look like you need to relax," a sweet voice whispered in his ear.

He turned to see a beautiful woman, her face pale white, her lips painted red, her eyes dark and enchanting. She put her hand on his shoulder and looked longingly with her deep, practiced stare.

"I'm not interested," Sheng countered. "Please let me be."

"Are you sure," she asked enticingly, her bright red lips pursing into a pout. "I can make you forget all your worries."

Sheng pulled a small looped chord of rope from around his wrist, quickly untying it and removing two coins that the rope threaded through. "Take these and move along," he said, returning the chord to his wrist. "Go make another man happy. I wish to be alone."

She bowed and accepted the money, then flitted off to find another vulnerable-looking target. This was not where Sheng wanted to be. The party would certainly last for hours and he'd had enough.

He took his leave and stepped out into the night. Stars lit the sky. The moon was full and bright as a warm summer breeze worked its way through the streets and passageways of Kamakura.

Sheng wandered the city as its people slept. Recent events had the city guard on edge as several attempts to invade had been swept aside by Master Hasegawa's private army. But as the home of the Hōjō regency, Kamakura had become a target for those looking to gain power and influence with the emperor in Kyoto being little more than a figurehead in the feudal society. The real power was in Kamakura. Siege from warring clans was an ever present threat. The guards patrolled in teams of two, fully armored and ever ready. Sheng had garnered a reputation on the battlefield and the men of the guard looked to him as a leader, even at his age. He was a young man with an old spirit. At least that's what they said about him. And he understood it, a sense of burden for every soul he cut down in war.

On this night, his spirit felt exceptionally old, even fragile. He was an exceptional warrior with unmatched skill. Opposing clans called him a devil in battle, believed he was un-killable. Maybe they were right. He seemed to supernaturally deflect incoming blows as if he could see them before they happened and counter with ferocious strikes of his own, his sword always finding the gaps in an enemy's armor. Yet his heart was heavy and his eyes lacked the hope they once had in his youth, even after the death of his parents.

The sound of hooves striking the ground pulled his thoughts from gloom as he watched a rider approach. Sheng recognized his robes. He was a messenger from the dojo.

"Master Hasegawa is looking for you, sir," the rider said. "He requests your presence in the castle immediately."

Sheng nodded, climbing onto the back of the horse and they galloped off. Hasegawa's request was a relief for Sheng, a distraction from his burdens and he was happy to follow his master's command.

Takeshi Hasegawa paced the floor within his private wing of the dojo's castle. Moonlight shone through the windows, casting his long, lean shadow on the wall. He'd extinguished the candles, smoke wisps curling from the blackened wicks. In the center of the room, between the windows and away from the moon's wash, was a figure, bound with rope and fastened to a chair. A black hood was draped over his face, leaving the cries of the gagged man hidden beneath the cloth a muffled and unintelligible mixture of grunts and groans.

"Who is it that conspires against the Hōjō regency?" Hasegawa asked tauntingly, knowing full well the man was helpless to reply. "Is it Emperor Go-Nijo? Is it the Jimyō-in family? The Daikaku-ji?"

The captive struggled against his tight bonds, writhing in agony from the ropes that cut into the flesh of his arms and legs. His stifled attempt to reply amused Hasegawa

"Kamakura is my city," Master Hasegawa continued playfully, like a cat pawing at a terrified mouse. "How dare you spy on this dojo and my people. You should wish that the guards who discovered you had simply killed you. Your fate would have been easier to accept had they done you such a favor. Now you will know why I am so greatly feared. You will know why…"

The door opened abruptly as two of Hasegawa's personal guard escorted Sheng into the room. The armored men remained with them as the door closed.

Smiling, Hasegawa continued to speak, "You will know why the Hōjō rightfully controls Japan."

Sheng stood silently by the door, observing his trusted master as he toyed with the prisoner. Something didn't seem right and Sheng found the situation very uncomfortable.

"Thank you for joining us, Sheng," Hasegawa said, motioning him to come closer. "I'd like you to see the face of our enemy."

Master Hasegawa turned and violently ripped the hood off of the man's head, revealing his severely beaten face; his eyes swollen and bruised, his mouth strained and his jaw taut from the tight gag. Fresh blood seeped from gashes on his cheeks and brow from where he'd been repeatedly struck. Sheng found it hard to look at the man. Seeing a fallen and bloodied enemy on the battlefield was one thing, but this – torture – was something he thought to be totally different and in his mind absolutely unacceptable.

"What is this?" Sheng asked, knowing his tone was sharper than intended.

Hasegawa's brows raised, "Should we not protect the dojo or this city we have helped to rebuild?"

Sheng was silent.

"This man is a spy," Hasegawa explained as justification for his actions. "He has come here to learn our secrets so that the imperial court might exploit them and gain leverage over the Hōjō regency."

"Do we not support the emperor?" Sheng asked, his voice calmer this time.

"We support a strong Japan, my young friend. And if the emperor is not capable of making us strong, then he is not *my* emperor."

The man made a muffled attempt to communicate, distracting from the tension between master and apprentice. Their attention returned once more to the beaten captive in the chair. Hasegawa pulled a short sword from his belt and quickly cut loose the gag. The man gasped, painfully working his jaw by opening and closing his mouth.

"What do you have to say for yourself, *spy*?" Master Hasegawa growled.

"I swear to you I am no spy. I am an ambassador from the court. I was sent to meet with the regency. That is all!"

"Then why do you ride at night?" Hasegawa pressed. "And alone, no less?! The roads into Kamakura are dangerous at night. Marauders watch the passages through the mountains."

"It's an urgent matter that the court has sent me on. I have a message for the regency. I must speak to the shogunate."

"You are lying!" Master Hasegawa exploded.

"As I said before, on my families honor, I am not lying," the man pleaded fearfully. "I have a message to deliver!"

"So do I," Hasegawa said as he plunged the short sword deep into the prisoner's chest.

Hasegawa withdrew the sword, blood gushing from the savage wound. Then, he kicked the chair over, the man slamming into the hard floor. He gurgled and coughed as he choked on his own blood. Sheng watched as the man's struggling ceased, a red, sticky pool oozing from beneath the dead body.

"You two," Hasegawa ordered, pointing at the guards. "Strip him, then burn his clothes and belongings. Take his naked corpse to the shikken and tell him you found this man on the side of the road just beyond the city's wall. Tell them he was beaten, robbed, and murdered."

The guards left their place at the door and cut the man free from the chair, then took him by his arms and drug his limp body from the room, blood smearing along across the floor as they did.

"And send some servants in to clean up this mess. Choose them from among the mutes so that they cannot utter a word of what they see here," Hasegawa added.

Sheng stepped aside as the guards pulled the body through the open door, "Master, was this necessary? Killing him, I mean. Could we not have learned more form him?"

"There was nothing left to learn from the spy," he replied.

"What about mercy? He was not an enemy on the field. Why judge him so harshly?"

"Mercy?" Hasegawa smirked. "You say he is not an enemy on the battlefield, but you are wrong. Open your eyes, young Sheng! The world is not so black and white. For the world itself is a battlefield and those who oppose a unified Japan are our enemy. The fight is real, my friend, and you must recognize that the war will find you whether or not you are armed and ready. Whether or not you engage in honorable warfare, you can still die at the hand of a dishonorable man. And that spy was a *very* dishonorable man. He would have just as soon plunged a knife into my own heart had I not handled him myself. Indeed, the war has now come to us!"

Master Hasegawa righted the toppled chair, the coarse ropes hanging from it bloodied. Sheng still stood near the door, purposefully putting space between himself and the grisly scene.

"So is this why you called me here?" Sheng finally asked, his focus returning to his master. "Did you wish for me to witness the spy?"

"In a manner of speaking," Hasegawa replied. "I wanted you to see what happens to spies when they are captured and interrogated. And I promise you, this scenario would be very much the same if you were discovered by our enemies. The mercy you mentioned would not be afforded by them either."

"But I am not a spy," Sheng reasoned. "I am a samurai. I fight with honor."

"Indeed you do. You have served me well in my army, Sheng. You have earned your position among the highest ranks of warriors. But I have something more for you to do. I believe it's time to put your special abilities to good use. I'm sending you to Kyoto."

"What?" Sheng replied. "I do not wish to be a spy!"

"I want you to think of it as being my emissary."

"I don't understand?" Sheng complained. "Why not send a messenger?

We have spies within our ranks."

"But none that can fight like you. You will leave in the morning. I've arranged passage for you on a merchant ship that will take you to the port in *Naniwa*. From there, a smaller vessel will take you up the *Yodo* and then to the *Katsura* river. Once you arrive in the city, you will meet with a contact I already have working secretly within the imperial court. He will explain to you your mission."

"And what of the classes I teach?"

"Master Wong will lead the lessons on your behalf. He is a more-than-adept swordsman."

"And what if I run into trouble when we reach Naniwa? As you said, it is dangerous to travel, especially alone."

"I believe you are more than capable of defending yourself, but I agree. You could use an ally," Hasegawa conceded. "Take Daisuke with you. After all, I might not be able to stop him from following you anyway."

"Alright."

"Do not pack. Travel light and fast. Wear simple robes and conceal your swords. Do this so you will not attract the attention of ronin. Carry only enough money to get to Kyoto. Once you arrive you will go to *Chion-in*, a Buddhist temple. There you will meet with a monk."

"How will I know him?" Sheng wondered.

"Do not worry about that. He will know you. The monk will provide you with more regal clothing, as much money as you need for your time in Kyoto, and also the details of the plan."

"Alright," Sheng replied. "Is there anything else, Master?"

"Not at this time. Now rest. You will need it."

Sheng and Daisuke set out early the next morning. The trip to Kyoto was a two-day venture, three if the wind was not with them. They'd taken care to dress as peasants. Carried with them was a meager store of food and a small number of coins, a rope threaded through the open center to secure them. Beneath their ragged robes were their swords, only to be used in the most extreme of circumstances. Sheng kept a small dagger at his side, hidden beneath his worn, outer cloak. Caution seemed prudent given the secrecy of their task. And with ronin, master-less and disgraced samurai, roaming the countryside and ports, even a competent warrior could be easily subdued if caught off his guard.

Master Hasegawa had given them a map of their route and provided them with papers that would guarantee their passage through the territories of regional lords. Once they'd travelled up river, they planned to blend in with the crowds and weave their way to Kyoto as non-linearly as possible, lingering among crowds of people in an attempt to avoid drawing attention. And though this would lead them at times off of the main road, slowing their pace, they knew this would lessen their chance of encountering bandits and ronin.

The sun shone brightly in the cloudless, blue sky as they looked out over the bay. Birds squawked overhead, searching for their next meal. Ships' battened sails billowed in the wind. To the west, Mount Fuji was visible in the distance, rising high above the heavily wooded landscape. The weather appeared to be on their side. They found the boat Hasegawa had procured for them, a Chinese-style *junk* with a carved and painted dragon adorning the bow, and climbed aboard. They were greeted by the captain who was pleased with their timely arrival as they showed him their traveling papers.

"Welcome, most esteemed friends of the great Takeshi Hasegawa," the captain said bowing low as he handed their papers back to them. "Right this way."

Sheng and Suke-chan followed, studying the crew as they passed the men who checked the rigging and prepared to cast off. The sailors seemed less impressed than the cordial captain and glared back austerely.

He hastily led them across the large, three-masted ship and beneath an elevated deck at the stern, "Please sit. Here you can eat and rest in the shade. We will leave shortly after we verify the manifest. We will sail through the day and night and, weather permitting, arrive in Naniwa before dawn."

"No fear of *wako*? Sheng asked as they graciously sat.

"Pirates know this ship," the captain smiled. "I assure you, my friends, that they are afraid of us."

With that, he turned and left Sheng and Daisuke by themselves. They stared out at the harbor, the smell of salt water thrilling as they were awaiting to embark upon the open seas. They'd explored much of the land around Kamakura and had battled many times to defend the mountain passes from raiders and rogue samurai factions. This was their first sea voyage and the furthest away from the dojo they had yet ventured.

The junk lurched as the seamen shifted the sails into the wind. Soon, they passed beyond the mouth of the bay, leaving Kamakura and the safety of the dojo behind.

14

WHAT LIES AHEAD?

White crested waves crashed against the bow of the merchant ship. The sails billowed as a strong easterly wind drove them on their course. Though the junk was sea worthy, the captain kept the coastline in view from starboard. Trees rose high above the steep cliff walls of the main Japanese island, the mountains beyond reaching even higher. In the distance, the bright blue sky touched the deep blue sea on the horizon. It was a perfect day and Sheng was content to enjoy the warm breeze and sunshine.

Daisuke sat beside him. They'd spent only an hour or so on the water and Suke-chan was already eating. He munched on some nuts and dried fruit, tapping his feet happily on the hardwood deck-planks.

Both were very impressed with the professionalism of the crew. The men were militant in their discipline and moved about the ship effortlessly as it yawed and pitched on the choppy water. Large wooden crates and barrels were tied down onto the deck of the junk with heavy rope. The captain stood watch from the stern, his eyes ever-scanning the waters for threats.

Sheng knew little of sailing and enjoyed learning from the crew. He'd spotted two trap doors in the deck that he assumed led to cargo compartments beneath them. And he'd noticed that as all the other men, even those obviously stationed to certain parts of the junk, scurried about to keep the ship sailing at its best, one large sailor, armed with a sword and strapped with leather belts across his chest, back, and waist, seemed to keep his position directly over top of the main cargo door, almost as if he were guarding the contents within.

"What do you suppose is hidden beneath the deck?" Sheng asked in a quiet voice, his head nodding in the guard's direction.

Suke-chan looked to where Sheng was gesturing and swallowed the mouthful, "Could be anything. Maybe food, maybe weapons?"

"Could be," Sheng shrugged. "Why do you suppose the captain said that wako pirates would be more scared of this ship than he is of them?"

"If this ship carries cargo that belongs to Hasegawa, then I suppose that in itself is enough to fear. And with the front of the ship decorated like an angry dragon, it's recognizable enough. Certainly even pirates aren't crazy enough to cross Master Hasegawa," Daisuke reasoned, shoving another fistful of snacks into his face.

"Sometimes you truly surprise me," Sheng smiled as he patted his large friend on the shoulder. "There is a brain in there after all!"

Suke-chan grinned, his teeth covered in crunched nuts and fruit. The two laughed again, loud and hard, just like when they were boys. It seemed they hadn't laughed like that in a long time. Hasegawa demanded control and poise at all times. Battle had hardened them. Perhaps this adventure would do them some good as the air seemed sweeter beyond the dojo's walls.

7

Hours passed as the hot sun beat down on the junk. Sheng and Daisuke were very thankful for the shade afforded beneath the poop deck. Only twice during the voyage so far had Suke-chan lunged heaving over the side of the boat, his stomach unused to the jostling of the water. He decided that sea travel, much like horseback, was not for him. Sheng however had no issues and had even stretched his legs, traversing the length of the ship and back while careful to remain out of the crew's way.

Their hair blew in the warm breeze as the ship cruised on steadily, the shore to their right, the open sea to their left. From time to time, they spotted fish near the surface of the brilliant blue water. Birds flocked behind the ship, following them as they sailed, hoping for scraps of food to be tossed over the side. As more time passed, the scenery, though lush and vibrant, varied little and soon, the waves rocked them to sleep. Suke-chan sat slumped over, his chin resting on his chest. Sheng rested alongside of him, leaning up against him, his friend's burly bicep a comfortable rest for his head.

Darkness covered the water. The moon replaced the sun in the sky, it's brilliant, glowing reflection on the cool water muddled by the rippling of the waves. It seemed the boat had stopped.

Sheng stirred, aware enough to recognize that they must have changed course at some point as he slept. Either the island of Honshu had disappeared in the darkness and the dense trees visible in daylight simply blended in with the mysterious shadows of the night or they were out at sea, the sky a vast black canvas bedazzled with wondrously twinkling constellations. His eyes returned from above as he heard a faint splash in the distance. In that direction, he saw the flickering light of distant torches over the water, dim and orange. He strained to see in the darkness. Then he realized what he saw: silhouetted in the moon's glow was another junk, larger than the one on which they travelled. It had a fourth mast and its battened sails were much broader. He imagined it could easily be a warship, or worse; pirates.

The splashing grew closer and Sheng managed to make out a small boat, known as an *ayubune* or *sampan*. He'd seen them many times used by fisherman, but only in the rivers and never in the open sea. A member of the crew walked by in silence, briefly obscuring his view. Sheng pretended to sleep.

"Put this down below," he heard the familiar voice of the captain say as the sampan must have arrived at their ship.

The words were followed by a heavy thud as whatever he was referring to hit the deck. Sheng wanted desperately to open his eyes, but he feared what he might see. And worse, that someone would see him watching! He dared not take a peek. Pretending to be asleep meant he was not privy to the captain's secret, a secret that could not be made but under the cover of night and at open sea. And if it were pirates, what seemed to be a trade or arrangement of sorts, would most definitely be a secret worth killing to protect.

Suke-chan suddenly snorted, shifting in his spot and then drifting back to sleep. Certainly someone would have heard that and looked in their direction. Sheng did his best to keep up the act. He heard many footsteps and then the sound of a hatch opening. Another thud was audible, though quieter than before. Whatever goods had been taken on board were now locked in the guarded compartment below the deck. Chances are he'd never find out what it was now.

The captain barked out orders and the junk lurched, steering westward as the wind carried the vessel back to its course. Soon the crew was once again working tirelessly and Sheng was once again asleep, his troubled mind tortured by the curious event.

Sheng woke to the delicious smell of food. He climbed to his feet and ran down the stairs to the first floor of the house.

"Good morning, son," his father smiled.

"Sheng, come eat while the rice is warm," his mother insisted.

His stomach growled and he took his place on the floor at the table without argument, "Thank you. I've never been so hungry!"

His parents laughed as he began shoving fistfuls of food into his mouth. As he did, he stopped and looked at his hands. They were not the hands of a warrior, scarred and calloused. No, they were the hands of a boy. He continued eating though he noticed that the bowls of food in front of his parents remained untouched.

"Aren't you going to eat too?" Sheng wondered, suddenly aware of his boyish voice.

"Son, the dead do not eat," his mother replied.

The room began to spin as his heart beat in his throat. He jumped up and ran to his mother, throwing himself forward, his arms outstretched, but he passed right through her as she seemed to evaporate into a mist. He hit the floor hard, splinters cutting into his palms and knees as he skidded on the wood floor. He turned to see where his father was, but Taekori, like Amikori, was gone. Sheng was alone, bruised and bleeding on the floor of his childhood home.

He sobbed, tears streaming down his face. What was he doing here? Where had his parents gone? Were they really dead?

"Sheng," his father's voice called from outside the house.

Sheng sniffed and headed for the porch. He could see the village, not as a happy memory, but smoldering and charred. There his father stood, pointing up at the tall, snow-capped mountain beyond the valley.

"You must climb the mountain," Taekori ordered. "There you will find what it is you are looking."

"What am I looking for ?" Sheng asked.

His father stepped down from the porch and began walking in the direction of the mountain, his back turned, his gaze focused on the crest, "Answers, my son. There you will find answers."

The floor cracked, then crumbled beneath him and he found himself falling into a deep pit of darkness. Sheng jolted awake. The bright sun hurt his eyes as he squinted in the glorious morning light. It was only a dream, a nightmare yes, but still only a dream.

Sheng righted himself on the bench. Daisuke was gone. To the north, he could see land once again. In the distance, he could see another island. Beyond that, foreboding dark clouds on the horizon. Apparently they were sailing headlong into a storm.

Perfect, Sheng sighed.

He stood awkwardly as he took a moment to get used to the rocking of the ship. Voices above caught his attention and he made his way onto the upper deck. There he found Daisuke talking to the captain.

"We wondered when you would wake," Suke-chan smiled.

"*We?*"

"The captain and me," Daisuke replied. "You got all sweaty last night and I thought you were fevered so I helped you lay down. You were mumbling in your sleep this morning so I came up here to see if I could help with anything on the ship."

"It appears your big friend here has an aptitude for sailing," the captain mused.

Sheng found this surprising, knowing that only yesterday Suke-chan could barely keep his food down, let alone keep his balance on the water. "You're serious?" Sheng questioned. Surely the captain was joking.

"Absolutely, my friend," the captain confirmed. "Daisuke here has spent the morning learning the parts of the boat and how the sails work, even when pushing into the wind."

"I see," Sheng chuckled, shading his eyes with his hand as he watched a flash of lightning flicker from within the dark clouds ahead.

"How far are we from Naniwa?" he asked.

"We'll reach the port by nightfall," the captain answered.

"And the storm?"

The captain grunted and mumbled, licking his finger and sticking it into the air, "It will be on us by midday. We'll be crossing into the channel between *Honshu* and *Futana-Shima*. There the winds will be strong, the waves large, and the journey slow…we might even *lose* a few men."

"What?" Suke-chan asked, startled and wide-eyed.

"Not to worry," the captain continued nonchalantly. "It happens every storm. It's the sea's way of showing who the real sailors are. If I lose a man from this ship, then he wasn't meant to be here."

"And what about us?" Sheng asked.

"I guess we'll find out, won't we?" the captain winked.

Thunder boomed. Rain pelted the deck as the crew raced around to secure the rigging and protect the cargo. A fierce wind howled, ripping at the sails, the bamboo battens rattling. The men fought with the tack lines, reigning in the sails as best as they could in the deluge.

Sheng held fast to ropes that hung on the underside of the elevated rear deck. Daisuke did the same, the terrified look on his face more than conveying that he no longer wished to be a sailor.

"Is this a typhoon?" Suke-chan shouted into the wind.

"If it's not, I can't imagine a typhoon could be any worse!" Sheng replied.

A loud creaking sound drew their attention to the center mast as it strained under the stress of the storm. The crew didn't seem to notice.

"That can't be good!" Sheng exclaimed.

Waves continued to batter the ship, smashing against its sides and crashing down on the deck. Even under the tightly tied ropes, the cargo shifted and swayed with the tossing of the craft.

"I don't think we're going to make it!" Suke-chan cried.

Another giant wave crashed down onto the deck and knocked one of the crewman off of his feet. He hit the wooden deck hard, his face bloodied as he lay unconscious. Without hesitation, Sheng ran from what little safety there was beneath the aft deck and out into the chaos of the storm. His vision blurred as the hard rain stung his face, his black hair matted to his head. He reached out for the man's arm, planning to drag him back to the rear of the ship. But, he didn't make it far. A massive gust of wind whipped across the ship from the port side and shifted the cargo. A rope suddenly snapped violently as a large crate teetered on the edge of another and began to fall, Sheng and the helpless sailor directly in its path.

Sheng fearlessly threw himself down on top of the man to protect him from the blow. He closed his eyes, bracing for impact. But it never came. He looked up to see Daisuke standing over them, his muscular arms holding the crate in place.

"Hurry!" Suke-chan urged.

Sheng did just that. He reached to grab the man under the arms and drag him to safety, but as he did, he realized that they were right above the compartment that was normally under guard. He knew he didn't have much time, but what he wouldn't give just for a peek inside at the captain's secret cargo?

"What are you waiting for?!" Daisuke shouted again. "Go!"

Sheng knew he shouldn't risk it, but he couldn't help himself. He might not have another chance! He reached for the iron-ring latch and began to lift. Another wave covered them and slammed the hatch closed once again. But Sheng had seen enough, the pit of his stomach knotted as he took hold of the still-unconscious sailor and drug him away from the cargo. Daisuke let the crate fall crashing to the deck and headed off behind his friend.

"What were you thinking?!" Suke-chan scolded once they were again under the aft deck. "You could have been crushed!"

Sheng wasn't listening, his attention focused on the man. He knelt over him, placing his ear above his mouth, listening for breath, but there was none. Daisuke dropped down onto his knees and thrust his fist into the man's chest. Water gurgled in his throat and bubbled up, trickling from the corners of his mouth. Suke-chan struck him again and again, water came up from his lungs. Sheng turned him onto his side and the man coughed to life. They helped him sit up against the side of the ship and he coughed again, in pain but happy to be alive.

"That was close," Sheng said in relief as he and Daisuke slumped down along the sailor.

Suke-chan pushed his sopping hair from his brow. "So what was that all about?" he asked.

"The hatch," Sheng answered deciding it best to whisper so that the man couldn't hear, "I wanted to know what was hidden inside."

"And was it worth risking your life?" Suke-chan quipped.

"I wish I hadn't."

"Why? What did you see?"

Sheng leaned in closer to answer. But as he did, they were interrupted by the captain.

"You there, sailor," he shouted as he glared at the man. "Why aren't you on your feet?"

The man stood and quickly ran back to his post, though he clutched his chest as he did, still clearly in pain. Perhaps Suke-chan had cracked a rib — *or two.*

"He fell, captain," Sheng explained. "The waves knocked him down and he hit his head. I brought him back to the rear of the ship."

"You saved his life?" the captain asked.

"We did."

"Then you have given him a second chance to prove he belongs on my ship. You just might have changed his fate, my young friends."

"Will the ship outlast the storm?" Daisuke asked as the captain began to turn away.

"This?" he laughed. "This is nothing! I was there when the divine wind drove off the Mongols. Now that was a storm! This is nothing but an inconvenience!"

Sheng and Daisuke shared a confused glance as the captain turned and headed back to the upper deck, the wind rustling his clothes. He shouted out orders as he did, facing the brunt of the storm and cursing the gale.

"So what was it you saw?" Suke-chan asked again, wanting desperately to find out what was in the cargo hold.

"Well, I didn't get the best look," Sheng admitted. "The rain was in my eyes and the compartment was very dark. I made out a few shapes. There was movement, but I couldn't see what was down there. But right before the hatch slammed shut, I did see one thing."

"What, Sheng? What did you see?"

"I saw eyes looking back at me," he answered solemnly, "too many to count."

"You mean the captain is carrying people below the deck?"

"I think they were children, maybe girls. He's smuggling them."

Daisuke thought a moment, staring out at the still-raging storm, "Do you think that Master Hasegawa is involved?"

"I don't know," Sheng answered, "but when we return to Kamakura, I'll be wanting an explanation!"

The storm soon passed and the sky was once again clear, the water calm. As the captain had promised, the port at Naniwa was visible in the distance. The sun was just setting beyond the mountains of Honshu. They would be there by nightfall. They would rest and then leave for Kyoto at first light.

15

A DETOUR OF FATE

The night spent in Naniwa passed quickly. After disembarking from the junk that brought them from Kamakura, Sheng and Daisuke found a tavern with an inn and rented a room for the night. They slept with ease, happy to once again stand on solid, dry ground.

Their appearance was innocent enough: simple travelers with little coin visiting the what was storied to be the first imperial capitol. Naniwa itself was a unique and interesting place. The market was like nothing they had ever experienced. Now that they were seeing the harbor in the new day's light, they recognized how many different types and sizes of ships were docked in this city of trade. They marveled at the dialects spoken all around them, tongues that were new to their ears, yet business was conducted without miscommunication. This was nothing like what they were accustomed to back home!

Sheng removed two coins from the rope he wore around his neck and paid a street vendor for their breakfast. Daisuke quickly ate the rice he'd been given.

"Hungry boy!" the merchant laughed.

"We had a long trip and haven't eaten in nearly two days," Sheng explained, intentionally exaggerating their situation.

"Where do you come from?" the old man asked. "And where are you going?"

Sheng thought for a moment, uncertain if he should tell the truth. "We're from the South," he lied. "My brother and I are on a pilgrimage to the shrines and temples in *Nara*."

"I see," the merchant nodded. "Be safe on your journey."

They bowed to him and headed away from the market, first in the direction of Nara, but when they sure they were out of the old man's line of site, they doubled back to the Yodo River.

"Why did you lie to the old man?" Daisuke wondered.

"If something were to happen and anyone started asking questions, he would never give us away," Sheng replied. "I don't want to draw any unnecessary attention. Two pilgrims traveling to Nara is common, so we will be soon forgotten."

As they spoke, they came upon a row of flat-bottomed *takasebune*, each one with a man ready to take travelers up river. At times, portions of the Yodo were full of fisherman and small cargo vessels and navigation could be difficult. One man in particular seemed to notice them and waived enthusiastically for them to approach.

"How far will you take us?" Sheng asked.

The man replied very happily, ready to serve his customers, "I know of a good fishing spot two hours from here. It's a family secret, but I'll take you. Come now."

"Is there a place where we can go to shore and eat once we're there?"

"Of course! Whatever you ask. Come now, I'll take you."

Sheng and Daisuke carefully stepped onto the long, narrow boat and their *captain* pushed off, steering the takasebune with a long pole used to push against the riverbed. The ride would be long and slow, but they risked even less chance of being discovered by travelling away from the crowds. Master Hasegawa had told Sheng to blend with the mass of people in Naniwa, but this seemed safer yet. As they glided along the surface of the river, Sheng pulled the hood of his robe up over his head, hiding his face from the other passengers on nearby boats.

"So what happens next?" Suke-chan questioned.

Sheng pulled the map and travel papers from his pocket and unfolded them. He studied Hasegawa's notes and followed the recommended path to Kyoto.

"We'll see where this man takes us," Sheng whispered softly as he leaned in close to Suke-chan. "When we land for lunch, we'll sneak away and find the road north."

"Do you think we'll reach Kyoto today?"

"I don't think so, at least not on foot. We don't have the money for horses and we can't follow the river into Kyoto. *And*, same as with the merchant in Naniwa, the less people we meet along the way who know about our destination, the better! After seeing the cargo hidden on that junk, I've lost some trust in Master Hasegawa. Certainly he knows what his friend is up to! I'm beginning to wonder if this journey doesn't have a darker purpose?"

"I guess we'll have to wait and see what Hasegawa's contact has to say."

"Certainly. And we should be prepared to camp tonight," Sheng planned. "We'll sleep in shifts so as not to be caught by surprise."

"Sounds good," Suke-chan agreed, laying back and kicking up his feet. "If we've got two hours to go, I'm going to get more sleep. After having nearly died yesterday, I think I deserve a little extra rest and relaxation."

Sheng smiled and shook his head in disbelief. If Suke-chan was ever to be counted on, it was for meals and bedtimes. One could tell the time of day by the grumbling of his stomach. This strange gift was only second to his loyalty. And for this, Sheng was thankful for such a companion. He decided he too may as well take advantage of the takasebune's leisurely pace. At one point, he was almost certain he'd seen a shadowy, hooded figure watching them from a distance, but when he glanced back, there was no one there. He decided his mind was weary and playing tricks on him. After watching the shoreline for a while, Sheng's eyes grew heavy and he fell asleep.

The boat jolted as the bow struck the grass-covered bank of the Yodo river. Sheng squinted as he opened his eyes, the bright sun high in the sky: they were nearing midday.

"Is this your family's secret fishing spot?" Sheng asked the man as he righted himself. "We must have travelled longer than two hours!"

"Right you are, friend. But you were sleeping so peacefully that when we reached the place where I recommended, I couldn't bring myself to disturb you. So, I kept pushing up river and here we are!"

"I see," Sheng replied, unsettled by the change in plans.

"Here is a good place to fish though too, and eat! It's very private here. No one knows about this place except for me and my family."

"Is that so?"

"Most certainly! As a matter of fact, it was my great grandfather who discovered this exact place. He brought home many, many fish from here over the years. Oh, great grandfather...I could speak of his legend for hours!" the man gushed with a big, toothy smile. "Anyway, did you bring food?"

"We did," Daisuke chimed in, suddenly awake and alert at the mention of eating."

The man pointed up the bank at a cluster of trees, beyond it a forest so dense that only small rays of light could be seen piercing the canopy of leaves, "There is plenty of shade there. Go ahead and eat! I will catch us some fish and we can have that to. My grandfather was known all over Japan for his skill, my father as well. They taught me everything I know. We'll be feasting in no time, my friends!"

Sheng stepped off the side of the boat and onto the rocky edge of the river, then into the tall, green and yellow grass. Suke-chan followed. As soon as they were out of earshot, Sheng glanced back. Their captain was dangling a bamboo rod out over the water, the line too thin to see from that distance.

"Does it seem odd that he continued taking us up river, travelling longer than he told us we would?" Sheng asked Suke-chan.

"Maybe not, if he just thinks we're tourists. He probably figured we wouldn't care where he took us to fish."

"Perhaps."

The two of them climbed the rest of the way up the bank and arrived at the cluster of trees. The shade felt good after being on the water. Sheng's face was warm from the sun. Suke-chan was sweating.

The trees were only a short way from the forest. A path could be seen winding into the overgrowth. As they stood amongst the thin trunks, they noticed that the grass in the center area was matted down, as if it had been visited many times before. The branches of the trees sagged, covered in beautiful white blossoms, forcing them to hunch over to best see beyond the shaded cover.

"He's a bit eccentric isn't he?" Daisuke laughed, looking down at the man swinging the pole around in an overly animated fashion.

If Sheng didn't know better, the man almost looked like he was dancing, his backside wagging and feet tapping as he moved. The man's voice began to carry across the water as he began singing a strange, unfamiliar song.

"That's no good," Sheng said. "He'll scare away all the fish carrying on like that! He won't catch a single thing."

He and Daisuke watched from the matted circle amongst the trees, unsure of the man's curious actions. For claiming such a lineage of famous fisherman, this man seemed to know nothing about the craft. His dance was oddly mesmerizing. They couldn't look away.

From somewhere behind them, a twig snapped in the thick forest. Sheng spun around.

"Did you hear that, Suke-chan?"

"What?" he asked, still focused on the crazy fisherman.

"That sound? Did you hear a branch break?"

"I didn't," Daisuke admitted, not turning to look into the forest. "It was probably just a deer."

Suke-chan immediately turned his attention back to the odd entertainment down below. Sheng continued scanning the tree line for movement, but everything was still. This should have been reassuring, but deep down he felt like something was very wrong. His eyes fell to the ground, better studying the trampled ring of flattened grass. Then he spotted it. He knelt next to one of the trees and examined a gouge cleanly slashed in the trunk. It was deep and clean through the bark. The mark was approximately at the same height as an average man's waste and the angle looked like it had been hacked in a sweeping, downward motion. He remembered the wooden posts used at the dojo when training students new to sword-craft. Sheng envisioned the marred and chopped wood, marked in such a way by nothing but a razor sharp katana. This was no doubt a mark made by a sword, and not that long ago!

Sheng looked at the forest once again, just in time to see the sudden movement of a roving band of raiders emerge at full speed from the brush, swords raised, screams bursting from their gaunt faces. This was an ambush, planned and precise.

"Suke-chan!" Sheng shouted as he quickly removed his heavy outer robe and unsheathed his sword.

There was not time to think. Daisuke realized what was happening and drew his sword as well, joining Sheng in his defensive stance. The raiders crashed through the low hanging branches and into the circle, six of them in all. These were not good odds and their lack of armor left them more vulnerable than they would normally be when facing such an attack. But the side effect, if it was any consolation, was their enhanced speed of movement without being encumbered by the weight of their samurai garb.

The first rogue lunged clumsily his sword missing the agile Sheng. An effortless flick of his blade dropped the attacker to the ground. Daisuke stopped the second bandit in the same manner, dodging a wild blow to deliver a devastating one of his own. These raiders were fearsome, but poorly trained and the samurai used this to their advantage. The third man shrieked as his blade cut into a tree, the blade striking the trunk as Sheng spun out of the way, his sword sweeping in an arc and cutting the man down, red blood droplets splattering onto the pure, white blossoms encircling them.

Sheng and Daisuke fought furiously. The fourth, fifth, and sixth fell just as easily. The samurai stood over the lifeless bodies of their attackers. This was not what they expected to face on this *diplomatic* journey.

146

Another shrill cry came from the direction of the river as the fisherman, armed with a sword, ran up on them. He took one look at the bloodied corpses and screamed, dropping his blade and running back to the boat. Sheng took chase and tackled him before he reached the shore.

"Why did you trick us?" Sheng growled, taking the man by his collar and pulling the short sword from his belt, holding it threateningly to the man's throat.

The man stared up at Sheng in terror, his wide eyes darting back and forth from the blade to Sheng's blood and sweat streaked face, "Please don't kill me, kind sir! Please spare my life!"

"Why should I?! You brought us here to die. What do I owe you?"

"Please," the man whimpered, "the raiders have my family. They have taken them into the woods. There is a cave to the north of here. I owe them money. This is how they force me to repay it. They said that I will not see my family till I repay the debt. This is the arrangement. I bring people here, they kill and rob them. Please, most honorable sir, you must believe me!"

"What's that smell?" Daisuke asked, his nose scrunching as he knelt down beside the two of them.

"He soiled himself," Sheng sighed as the man began crying in shame.

"Please believe me," he sobbed. "I only want to see my wife and children again. I know now that you two young men are great warriors. Surely you can show me mercy. Please, will you help me get my family back?"

Suke-chan rolled his eyes at the man's sniveling. What was worse, he knew that Sheng could never live with himself if he left an innocent family to suffer who-knows-what indecencies at the hands of heartless raiders. Sheng's self-ascribed defense-of-the-little-guy mentality had only grown over the years and certainly his sense of victimhood fed this purpose, having known the pain of being ripped from his family against his own will. Daisuke knew that this *side-quest* was unavoidable. Their current task – Kyoto – would have to wait.

"How far is the cave," Sheng asked, fulfilling Suke-chan's prediction.

"Bless you, kind sir. The cave is not far. I am your humble servant."

Sheng put away his short sword and helped the man to his feet, "I will help you. But know that if this is another trick, you will not be shown further mercy. I will strike you down, you and whoever is waiting for us!"

"Certainly, my friend, certainly. I swear on my family that I am telling the truth. Now follow me!"

The man raced back up the steep bank of the Yodo and past the gory scene at the grove of white-blossomed trees. Sheng and Daisuke followed close behind, wary, their hands on the hilts of their swords as they moved. They took the narrow, winding path into the forest. Birds sang happily in the branches above. Small, furry creatures scurried out of their path, taking refuge in the surrounding thickets as the strangers tromped through.

"I must warn you," the man called back over his shoulder as he led them along, "there are bears in this forest, so we should be careful!"

"Oh, that's just great," Suke-chan huffed from the rear. "Bears. Perfect. As if raiders hiding in a cave weren't enough!"

"We'll be fine," Sheng grinned.

After they'd been on the path for some twenty minutes, they came upon a small clearing. The mouth of a cave was visible. Crates were stacked near the entrance. A lone sentry stood guard, resting against the mountainside, his eyes closed.

"How many do you think are in there?" Sheng whispered as the three of them stared through a gap in the branches.

"Could be ten, could be twenty," the man estimated. "Their numbers are different each time I see them."

"Alright," Sheng continued, formulating a plan on the spot, "here's what we'll do. I'll sneak around to the other side of the clearing. When I signal, Suke-chan, grab that stick there on the ground and smack it hard against the tree trunk next to you. It should draw his attention this way. When he's distracted, I'll sneak out and take him down from his blindside."

"And what if the noise brings more men from inside the cave?" Daisuke questioned.

"Then I'll attack the man closest to me. When I do, they'll come to his aid and you can strike unexpected from behind."

"What should I do?" the old man asked.

"You'll wait till the area is clear. We're not risking our lives rescuing your family just to have you killed in the process."

"If I were to die while trying to set them free, it would be an honor!"

"Well you'll soon have your chance," Sheng said. "Ready your swords."

Suke-chan and the captain did as he instructed and then watched as Sheng slipped away silently into the lush forest. He moved quickly, nimbly, careful not to upset branches as he went. Before long, they saw his face poking out from the trees. The man had remained undisturbed.

Sheng nodded and pulled the short sword from its place on his belt. Suke-chan followed his cue and grabbed the thick, broken stick that lay at his feet. Without hesitation, he smacked it hard into the nearby tree trunk. The sharp *thunk* resonated in the clearing and, just as expected, the guard jumped to life, startled by the sudden noise. He placed a hand on the grip of his sword as he scanned the trees. Cautiously, he approached where the sound seemed to have come from. His hearing was good because he was heading straight at them!

There was no time to lose. Sheng double checked the entrance to the cave to make sure no more guards were emerging before he darted out from his hiding spot, the knife-like blade in hand. He was on the guard without being detected. Sheng placed his hand over the unsuspecting man's mouth as he plunged the sword up into his ribs. There was a brief struggle, a few guttural gasps, then silence as his body went limp.

"We have to hurry," Sheng urged, quickly turning back to the cave.

Suke-chan followed, the captain close behind. "You'll wait out here for us," Sheng told the old man as they stood at the mouth of the cave. "We'll go in and clear it out. We'll call for you when the coast is clear."

The man watched nervously as Sheng and Daisuke disappeared into the blackness of the cave. After a moment, he heard shouts and cries followed by thumps, bangs, and clanks. Again more agonizing screams, and then nothing, not a whimper nor footfall. He peered into the darkness, trying to make out a shape or detail, but he couldn't see more than a few feet in front of him. The cave seemed to swallow all light.

He began to pace. Would these warriors find his family alive? A flicker of light began to show from the rear of the cave. It approached quickly and the man cowered, fearing his would be-victims had failed and now retribution for his betrayal of the gang was coming to finish him off as well. But fortune was certainly with them and he saw the familiar face of Daisuke emerge from the depths, his face reflecting the orange glow of a fiery torch, his hand motioning for him to follow.

They trekked deep into the cave, making several turns. Scattered about were the bodies of the raiders, caught unprepared and cut down where they stood as the samurai blitzed through the tunnel. At last they came to the rear of the cave. There, they found a makeshift dining hall and sleeping area. Beyond that, in a narrow alcove, was a crude cage made of bamboo shafts, crossed and tied tightly together. A woman sat back against the wall, lean and sickly, her age difficult to discern as dirty and careworn as she was. Beside her sat a young girl, eleven or twelve-years-old, her eyes forlorn as she looked up at them from the hand-made prison. A third body rested in the corner, hidden beneath a blanket: apparently male and very frail, only a little bit of dirty black hair visible on the top of his head.

"Is this your family?" Sheng asked as Daisuke held the torch close to the cage so the old man could see.

The man did not need to answer. Their smiles were confirmation enough. Happy tears streamed down his face as he looked upon his wife and daughter.

"Where is he? Where is our son?" the man questioned his wife, suddenly realizing that whoever was under the blanket was not who he thought it was.

His wife's eyes grew sullen as she formed her reply, "Not long after we were taken, he managed to escape. He wanted to try to get help and set us all free. He killed two guards, the second with a sword he took from the first. But, he didn't get far before the rest of the gang swarmed him. The raiders overpowered and killed him, right in front of us. He fought bravely, but they killed him!"

"My son is dead?" he moaned, mourning in his sad voice. "No! Please, no!"

Daisuke swung his sword down on the rope that secured the bamboo gate of the prison cell. The mother and daughter clung to the father, all three sobbing. They were reunited, but it was bittersweet. The young man in the corner did not move.

"Do you suppose he's dead?" Suke-chan asked as he helped the grieving family to their feet and moved them aside so he could check the other stranger in the cell.

As he reached down to take hold of the blanket, a hand shot up from beneath the woolen cloth and took Suke-chan by the wrist. Though frail in appearance, whoever it was beneath the blanket was very much alive, and surprisingly strong! Daisuke pulled back with all of his might, his weight shifting rearward, but the person held on tight, being pulled unsuspectingly right up onto his feet.

Sheng and Daisuke both laughed. It wasn't a frail man at all, but a *girl*. Her hair was cut short like a boy and she wore clothing that hid her figure, but *he* was most certainly a *she*. The girl was younger than the two of them, though not by much. She was not yet a woman and there was a child-like twinkle in her eye. She still gripped Suke-chan's arm. Again, he pulled back, this time lifting her up off the floor.

"We're friends, I promise," he said, easily throwing her over his shoulder.

"Let's get out of here," Sheng urged.

The light from the torch guided their steps till they reached the cave's entrance. The girl struggled in Suke-chan's strong grip, shouting at him to put her down. He chuckled as they stepped into the bright sunlight, finally giving in to her demands. As soon as her bare feet hit the grass, she reached up and slapped the towering Daisuke right across the face.

"What did you do that for?" he whined, his cheek red from her quick strike.

She didn't back down. Without hesitation, she stood toe-to-toe with her unwanted rescuer and wagged her finger in his face, "Because I told you to put me down, that's why!"

Daisuke didn't react angrily; in fact, he seemed speechless. In the daylight, even with smudges of soot dirtying her face, she was beautiful. Big Suke-chan just stared at her bashfully, his mouth agape as he accepted her admonishing.

"Calm down, girl," Sheng scolded. "Be glad we came along and rescued you. If not, who knows what those men would have done to you!"

"I had everything under control. I had a plan and I was going to escape. I'm not scared of anything, okay?" she spouted back with as much attitude as she could muster.

"I believe you," Daisuke finally uttered, breaking free from his trance.

As they stood there, a rustling came from the perimeter of the clearing. The branches parted and a black bear lumbered into view. The girl screamed, scaling up Suke-chan's back and wrapping her arms tightly around his neck, putting him between herself and the creature.

The bear sniffed the air, sizing up the humans it had stumbled upon. With a snort, it backed away and disappeared again into the forest.

"Not scared of anything, huh?" Sheng mocked.

She still clung to Suke-chan. He didn't seem to mind, a goofy grin on his round face.

"This is where we part ways," Sheng said, turning to the old man, his wife, and his daughter.

"Thank you so much for rescuing my family," he replied, bowing respectfully.

Sheng bowed as well and continued, "If I were you, I'd leave Naniwa and never look back. If these raiders are part of a larger group, then there will be a price on your head. Go far north or far south, but as *far* away as you can. Start a new life and be thankful you did not lose your whole family to your debts. Be content in your circumstances and love those around you."

"I will."

The girl listened to Sheng, his words wise and true as she watched the family walk off in the direction of the river. Her feet once more found the soft grass, but she stayed close to Daisuke.

"And what about me?" she asked as Sheng turned his attention to her. "What would you have me do?"

He smiled, thinking back to her claim of being fearless, yet cowering at the sight of the bear, "I would tell you to know that accepting help from others is not cowardice, but wise and shrewd. If you never trust anyone, then you will certainly never be disappointed; but, you will always be lonely. One's self is a poor companion on a lonely road."

"Then I accept your help," she beamed happily. "I will join you wherever it is you are going."

"What?" Sheng laughed, more out of shock than amusement. "What makes you think we would want you tagging along with us? And what makes you think we're going anywhere?"

"Well you must be going *somewhere*," she replied sharply. "I know this region well. No one lives in this area. The raiders chased them all away a generation ago. Travelers use the river and the road. We're all travelers here."

"I see," Sheng said, now intrigued.

"So where is it you are going?" she pressed. "You're heading north, that is for certain. And, all that is north is Kyoto. There's no other reason to take the Yodo this far and not continue on to the imperial city. That's it isn't? You're heading to Kyoto!"

"No," Sheng lied.

"Yes," Daisuke blushed.

"Excellent. Then I'm coming with you," she decided.

"Suke-chan!" Sheng yelled at his friend.

"What? What would it hurt? We can't leave her out here all alone."

"We can't?"

"Well of course not," Daisuke challenged. "There are raiders…and *bears*! How can we just leave her here?"

"Fine." Sheng agreed. "She can come with us to Kyoto, but that's it. Once we're there, she goes her way and we go ours. Do you have a name, girl?"

"Hayami."

"Well then, *Hayami*," Sheng responded sternly. "Onward to Kyoto."

16

SAFE, BUT NOT SOUND

The forest was alive with sounds. Crickets chirped as the darkness of night enveloped the three travelers. After leaving the cave, they returned to the Yodo River and followed the path along its banks. Hours passed full of conversation, mostly between Daisuke and the relentless Hayami, her words fast and her wit faster. Sheng was content to listen to his best friend share tales of their battles and feats of might. Suke-chan made the two of them seem like warriors of legend. Hayami ate up every word. She seemed to have a special liking for Daisuke. Sheng was glad to see how happy his friend was, if only for this one night.

They'd found a spot to camp and had once again left the visibility of the path for the security of the woods. The dense brush did well to hide their small campfire from view. Now, they rested, lying on the ground and staring up at the bright, twinkling stars through a gap in the treetops that towered high above them, the trunks glowing in the flickering firelight till they stretched up beyond the orange glow's reach, becoming black silhouettes against the dark night. Fireflies danced around them. Bats fluttered back and forth above.

"Tell me about your childhood," Hayami asked as she snuggled in

154

close to Suke-chan.

"Well," he began, "we both grew up in the same village, somewhere east of here, a day's and night's journey from Kamakura. I don't remember exactly where the village was, but it was in a beautiful valley full of flowers and rolling hills…"

"It was more than beautiful," Sheng added, his hands clasped behind his head, "it was perfect."

"It was," Suke-chan smiled, reminiscing. "There were many children in the village and we would run through the fields, chasing each other. We would play games after our tutoring and wade through the creek that watered our crops. I remember one time, we were looking for *treasure* in the stream. Sheng packed a ball of mud in his hands and turned, throwing it quickly without really looking. I was his intended target, but Kimi-chan had stepped right in the path of his throw. The mud ball hit her square in the shoulder and splattered all over her kimono and face. It was in her hair. Boy was she ever cross! Do you remember that, Sheng?"

"I do," he smiled. "That was the day I found that strange stone in the water and I made her a charm out of it to say I was sorry."

"Oh yeah!" Suke-chan laughed. "She never took that off."

There was a long pause in the conversation as Sheng and Daisuke thought about their long-lost friend. Hayami sensed the regret that neither man would speak of but was clearly there.

"Did you have many other friends?" she prodded, finally breaking the silence. "Or was it just the three of you?"

Sheng cleared his throat. Hayami wasn't certain, but she thought that perhaps he had been crying.

"There were a few kids that ran around with us, but it was normally just Suke-chan, Kimi-chan, and me. You know, Suke-chan was the biggest kid back then too. He could spar with the oldest boys, even hold his own against a few of the men if he wanted to, but some of the children still bullied him. They made fun of him for his size. They would hit him and run away laughing. They would call him fat and slow. I never understood why. To this day, I still don't understand why they singled him out. I got picked on too, but my temper was hotter and I would hit back. But Suke-chan, he knew how strong he was. And even though he could have swatted those bullies like they were flies, he always held back. There were many times I

155

fought for him because I couldn't stand to watch him be teased, but he always controlled himself. It's something I admired – still do. Suke-chan was – *is* – a gentle giant."

Hayami sniffed as she wiped tears from her eyes. "I'm sorry," she sighed.

Daisuke reached over and took hold of her small hand, wrapping his enormous fingers around it, "It took me a long time to understand. I don't know that I've ever gotten over it: the bullying. I was nice to everyone. Sheng and I always stood up for the ones who would get picked on. But I just couldn't seem to fight for myself. For years I believed their words and thought I was worthless. I just put on a happy, chubby smile and continued being the butt of their jokes. It hurt. It was hard. But, here I am."

"And he's still huge," Sheng added.

Suke-chan laughed, "And I'm okay with that. It's just difficult finding samurai armor that fits is all!"

"So you are samurai?" Hayami mused.

"Like our fathers," Suke-chan confirmed.

"Did they fight many battles?" she continued.

"They did," Sheng replied. "They defended Japan against the Mongols. That's where they became friends. After the invasion attempt was foiled by a great storm, our fathers left together and moved to the village where we grew up, far from the threat of invasion. There were still battles, but none like the invasion of the Mongols!"

"I could have taken Kublai Kahn," Suke-chan smiled, "if it was just him and me!"

"We're from a line of warriors. Certainly you could have," Sheng grinned. "We are both Shimazu clan by lineage. I believe we even have distant relatives still living in *Kyūshū*. Maybe someday we'll travel there as well."

"So what happened to your parents?"

"They're dead," Sheng answered, almost coldly.

"Our village was attacked by raiders when we were just boys," Suke-chan explained. "All the children were taken away. The parents were killed."

"That's awful!"

"That's life," Sheng said flatly.

"So we ended up being taken to Kamakura," Daisuke continued. "We were trained and educated at a dojo by the samurai master Takeshi Hasegawa."

"Hasegawa?!" Hayami exclaimed. "I know his name!"

"He is a warrior of great renown," Sheng confirmed. "And yet..."

"What?" she prompted. "It's okay. You can tell me."

"I shouldn't be saying this," Sheng said, "but, I don't know if Hasegawa is to be trusted."

"Is he the reason you're going to Kyoto?" she figured.

"I've said enough," Sheng decided, rolling over, his back to Suke-chan and their new friend. "We should get some sleep."

Morning came quickly, bright sunlight bursting through the trees, outlining the green leaves with brilliant, yellow halos. Sheng stirred, waking to see Hayami tucked up closely to Suke-chan, cradled in the nook of his arm, his chest a makeshift pillow. The fire was smoldering, gray smoke rising from the last of the faintly glowing embers.

"It's time," Sheng called out climbing to his feet.

Daisuke yawned, as did Hayami. "The ground was harder than I thought it would be!" Suke-chan exclaimed with a grimace, suddenly aware that for the better part of the night, a rock had pressed against his ribs. "What I wouldn't have given for a nice soft straw mat or even a blanket!"

"I thought it was nice," Hayami smirked.

Sheng was fully aware that he was now the odd man out. But all that would change in Kyoto. Hayami would go her own way and Daisuke would be able to focus on their task. They just had to keep moving.

"We'll eat while we walk," Sheng said. "There are still cakes from yesterday. And, we should watch for berries and nuts growing in the wild. Kyoto is reachable by late afternoon if we keep a steady pace."

Without argument from Hayami, they set out once again on the path that lay before them. Kyoto was just shy of a day's hike north. They kept the forest to their right, the river on the left. Visibility was good as they travelled. It would be difficult for more raiders to catch them unaware, still they listened for the slightest sounds and moved swiftly.

The terrain was easy enough with no obstacles to clear. The well-worn path showed signs of daily use, the dirt packed hard under their feet. Occasionally, they came upon another traveler who they would greet with cordial, if not too friendly, nods of their heads as they passed. Boats could be seen carrying small loads of goods up river. Certainly the Yodo would be faster, but the water also came with its share of risks. For one, the passengers on the boats were out in the open, widely viewable and easy to stalk. And two, an ambush was almost always possible as well-maneuvered boats could trap a smaller craft easily and overtake them, then allowing for arrow strikes from the shore. Sheng believed the path was safest and his companions followed his lead.

They ate as they walked. Every hour or so, they would pause and rest briefly, either under a tree for shade or down at the water's edge where they could drink and be refreshed in the heat. Then they would once again move north, ever closer to Kyoto and Hasegawa's contact. Halfway along, they came across a grove of apple trees. They'd stuffed their pockets with as much of the sweet, juicy red fruit as they could and were thankful for such a find.

As the sun sank into the west, the trio arrived at a crossroad; a much broader path clearly marked as leading to the imperial city. A small series of wooden docks as well as several carts carrying the wares of vendors were seen on the western road.

"So this is it," Sheng said, looking up each pathway. "This is where we part ways, Hayami."

"But you said she could come with us to Kyoto?" Suke-chan protested, a lump growing in his throat.

She smiled at Daisuke and took him by the hands, then stood on the tips of her toes and stretched to give him a kiss on his rosy cheek, "It's alright. I have a feeling we will see each other again."

Daisuke held on to her as long as he could, his heart sinking as he felt her pull away, her fingers dragging reluctantly across his till their connection broke and the big bear-of-a-man was left standing in listless despair. Sheng felt horrible as he witnessed his best friend's dejection, but there was really nothing that could be done. They had a mission to complete. Hasegawa was not a man to dissatisfy and Hayami was a certain distraction. Perhaps had they met under different circumstances…still, they had to focus on the task at hand. This was no time for love.

Hayami stood just off the eastern path, out of view from the road to Kyoto. She'd travelled along far enough to give Sheng and Daisuke ample time to set off north before she doubled back. The sun had all but disappeared beyond the mountains and the darkness of night had overcome the last rays of light.

The soft glow of a hand-carried lantern caught her attention and she moved in its direction. She seemed to have expected the signal and was happy to answer its beckoning call.

She reached the source of the light and was greeted warmly by a hooded figure, his face obscured in shadow beneath the heavy, hooded cloak. Hayami bowed as she stood in the man's presence. "Master," she said graciously.

"My dear, Hayami," he replied. "I see you are well. How was your trip?"

"There was no trouble at all."

"Did the samurai rescue you from the raiders' den?"

"They did, Master."

"I thank you for taking such a risk," he said, "allowing yourself to be captured with no certainty that a rescue would even take place."

"It was a calculated risk and a risk worth taking," she replied with a smirk. "And if they had not come along, I'd have escaped without their help!"

"There is not a doubt in my mind that you would have, young Hayami."

"Thank you, Master."

"Did you tell them about me?" he asked.

"No, Master. I did as you asked. They have no idea that you are watching them."

"Thank you for respecting my wishes."

"I must ask. Will you reveal yourself to them in Kyoto?"

The hooded figure shook his head *no*, "I do not want to distract them while they are on this journey. This is a test of their abilities, their character. They must see their task through to completion. If they knew I was here, I could put their mission in jeopardy. They must do this on their own."

Hayami and the shadowy man paused as they spoke, careful to avoid being overheard by a small group of passing travelers. As soon as they were out of earshot, they continued.

"Do you believe they will be able to complete their task?" she wondered.

"That remains to be seen," he replied thoughtfully, the soft glow of the lantern briefly revealing his bright green eyes. "They may yet need your help and if that time comes, you must be ready."

"Of course, Master!" she nodded emphatically.

"I want you to follow along to Kyoto. Stay hidden. Do not let the samurai detect you. I will return and prepare for the next part of the plan. Hopefully Kyoto will be a success and we will be a step closer to restoring the balance of power in Japan."

"As you wish," Hayami agreed. "I will follow the samurai. Safe travels, Master. I will see you soon!"

"Good luck," the man replied, extinguishing the lantern and disappearing into the darkness of the trees.

Lights glowed ahead. Torches illuminated the entrance to the city. Sheng and Daisuke quickened their pace, Kyoto now within sight. They'd discussed their plans after leaving Hayami behind. Finding Chion-in was their first priority. Food and rest could wait. Sheng would have been happier knowing exactly who they were meeting, and why, but Master Hasegawa had assured him that the monk they would meet at the temple would recognize them.

They passed through the gate, expecting to see a grand, rich city – and certainly it was wealthier than Kamakura – but they were gravely disappointed. Arriving in Kyoto looked very much like returning home to Kamakura. By lantern light, they could see the frontages of shops and houses, the buildings very similar in construction, crafted meticulously from hand-hewn stone and wood.

Having passed through the city gates after nightfall carried both risks and rewards. For one, they streets were clear of the normal bustle associated with Kyoto traders. Sheng and Daisuke easily navigated the city free from the entanglements of a crowd. But in that was also great risk: it's very difficult to blend in with the local citizenry when the streets are bare. They were aware that they had no place to hide and decided to keep to the main roads and be seen as journeymen rather than slink through the shadows and run the risk of being thought thieves or robbers.

Finally they reached the stone stairs of Chion-in and looked up in wonder at the magnificent temple. Beyond, the silhouette of the mountain, *Kachozan*, blended with the night sky. Trees and gardens, meticulously maintained, encompassed the surrounding buildings that made up the complex. Chion-in was larger than they expected. How would they find their contact?

This question was answered sooner than expected. The samurai-in-disguise had only just reached the top of the steps when a gesturing shadow of a man whistled sharply to get their attention. Their guard raised immediately, the hair one their necks bristling. Cautiously they moved in his direction. Was this their contact? Hasegawa had said his man in Kyoto would find them. Surely this must be him.

"*Konbanwa*," Sheng bowed in greeting as they approached the man.

Suke-chan mirrored the greeting of *good evening* and bowed as well.

The man, dressed as a monk, returned the greeting, graciously bowing his bald head as he urged the conversation forward, "We must not speak here, my friends, where we are so visible. The city has many eyes and ears, both friend and foe. We must be cautious. Please follow me into the gardens."

Curiously, as he motioned for them to follow, his gaze seemed distant, off somewhere else. But his eyes, what they could see of them in the moonlight, looked hazy and glazed. Sheng stared at the monk, unsure what to think. Was this man actually *blind*? If so, how did he know it was friends who approached? How did he even know they were there? His mind was racing with questions.

On the outskirts of the temple grounds, narrow, deep houses fronted with shops lined the dividing street. From there, Hayami watched them make contact. She'd hidden behind a stack of barrels between two buildings, just the whites of her eyes visible, peering out as she observed Sheng and Daisuke. But she recognized the man's gaze had fallen in her direction and she ducked further into the shadows, obscured from his view but also unable to see the samurai as they disappeared into the dense darkness of the garden. She would need to be more careful.

"How were your travels?" the monk asked, satisfied that their words would not be overheard as they stood amongst the trees and bushes.

Sheng recalled the sudden storm at sea and the marauders on the road, but said nothing of them. "We are happy to have arrived in Kyoto – safe and hungry," he smiled.

"We will see that you are given provisions immediately," the monk replied. "But first tell me of Hasegawa. I was hoping he would accompany you on a journey of such importance. I would have thought he would have wanted a task like this completed by his own hands, if only for the satisfaction! But he believes you to be capable, so I will trust you as well."

"What satisfaction would Master Hasegawa receive from this *journey*?" Sheng pressed. "What is it we are truly here to do? He said I was an emissary to the court."

"All in good time," the monk laughed. "I will tell you all you need to know in the morning. But first, you are hungry, you said so yourself! You will eat and sleep. Tomorrow, we discuss your task. Follow me now."

The man turned and headed deeper into the garden, walking along a path that was barely discernible in the dark. Sheng and Suke-chan looked at each other uncertainly. There seemed to be something more sinister than they suspected behind this quest of Hasegawa's. Perhaps this simple garden path was truly leading them somewhere they did not want to go?

"Well come on then," the monk called out, "keep up or you'll be lost till sunrise!"

They'd come this far already and knew they had little choice but to continue. They followed after the sound of the monk's footfalls, the garden soon ending as the path opened up into a courtyard. From there the man led them to a small outbuilding. The samurai ate a simply prepared meal of bread and fruit before being told they would sleep there as well.

"No one will bother you here, my friends. I will bring you more food in the morning as well as the supplies Hasagawa requested. Rest well."

With that, the monk was gone and they were alone. Neither Sheng nor Daisuke spoke. They really had nothing to say, though they could see in each other's eyes the same questions and reluctance. What had they gotten themselves into?

Birds chirped as the warm morning sun bathed the temple grounds in a wash of brilliant light, the gardens aglow with color and life. The young men woke, stretching and rubbing the sleep from their eyes.

Suke-chan cried out, suddenly startled by the unexpected presence of the monk who sat in silent meditation in the corner of the room, his cloudy eyes open, staring straight into Daisuke's. The monk then let out a cry. He too was just as startled by Daisuke's outburst.

"What is wrong, my friend?" the monk asked.

Suke-chan calmed down as he glanced around the room. "Nothing is wrong," he chuckled. "I just woke up and didn't expect to see someone staring at me, that's all."

"I wasn't staring at you, boy," the monk stated matter-of-factly. "I was looking beyond you."

"Excuse me for being blunt," Suke-chan said, apologizing in advance for what he was about to ask, "but you're blind, are you not? How can you be staring – or looking – at anything?"

"I take no offense, my friend. But you should know that simply because one is blind, it does not mean that he cannot see. Do you understand?"

"Not in the slightest," Suke-chan admitted.

"There is sight and then there is *sight*," the monk explained. "I know you already, my friend, though we only just met. You see many things, yet there are many things you do not see because you are too busy *seeing!* "

Daisuke stared blankly at the old monk, trying to understand what he meant. He was never one for riddles and this man certainly was one. Suke-chan's head was spinning.

"By your silence, I take it you do not understand me," the monk continued. "A warrior must know that what he sees with his eyes is not always the truth. What he sees with his mind or his heart is also not always true either. One man's truth is another man's deception. So though one may see, that does not mean he truly *sees*."

"You still lost me," Suke-chan laughed aloud, again startling the blind monk with his sudden, loud outburst.

"I get it," Sheng said thoughtfully. "You're saying that things are not always as they seem. There are some truths that seem like lies and some lies that seem like truths. But how can one tell the difference?"

"I don't know?!" the monk snorted happily, clapping his hands together as he climbed to his feet. "But it is time to begin. Come now, leave your youthful dreams behind and help me with this trunk."

The samurai looked to the opposite end of the room and saw a wooden chest, its lid secured tightly with rope. Sheng didn't remember seeing it there the night before. The monk must have brought it in before morning.

"In here are your new clothes, armor, weapons, and money as well as documents that provide new identities for you so as to complete your task," the monk explained.

"New identities? Weapons? What is it exactly we are doing here? Why is it that Hasegawa has sent us to Kyoto. We are samurai, not spies."

"But that, my young friend, is exactly why he sent you. Your new identities will grant you admission to the court. These new clothes are provided so that you look the part. Beggars would never be allowed in the presence of the emperor."

"Wait, we're going to meet the emperor?!" Daisuke beamed excitedly.

"Of course, my boy."

Suke-chan continued on, "I thought we were just going to end up delivering a message to the court?"

"Certainly you will," the old man chuckled.

"And what about the armor…and the weapons?" Sheng pressed. "Why do we need those if we are to be an envoy on behalf of Hasegawa to the emperor?"

"Oh my friend, haven't you figured it out yet?" the blind monk replied. "You are not here to treat with the emperor. Hasegawa has sent you to kill him."

17

TRUTH & CONSEQUENCES

Sheng, fully dressed in the fine clothes provided by the old monk, paced about the small room. His armor was firmly fastened. A katana hung at his side, its razor-sharp blade confined to its sheath, only waiting to unleash bloody furry. *How did I not see this coming?* Sheng pondered. Certainly he knew that Takeshi Hasegawa hated the emperor, but killing him? He and Daisuke were no assassins! They were honorable samurai, living by the code. Surely there were other samurai at Hasegawa's disposal, others who would gladly chance certain death for praise from their master.

"What are we going to do?" Suke-chan asked. "We can't do this, Sheng. It's wrong!"

"I agree," Sheng answered. "But our orders are clear. Do we disobey our master, our sensei?"

"This is the emperor we're talking about!"

Sheng sighed, "And certainly we will die for killing him."

"So we obey our master, kill the emperor, and die at the hands of his imperial guard. Or, we spare the emperor, disregard our order, and meet the same fate – or worse – in Hasegawa's wrath. Either way we're dead!"

Suke-chan began to panic, his breaths shallow and short as he considered their fate. His face grew red. Beads of sweat glistened on his furrowed brow. "Maybe we could talk to the emperor," Suke-chan suggested. "If we plead our case, maybe he would allow us to remain here and live in peace. We could forget all about the dojo…and Hasegawa."

"We could never forget about Hasegawa because he would never forget about us," Sheng reasoned. "We would spend the rest of our lives looking over our shoulders, sleeping with one eye open, wondering when or how Hasegawa would strike. That is no life to live, Suke-chan. And that's if the emperor even believed us. Even if we told him the truth it could still seem like a plot against him and he might treat us like spies all the same!"

Sheng had yet to put his helmet on. He stood with it in his hands, looking at the snarling, demon-like mask that was meant to strike fear into its enemies as it hid the identity of the wearer. "I need some air," he decided.

Daisuke followed Sheng out onto the porch. The old monk had wandered off. The garden was nearby and a walk would allow Sheng an opportunity to focus his thoughts and perhaps formulate a solution. Together, the best friends left the small building behind and were greeted by perfectly manicured trees and shrubs as they followed the flower-lined footpath into the garden. Small stones crunched beneath their feet. Ahead, they came upon a koi pond and paused to look at the huge, orange fish.

"They have it easy don't they?" Suke-chan said, speaking softly.

"What do you mean?"

"All they have to do is swim and eat, swim and eat, and they live happily day after day. There's no danger in the water, just swim and eat."

Sheng grinned and pointed to a cluster of large rocks that decorated the edge of the water. A cat sat perched on top, its tail twitching as it looked down hungrily at the fish, its head following their darting movements as they swam around in circles.

"There's always a predator, even if you don't know it's there," Sheng mused.

"So which one are we, the cat or the fish?" Suke-chan wondered.

"I have no idea," Sheng laughed, "but I'd rather be…"

His words were cut short by a sudden sound from somewhere off in the distance. They were not alone.

"Maybe it's the old blind monk?" Suke-chan whispered, his eyes scanning the garden ahead for any sign of movement.

The noise continued: a grating, swishing sound, like waves of pebbles breaking on a shore of stone. They followed the path cautiously as it bent around a tree-obscured corner, their hands instinctively clasping the grips of their swords. The volume grew as they approached till finally they had found the source of the sound. Fifty yards ahead, a large man raked the pebbles of a *Zen* garden. His back was to them and they couldn't see his face. Long, stringy gray hair covered his head, resting on his shoulders as he worked. A scruffy and patchy gray beard could be briefly seen as his head turned towards them for just a moment. Still, there was something about the man, his size, shape, perhaps the way he moved, that seemed hauntingly familiar like a long-forgotten dream.

"I suppose he's just a gardener," Daisuke sighed in relief, his hand relaxing as he released the grip of his sword.

A sad melody could be heard in the quiet tranquility of the garden. The hummed notes were held out long and lingered slowly like a dirge. The gardener's melancholy song was in stark contrast to the playful chirping of birds and the occasional buzz of an insect.

"I've heard that song before," Sheng mused.

"You have?" Suke-chan whispered. "Where?"

"My mother used to sing it when my father would leave for war. But I haven't heard it since. I thought it was her own song. I'd never have imagined that anyone else would know the melody."

The two friends stood in silence, listening to the gardener's sorrowful refrain. They'd all but forgotten their own situation as they looked on from amongst the blossoming branches.

"How do you suppose a gardener in the imperial palace came to know your mother's song?" Suke-chan wondered.

Sheng was about to answer when a hand clasped down firmly on his armored shoulder. Both he and Daisuke were startled to see the old blind monk standing at their side.

"The gardens are lovely aren't they?" the monk smiled, taking a long, snorting sniff of the air. "It makes me forget all about the stink of the city, or at least the fish market!"

They stood and stared in amused awe at the strange old man. The gardener's song had ended.

"The gardener," Sheng asked, "does he always sing that melody?"

"*Sing?*" the monk asked.

"Yes. That song – didn't you hear it?"

"The gardener is a deaf mute, my boy," the old monk replied. "He doesn't sing, can't even whistle! He was badly wounded in a long-forgotten battle. He seems to have once been a samurai. But he'll never speak a word of his past. Perhaps he betrayed a former master?"

"Why do you think he may have betrayed a former master?"

"Well, we'll never know for sure," the monk explained, "but he has a mark on the side of his neck where he was branded by whomever he betrayed. It's a Mitsu-uroko, the mark of the Hōjō Clan. Regardless, he is happy here amongst the trees and the flowers. Whatever happened in his past, that was another life. Here he has found peace!"

Sheng took a final, long look at the gardener as the monk took hold of his wrist and led the two friends in the opposite direction. "It is time to meet the Emperor," the old man grinned.

The Emperor of Japan sat in a chair opposite Sheng and Daisuke. His seat was not the *Chrysanthemum Throne*, nor were they in the proper palace. They met with the emperor in his private living area, a space afforded him graciously by the nobility that typically surrounded him. The monk had manipulated the emperor's schedule in an effort to arrange for his death with the least amount of struggle possible – the smallest amount of struggle and *witnesses*. Here, they were alone, or in the least as alone as they could be with the most powerful man in all of Japan. Members of the emperor's imperial guard stood at the entrance to the room, another two armored warriors flanked the emperor himself. But by the monk's calculating, four guards, even trained as they were, would be no match for Takeshi Hasegawa's protégé. He excused himself with a humble bow, certain that this would be the last time he stood in the Emperor's presence. Soon all the plotting and planning would come to fruition and the rebellion against the imperial order would begin!

Emperor Go-Nijo was much younger than Sheng and Daisuke expected; in fact, he was younger than them – just nineteen. His father, former emperor Go-Uda, lived there as well, now a cloistered advisor to his son. Go-Nijo was more of a symbol than a ruler, especially with the military might of the shogunate. Still, the seat of the emperor was highly respected in Japan. Certainly this is why Hasagawa wanted this young man eliminated.

"Tell me then," Go-Nijo said softly, "why has the great sensei Takeshi Hasagawa sent you to me? Our relationship with the Kamakura shogunate is strong and your master does not represent the shikken, *Hōjō Morotoki*. My father says Hasagawa is ruthless and a threat to the peace and order we have established in Japan."

"Peace and order?" Sheng mused. "With all due respect, Emperor, the world outside this compound, outside of Kyoto, is far from peaceful. Bandits terrorize the roads. Pirates plague the sea. And Hasagawa...*our master*...plots your demise."

"*WHAT?!*" Go-Nijo asked in surprise.

"It is true. Hasegawa has sent us to kill you," Sheng admitted.

"*GUARDS!*" the emperor shouted.

"Please, we did not come here for a fight," Daisuke pleaded as the men who swore to protect the emperor drew their swords and leapt between the samurai and Go-Nijo.

The razor sharp blades brandished by the guards whistled as they sliced through the air in defense of the Emperor. Sheng and Daisuke dodged the attacks, striking back with graceful kicks and punches, their swords never drawn in return. Sheng artfully disarmed his opponent and sent the stunned guard reeling into unconsciousness with a roundhouse kick to his jaw. Suke-chan, by pure brute force rather than practiced skill, managed to grab hold of the other guard's shoulders and tossed him effortlessly across the small room, his body thudding first into the wall before dramatically settling in a heap on the floor.

Emperor Go-Nijo took a step back in fear, his own personal guard defeated easily by these *assassins* from Kamakura. He positioned himself behind the chair so that it stood as a barrier, even if only a meager one, between himself and the samurai.

"Please listen," Sheng urged. "We were sent to kill you, but we have chosen to warn you instead. When Takeshi Hasegawa learns that we have not done as he asked, he'll send more men, a whole army if he has to. You must believe me that your life is in grave danger, just not from us."

Go-Nijo focused intently on Sheng, listening to his argument, weighing his words, "Why should I believe you? The Shogunate controls the military, not Hasegawa. My title is of little value to a man with swords."

"But that's just it," Sheng reasoned, "you're of great value to Hasegawa because of what you represent to the people of Japan. I don't know what Hasegawa is plotting, but if his goal is to take both military and political control of our country, then he needs to create chaos. Killing you would certainly do that."

"Let's say I believe you," the Emperor contemplated, "what happens to the two of you if I let you live? You have come to me as treasonous spies, assassins. Will people not question my authority if I let you live?"

"You're the only one who knows the truth," Sheng said in an effort to reason with the young emperor. "No one else of consequence even knows we're here. We travelled as vagrants by day and arrived in Kyoto, at the palace grounds, under the cover of night. We can leave the same way. No one will know."

"And what if this is a trap?" Go-Nijo asked. "What if you are only saying this now to save your lives? Surely you have come this far, why not finish me off in my sleep all because you tricked me into trusting you?"

"We could easily kill you now," Sheng replied, his hands raised palms-out as he nodded towards his still-sheathed sword, "but we know that is not the right thing to do."

"I cannot allow spies in my court, even if they've had a change of heart."

"Well you already have, and for who knows how long!" Daisuke chimed in.

"What do you mean?" the emperor asked, his head cocking slightly to the side at the accusation of treason.

"You already harbor a spy," Sheng continued.

"Impossible! All of my council is loyal – loyal to me, my father, and Japan!"

"The old blind monk," Suke-chan continued, "we were told by Master Hasegawa that there would be a contact waiting for us here in Kyoto. He is that contact."

"It couldn't be," Go-Nijo argued defiantly. "He has been loyal to my family for years, since the Mongol invasions."

"You don't have to believe it for it to be true," Sheng pushed back.

Just then, shouts came from beyond the entrance, "The Emperor is in danger! We must hurry!" They all recognized the voice of the blind monk, his cries accompanied by the thunderous footfalls of the heavily armored imperial guard. Things just went from bad to worse and the two companions knew they had little choice but to fight their way out.

"I told you he was loyal," the emperor smirked.

The door quickly slid open. A half-dozen warriors stormed into the room, their swords drawn and ready to strike.

"I pray we're not too late!" the monk shouted. "Is he dead? Is the emperor dead?! Tell me what you see!"

"The emperor lives," one of the guards confirmed, spotting Go-Nijo behind the two companions.

For a moment, the blind monk looked surprised, even disappointed. Only Sheng and Daisuke saw his treacherous reaction. Everyone else's eyes were on them.

"Protect the emperor," the monk shouted. "KILL THE ASSASSINS!"

With a shared expression of disappointment and reluctance, Sheng and Daisuke drew their katana from their sides and took a defensive stance. "Try not to wound them too badly," Sheng whispered to his friend.

Four of the guards lunged forward as the samurai deflected the strikes with their blades and countered with punches and kicks. The speed of the fighting was dizzying, their movements lightning quick and precise. The remaining two guards did not join in the battle but flanked Emperor Go-Nijo, pushing him to the corner furthest from the chaos.

Their swords clanked furiously, the razor-sharp edges shrieking with each blow. Sheng and Daisuke could easily end the fight, but they did not want to kill the emperor's guards. Keeping the men alive was much more difficult than wounding them.

Sheng struck out in a flurry of sweeping strikes. In seconds, the four guards fell to the floor in pain – bloodied, but far from dead.

"*RUN!*" Sheng ordered.

The companions never looked back as they raced through the corridors, pushing past startled and confused palace servants, sending a tray of tea service unceremoniously crashing to the ground before reaching the sun-drenched courtyard. They stood out like peacocks on parade in their armor, but there was no time to change. Word of an attack on the emperor must have spread by now: guards would certainly be searching the grounds for the assassins.

"The main gate is sure to be heavily guarded," Daisuke growled. "Where do we go?"

"Think, think," Sheng mumbled.

The sound of running soldiers echoed from the halls of the building behind them. The samurai had to move.

"This way," Sheng decided, sprinting toward the gardens. "We can hide there amongst the dense trees till nightfall, then escape under the cover of darkness."

"And what about the gardener?" Suke-chan asked as he huffed alongside his friend. "Won't he hear us coming? Certainly he'll turn us in!"

"Remember what the monk told us. The gardener is deaf and mute. He'll never know we're there."

The walkway through the garden twisted and turned as the two searched for a place to lay low. Some areas they passed by were wide open and would not do. They needed dense shrubbery, low hanging branches, even tall grass would be better than nothing. Ahead, they found a cluster of trees, far from perfect but away from the main path. This would have to do.

They raced from the walkway and under the drooping branches, relieved to find that the ground beyond the trees sloped deep enough to add additional cover if they laid down and stayed low.

Minutes passed with agonizing anticipation as the samurai expected a full unit of armored soldiers at any time, but the garden remained eerily quiet. Perhaps the search was over? Maybe the imperial guards assumed that the assassins had escaped into the city and were now far from Kyoto? Even so, they remained still and silent.

Sheng woke to a strange sound: Suke-chan's stomach was growling incessantly. The day was gone. Night shrouded their hiding place.

He couldn't believe he'd been so foolish as to fall asleep, but they'd laid so still and the garden was so peaceful that the two friends had lazily drifted off even in the midst of such dire circumstances. Tranquility, it seems, had been the only pursuer to find them as they remained cloistered beneath the cover of welcome darkness.

"Wake up," Sheng whispered as he nudged Daisuke in the ribs. "It's time to go."

Suke-chan stirred, his eyelids heavy with sleep. "Have we been found? Are the emperor's men here?" he managed to ask.

"No," Sheng grinned. "I think they've given up the search. Nevertheless, we must remain cautious. Certainly the guard has increased the number of patrols after our...*misunderstanding*...with Go-Nijo.

The two friends climbed to their feet, their eyes ever-scanning their surroundings. Though sleep seemed an unaffordable risk, Sheng was thankful for it now. At least they would not be tired as they tried to escape beyond the palace walls.

Moonlight shone down through the silhouetted trees, casting sporadic shadows as the samurai quietly crept through the gardens. They used these patches to their advantage, hurrying methodically from one to the next. Other than the chirps of crickets, they were engulfed by a foreboding silence. This too, however, was to their advantage as approaching patrols could be easily recognized in the stillness of night.

Finally they came to the place where the garden path met the courtyard. To their left was the palace; ahead, the courtyard and main gate. There did not appear to be any additional patrols. The gate was open, unguarded as it had been the night before. Beyond earshot, Sheng spotted two guards walking away from them, a torch lighting their path.

"If we go now, we can slip away into the streets and no one will be the wiser," Suke-chan smirked. "This was easier than I expected."

Sheng hesitated. His friend was right: this had been too easy. And now, the unguarded gate that tempted him to break into a sprint for freedom also seemed a perfect trap to draw them out.

"Hold on," Sheng whispered. But he was too late. Daisuke had left the shadows and was now tiptoeing across the fully exposed courtyard, brightly awash in the moon's cool glow.

"You must think you are very clever," the blind monk's voice spoke, echoing across the courtyard.

Daisuke froze in place. Sheng's thoughts raced as his eyes darted about the expanse. Where was the monk?

"Get them!" the monk ordered with a shriek.

Sheng watched helplessly as a dozen heavily-armed guards came rushing from beyond the gate. They'd been hiding outside the wall. Suke-chan looked back at Sheng, his eyes wide as another dozen guards raced out from the palace. Not only was their exit blocked, but the threat also stood between the two samurai. Suke-chan was trapped in the middle.

Daisuke drew his sword as did all the imperial guardsmen. Certainly the odds were against him. There was nothing Sheng could do but draw his own sword. With a heavy heart, he hurried towards the guards. The time for caution – and mercy – had come to an end.

Chaos followed. Before the men knew what was happening, Sheng had already cut two of them down, his strikes fatally true. Daisuke took advantage of the sudden panic and struck out as well, cleaving at the attackers, his blade taking another three men out of the fight. The two friends met in the middle of the guardsmen. With their backs against each other, they worked in tandem to deflect blows and strike back with exacting fury.

The blind monk listened in horror to the fighting. He could discern from the lessening grunts and clangs of warfare that his numbers were dwindling even though the battle clearly continued. Despair filled the monk as the would-be-assassins quickly dispatched the twenty-four men he had hand selected to fight Hasegawa's students. Now their bodies lie in crumpled, bloodied heaps in the emperor's courtyard. Sheng and Daisuke had whittled down the guardsmen and now a mere half-dozen swords remained raised and ready to continue the onslaught. With another shrieking cry, the blind monk rushed into the fray his staff readied as a weapon. Another two-dozen guards accompanied his as reinforcements, following his call to arms.

Again the samurai found themselves outnumbered. Sweat stung their eyes and the stench of death and blood filled their nostrils. There was no time to think about it. They had to keep up the fight.

The monk thrust out with his *bo* staff, deflecting the blow from Daisuke's katana as the blunt weapon slammed into Suke-chan's chest. Even with the armor, the fierceness of the strike knocked the breath from his lungs and Daisuke stumbled back, gasping for air. Sheng turned his attention to the blind monk, but was too slow. The man had whipped his bo around and caught Sheng squarely in the side of the head. If not for the helmet, the strike would have surely killed him. Staggered, his ears ringing, Sheng struck back fiercely, but the monk's *kung-fu* was brilliantly quick and without the encumbering effect of armor, the blind man was nearly unstoppable. Another swift strike from the staff and Sheng's helmet was violently knocked from his head, exposing his sweat-soaked hair and now-vulnerable face. The monk raised his staff high and readied to strike. As the wooden bo crashed down with crushing force, Sheng watched in disbelief as a blade swept past his face and met the staff in mid strike, splintering the wood and startling the blind monk. In the moonlight, Sheng struggled to make out the figure: it was the gardener!

"NOW!" the supposedly mute gardener barked into the night.

A sudden volley of arrows came from over the wall, the sharp points of the heads finding their marks and driving back the guardsmen. The emperor's men began to retreat back into the temple, many of them wounded, arrows deeply puncturing their flesh.

Still the monk persisted, now disarmed, his fists bludgeoning the gardener with precision. A blow to the head stunned the man who had come to the samurai's aid and Sheng quickly defended him. Suke-chan had regained his breath and did the same. Still, the blind monk deflected their blows and countered with thrusts and kicks. The stone blocks that paved the courtyard grew slick with the blood from the dead and the fighting became more treacherous as they maneuvered around the fallen guardsmen's lifeless bodies. Quickly, the gardener recovered and made the fight three-on-one. Even so, the blind monk continued on.

An unexpected arrow whizzed between Sheng and Daisuke and struck the monk in the shoulder, sending him reeling, spinning on his heels and crashing to the ground. The men looked back to where the arrow had come from and there at the gate stood Hayami, bow in hand, flanked by six more archers.

"Come now," she urged.

There was no argument from Sheng, Suke-chan, or the gardener as the three of them hurried away from the brutality of the courtyard and into the dark streets of Kyoto. Still the question lingered in Sheng's thoughts as they made their escape – had they done the right thing by sparing the life of Emperor Go-Nijo?

18

REUNIONS

The thundering of hooves broke the stillness of night as ten hooded riders rumbled on horseback through the moonlit forest. The gardener rode in front, Sheng behind him. Daisuke and Hayami rode next in line, side-by-side. The six archers brought up the rear. In whole, they looked formidable, even savage.

The trail led them the north and then, after two hours of hard riding, east through a rocky pass. The terrain had changed and slowed their progress. Even so, travelling under the cover of night, beneath the dense canopy of trees, they had no issues, experienced no delays.

Soon, they came to a river. The gardener stopped and dismounted, leading his horse to drink and rest. One by one, the companions did the same.

To this point, the gardener had remained silent. Sheng struggled to get a good look at the man's face, even now as he stood alongside him at the river, the gardener's face was shadowed by his hood.

"How much longer do we ride?" Sheng asked. "Are we returning to

Kamakura? Or heading further north to *Edo*?"

"One question at a time," the gardener chuckled. "I know you're anxious, but all will be answered."

"I'm sorry," Sheng admitted, "it's just that everything has changed. I have no home, no master, no students. I guess I'm just looking for some hope."

The gardener turned to face him, "Young Master Sheng," he smiled, his gruff voice suddenly so familiar, "you have grown into a strong, courageous man. I've wanted to find you – speak to you – for so long, but the time was not right...*till now*. Let my old, tired face bring you hope. I know it's worse-for-wear but it's the best I can do!"

He lowered his hood so they could see each other face-to-face. Sheng felt like he was going to explode from happiness. In fact he may have never been happier to see anyone in his entire life.

"Scar!" Sheng cried out, throwing his arms around the old man and embracing him tightly. "I thought you were dead!"

"Easy now," Scar chuckled. "Don't knock me down, I might not get back up!"

Daisuke joined in the joy of reunion and threw his big arms around the both of them. The three stood embracing till Scar finally spoke, "We need to be off, boys. We're not that far from Kyoto and we still have to ride till morning."

"Where are we going?" Sheng asked.

"There's an old abandoned temple deep in the woods a day's ride west of *Fuji-no-Yama*. No one goes there anymore, in fact many may not even remember it exists."

"Fuji-no-Yama," Sheng smiled, "the great mountain. Its snow-white peak has been the only constant in my life, from childhood to adulthood. I remember playing in the mountain's shadow when I was young, dreaming of what mysteries and adventures might lie at its summit. Then, in Kamakura, at the dojo, I could look up at the mountain and be reminded of home. In a way, Fuji-san feels like the only family I have left."

Daisuke laughed, his heavy hand slapping Sheng on the back, "We're your family now and we aren't going anywhere."

Scar and Hayami nodded in agreement. Sheng had never been nor would he ever be alone.

"Come," Scar urged, "we must ride once again. You will have more time for reminiscing and reunion when we reach the temple, but we must be off the trail by sunrise. Let's go."

Sunlight streamed down to the forest floor, fragmented as it filtered through the dense branches above. Thin spider webs glistened, the taught strands sparkling with dew – a beautiful trap waiting to ensnare.

The horses turned off the main trail and down a lightly used path engulfed by heavy growth. As they pushed through, the riders ducked beneath the low branches, shielding their faces with their arms as the trees scratched and clawed at them. Finally they broke beyond the natural wall and found the quant, weathered *pagoda* that served once as a temple and now as a veiled refuge. Moss had long ago overtaken the walls and peaked rooves, the highest point of the temple now undistinguishable from the green, leafy surroundings.

"We have plenty to eat, so eat as you please," Scar explained as they dismounted and tied the horses near a trough. "We also have a place you can rest and wash up. There's a training room too. You'll see recruits, men and women loyal to the emperor, around the temple. They'll certainly enjoy sparring with you if you would be so willing. Scouts come and go, usually under the cover of darkness, bringing reports from all over Japan. Come on now, into the temple."

Sheng and Daisuke followed their old friend across the once-manicured grounds and up the weathered stone stairs to the main floor of the pagoda. The structure had been repurposed on the inside. Wooden benches lined each side of a tightly woven grass mat, twenty feet wide and twenty feet long: the perfect place for sparring. Beyond that stood an armory of sorts. Racks filled with swords and daggers, bo staffs and spears, *nunchucks* and *kamas*, throwing stars and *caltrops*, bows and arrows lined the interior wall. With that were also assorted gear and ropes used by ninja. An ancient table then stood in the middle of the weapon racks, its top covered with scrolls and maps. A candle lit shrine graced the opposite wall and was flanked on either side by large bookshelves filled with history, knowledge, and legends. A small room in the rear of the temple had been converted into a simple kitchen. Beyond that space was a bath area that opened up to the gardens. A courtyard sat nestled amongst the trees on the north side of the grounds. There, a blacksmith had set up a furnace and anvil, his tools and barrels of water organized and used daily. There was also a small stable on the property and the occasional bleats of sheep and crows from roosters broke the eerie silence of the woods. The floors above were reserved for sleeping space and what little personal belongings refugees brought to this sacred place.

Scar led them to a room on the second floor after giving them the tour. There, the two friends were left to rest after a night of riding. They undressed, leaving their armor — stained in the blood of their enemies — to the side. The clothes they wore beneath the armor were also bloodied and not worth the time to clean. They found robes folded neatly on a shelf in the corner and changed into those, then laid down on the grass mats. No sooner had they closed their eyes, the best friends were asleep, hidden away from Hasegawa and his wrath.

Sheng blinked awake, candlelight reflecting in his eyes. Scar and Hayami knelt above the two samurai.

"There's someone who would like to talk to you," he said, smiling down at them.

"Who?" Sheng asked excitedly.

"Another ghost from your past. Come on."

Hayami took Suke-chan by the hand and they all followed Scar back down to the main floor of the temple. The sun had set, darkness once more overtaking the light.

I can't believe we slept all day, Sheng thought to himself as they walked down the old, narrow, thin-planked stairs. *Who else knows we're here?*

The large main room was much busier now than when they had arrived. A pair of wiry youth sparred on the mat, taking turns striking and blocking while the next contestants awaited their turns to prove their skills. Others had gathered near the kitchen where the enticing smells of a variety of foods lingered and mingled amongst the many conversations. Sheng didn't count, but estimated near sixty people in the temple. Scar had assembled an impressive group of men and women in opposition to Hasegawa. Hopefully their prowess in battle surpassed their numbers.

Scar continued through the bustle of the ground floor and out to the courtyard. A pair of torches illuminated the shape of a man, his back to the temple, his hands clasped behind his back as he waited patiently to speak to the samurai masters.

"He's waited many years for this," Scar said. "We'll leave you three to get reacquainted."

Hayami nodded and stood on her tiptoes to give Daisuke a small kiss on the cheek. "I'm so happy you have found your way here," she whispered. "There is greatness in your destiny."

Suke-chan blushed and smiled as he watched her return to the temple alongside the aging warrior, Scar. He would have never thought a girl as beautiful, as kind, and as fierce as Hayami would be interested in him, but she was and he wasn't about to question her interest. Sheng tugged on Suke-chan's sleeve, literally pulling his attention back to the man in the courtyard.

"Konbanwa, friend," Sheng said in greeting the stranger.

"Konbanwa," the man replied, turning to face his old friends.

The two samurai looked on intently, taking in his features, studying his face. There was familiarity in his eyes, his stern mouth and brow, yet the fog of time clouded their memories.

"Do you not recognize me?" he asked, a little surprised. "I certainly recognize the both of you, especially you, Suke-chan – you are a mountain amongst men, strong and brave-hearted as ever. And Sheng, your eyes may no longer shine with the naivety of youth but they do still burn with the same fire for justice that I remember."

Memories replayed through Sheng's mind, searching for recollection when in a sudden explosion of emotion, Sheng threw his arms around the man. "Tatsuo!" Sheng laughed and cried simultaneously. "You live!"

"Of course," their old mentor smiled.

Daisuke slapped him solidly on the shoulder as Sheng stepped back from the heartfelt embrace. "Is it true what they say? Did you really kill your own father?"

"Not wasting any time catching up are you, Suke-chan?" Tatsuo laughed. "That is a conversation for another time. Tonight we celebrate this happy reunion. Tomorrow we can face the sobriety of truth."

The three friends met Scar back within the temple's walls. There they ate and drank, reminiscing of their days spent in Kamakura. The dojo held both good and bad memories for all of them. Though in the midst of Hasegawa's plot to destroy the emperor such frivolity seemed almost indecent, there was a calm brought on by their recollections, a peace that came from their kindred bond. And in that peace, Sheng and Daisuke felt assured that they had made the right decision in warning the emperor, even if it ended in bloodshed. For now, Go-Nijo still drew breath and it was because the two friends had defied their sensei.

Hayami listened and laughed along as the wistful stories of their youth brought a welcome relief from the normally serious goings-on of the makeshift rebel camp. After all, it's not every day long lost friends find their destinies once more converging on the same path. She found herself wishing she had some of the same memories. But her past was her own: the daughter of a wealthy landowner and raised without want in Kyoto. Trained in archery and handy with her fists, she was never one for tea ceremonies and the rigid social hierarchy. She preferred to play with the boys, spar alongside them, and in the end best them in a fight, not by strength but with speed and wit. This is how she came to the attention of Scar and Tatsuo. By birth she had access to the influential wealthy class, but she earned her credibility on the street – all unbeknownst to her family.

A single rider galloped down the dark streets of Kamakura, a torch held high to light his way, a stream of smoke trailing behind. The animal's hooves beat violently against the stone pavers as he pressed on frantically towards Hasegawa's dojo.

The dojo's gate blocked his progress as he came upon the entrance. "Open at once!" he demanded.

With a loud creak of the hinges, the guards began the task of admitting him through the gate. No sooner had the heavy wood and iron doors opened just wide enough for his horse to slip through, he once more raced on, pushing the snarling beast at full pace across the narrow pathways of the dojo grounds.

He reached Hasegawa's personal quarters and was admitted without hesitation by the armed guards standing watch. The glow of his torch could be seen floating down the hallways as he searched for his master, finally finding Takeshi Hasegawa alone in his study.

"What is it, rider?" Hasegawa demanded, startled as the man burst into the room.

"The emperor…"

"What news do you bring from Kyoto?!" Hasegawa asked anxiously, quickly standing from his chair. "Is he dead?!

"He lives. Master Sheng has failed you, my master."

Hasegawa stared sternly into the distance, his gaze fixed intently yet on nothing in particular. The rider stepped back slowly towards the door, uncertain of how his master would react to his words. He was wise to do so.

In the next moment, the normally well-composed sensei let out a roaring scream and flipped the table in front of him, sending its contents flying through the air as it crashed to the ground. Hasegawa then took hold of his chair and sent it smashing into splinters against the wall. But his anger was not quenched. He drew his tanto from his belt and moved so swiftly the rider could not react. The blade thrust deep into his stomach as Hasegawa seethed, his teeth gritted, his eyes wild with bloodlust. The rider shook as his life left him and Hasegawa, covered in the innocent man's blood, let him slip to the floor, the dagger still in his belly. The room then echoed the sound of Hasegawa's demented laughter as he ran his shaking, blood-stained hands across his brow and through his sweaty hair, leaving the blood to cover his face and head in a hideous display of his misplaced fury.

Not once did Hasegawa question what he had done. He was satisfied with the rider's death even if it didn't change the circumstances. In his mind blood had to be spilled and the man's proximity made him a convenient outlet.

Hasegawa collected himself and summoned servants to take care of the mess, leaving his own bloodied robes behind to be burned along with the victim. He then walked slowly, thoughtfully to his dressing room and put on a new, clean robe. *What am I to do?* he asked himself as he looked out of his window at the expanse of the dojo grounds. *What can be done?*

Though his outrage had subsided, his thoughts still burned with Sheng's betrayal. He carefully weighed his options, uncertain of which scenario he envisioned was the truth. Had Sheng tried to follow through and was simply overcome by the emperor's well-trained guards? *No!* he thought, slamming his fists down on the window sill. Sheng was too skilled to fall to Go-Nijo's men and Daisuke was with him, a certain asset when faced with dozens of foes. Perhaps he was killed along the way? Perhaps Sheng never arrived in Kyoto? *Not a chance*, Hasegawa answered himself. Maybe Sheng did the unthinkable? Maybe Sheng sided with the emperor, telling him everything about Hasegawa's plotting and treachery, and at this very moment a legion of Go-Nijo's finest men were on their way to Kamakura to stop his treason. This made the most sense to him. And though it made him furious, it also deeply saddened Hasegawa.

Sheng was one of his most trusted teachers at the dojo, a master into whom Hasegawa himself had poured insight and knowledge, strategy and lethality. Much of who Sheng was now as a warrior was due to Hasegawa's tutelage and this is what made Sheng's betrayal all the more bitter. Hasegawa, with his focus so strongly fixed on the dojo, politics, and war, had never married, never fathered a child and Sheng, the son of a good man he ensured was murdered more than a decade ago, had become like his own flesh and blood. This was not a betrayal of master and student, no this was family. And again, Hasegawa's blood boiled.

The truth had to be found out. Hasegawa went to the door and peered into the hallway, spotting a servant walking down the corridor.

"You there, girl," he called out. "Fetch me a rider. I must send word to Kyoto at once."

She bowed low and hurried away to find one of her master's couriers. She certainly did not wish to disappoint him. Hasegawa returned to his study and quickly found a small bit of *washi* paper and began writing in kanji script. The sharp tip of the quill scratched on the hand-made paper as he hastily wrote the letter. He paused briefly to refresh the quill with ink, then continued on. When he had finished, Hasegawa took the lid off of a small ceramic jar at his desk, touched a *hanko* stamp gently on the red paste within, and then firmly left the impression on the bottom corner of the letter. He then rolled the script up tightly and tied it with a small piece of twine just as a knock came at his study door.

"Enter," Hasegawa commanded.

The courier stepped reluctantly into the room, doing his best to ignore the faint remnants of his predecessors blood on the floor and wall, "How may I serve you, Master?"

"Take this letter. Deliver it by hand to the blind monk in the emperor's court in Kyoto. You should have no trouble finding him. Give it directly to the monk and no one else. When you are certain the two of you are alone, read it to him and then ask him for his response. Write it down word for word. I must know what happened in Kyoto! When he is finished, return to me at once. Do not tarry on the road. I believe there may be rogue samurai on the roadways. This correspondence must not fall into their hands. If so, they would use bitter lies to destroy this dojo – *your home*. We must not let that happen!"

"Yes, Master Hasegawa, on my honor," the soldier replied. "I will ride at once!"

"So let me get this straight," Tatsuo said, reviewing Sheng's given account of the events at the emperor's palace in Kyoto, "the two of you were sent by Hasegawa to assassinate Go-Nijo, but instead you told the emperor the truth? Then the two of you fought off two dozen of his imperial guard in an attempt to escape because he didn't believe you?"

"Don't forget the blind monk!" Suke-chan reminded.

"Yes," Scar laughed, "Hasegawa's man inside. I never even suspected he was working to betray the emperor. I'd known him for years, not well of course, but he was at the palace long before I managed to work there as eyes and ears for our movement. I figured it was my best chance to ensure the safety of the emperor while communicating all I learned to Tatsuo and our order here at this temple. Am I ever glad I did now!"

"Where does this leave us?" Sheng questioned. "Suke-chan and I cannot return to the dojo and we certainly will not be welcome again in Kyoto. In fact if we travel anywhere throughout Japan, Hasegawa will know and we will live under the shadow of his threat for the rest of our lives! Do we remain here then like outcasts living in exile?"

Tatsuo thought for moment, he and Scar staring at each other, searching each other's eyes for wisdom. Had the time come to tell Sheng the whole truth? Was Sheng even ready to hear such a revelation? The two men wordlessly decided otherwise.

"There's something you need to know Sheng, but now is not the time and I don't think either of us are the one to tell you," Tatsuo finally replied. "I do know you are meant for much more than a life of exile, both of you."

"What are you talking about?" Sheng argued, frustrated by the aloofness of his old friends. "Don't speak to me like a child. I can handle whatever it is you need to tell me. If you're truly my friends, then you would respect that."

"We do respect you, Sheng," Scar continued. "But, and this is what will be hard for you to understand, there is someone else who will tell you everything. This person does not wish for us to reveal all to you. You will certainly understand in time."

"Fine," Sheng said as he took a deep breath to regain his composure. "I will trust you and wait to learn what you know. Till then, what do we do?"

"I think the first thing to do is rectify this situation with the emperor," Scar suggested.

"And how do we do that?" Daisuke laughed. "He *only* thinks we tried to kill him."

"That's right," Tatsuo agreed, "so we can't talk to him in person. I doubt he would even grant us an audience after all the bloodshed. But perhaps your story could convince him."

"What are you saying?" Sheng questioned.

"I'm saying you should write the whole thing out; not just what happened in Kyoto, but everything…all the way back to how you came to be in Hasegawa's dojo in the first place. Tell him your story in a letter and then, after he has had time to read and think on your words, we arrange a meeting at his court, in front of his most trusted advisors and under total submission to his guards."

"You mean no armor, no weapons, just words?"

"Exactly!" Tatsuo nodded.

"How do we deliver the letter?" Sheng asked.

"If you can write it tonight, we'll set out first thing in the morning.

You and I will return to Kyoto and I will deliver it to the court myself," Tatsuo explained. "I'll have you wait in the market while I'm at the palace."

"I don't know that I like the idea of Sheng going with you, let alone wandering a market in broad daylight after what happened only yesterday," Scar argued. "Certainly Go-Nijo's guard will be alert and searching for the assassins. Why must Sheng go at all? Why not just have one of the others travel with you?"

Tatsuo shrugged as he replied, "It's not something I can explain so easily. I just have this feeling that Sheng is supposed to go, like there's something yet to be learned in Kyoto and only he will recognize it. Call it destiny – maybe insanity – Sheng is going with me."

Hasegawa walked the dojo grounds in the moonlight. His mind was still unsettled at the news of Sheng's failure. Little would console him, only one thing was on his mind. He made his way through the gardens and into the densely wooded area Sheng and Daisuke had discovered so many years ago. The old shack still stood. Though weathered and forlorn, the small outbuilding always reminded him of his purpose. The outside of the building was now almost entirely covered in moss and vines. Time had made it part of the garden, the natural overtaking the unnatural, reclaiming what man had made.

Deep in thought, he stepped up the simple plank stairs, each one creaking under his weight, and stood on the small porch as he faced the dirt-crusted door. Hasegawa closed his eyes and reached out, placing his hand over the carving of the Hōjō clan symbol. With his fingers he traced the edges, dislodging years of moss and grime. Hasegawa once more opened his eyes as he withdrew a key from the folded belt wrapped around the waist of his robes, then pressed the key into the lock, fighting against rust and natural debris. With great effort, he twisted the key and the door to the shack stubbornly opened. He then pushed hard against the door as the hinges whined and the bottom of the door scraped against the rotting floor boards.

An odd, musty scent lingered within the stale space. Moth-eaten scrolls hung on the walls, many depicting the failed Mongol invasions. A small round table stood in the middle of the room, its top covered in melted wax from the dozens of candles that sat embedded one into the next. He picked up a piece of quartz and a steel striker, and with a few solid cracks ignited the paper wick on a candle that sat on its own stand at the edge of the table. With that, Hasegawa then lit the rest of the candles, providing a warm, yellow glow. At the end of the small square room, opposite the front door, sat a rustic, hand-made chair directly facing the wall. In the flickering light, the shape of a round mass could be discerned beneath a black cloth.

Hasegawa locked the door and then headed for the chair, slowly sitting ceremoniously, almost fearfully, the candlelight at his back, his shadow darkening the cloth. He whispered something unintelligible as he reached out and took hold of the black fabric, pulling it free to reveal a bronze mirror on a stand. Again, he appeared fearful and avoided looking directly into the mirror as he whispered more soft words. Sitting on the stand just in front of the mirror was a small vase holding three sticks of incense. Hasegawa removed them and turned, lighting them in the small flames of the candles. They were returned to their holder as thin wisps of fragrant smoke swirled between Hasegawa and the mirror. And again he whispered softly.

In absolute silence, he sat. His hands rested on his knees and his eyes stayed trained on his fingers as they tightly grasped the cloth of his robes, his knuckles white as he clenched then unfurled his fingers over and again in a nervous display. The sweet scent of the incense tangled with the mustiness of the space, the resulting odor a foreboding convolution of tranquility and death. Suddenly, a rogue wind like that of a violent storm blew through the closed room, extinguishing the candles and leaving Hasegawa in total darkness. Beads of sweat rolled down his brow as his hands and feet shook from his fear. Just as quickly, a faint humming sound, something Hasegawa could not describe, started in low and then grew till the hair on his arms stood on end. The hum vibrated loudly now in his ears, pulsing, pounding, he thought his head was going to explode and he clenched his teeth in agony. The vibration thumped in his chest, beating rhythmically as it swelled and waned, swelled and waned, again and again. And then, it stopped. The candles relit themselves.

"It has been a long time since you visited us," a raspy voice spoke from somewhere within the room.

"We were worried you'd forgotten all about us," another, deeper voice growled.

"But we are pleased to see you," a third voice whispered.

Hasegawa's gaze still remained fixed to the floor. "I seek your council.

Things have not gone as I had planned and I'm unsure of what to do?" he admitted to the voices.

"Is this the madness that has driven you to kill innocent men?" the deep voice replied.

"How do you know this?"

"We see many things," the raspy voice answered. "We watch you, hear you."

"Did you think you could do this without our help?" the whispering voice questioned.

"I thought you had already given me everything I needed to succeed."

"When we spared you those many years ago, you made us a promise," the deep voice said. "Do you remember? You promised to kill for us, but now you kill for yourself!"

"I could leave, I could never come back. You three are trapped here, but I am not."

"We are no common *yōkai*, not simple spirits who haunt forests or torment unfaithful husbands. No. We are the nightmares that plague good men, turn their hearts from light and drive them into darkness like nails through hard wood."

"I'm sorry," Hasegawa said softly. "I remember my promise. I will always honor our agreement."

"Then look at us…" the whispering voice said.

Hasegawa hesitated. His head raised ever so slightly.

"Look at us…" the raspy voice pleaded.

Hasegawa tried, but his fear was too great.

"*LOOK!*" the voices all shrieked in unison, the sinister power of their wrath shaking the very room itself.

Hasegawa finally lifted his eyes and gazed into the old bronze mirror. His own reflection was accompanied by three jaunt, hairless figures, undiscernible as male or female, their eye sockets deep sunken black holes, their mouths listless and agape, insatiably hungry and fiendish.

19

FORGOTTEN FRIENDS

Sheng could hardly believe he was once again in the capitol city of Kyoto. Tatsuo led the way, both men on horseback and dressed in modest robes that disguised their identities as samurai. They travelled light, knowing that food nor weapons would be required, not even a dagger or throwing star. This was a peace mission and Tatsuo was not going to allow failure. Any form of aggression, even as a defense, could jeopardize their very purpose.

"When we reach the market," Tatsuo said, "I will leave you and go on to the palace myself. You must blend in, avoid conversation, and always keep moving. Do not linger in one place for too long."

"Are you certain I should not come with you to deliver my letter?"

"I am. Just stay aware. I will find you when I am finished."

The time had come to dismount and they tied their horses securely to the wooden railing of a stable at the city's edge. There, they paid the owner for food and water for their horses, and then continued on foot into the city. Like most days, Kyoto was bustling, the sights and sounds of commerce filling the market. Sheng and Tatsuo had left the hidden, wooded-sanctuary before dawn and had arrived in Kyoto shortly after mid-day. They'd managed to travel faster as just the two of them, especially without the additional weight of armor and weapons burdening their horses. Sheng raised his hood to help hide his face as they entered the main market.

"I'll meet you back here," Tatsuo said confidently. "I won't be long."

Sheng watched as his friend slipped into the crowd and disappeared from sight. A passerby looked at Sheng curiously. The old woman's gaze convinced him that tarrying too long in one place was against his best interests, so he quickly moved on, zigzagging amongst the heavy foot traffic in the densely-packed market. He wandered around the vendors' stalls and carts with no direct path, no purpose. With all the distractions around him, Sheng still couldn't take his mind off of the letter he'd written to the emperor. Would he believe Sheng's words? Would he even read it?! The minutes past slow and arduously as he contemplated all these things.

As he was perusing a food cart filled with delicious-looking, doughy cakes, Sheng was startled as a small girl, no older than seven or eight, collided with him. He looked to where she'd ended up falling to the ground at his feet. Her eyes were wide with panic and her lower lip quivered in anticipation of the scolding that would surely follow.

"It's okay," Sheng smiled, kneeling down and speaking softly, his hand reaching out kindly for hers.

The girl hesitated and just as their finger tips met, a voice cried out from several stalls down from where they were. "Thief!" the man screamed. "Stop that girl!"

Her scared pout instantly turned to a mischievous grin and before Sheng could react, she was on her feet, dodging artfully through the crowd of onlookers. He stood, watching to see where it was she headed. As he did, he placed his hands on his hips, his palms resting on his belt. With great surprise he realized that the small bag of coins he'd tied to his belt was gone.

Tatsuo stood in front of the entrance to the palace grounds. Four guards, heavily armed and ready, watched the gate. Beyond them, a patrol could be seen marching through the courtyard. Blood still stained the gray stone pavers. He approached the gate, but the guards blocked his path.

"What is your business here?" the guards demanded.

"I bring a message for the emperor. I am his humble servant," Tatsuo replied with a gracious bow.

"The court is not receiving anyone today," one of the guards answered.

"Please let me pass. I do not need any more than just a brief moment with the great emperor. It is imperative that I deliver this message."

The same guard partially drew his sword, the razor sharp edge a visible threat, "None pass who do not have official business – by order of the emperor's council."

"Then could you please deliver this letter for me?"

"What does it say?"

"I do not know for certain, only that this letter contains news for the emperor regarding his enemies in Japan," Tatsuo answered. "It must reach him safely!"

The guards looked at each other, silently weighing the request. Without words, they decided to accept the letter, much to Tatsuo's relief.

"This letter will be taken directly to the emperor and given to him in person," the main guard explained. "What he does with it after that is beyond my control. That is the best I can do."

"Then it is all I can ask," Tatsuo said, bowing once more before taking his leave.

Sheng pushed through the crowd, trying to catch up to the young thief, but he was not nearly as quick through the sea of people as the much smaller girl who darted her way in and out of the shoppers with ease.

He finally reached the edge of the market just in time to see the girl's heels race around the corner at the end of a narrow corridor that led between the tightly spaced buildings. At full speed, Sheng made chase. She was fast, but his long strides more than made up for her advantage and he managed to catch up enough to follow after her on the winding path she chose through the city.

Sheng mused as he tried to keep up: having been his second trip to Kyoto, he was seeing more of the city chasing a simple urchin than in his quest to speak to the emperor of Japan. This was not his idea of sightseeing, and yet this was a great distraction from the stress of their quest and the new questions Hasagawa's treachery had brought into the light.

Every so often, the girl looked back to see if he still followed and Sheng noticed that her face displayed a peculiar look of playfulness rather than fear. It was like she was toying with him, making it a game. And in that he questioned their game of cat and mouse – who truly was the cat and who was the real mouse? In his stomach, he began to feel that knot that grows from a sense of certain impending doom and perhaps he was right, perhaps the jaws of the cat were closing down on him with each tangled turn this young girl led him down. But now he was committed and against his better judgment, his curiosity outweighed his caution.

The alleys narrowed and shortened till he had nearly caught her; but just out of reach, she dodged down one last path. A dead end! He had her now. Sheng watched in confusion as the girl continued on headlong towards the stone block wall ahead of her. Why wasn't she stopping?

"Hey – girl – *STOP!*" he called out, afraid she would run right into the wall.

But she didn't. And to his surprise, just short of the wall, she dropped down and slid along the ground, impossibly low as the bottom blocks of the wall seemed to swallow her up and she disappeared right before his dumbfounded eyes.

He raced to the wall and pressed against it with all his might, but it was all-for-naught as the heavy stone was unmoving. Sheng kicked at the lower blocks through which she had escaped and they too were solid. There had to be an answer to the illusion. He stomped the ground and noticed a peculiar hollow sound beneath where he stood. The stone looked less like

194

the others around it, but there was no flex. And after all, how could stone be used to manufacture a false floor? And what would be the reason for a false floor in a dead-end alleyway?

The wall reached up high above him and the houses on each side extended even higher, their pitched rooftops sloping into the alley beneath, the walls showing weathering from many years of rain runoff down to the dirty floor below. Crates and barrels, some broken, littered the corners but no place to hide. The only answer was a secret trapdoor.

As he pondered the mechanism and its workings, he heard the soft landing of a person behind him. Someone had managed to sneak up on him, probably dropping down from the rooftops above like a hawk swooping down on unsuspecting prey.

"How did she do it?" Sheng asked without turning to see who stood behind him. "How does the trapdoor work?"

He could feel someone's presence, the person's gaze boring into him. But there was no reply.

"I did not come to Kyoto to fight," he assured, slowly turning to face his confronter.

What he saw was not at all what he expected. Looking him intently in the eyes was not a warrior or an assassin as the soft ninja-like footfall had implied. No, he found himself staring into the beautiful face of a bright eyed young woman. Her black hair was long and flowing, swaying slightly in the gentle breeze. Her pale complexion only emphasized the enchanting, large green eyes that graced her flawless porcelain face. Slender and mysterious, she remained silent.

Sheng managed to close his gaping mouth. But words escaped him and he feared any utterance would surely make him look a fool. He could tell she was searching him with her eyes, determining his level of threat. Perhaps her looks were deceiving? She just might be an assassin. What if Hasegawa had sent her?

She broke the silence first. "There was an attack on the emperor within the walls of his own palace, just two nights ago. Do you know of this?"

He tensed up, clenching his jaw at her words, "I have heard so much,

195

but nothing more. I thought maybe it was just a rumor?"

"It is no rumor," she replied curtly. "You can go see the blood that yet remains in the courtyard for yourself."

"Wow," Sheng frowned, "scary."

"The word here on the streets of Kyoto is that two samurai infiltrated the private residence of the emperor and, with the help of an old accomplice, killed many of his men and then escaped into the night…all this after failing to kill the emperor himself."

"Those are a lot of words. Who says so much?"

"The whole city whispers," she smirked coyly.

"Well I had nothing to do with it," Sheng replied.

"But that's not what I asked," she smiled.

He stared back at her. Not only was she smart, she was tightening her snare.

"I would appreciate your honesty rather than false answers for the truth is written on your face."

"Is it now?"

"Certainly. You are one of the samurai."

"Am I?"

"Of course. Your eyes are truer than the lies of your lips."

"If you think me so deadly, why would you confront me?" he questioned. "And unarmed!"

"Leverage," she answered, her eyes narrowing as she took a fighting stance, her hands raised, feet apart, and breathing calm.

Reluctantly, Sheng stood in defense, prepared to block her strikes. He'd never fought a woman before and he had no desire to do it now. But she clearly meant what she said and allowing himself to be beaten to death in an alleyway while he refused to defend himself from an attacker, woman or not, would certainly aid Hasegawa and greatly hinder whatever hope Scar and Tatsuo had of protecting the Emperor from the unknown plots against him. If anything, he decided, he would only defend, not strike, and create a diversion to make his escape.

There was no fear in her eyes as she lunged forward, thrusting her outstretched fingers toward his throat. Sheng lithely deflected the move and just as quickly turned away her next attempt. She pushed harder, faster, her attacks growing in intensity, her strikes fluid and precise. She was excellent and well trained. She fought not with one style, but blended multiple moves into a string of graceful thrusts, kicks, and punches. Her long hair and silk robes twirled about her as she spun and pounced over and over, pushing his defense to its limits. Sheng was greatly impressed, and growing more concerned. Her skill was putting his honor at a disadvantage. To escape, he realized he would actually have to fight back.

She continued her onslaught and Sheng knew he had to act. He had been gone from the market for far too long and he now worried that Tatsuo may be looking for him. After deflecting her next series of strikes, he made his move. He pressed back defiantly, putting her on the defensive, his measured blows pushing her back till he managed to gain the total advantage and she stumbled, caught on her heels and unbalanced.

The beautiful woman fell to the ground, her eyes shocked, yet still surprisingly calm. As she lay there staring up at him, he saw that her robe had opened slightly, exposing a necklace with a small stone charm that hung around her willowy neck. He recognized the token immediately as memories of his childhood flooded his mind, bringing tears to his eyes. That necklace had been given to a long lost friend, a friend assumed dead – now very much alive!

"Kimiko," he stammered, rushing to help her to her feet.

"Sheng," she cried, her smile wide, her eyes wet with happiness.

Tatsuo was panicked. Sheng was nowhere to be found in the market. And what might be worse, armed guards were speaking with a merchant who could be seen pointing off towards the city. There must have been some sort of altercation. Was it Sheng? What could have happened?

Reluctantly, he began the walk back to their horses alone and worried. But he had only reached the edge of the market when he felt a hand take hold of his shoulder.

"You'll never believe what I have to tell you!" Sheng beamed. Tatsuo turned to see his friend, a beautiful woman at his side. "This is Kimiko," Sheng said in introduction. "We grew up together in my village. I haven't seen her since we were all taken away and the village destroyed. I thought she was dead!"

"It's an honor," Tatsuo replied with a hasty bow. "But I must ask, does anyone else know you are here, Sheng? It is now too dangerous for us to linger. Your message has been delivered to the emperor. We must go."

"And what about Kimiko?" Sheng asked.

"Can we trust her?"

"I have no doubts," Sheng smiled.

"You can trust me," Kimiko assured sincerely, "I promise."

"Then you can come with us," Tatsuo offered, "but know that you will be sworn to secrecy. What you see can never be spoken of to anyone. There is no turning back. Your life will no longer be yours, it will belong to our cause."

Kimiko took Sheng by the hand, "My broken heart has been mended, if only just a little. I thought my friends dead, but Sheng told me that Suke-chan lives as well. I have a life here, but I belong with Sheng and Daisuke. They are the only family I have left."

Tatsuo studied her with narrowed eyes. Surely she had attachments in Kyoto. What was she leaving behind to follow? Tatsuo's trust was hard earned and there was something about Kimiko that just felt *off*. He feared that Sheng was blinded by the excitement of their reunion – her beauty – and was perhaps lacking judgement. Regardless, there was no turning back now. Tatsuo resigned to welcome her into their faction, but he would most certainly keep an eye on her.

They returned to their horses on the outskirts of the city. Sheng mounted, then reached down to help Kimiko climb up. Tatsuo took the lead as they rode single file away from Kyoto. She sat behind Sheng, her arms wrapped around him, her head resting on his shoulder. As they neared the turn that would take them on the journey to the hidden temple, Kimiko looked back one last time. There, in the distance, following swiftly and keeping to the trees, was one of the young girls from the thieves guild.

Night had come. The chill of fall was in the air, the warmth from the torches that also gave them light a welcome comfort. They neared their destination, slipping through the dense, low branches. Kimiko grinned widely as the pathway once again opened up, revealing the hiding place of the resistance army: something of which she'd heard growing whispers through Kyoto's secretive underground over the last several years.

Friends had assembled on the temple steps as they awaited the return of Sheng and Tatsuo, hopeful that words of a successful mission would follow. Daisuke could hardly believe his eyes when he saw the horses return with a third rider. He raced to their side and helped Kimiko down, smothering her with an enormous hug as he wrapped his arms tightly around her. There were tears in both their eyes as they embraced. Hayami followed and was quickly introduced to Sheng's and Suke-chan's long lost friend.

Tatsuo dismounted and handed off the reigns of his horse to a man who cared for the animals on the grounds. He nodded at Scar as he hurried past him on his way up the stone stairs.

"We need to talk," Tatsuo said in a hushed voice.

"The girl?" Scar questioned, watching the happy gathering below in the courtyard.

"I fear she's a distraction."

"She's beautiful," Scar snorted in amusement.

"See what I mean?" Tatsuo said in frustration as he continued on, leaving the reverie behind.

Scar saw that Sheng was waiving him down to join them so he put aside Tatsuo's words and hurried to welcome them back as quickly as his old, tired legs could manage. Sheng was wise enough to manage both a military campaign and a woman, regardless of how beautiful she was – or at least Scar hoped.

"Meet Kimiko," Sheng smiled, his arm outstretched to guide Scar into their circle.

"Any friend of Sheng's is a friend of mine," Scar said, bowing respectfully.

"Thank you," she replied.

"Especially when she's as pretty as you!" the old samurai added with wink.

Kimiko smiled. She was used to such compliments from older *gentleman* and she took it in stride.

"Come along everyone, I want to show Kimiko around," Sheng said as he urged the group towards the temple.

"Alright," she replied, "but could I have just a moment to prepare myself? Honesty this is all just a little overwhelming. I'll join you in a moment."

"We'll be just inside the entrance. Come up when you're ready," Sheng nodded and they left Kimiko behind in the courtyard.

She waited till they were out of sight, then turned towards the shrubs nearest the path at the very edge of the courtyard. Kimiko studied the leaves for a moment, searching amongst the branches till a soft coo like a dove pulled her attention to a set of small blinking eyes hidden amongst the overgrowth.

"You managed to keep up?" Kimiko whispered.

"Of course, my lady. The horses never broke from a trot and I was able to keep watch on you from a distance. The light from the torches helped too."

"Do you believe you are in danger, madam Kimiko?" the voice asked.

"No. I couldn't be safer, in fact."

"How long do you plan on staying here?"

"I do not know," Kimiko said shaking her head reluctantly.

"Usagi and Asami will be most worried when you do not return. What would you have me tell them?" the girl questioned.

"Say that I may have found a wonderful opportunity for us, one that will lead us out from the underground and legitimize all that we are. I don't know the details yet, or how I can work this to our advantage, but tell her that the resistance is real. Tell her that I am among friends but that I am, as always, loyal to the sisterhood."

"As you wish," the young girl replied.

"I want you to report back to me here in one week. I will have a letter ready for you to take back to Usagi and Asami. For now, keep this between the four of us. No one else can know where I am. Now go and be safe on the road."

"Yes, my lady," she replied, slipping away into the night, leaving Kimiko to her reunion.

20

PEREGRINATION

The fall months passed quickly. Sheng and his fellow masters had seen much progress regarding the training of their recruits. Nearly every day, or so it seemed, more men and women came to join them in their resistance. Their volunteer army swelled in ranks with members from all throughout the region. And with these new recruits came a new hope. Scar and Tatsuo, Sheng and Daisuke, even Hayami and Kimiko – six fearsome warriors in their own right – could not overcome Takeshi Hasegawa and his imposing samurai force.

During this time, Scar and Tatsuo had revealed to Sheng and Daisuke the true purpose of this hidden temple-made-dojo and emphasized the need to prepare for war against Hasegawa. Scar had always known of Hasegawa's aptitude for treachery when he had taken over the dojo in Kamakura for himself all those years earlier. Tatsuo learned of it after the betrayal by his own father. After leaving the dojo, he hunted down his father and demanded he reveal the truth before exacting revenge in the name of honor and watching his father fall on his own blade in ritual *seppuku*. Sheng's journey to Kyoto, the wako pirate slave ship and Hasegawa's plot to murder the Emperor, had opened his eyes to the truth and emboldened his resolve to avenge his family and the plundering of his village when he was just a boy. And now, with a small, but effective army of archers, martial artists, ronin desiring to regain honor, and farmers who had simply had enough of Hasegawa's threats and disregard for the emperor *and* shogunate, the leaders of this dojo were deciding how and when might be best to face Takeshi Hasegawa.

War was not all that grew closer as the cold of winter descended on Japan. Daisuke and Hayami had pledged their love for one another and were married according to tradition. Sheng and Kimiko also found themselves spending much time alone, walking through the woods and discussing their lives – everything that had happened to them since they'd been separated all those years ago. Kimiko explained her role in the underground thieves guild of Kyoto. Though Sheng disagreed with the actions used by the guild, he respected the tenant of helping young, destitute girls escape the inevitable servitude and abuse that would likely hang over them for the rest of their lives. Sheng also recognized that a conflict with Hasegawa would most certainly be nonconventional. It would require stealth and espionage, not open conflict. The battlefield would be as psychological as it would be physical. The thieves guild would be an excellent ally, he reasoned, because the women were trained in the art of *ninjutsu* – guerilla warfare and stealth – and this would give them a stark advantage since Sheng and the other leaders knew of Hasegawa's specific martial tactics and the training each of his samurai received. They could leverage that knowledge to their advantage and add Kimiko's skills, both lethal and nonlethal, to destroy Hasegawa's army. But that of course would still leave Hasegawa who alone would be a formidable foe.

The temple's grounds lent itself well to such diverse and specialized training. The trees afforded the opportunity to practice stalking a target from the branches, then strike without detection, whether by bow or by sword. Stone walls and outbuildings made urban stealth tactics a reality and gave the opportunity for the fighters to learn that shadows and cover were indispensible assets when one must remain hidden before unleashing an attack, especially to remain inaudible while doing so. Battling from horseback, learning new weapons, forming solid defenses: all was a lesson to be learned and the members of the resistance, young and old, man and woman, skilled and novice applied themselves to the cause. It was exhausting. It was time consuming. But every one of them knew that it was worth every drop of sweat, every painful tear, to see evil vanquished.

Mist lingered in the stifling air. A fog covered the land, making visibility beyond one's hands difficult at best. Sheng peered into the gloom and searched for the source of the voice, his hand on his sword as a necessary precaution.

The woman called out again in a faint, haunting whimper, "Help me."

Where was she? Sheng searched, stepping over debris left behind from the long-fallen village. "Can you hear me?" he called to her. There was no reply.

He continued on, wishing he had a torch or a lantern to light his way. As he followed the path, he felt like he'd been here before. The hair on the back of his neck tingled and stood on end. Ahead, he spotted a strange blue, ball-like light glowing through the fog unlike anything he had ever seen. The light pulsed and moved along gracefully. Again, he heard the voice and now the enchanting light seemed to be drawing him towards her.

Sheng quickened his pace, the blue orb now moving faster, darting back and forth up the moss-covered, old stone walkway. He followed it to the end of the path, then across a stretch of grass and up onto the porch of an abandoned, burnt shell of a house. The fog dissipated as black ash now seemed to fall from the sky like a chalky, sulfurous rain.

The blue light twirled manically as it took the shape of a woman, her face young, loving – familiar. "My son," the voice spoke with an eerie resonance, "come find me. Climb the mountain and find me."

"*MOTHER!*" Sheng shouted, throwing off his blanket violently and sitting up from where he lay sleeping on the floor of the temple.

Everyone in the room woke, startled by his sudden, panicked outcry. Kimiko hurried to his side.

"What's wrong Sheng?" she asked. "Was it another dream?"

"It was," he sighed, "another dream about *her*, my mother – just like last night and the night before, and the night before that."

"What does it mean?" she pondered, wiping the sweat from his brow.

"I do not know for certain," Sheng said, taking hold of her hand and pulling her close, "but I know what I must do."

"You couldn't pick a worse time to leave!" Tatsuo argued. "We are relying on your leadership. The training we do here will suffer in your absence. And with new recruits coming all the time, they need to hear your experiences first hand. As a defector from Hasegawa's dojo, your words carry weight with our people. Many of them are joining because of you!"

"I won't be gone long," Sheng replied. "This is something I must do. There are questions left unanswered and I have to know the truth. I have to see the village where my parents lived with my own eyes. I must come to terms with the past. I won't be haunted any longer!"

Scar paced the room as he listened to each man reason with the other. The door was closed, their conversation private.

"And what of the snow then?" Tatsuo huffed as he pointed in the direction of the outer wall as he spoke. "This is the worst winter we have seen in years. You will face cold and exposure. A horse will be no good this time of year. In this weather, a one day's ride will be a two day hike. Where will you make camp? How about eating and sleeping? What if you never come back? What if you die out there?!"

"That won't happen," Sheng assured.

"You don't know that! You could be ambushed. You could fall ill…even starve."

"Tatsuo!" Scar barked, startling the friends. "There's no stopping him."

"But…"

"Let him go," Scar answered, cutting Tatsuo's rebuttal short. "We'll continue on in his stead."

Sheng nodded his appreciation and left the two masters alone, closing the door once more as he headed down to the main floor of the temple. Scar waited to make sure he was gone before he continued. "You knew this would have to happen eventually."

"I did, but when the weather would be better, safer," Tatsuo shrugged. "Why would *he* want the journey to be harder for Sheng than it needs to be? Is this a test?"

"I don't question what *he* asks of me. If he wants to test Sheng in such a way, that is up to him and not me," Scar explained. "And you shouldn't question *him* either. In fact if it weren't for him, none of this would be possible. I'd be dead, of that I'm sure. This man has saved me more than once and the least I can do is honor his wishes. If *he* says Sheng will find purpose in this journey, then I believe him."

"But why now? Why would Sheng feel the need to go now?"

"That's beyond me," Scar chuckled. "Perhaps we're just not meant to understand. Just know that when Sheng returns…"

"*If* he returns."

"…*WHEN* he returns, young Tatsuo, everything will be different."

Sheng stood in the courtyard. The sun was only just beginning to glow on the far eastern horizon. Night still lingered in the early morning hours. A heavy fur coat warmed his torso. Thick leather pants protected his legs. His feet were clad in heavy boots, fur-lined and sturdy. He wore a pack made of leather and rope on his back, in it the provisions necessary to make the journey to his childhood village. He knew what awaited him. This would be no easy task. A sword would be too cumbersome. Instead he carried a small dagger-sized blade on his belt – hopefully he would not even need that.

"Are you sure I cannot go with you?" Kimiko pleaded.

"This is something I have to do alone," Sheng answered. "I wish I could take you. I'll miss you greatly, more than you'll ever know. But something deep inside me tells me that this is how it needs to be. We will have many adventures together, of that I'm sure. But for now, I go alone."

"I don't understand," she sighed, "but I respect your conviction. If this is what must be done, then go with my love. Just promise you'll return to me. Promise me, Sheng!"

"I promise, Kimiko…with all my heart."

With those words, she threw her arms around him. She'd lost Sheng ten years ago, fearing he was dead after their capture. Now, having been reunited for what seemed like such a short time, she could barely stand the thought of losing him again. Their embrace continued, neither one wanting it to end. But Sheng knew he must take advantage of every minute of daylight.

"It's time," he whispered in her ear, lessening his grip as a signal for her to do the same.

She kissed him and then reluctantly smiled as he gave a farewell wave to the leaders of the dojo. Kimiko, Daisuke, Hayami, Tatsuo, and Scar watched, their thoughts full of uncertainty and dread, as the greatest hope of defeating Hasegawa journeyed into the near-certain death of winter's grasp.

The morning passed quickly and Sheng managed a steady pace. He thought of stopping briefly to eat, but chose to snack as he hiked on. The sun was warm on his face, his hood causing him to sweat.

Afternoon came and passed as the sun drifted across the sky. Night would fall soon. He was tempted to press on, but he estimated he had made it nearly half of the distance to the village and chose to use the last of the sun to grant him welcome light as he set up a simple camp. He found a large cluster of rocks that provided a slight overhang at their base. They worked well to shield him from the wind. He quickly gathered the driest sticks he could find, and then removed a small piece of cloth and a container of lamp oil. With a few strikes of his simple tools, the oil caught a spark and he soon sat in the warmth of the small crackling fire, the orange glow flickering, casting his shadow against the rocks at his back. Though the ground was hard, he made the best of his situation. Now that he was resting, the day's travel had caught up with him and he fought cramping in his legs. Even so, he ate and rested. Wrapped in a blanket he'd pulled from his pack and laying close to the fire, he was soon asleep.

He woke the next morning before sunup, shaken awake by his shivering. The fire now stood as a crumbled pile of ashes with only a few still-glowing embers too small to overcome the cold. His toes ached and his fingers hurt as he worked them open and closed to get the blood flowing. Deep pain coursed through his stiff neck and back. Sheng took food from his pack and ate the small, flat cakes quickly as he considered building a new fire. But, he decided, he would save his supplies for that following night; after all, he did have the return trip to consider and he would have to ration what he'd brought along just in case the trip took longer than anticipated. With the orange morning-glow of the sun peeking over the horizon, Sheng climbed stiffly to his feet and greeted whatever challenges the new day would bring.

At parts, the snow was too thick and deep for him to follow the road so he continued on blindly in the direction he knew the village should be, uncertain whether or not he had left the path. Much of the terrain was a surprise and firm footing a relief as he would step forward into assumed solid ground only to find himself stumbling as the land dropped out from beneath him unexpectedly, hidden beneath the fluffy white drifts. Where the road was clear, the dirt was often rutted from the wheels of horse drawn carts. Here the unevenness only added to his growing fatigue. Even so, he continued on, knowing full well that each stride brought him a step closer to his home and the answers he hoped to find.

After spending most of the day trekking along the lonely, barren road, he came across an active stream, the water moving too fast to freeze solid. He pulled off his leather gloves and knelt down, scooping up the frigid water with his cupped hands. He desperately drank, greedily repeating the movement over and over till his fingers had gone numb. And there, on his knees, he realized that this was the same stream from which he pulled the stone that even now hung as a charm around Kimiko's neck. He was almost there.

Refreshed and with new vigor, Sheng climbed to his feet, putting his cold hands back into his gloves, and hurried on. It didn't take long for him to reach where the main gate once stood and looking beyond, he saw the odd snow-covered mounds that raised above the ground like burial sites of the former homes that stood in neat rows, staggered on both sides of the central path. There was an eerie silence here and it felt, in a way, sacred – it was, after all, the final resting place of the adult villagers who were slaughtered on that horrid day.

Sheng found himself wondering if anyone had buried the bodies? Was there a mass grave or were the fallen left as carrion for birds and predators to scavenge? *No wonder I've had nightmares of this place,* he supposed.

In solemn silence, he imagined what it looked like as best as he could remember, when the grass was green and lush, and the children played while the elders pondered. He could almost hear the sound of the small marketplace, smell the food that cooked in pots and over fires. This village was surely haunted for his thoughts were filled with ghosts.

He continued on, following the snowy, central path to where his family's house once stood. Tears began to form in his eyes as he pictured his mother standing on what was left of the porch, rotten planks peeking out from beneath their wintery shroud. He fantasized that his father had joined her and together they reached out to him with open arms, welcoming him home.

Sheng sobbed as he dropped to his knees. Furiously he brushed away the snow and desperately thrust his fingers down into the frozen dirt, fighting to grasp at clumps of earth as if to take hold of his parents' hands where they had fallen and become one with the ground. Rolling onto his back, he stared up into the sky, tears streaking his face. As Sheng laid there, he remembered possibly the most important thing he'd forgotten over time and was angry at himself for ever letting the memory go. This all began because of Hasegawa's desire to fill his dojo with youth who would become his army. This was all a result of Hasegawa's scheming against the leaders of the shogunate and treason against the emperor. And to make it all worse, Sheng had tolerated, even accepted what Hasegawa had done all those years ago, what Hasegawa had continued to do to that very day: destroy lives for his own purposes. Hasegawa was the cause of all Sheng's greatest sufferings and Sheng had supported this man, imagined him and the dojo as family all because he longed so desperately for the bond that comes with a father. Hasegawa would pay for what he had done.

Hate suddenly consumed him. Sheng burned with rage. He forgot all about the cold, all about those who loved him and waited for him to return. All he wanted was revenge and it was driving him mad. He ripped his knife free from its sheath and searched the area for sticks, branches, anything that would burn. Returning with some thick, dry twigs, he began hacking them into smaller pieces with the blade. A pile slowly formed as he continued chopping, retrieving more, and chopping again. He finally returned with some larger pieces and stacked those over top of the smaller kindling.

Hastily, Sheng tore open his pack and prepared to build a huge fire. He would eat and remember all that he could as an honor to the dead. He would sing songs and speak tales of war and victory even if he alone would hear. He would celebrate the elders and children alike. Tonight the village would live once more.

Something startled Sheng from his sleep. The fire still roared, keeping him warm and dry. He stood, looking up into the cloudless night sky – the vastly infinite chasm of space – where the twinkling of the stars was both inspiring and mesmerizing. Rubbing the sleep from his eyes, Sheng stared out across the snow covered valley. There was no movement in any direction. Even the air seemed still and somber. He turned his back to the hot flames as a faint flicker of light drew his attention.

What is that?! he wondered.

Far beyond the remains of the village, even beyond the outskirts of the valley, a light shone from halfway up the mountainside. It was a wonder he could even see it from where he stood; yet there it was, a ball of fire flickering on the sloped face of the snow-capped mountain.

A whisper came to him on the wind. *Climb the mountain*, it urged. Sheng shivered, not from the cold but from the revelation. The dying words of the old master sword maker, Masato Katsumi, came back to him as he recalled that fateful day in Kamakura when Tatsuo's father struck him down. *Climb the mountain*, Katsumi had instructed with his last breath. And with that, the dreams he had of his mother when she said it as well, *Climb the mountain*.

Without knowing the hour of night, Sheng hurriedly kicked snow over his campfire to extinguish the flame. He checked his provisions, but found he had eaten all the food the night before. The last of his kindling had been used as well. He threw the pack down on the ground in frustration, knowing now that it was useless and would only add weight as he climbed; not that the kindling would have done him much good on a snow covered mountainside. Sheng resigned himself to the fact that his journey up the Fuji-san, with no food and no fire for his return to the far-away temple, would most likely result in a one-way trip. Death most likely awaited him, yet he did not fear it. Certainly he could turn around, run back to the warmth and food of the dojo in the woods. He would be hungry, but most likely not starve in just two days. Exposure to the icy cold was the greatest threat, especially at night. And most definitely, Kimiko and his friends would no doubt be thankful for his safe return. But Sheng still didn't have the answers he wanted so desperately; and now, he felt like the only place he would find them was at the source of the mysterious fire. Snowflakes had once again started to fall, but it didn't matter. He had already made up his mind to continue. Somehow, Sheng knew that his past, the present, and his future were all connected to that light shining in the darkness.

21

DÉJÀ VU

Snow crunched beneath his feet with each labored step. He'd traveled on foot for days, climbing to the crest of the tallest peak in the treacherous range of mountains that surrounded the quiet valley below. The air grew thin and he found himself short of breath, exhausted by the arduous terrain.

He stopped momentarily to rest, turning to look back down the snowy mountainside, the fading trail of his solitary footprints a reminder of the lonely burden only he could bear. Slowly, he pulled back the hood on his thick leather-hide wrap, revealing his young, tired face. He looked but a boy, his cheeks still round with youth, but his body was strong, lean, and tall. A long black braid fell from his shoulder and hung at his waste. His dark, piercing eyes squinted in the bright sunlight.

Sheng's journey was far from complete. He turned his attention to the unmarked snow that lay ahead, the top of the mountain still a half-day's climb away. The twinge of hunger haunted him as the cold wind bit at his face and he knew he could not linger. Amidst his pain, his desire for warmth, for food; he pressed on.

With another heavy step, he continued onward towards the summit.

The slope of the mountain grew steeper with every step and all too soon he felt his legs go numb, falling headlong into the snow, his eyes slowly closing as his body gave in to the elements.

His unguarded mind flooded with memories. They flickered quickly: his home, his family, the other children he grew up with; all orphaned in the same attacks that spread across the entire valley. No village was spared.

I must not fail, he warned himself, managing to open his eyes.

With great difficulty, he tried to raise himself up, but his weakened arms gave way and he collapsed back down once again. This time, he did not struggle. Sheng passed out, surrendering to the elements.

"Sheng? Sheng? Sheng!" a woman's soft voice called out, startling him awake.

"Kimi-chan?!" he wondered, unsure of what had happened.

Sheng sat up from where he lay beneath a large, furry animal skin blanket. He realized he was shirtless, but very warm. Kimiko smiled at Sheng, holding his hand tightly as he looked around the room in confusion.

"Where am I?"

"You are safe," she replied.

"What happened?" Sheng asked as he laid back down, his head pounding.

"You've been asleep for days, fevered and thrashing about like you were having some sort of nightmare. I was afraid you might not wake."

"I mean before that, how did I get *here*?"

"It's not my place to say. But it was certainly destiny that brought you here," Kimiko grinned as she continued excitedly. "I'll let everyone know you are awake. I'm sure *he* will see you soon."

Sheng closed his eyes as she left the small, dimly lit room. The scent of incense lingered in the air and candles flickered, ceremoniously placed on a finely crafted wooden table near the straw bed where he lay. What was this place? And who is this *he*? Scar and Tatsuo had both referred to some man the exact same way. Sheng wrestled with these thoughts as he tried to reason through all that had happened. He'd gone on this journey to find answers, not more questions. Muffled voices could be heard from outside the room, but he didn't care. Right now all he wanted was for the world to make sense. With that, he drifted back to sleep.

"You're so close," Sheng heard his mother say. "Do not give up now."

"There's just so little that I understand at this time. What is happening to me?" he replied.

Together, Sheng stood with Amikori, their feet firmly planted on a boulder-like rock that seemed to float effortlessly within the infinite void that enveloped them. There seemed no way to gauge time or distance or scale: they were just *there*. A purple and gray mist swirled about them and far away, high above their heads, a pinhole of light glimmered from above in the absolute blackness of the beyond.

"What is this place?" Sheng asked.

Amikori did not answer. She simply stood in silence, satisfied to look her son in the eyes. Sheng knew this couldn't be real. This place defied all logic and reason. Yet in his heart he longed for it as well. Suddenly, the tiny dot of light overhead erupted into a broad, blinding beam that fully engulfed them in its energy.

"The truth is near. Do not be afraid," she urged.

Sheng squinted as he opened his eyes. A lantern hovered just above his face, the sudden light disorienting. He struggled to see from who's hand it dangled.

"Come on, Sheng," Scar said, his haunting face coming into focus. "It's time for you to get your answers. Kimiko brought clothes for you from the temple. I'll be waiting just outside of this room when you are ready."

Scar left him to get dressed. Sheng stood, finding himself at first very unstable as he fought against the aching in his legs. He put on the robes quickly in spite of his pain and took a quick look around the room. Nothing was familiar. He'd certainly never been there before.

He slid open the door and found not only Scar and Kimiko, but also Daisuke, Hayami, and Tatsuo. "You all came?" he asked a bit surprised. "Who's watching over the dojo?"

Tatsuo was first to respond, "The students are very capable. You, having trained many of them, have made it possible."

Sheng nodded. "I trust your judgement," he smiled before hugging each of his friends.

"That's all fine and well, but we need to move this along," Scar winked. "I don't trust the resistance on their own without any of us there. The sooner I get back to them, the better."

Scar tugged at Sheng's sleeve and the two walked down a narrow corridor, leaving his friends behind. This was a strange house, Sheng observed. There were not many rooms, but many corridors, and the layout was *unique* to say the least. By all appearances it felt like a house – still, there was something strange about it, almost false. *Who lives here?*, he wondered.

They reached the end of the path. Scar bowed, then slid the door open and motioned Sheng into the room. As soon as he passed through, the door was closed behind him. Two men sat opposite Sheng where he stood. The first he recognized immediately – the blind monk from the Emperor's court in Kyoto. The second man's face was hidden beneath the shadow of a black hood. Sheng's anger and confusion was overwhelming. He seethed, clenching his fists, paying no attention to the banners and wall-mounted weapons that decorated the room. How could this be? Had this been a trap? Had the last several months been all for naught? Why would his friends do this to him? This betrayal was unimaginable!

"*Takeshi Hasegawa!*" Sheng growled.

"No," the hooded man's voice replied calmly. "Hasegawa, I am not."

Sheng stared back, his jaw unflinching. But hidden behind his sternness was a creeping doubt. There was something authoritative and sincere about the voice that made Sheng believe him.

"Then who are you?" Sheng questioned, his brows furrowing. "You sit here with one of Hasegawa's agents, a man who plotted to aid in killing the emperor."

"Do you not believe in redemption?" the man asked. "Can a man not turn away from the sins of a past life and find a life of peace and goodness?"

"But his loyalty is with Hasegawa. He even tried to see to it that I was killed, and my friend Daisuke as well, when we decided we could not assassinate the emperor, that it was the wrong decision."

"This I know," he replied. "But until just a few months ago, were you not also an agent for Hasegawa as well? Did you not even teach in his dojo? Did you not travel to Kyoto to do his bidding?"

Sheng stared at the blind monk intensely. The hooded stranger was right. He knew that he and Daisuke had made the choice to do what they thought was right. Perhaps the blind monk had done the same?

"How do you know that you can trust him then, knowing that he was – *or is* – a friend of Takeshi Hasegawa?"

"Have you never heard it said, the enemy of my enemy is my friend?" the man countered. "Speak, Monk, answer for yourself."

The monk turned his attention in the direction from which he'd been listening to Sheng speak, "It is true that I helped Hasegawa plot against the emperor, even ensured you would have an opportunity to kill him when the time came. And yes, I tried to kill you and your friend. I cannot excuse my past, but I can make up for it. I know all of Hasegawa's plans!"

"That's fine. You might even be telling me the truth. Perhaps you do wish to make things right. But why would you suddenly betray Hasegawa. When last we met, you seemed adamant that his wishes be carried out. Why the sudden change of heart?"

"When Hasegawa found out what had happened, that you failed to kill the emperor and I in turn failed to kill you, he sent notice to me that another assassin would be sent. He specifically asked me to meet the man at a location outside of the palace walls. I agreed. But as it turned out, the assassin was sent for me: punishment for my failings. He tried to kill me, but I escaped and fled. I didn't know where else to go so I wandered, nowhere in particular, just away from Kyoto. After all, road signs are of no use to a blind man! Fate led me to this place. I was seeking to hide in a temple or a shrine, someplace quiet to pray and reflect on my life to that point. I wandered and wandered till I found myself at what must have been the foot of a mountain. A voice in my head told me to *climb* and I followed. Now I am here with you. For whatever it is worth, I'm sorry."

"This man is no longer a friend of Hasegawa's," the hooded stranger assured. "Just as you are no longer a sensei in Hasegawa's school."

Sheng had lowered his guard and softened his jaw. The blind monk seemed genuine in his words. His focus returned to the man in the hood, the man that seemed so much like Hasegawa, yet so different.

"Then tell me...are you the man I saw in the garden, back in Hasegawa's dojo? I was just a boy, but I remember. You climbed over the wall and disappeared. That was you wasn't it?"

The man shifted in his seat, leaning forward as candlelight briefly lit his face. Sheng glimpsed his bright green eyes.

"I have been watching you for a long time, Sheng. I watched you during your studies and training, I watched you grow into a man; I even watched you as you travelled to Kyoto. And I am the one who found you when you collapsed in the snow on the side of this mountain."

"We're still on the mountain?" Sheng questioned, clearly surprised. "This house is on the mountain?"

"Not on, but *in* the mountain. And it's less of a house and more of a cemetery, but that too will be explained in time."

Sheng weighed the man's words before he continued. "The last time I saw Scar when I was a boy, he was being interrogated – *tortured* – by a masked man in a hood. That was you? And that day in the Kamakura market, the bearded man with the brilliant green eyes, that was you as well?"

"Yes."

"And Scar is here with you now?"

"Indeed. He has been my friend for a very long time, long before the dojo in fact."

"So what I saw in Kamakura was a show? Scar's torture, the girl I thought was Kimiko, even the times you posed as Hasegawa on the dojo grounds?"

"Very good insight," the hooded man replied. "Everything you saw that day between myself and Scar was what you needed to see. That day was hard for me. I hadn't been that close to you in over a year. I wanted so much to just take hold of you and tell you the truth. But you were not ready and that is why Scar had to leave the dojo. It's the reason for the theatrics. He wanted to tell you the truth, but I wasn't ready for you to know. And later, when I spoke to you in the market, that fake beard itching my face as I looked so proudly upon you, I wanted nothing more than to open your eyes to all you did not know."

"So you thought it better for me to think that Scar was dead...and...and Kimiko!" Sheng said boldly. "You made me think she was dead too! Why would you do such a thing?"

"I'm very sorry that I did that to you, Sheng. I'm sorry that you had to live all these years believing a lie, but I needed to make sure you had reasons to always doubt Hasegawa, never trust his intentions. And it worked! You are here, with me, not at his side!"

"Who are you?" Sheng finally asked. "Why would you care whose side I'm on or want to be close to me? Why would you watch me for all these years?"

The stranger stood and slowly lowered his hood. Sheng stared into the man's deep green eyes. He studied his brow and the shape of his chin, pondered the positioning of his nose and the size of his ears. The man's hair was jet black, though graying around the temples. It was pulled back into a tight braid, just like Sheng's. A manicured beard peppered with gray tones graced his chin and jaw. His left eyebrow was split with a narrow scar as was both his upper and lower lip on the right side. Broad shoulders supported his cloak. Though hidden beneath his clothing, Sheng could tell that this man, certainly a warrior in his time, was muscular and still fit. They were nearly the same height as each other and Sheng estimated him to be at least twice his own age.

"Do you not know who I am? Have you forgotten me?"

Sheng suddenly tensed up, his heart beating out of control. He felt like he was going to vomit.

"Father!" he cried out rushing forward.

"Yes, Sheng!" Taekori replied taking hold of his long-lost son.

The men stood weeping, their arms wrapped tightly around one another. Sheng could hardly believe it – after all these years, his father was alive! And what was more, he was the apparent leader of the very movement against Hasegawa that Sheng so adamantly supported. And yet, in the midst of this revelation, there was also the sting of deceit. Sheng had thought himself an orphan for so long, had accepted the fact that his parents were gone. He understood his father's reasons for never revealing that he lived, but the hurt was real then just as it was now. Sheng had a decision to make as he embraced his father. Either he could accept his return with joy and hope, or he could resent his father for letting him think he had been dead all this time. After all, couldn't Taekori have trusted his own son with his plans? Shouldn't Sheng have been involved all along? *No*, Sheng answered his own thoughts. *Sometimes decisions—hard decisions – must be made for the sake of all, not the consideration of a few.* In that moment, Sheng forgave Taekori and another fragment of his broken heart was restored.

"I know you certainly have more questions and I will do my best to answer them as they come up," Taekori assured. "But there is one last thing you must see before we discuss the clan and Hasegawa."

Sheng was suddenly aware of the surroundings he had ignored upon first entering the room, his focus fixed on the blind monk and the hooded man. There were banners, tattered from weather and war, hanging on the walls. He now recognized their meaning immediately for they bore his family mon: the mark of the Shimazu clan. He gazed upon the symbol, admired the design. He'd seen this circled-cross all his life as a child, but never since his village was destroyed. Now, it was a sign of hope. From a certain perspective, he was finally home.

Beyond the chairs where the two men had sat, was a simple table. In the center was a wooden sword stand flanked on both ends by many glowing candles. There on the rack was a sword, ordinary and unadorned. Why was a sword of such lowly esteem in such a prominent place of display?

"Come, Sheng, follow me," Taekori said, pulling Sheng's attention back to their conversation.

The two of them – father and son – left the room behind and returned down the corridors. They passed the room in which Sheng had remembered waking. Shortly after, they came to what looked like the main door. Sheng expected to walk out onto a front porch, and certainly they did; but, it was unlike any porch he had ever seen. The house itself was concealed inside of a cave! The ceiling was low, but the space was deep and the walls had textured striations in them, moss growing in the crevices. Sheng stepped up to its mouth and looked out at the world beyond. He could see for miles and miles. And, he realized that he also looked directly down upon the valley below and the nightmares of his childhood.

"This way," Taekori called, drawing Sheng back from the mouth of the cave.

They walked along the side of the house and into a stone garden. In the center, a tree grew, crooked and mysteriously alive.

"What is this place?" Sheng wondered. "How does a tree grow inside of a cave? And why is it so warm in here, even when it snows outside?"

Taekori chuckled aloud, "One question at a time, my son!"

"I'm sorry," Sheng smiled. "There's just so much I want to understand."

"I would expect no less! The answer to your first question: this place is my home. After our village was destroyed all those years ago, I recovered what lumber and materials I could and then brought them up here piece by piece. I had discovered this cave many years before when I, in fact, was just a boy. There was nowhere else I could think of as far removed from the world. I believed I could be safe here and this cave also offered both shelter and a place for me to grieve the loss of my family."

"That's incredible," Sheng replied, enamored with the feat managed by his father. "And the tree? How does it grow?"

"The tree is more than just a tree. It is a *living grave*."

"How so?"

"On the day your mother was killed by Hasegawa's samurai, I and the other warriors from our village had done our best to stave off their attack. But being caught off guard has its disadvantages and we were not able to fight back as a unit, rather we were scattered and desperate. I, too, was overwhelmed in the chaos. My horse was struck with a spear and it toppled backwards, landing on me and trapping me beneath its weight. I must have hit my head because the last thing I remember was feeling the labored breaths of the horse as he succumbed to his mortal wound and died, me still trapped beneath him. I hated myself for this failure for many years. I try not to ask myself the *what if* questions, but even so they haunted me. When I woke, I fought to free myself and then headed straight to our house to find you and Amikori. As I raced through the village and I did not come across a single survivor, my heart sank. And, when I finally came to our house, my worst fears were realized. There was Amikori – your mother, my wife – dead on the porch. I took her up in my arms and cried till I had no tears left. Even so, I couldn't let her go and I held onto her till nightfall."

"I saw her too," Sheng said sadly. "It's my last memory of her, just as you had described. I said goodbye to her from the caged wagon that took me far from home."

"I wish you did not have to see such a thing. I wish a great many other things had not happened as they did, but..." Taekori paused, "...well, when I had spent all my tears, I looked into your mother's still face and suddenly remembered not seeing a single child among the dead – not one! I gently laid her back on the porch and then searched the whole village and surrounding valley for you, but I never found your body and in that I received a glimmer of hope. My son lived! After that, I began the dreadful work of collecting the dead. I constructed a simple pyre and burned all of our friends and neighbors before their bodies could be defiled by beasts. But I could not bring myself to add your mother to the fire. Instead, I carried her to this cave. Exhausted, I laid her down here, on this very spot, and then collapsed, sleeping beside her one last time. In the morning, I found the moss-rich soil beneath me soft and warm. I began digging with my bare hands, thankful to find such a miracle in the midst of such dire heartbreak. To my surprise, I dug down deep enough to provide a grave for Amikori. Over the next several months, I took to the task of building this new home out of an old life. During that time, I noticed a sprout growing from where I laid your mother to rest. I began watering it and talking with it – long conversations, often about you and where I hoped you might be! And through all that, that sapling became this tree. From her death came life and this tree reminds me that she is still with me every day, even if only in my heart."

Sheng looked at the twisted, almost wretched branches. With nearly no direct sunlight shining beyond the cave's mouth, the tree had grown as if stretching out for the light, reaching away from the darkness in the back of the cave. The tree's leaves had fallen victim to the changing seasons and its long-dried leaves still rested where they'd fallen to the floor of the cave. He reached out and took hold of an arm-like branch with fingerish twigs at its end. A peace filled him and he was satisfied to know what had happened to his mother after her death. He felt that she too was at peace.

"I later discovered that this mountain is actually a volcano," Taekori continued. "That is why this cave is so warm. It's fed by the heat at the core of the mountain. There are vents in the rear, old lava channels, which have led me to conclude that this cave was created by an ancient eruption This volcano is why the valley below is so fertile. In a way, this mountain provided life for us before all these events and it sustains us now."

Sheng had always known that Fuji-san had been regarded as sacred; but now, with his mother a part of the mountain herself, he gained a new respect for those who revered the mountain as holy. As he stood alongside his estranged father, Sheng contemplated the irrationalism of all that he had experienced in such a short time. Not only had he, by sheer happenstance, reunited with Kimiko, but now he was once more with his father: the bravest man he had ever known. Their reunion had been bittersweet as Sheng had finally learned the fate of his mother and the village; but at the same time, it also birthed a new hope. His friends soon rejoined Sheng and Taekori next to the tree.

"Thank you, Scar," Taekori smiled, "for reuniting me with my son. Thank you for watching over him when he was young and for coming to his aid at the emperor's palace."

"Think nothing of it. Certainly you would have done the same for me, my old friend," Scar said sincerely. "But remember that I left the dojo in Kamakura when he was still just a boy. Sheng has as much to do with the man he has grown into as does anyone else. Even without your influence, Taekori, he has become like you: humble, yet strong."

Taekori threw his arm around Sheng and embraced him, "I might never be able to make up for my absence, but I will do my best."

"So not to take away from this joyous moment, but now that Sheng knows the truth, what do we do about Hasegawa? After you left the temple on your journey," Tatsuo said, turning to Sheng, "a scout returned and reported that two villages had been raided, the destruction absolute, both reportedly attacked by riders in black armor."

"And the children?" Daisuke asked.

"Gone," Tatsuo confirmed. "Their bodies were not found amongst the dead."

"Black riders," Daisuke frowned. "That has to be Hasegawa, just like before. It has to be!"

"It's been years since Hasegawa's men raided a village," Taekori said, his brow furrowed. "Ronin mercenaries and pirates have become more prevalent, but just as ronin have joined our cause, perhaps Hasegawa has added them to his ranks as well?"

"Whether he *has* or *hasn't* is not really an issue, "Scar growled. "The tyranny of Hasegawa has threatened the cities and countryside of Japan for long enough. We must put an end to his treasonous madness and we must do it now!"

"I don't think this is the time or place to make such a decision. We should return to the temple," Tatsuo reasoned. "From there we can strategize and strike. Hasegawa has weaknesses, but if we act in haste we may not manage to exploit them to their full potential."

"What say you, Sheng?" Taekori questioned, turning to his son.

"Well," he paused, composing his thoughts, "the dojo in Kamakura is a fortress and will be protected by Hasegawa's most loyal – and skilled – guards. I know he has outposts throughout the region. Perhaps we could strike those first and weaken Hasegawa's grip of the land. But regardless, I agree with Tatsuo. We must regroup and consider all our options."

"Then that is precisely what we will do," Taekori replied proudly as he patted his son's shoulder. "Let's gather what we need and return to the temple. Hasegawa's reign is coming to an end!"

22

ONE LAST THING

Sheng needed the next several days to recover before setting out once again into the snowy cold. Taekori, in his wisdom, had recommended they give his son this time knowing full well that Sheng, if he was anything like his father, would never ask for it himself nor would he let on that he even needed the rest. But everyone, especially Sheng, needed to be at their best and he knew this. Though Scar and Tatsuo both reminded the group that every day they did nothing about Hasegawa, his grasp over the region tightened evermore. They too knew that Sheng was the lynchpin that held their secret rebellion together. The fighters at the temple had come to respect Sheng as their leader and his skills surpassed the best of the resistance's warriors – even Taekori, whose age had slowed him, if only slightly.

His recuperation was swift. Through it all, Kimiko never left Sheng's side. She helped him dress and bathe. Daily she tended to the frost wounds on his bandaged hands. And in these moments, their love blossomed, evolving from the passions of youth to the deeper realizations of care and commitment, a desire for mutual well being and not simply satisfying the senses.

In the mornings, Kimiko helped Sheng up from his bed and then out to the tree that was rooted in his mother – a living shrine – her death sprouting life from the bosom of the dirt. There, in silence, Sheng contemplated his life and longed for a time when this could all be placed behind him as a memory and not a wound, knowing full well that he would carry the scars with him forever. He realized that stopping Hasegawa should not be an act of vengeance, but rather a plea for peace. For revenge, he reasoned, was every bit as great a killer as Hasegawa himself, though the only victim of the violence was the one who harbored such a desire. If he allowed vengeance to consume him, then he would be no better than Hasegawa and his own hate would become a greater threat than his fiercest enemy. His hate for Hasegawa would rot inside of him, killing him from within.

The days then were spent exercising, taking progressively longer walks and testing his endurance. The snow had ceased and the temperature had risen. Even at their elevation, the air had grown warm as the sweetness of the coming spring revealed its fragrance.

When evening arrived, Kimiko would bring Sheng his food and the two would eat together, sharing secrets and dreams, fears and aspirations. Finally they would sleep, knowing that when they woke, there was hope to be found in the risen sun.

On the third morning, Sheng woke while Kimiko was still asleep. He moved quietly through the house finding that he was the only one up at this hour. The mouth of the cave faced west. Not a hint of light was to be seen. Sheng continued on with small, careful steps as he left the porch and headed for the tree. He felt much stronger and was certain that this would be their last morning in the cave. Sheng reached out and took hold of the leafless branch he'd grown to imagine as his mother's own hand. He closed his eyes and thanked her for leading him to the mountain, to his father. The dreams he had always considered nightmares had become welcomed glimpses of the woman he tried so hard to never forget.

I'm proud of you, her voice whispered in his mind.

Sheng smiled as tears formed in the corners of his tightly closed eyes. "I love you," he said aloud. As he did, his fingers found a bud on one of the branches. Excitedly, he snuck back into the house and returned to the tree with a knife. Carefully, he cut the twig with the bud off where it stemmed from the branch. He knew exactly what he would do upon returning to the temple.

"Here you are," Sheng heard from over his shoulder. He turned to find Kimiko yawning, her arms stretched high over her head as she greeted him with a kiss. "You're father was looking for you, wondering if today was the day we head to the temple. I'd say it looks like it is!"

"Yes," Sheng grinned. "I'm ready to return."

"Perfect," she said with a playful wink. "I'll tell the others and we will prepare for the journey. In the meantime, your father is waiting for you in the room where you first spoke to one another. Do you remember?"

"The room in the back of the house…I remember."

They returned to the house together, but parted in the main corridor. Sheng followed the hall to the rear room where he found his father waiting for him just as Kimiko had said. Taekori was silently meditating with his back to the door.

"Father, I am here," Sheng spoke reverently as he quietly entered. "I'm ready to return to the temple."

"Very good, my son," Taekori replied, his eyes still closed, never turning to address his son face-to-face. "Come, sit beside me."

Sheng dropped to his knees alongside his father and looked at the table that sat directly in front of them. Candles and incense burned. The modest sword stood as the centerpiece. Dried wax and small scrolls covered the wooden tabletop.

"What do you see?" Taekori asked, his eyes still closed.

"I see the candles. I see your writings. I see a sword. Is it yours? It does not look like the one I remember you carrying when I was a boy," Sheng explained.

"It is mine, in a manner of speaking," Taekori replied. "But you are correct. Only under very rare circumstances did I ever carry this sword, I have never worn it for ceremony, nor have I ever used it in battle. The times this sword was at my side was for *its* protection, not my own."

"Then whose is it, Father, and why is it here?" Sheng asked.

"This sword belongs to no one, and yet everyone. You do not wield it, it wields you, if you understand me. For that reason, I have never even removed the blade from its sheath in anger or at times of conflict. This sword has not tasted blood, at least not since it was handed down to me by my father. This blade is mysterious and powerful."

"I don't know what you mean? How can a sword *wield* the one who holds it?"

"This is no ordinary sword, my son. This sword has no known origin, no known maker. A master swordsmith, a friend of mine from before you were born, inspected it long ago and said it was nothing like anything he had ever seen."

"Was it Masato Katsumi?"

"He was, but how do you know his name?" Taekori mused.

"I was with him when he died, murdered in Kamakura by Tatsuo's father."

"That's right!" his father recalled. "Tatsuo did tell me that, but that was a long time ago."

"What makes the sword so special?" Sheng wondered. "There is no ornamentation on the grip or sheath…"

"The shank is bare as well," Taekori interjected. "But Katsumi said it was one of the finest folded steel blades he had ever seen. The simplicity only adds to the mystery as its craftsmanship is unmatched. He admitted that even his finest work was no match for this sword. This sword has been entrusted to our family as guardians for generations and we have kept it secret – kept it safe – hidden away for centuries. I recovered it from the charred remains of our house. I expected it would have burned along with everything else, but it was found completely intact with no trace of damage! Then, I brought it here fearing that our family line had ended and that the whereabouts of the blade were in jeopardy. I thought it best that the secret die with me rather than the sword find its way into the hands of someone who might misuse its power."

"Someone like Hasegawa," Sheng acknowledged.

"Exactly! After all, the sword Tatsuo's father killed Masato Katsumi to acquire was made for Hasegawa who demanded an equal to this sword which he had heard of but never seen. He demanded the original, but I refused, falling from Hasegawa's favor."

"What do you mean?"

"I along with Scar and Hasegawa founded the dojo in Kamakura. Surely you know this?"

"You were the third founder?!"

"Indeed. Didn't Scar tell you? I thought you knew," Taekori said, perplexed.

"He didn't, not directly at least. Though in hindsight it all makes sense. You were the tiger clan, Hasegawa was the dragon, and Scar was…"

"The monkey," Taekori continued, "When I refused to give the sword to Hasegawa, he was furious. He lashed out, trying to kill me. We battled, neither really winning. I fled south to the safety of my clan, but he left me with the scars to remind me of our conflict. He was wounded as well, but not as severely as was his pride. That hate for me fueled his mission and I have long wondered if his terror, the attacks throughout the countryside, was not a veiled quest to find me and claim the sword once and for all."

"What does the sword *do*?" Sheng asked curiously, staring at the simple weapon that rested on the stand in front of him. "What *power* does it hold?"

"I only know what my father told me as the blade was passed on through tradition. He said his own father told him, and his grandfather before him, and so on. This sword, devours the souls of whomever falls victim to its razor sharp edge. Their souls, both good and evil, are consumed by the blade and then influence the one who wields it, bending his deepest desires and morality to its will. In the hands of a good man, the sword may be used for good, but in the hands of an evil man…well, I don't even want to imagine. The sword itself vibrates with the life-energy of its many victims – good and evil. I've heard it feels like taking hold of lightning and striking your foes down with the sheer force of nature. Your whole body tingles as you grip the blade, the weapon a direct extension of your soul's will. That is, at least, the legend. I give this sword to you now, Sheng. Do with it what you see fit."

The sun had only just peeked over the eastern horizon as Takeshi Hasegawa stood on a dock in Kamakura's harbor. He awaited the arrival of a ship, a ship which was promised to ferry a secret weapon, an invaluable tool in his quest for power. The spirits in the mirror had told him where the relic might be found, but it was a long journey, possible only by boat, and required trade connections with the West.

He enlisted the help of the wako pirates whom he had partnered with and profited from time and again. Smuggling was their specialty: weapons, precious stones, wine, even women and children, as Sheng had learned by accident on his trip to Kyoto. These pirates in particular were especially effective because their skillset included murder and they had never been afraid to get their hands dirty for Hasegawa. His hopes rose as he recognized the wako ship's sails as it navigated the busy harbor congested with fishing traffic. Eagerly, Hasegawa awaited his prize.

The ship docked and the manifest was checked as the *legal* cargo was unloaded. After that, money was secretly exchanged and the *true* cargo was managed. This was the arrangement. Questions were never asked as long as the wealth was shared.

The captain soon disembarked the junk and greeted Hasegawa with an honorable bow. Accompanying him was a man with a small box made of cedar wood, the outer shell covered in beautiful Arabian designs.

"Is this it?" Hasegawa smiled excitedly, looking down at the box in the man's hands.

"It pleases me to answer *yes*," the captain said, his words again accompanied by a bow.

"Excellent! Let us go continue this conversation somewhere more *private*," Hasegawa urged, his voice growing quieter and more secretive as he spoke.

He spun quickly on his heel and the three men silently headed to a nearby tea house where they were promptly led to a secluded room in the rear of the establishment. The proprietor excused himself and left them to their business.

"So tell me," Hasegawa continued, certain that they were now safe from prying ears, "was it difficult to find?"

The captain nodded as they resumed the conversation where they had left off at the docks, "We sailed along the Arab Sea, making berth in Memphis. From there, we headed north and searched in Jerusalem – finding nothing – then Damascus and Antioch. New, hopeful, information then led us to Rome; but again, we found nothing. We almost gave up, moving on to Constantinople on our own business when by what seemed pure happenstance, we came across a European man living there as a merchant. He had been injured in the Crusades and never made it further home. This merchant told us of a man, a Frenchman, who had fought valiantly against the Mussulman fighters. According to his story, this knight was supposedly wounded mortally, but miraculously recovered and from then on was untouchable, telling us that swords and arrows bounced right off of him."

"Unbelievable," Hasegawa laughed. "Please continue."

"As it turns out, the man was believed to possess what many soldiers came to believe was a holy relic of some sort because he seemed to possess almost a supernatural ability for combat. Mysteriously, the origin of this relic is unknown!"

"And it's in the box?" Hasegawa asked, suddenly changing from jovial to stern in his posture and speech.

"Yes."

"And did you open it? Did you look upon the relic?"

"I did," the pirate captain admitted, "but only to ensure that it was there. I never touched the relic itself. I will say though that it seems you sent us on a great quest for something so trivial. It doesn't seem to be anything of value, of course I'll leave that for you to decide."

"What would you say it is worth?" Hasegawa pressed.

The captain looked at his companion and then decided on a value, "Five hundred Chinese Ming coins, my friend. And that is a bargain for you."

Hasegawa reached inside of his robe and retrieved four leather pouches full of coins and tossed them onto the table in front of the captain, "I'll give you one thousand for your effort as well as your word that you never speak of this to anyone."

"You must know something that we don't know!" the captain smiled as he pulled the jingling bags towards himself as if he'd won some great prize.

"It's worth every copper in those sacks," Hasegawa replied confidently. "Thank you, Captain, for your commitment to the task and for your silent discretion. I must now return to my dojo."

Hasegawa remained seated at the table as the two men left to return to their ship. Slowly, he lifted open the ornate lid of the small cedar box and as his eyes fell on the contents, he couldn't help but smile, his mouth curling into a devilish grin as he looked upon his secret weapon, the item that would make him invincible. With this relic, absolute control over the shogunate and the Chrysanthemum Throne were within his grasp; and with them, all of Japan.

Sheng and the group said goodbye to the old blind monk who chose to stay behind in peace and solitude, wishing him well as they set out from his father's mountain refuge and began the return trek to the dojo. The hour was still early and the position of the sun told them that they were still hours from midday. Their plan was to camp and rest briefly, but continue on through the night as long as Sheng could manage after only just so recently succumbing to the cold.

As they exited the cave, Taekori pulled Sheng to the side and together they headed over to a nearby ridge that allowed them to look east. The sky was clear and visibility was excellent, especially from the vantage point of a mountain. From here, they could see for miles. "Do you see that out there?" Taekori asked, pointing Sheng's attention to the distant city. "Do you know what that place is?"

"It is Kamakura," Sheng replied.

"Yes it is, Sheng. For all these years, I lived where I could keep a watchful eye over the man who stole everything from me. When I discovered that you still lived and that fate had put you in not only Kamakura, but in the very presence of my despised enemy, I had to reconsider my hate for the man. How could I love you the way you deserved if I was so consumed with my hate for Hasegawa?"

"I'm not sure I understand, father. Hasegawa is a traitor and as such, does he not deserve a traitor's death? After all, he destroyed our family, our village...and many, many others as well. If he is not stopped, he will destroy all of Japan with his lust for power."

"I agree with you, Sheng. But you must listen to what I tell you now for it may be the most important lesson I could ever share with you. The lust for revenge is not so different from the lust for power. In the end, revenge destroys both the one who did the wronging and the one who *was* wronged. Revenge will do more harm to you than your enemy. Instead, examine your motives, your thoughts regarding my one-time friend, Takeshi Hasegawa. Do you wish to see his end for your own sake or for the sake of all the others around you? There is a considerable difference between vengeance and justice, my son. You must know which reckoning you seek for Hasegawa. Justice defends the weak while vengeance soothes the ego. Vengeance breeds only a hunger for more vengeance, but justice seeks to set things right."

Sheng turned his gaze from the far off city of Kamakura and focused on his father. In his eyes, Sheng saw the real struggle his father had lived regarding vengeance and justice. His father's words were not simply a monologued philosophy, but a sincere knowledge hard won by defeating his own demons. And if Taekori could spare his son the pain of going through the same process he most certainly would. But a man's demons, like most experiences in life, are something no one can face for another, rather it is the individual's chance to prove his mettle.

Not another word was spoken as the two men rejoined the rest of the party in their descent down Fuji-san. Daisuke acted as a pack mule and carried not only his own gear but also that of Hayami and Sheng. Scar limped alongside Tatsuo as Taekori came alongside them. Kimiko took hold of Sheng's hand as they began the return to their improvised home. Sheng was thankful that Daisuke had so generously offered to carry his share of the supplies as he found his legs still a little weak even after days of rest. All he carried was the sword and his own burdened thoughts.

Takeshi Hasegawa sat alone in his hidden shack deep within the Kamakura dojo's grounds. The candles flickered, providing light in the dark room. He sat in front of the mirror, the ornate box resting on his lap. Again he whispered the soft words that would conjure the spirits. And just as before, he was anxious as he recited the summons. Suddenly, the room shook violently and the candles' light vanished.

"*Hasegawa*," the three spirits said in unison, a single voice then continuing, "have you brought us the relic?"

"I have it here," he replied. "My associates removed it from the possession of a man who lives in a distant kingdom they referred to as

France."

"That's interesting," the spirit replied. "The last I had heard it was in the possession of a man with similar interests as yourself, a European seeking wealth and power in the Holy Land."

"Yes," another voice added. "He is a well-travelled man full of ancient wisdom."

The third voice chimed in, "He must have given the relic to this *Frenchman* you speak of."

"Why would you say that?" Hasegawa wondered curiously.

"Because had your associates encountered the man we speak of, they would have never returned," the first spirit spoke again.

"Suppose my pirate friends murdered this man, took my prize from his corpse and returned with it to me?"

"No human can kill this man. He is immortal, like us."

"Just like us," the spirits said in unison.

"Now," the second spirit encouraged, "open the box. *Try it on.*"

Hasegawa slowly opened the lid and removed the neatly folded black cloth that was carried within the wooden reliquary. "It is so simple," he said, doubting what great power something so unassuming could possess, "how will this help me conquer Japan?"

"Put it on," the third spirit urged.

He unfolded the cloth and tried to determine the proper way one would wear such an item. The darkness only made the task more difficult. On what he decided must have been the front of the cloth, he found the only distinguishable feature: two small openings about an inch apart. His anxiousness peaked and his heart felt like it was ready to burst from his chest. It was now or never. Hasegawa inhaled three long and steady breathes, then pulled the black cloth down over his face. The openings, he realized, were the eyes of a mask. His head pounded with sudden, intense pain, and yet in the midst of the agonizing hurt, there was an instant and addictive pleasure as all the secrets of the world were suddenly known to him! The darkness was irrelevant and he could see as if the sun itself was shining from behind his eyes. Energy coursed through his body and as it did, Hasegawa beheld in the mirror the specter he had become. His eyes glowed intensely white as the spirits took hold of him and wailed like a shrieking wind before dissolving into a ghostly cloud of smoke which he inhaled, gasping as they entered. The spirits had become one with him.

Hasegawa threw his head back in hideous laughter, his voice a deep and contorted chorus of ghastly, haunting octaves as the spirits laughed from within their unwitting host. The pain subsided as he grew accustomed to their power and he suddenly felt invincible, that he could defy all the limitations of the natural world. He was certain that if he wished, he could take flight and leave the very earth beneath his feet behind. Ancient knowledge flooded his mind and he became aware of memories that were not his own, like the mask itself was alive and had been for a very long time. And then, all of a sudden, something felt *wrong*. Hasegawa's whole body went limp as he slid off of the chair and collapsed awkwardly to the floor, overcome by the spirits which had possessed him.

23

BEGINNING OF THE END

Sheng and his companions had returned safely to their hidden refuge in the woods. They were thankful that their trip from the mountain was free of any trouble – no bandits, no injuries, even the weather grew warmer in that time. It was what they discovered upon arriving at the dojo that caught them un-expecting. In only a matter of days, not even a week, the temple was swelling beyond capacity with unfamiliar faces. Dozens of strangers filled the courtyard, most huddled around small fires built to offer warmth. Children of all ages laughed and played, the dojo was alive with the promise of new life.

One of Tatsuo's scouts greeted them as they entered the courtyard. The man's eyes were full of worry as he welcomed them home.

"What is going on here?!" Sheng asked, knowing that the whole party certainly shared the same confusion.

"They are refugees, from surrounding villages!" the man replied. "They are all that is left after raiders destroyed their homes. Many people were lost in the attacks. Some of these children are now orphans and the onslaught made many widows."

"How did this happen?" Tatsuo pressed.

"There was no warning, no provocation," the scout explained. "The sieges all happened within hours of each other, but the villages were not nearby each other. They all lie in different directions."

"So this was coordinated," Scar decided. "There are no raider groups large enough to wipe out three villages at once. This was done by an army — Hasegawa's army!"

"It's been a long time since he's done something this brash," Taekori considered. "Why such a sudden, aggressive move?"

"Perhaps Hasegawa is finally ready to move against the emperor in force rather than in secret?" Daisuke offered as a justification.

"But the Shogunate would never allow these attacks and they would certainly put an end to his terror quickly if this is the case," Tatsuo reasoned.

"Now is not the time for this conversation," Kimiko interrupted. "Sheng should rest now that we are home *and* we have people in need of food and care. Hasegawa will be dealt with in time. For now, these refugees are our first priority."

There was no argument from the group. Kimiko was right. *Justice, not vengeance*, as Taekori had said. Tatsuo ordered out the hunters to go and bring back game. Hayami ensured the makeshift kitchen went to work preparing rice and breads as well. And in all this, Sheng found new purpose as the words of his father rang true in his mind. The very temple that had been repurposed to train a rebellion against Takeshi Hasegawa would now house the victims of his terrible plot. Justice, not vengeance.

Hasegawa, whether by blackmail or sheer terror, had managed to take control of the shogunate in Kamakura. The shikken secretly promised the allegiance of the *tokusō* and the shogun. Their agreement was made all the more effective as the shikken, like Hasegawa, was also Hōjō clan. And though Hasegawa did not assume power publically, his machinations were put into action indirectly as subversive rumors and lies spread throughout the shogunate, whispers meant to convince the formal military that the emperor in Kyoto was plotting against them in order to return the power of rule to the imperial court. This threatened an end to the reign of the Hōjō regency and the Kamakura shogunate, something that the tokusō feared and simply would not tolerate.

The new-found power unlocked by the mask emphasized the worst elements buried within Hasegawa's psyche. His actions had never been so brutal and his boldness had never been greater. Diplomacy was a thin veil that did little to hide his true motives, yet the loyalty of those in league with him never waned, most likely out of fear that they might become the next victim of his wrath.

What was stranger, Hasegawa seemed active at all times, tireless, never sleeping or resting. He pursued whatever he desired at that moment, his lust for anything and everything only fueled by the spirits that drove him mad. At times, he was heard talking to himself at great lengths as he stalked across the dojo grounds. Many of the students had witnessed this and questioned what was happening to the headmaster of the dojo. At the same time, he had never been so feared by his servants or the fellow sensei teaching at the school. His temper had grown all the more terrifying and his outbursts had become more intense and frequent. He seldom wore the mask in public, but always kept it with him and close at hand. At night, Hasegawa would lurk in the shadows, the mask pulled snugly over his face, his eyes two white orbs in the darkness. The spiritual world had been revealed to him and he could see all that existed between the dimensions of the physical and the supernatural. He had entered the realm of incarnate nightmares and he himself had become a living oni.

On this night, Takeshi Hasegawa stood atop the highest point of the dojo's steeply peaked, pagoda-styled guard tower. The glow of his eyes was rivalled only by the large, full moon that hung in the cloudless, star-laden sky. From there he could look down upon the whole city of Kamakura, and in any direction he pleased. The cold wind brought whispers to his ears as invisible spirits shared the inhabitants' deepest secrets. Nothing could be concealed from him because the yōkai saw everything. The power he now held was more than any one man deserved and he reveled in it.

The next several months passed with relative peace. Hasegawa had grown only more mysterious and secluded, so much in fact that the dojo buzzed with rumors that he had fallen severely ill. When he did venture into the ever-watching eyes of the public, he'd begun to wear the mask as a show for all to witness. A few of the more imaginative boys had many others convinced that his face must have become, in some way, deformed beyond recognition and that was why their sensei wore a mask at all times; to conceal his horrid appearance or battle scars. Regardless of the truth, Master Hasegawa's absence and curious behavior had not gone unnoticed.

Far beyond the reach of Hasegawa's spying yōkai, deep in the woods between Kyoto and Fuji-san, the temple haven had exploded in growth. Scar had overseen the expansion of the facility, putting the refugees to work alongside the band of warriors as trees were cleared and dormitories erected. Sheng, Tatsuo, and Daisuke saw to their training in armed combat as Hayami instructed them in archery and Kimiko shared her knowledge of ninjutsu and guerilla warfare. Taekori couldn't have been more proud of his son, but within him also grew a fear. He knew that with all that had happened, all that was going to happen, Hasegawa would have to be confronted. His skills in battle were not underestimated, nor was the danger of facing such a ruthless man, these facts ever-known and present in their discussions. Still, it was of little comfort as Taekori recognized that his son was the only one of them who stood any chance against the fearsome warrior. He also knew that Sheng was willing to sacrifice himself if it came to that, but Taekori was less sure he could live with allowing such a decision if the worst should come to pass.

This is not to say that Hasegawa was unaware of the secret dojo, nor the growing opposition to his dream of dominating all of Japan. Rather he tested the fledgling band of rebels. It had come to his attention that the raids he ordered on villages and small towns had been growing less successful. This is how he learned of his old friend's existence. Taekori had been a thorn in his side for a very long time. Hasegawa decided that he would see to Taekori's death himself. Word had been brought by one of his samurai captains: warriors bearing the banner of the Shimazu clan had been protecting the people. Outposts had been established throughout the land and their scouts were able to anticipate and bolster the fighting men of the villages. In return, the people pledged loyalty to the emperor and the shogunate's reputation suffered outside of the cloistered Kamakura. This put pressure on the feudal leadership to address Hasegawa's abuses and the insurrection that was certain to follow. The Shogunate recognized that the balance of power was necessary to maintain stability and military control over Japan. They did not want the emperor growing beyond a powerless title, but that was exactly what was happening. Still, none of this mattered to Hasegawa. All he wanted was more power. And because of his lust, he was growing more and more impatient as long as both the emperor and the shogunate remained in place.

Soon, Hasegawa would formally take control of the shogunate, or at least that was his plan. He would then command an army of more than a thousand samurai loyal to the shikken, this force in addition to his own army of hundreds of trained and fearsome warriors as well as a wako pirate fleet ready to answer his call. If it was war Taekori wanted, then Hasegawa was pleased to oblige. And in an unprecedented move, Hasegawa even managed to plant a spy amongst the refugees taken in by his enemies. Reports were always brief and highly ambiguous, as if written to a distant family member; but to this point, the spy had remained undiscovered which emboldened Hasegawa all the more.

What Master Hasegawa did not know was that the emperor and his advisors were also strengthening their forces and secretly recruiting wealthy daimyō to join the fight against the shogunate. And since the daimyō commanded a vast number of samurai, a possible alliance with Taekori and his army would greatly jeopardize Hasegawa's victory. But there would be no such union as the emperor had rejected Sheng's letter and refused to welcome him to his court, reasoning that his words were just another ruse to attempt assassination. The haughtiness of his council had made itself known by their advisements and they afforded the emperor no leeway for deliberation in this matter.

All of this was unknown to the majority of the people in Japan. Their lives went on day to day with little reason to question the authority that ruled their land. Unless Hasegawa's violence came to their homes, there were very few outside of Kamakura who had ever even heard of his name. And in that was possibly the greatest danger: a nameless threat gives little to fear and life goes on, inching ever-closer to destruction.

"Sheng," Scar smiled, calling the young leader into the armory within the hidden forest refuge.

"What is it, my friend," Sheng replied as he stepped into the space designated for weapon storage.

Scar stood at the table, a wooden crate in front of him. Straw had been displaced from within the container as the lid had been hastily removed. "This package just arrived from China – something special I wanted to try against Hasegawa's warriors." He reached out his hand towards Sheng, an oddly shaped, tube-like piece of metal resting in his palm.

Sheng took hold of the simple bronze device, an inquisitive smirk on his face. One end was open while the other end was closed. "What is it?" he asked curiously. "Is it a weapon? It seems too small to strike with...how would I use it?"

Scar, giddy as a school-aged boy, retrieved a simple leather sack from the crate as well as a small, but heavy, iron ball, "The Chinese call it a *huotong* or *gonne*. You'll like this. Come with me!"

The two men hurried away from the crowded main floor of the temple and out to the archery range. There, Scar had already prepared for the demonstration. A fire burned hotly within a small metal bowl, long and narrow metal rods extending beyond the bucket-like lip. With his tongue licking at the corner of his mouth, Scar happily opened the mouth of the leather pouch and took hold of the small bronze pipe. He poured a strange powdery granule into the open end, then winked at Sheng as he stuffed the iron ball into the throat of the device and tamped it down tightly with a short wooden dowel.

"What is all this about?" Sheng asked as he looked on excitedly.

"You'll know in a moment," Scar chuckled. "Now take hold of it, like this." Scar forcefully placed Sheng's hands into position on the outer tube, mindful to keep his fingers clear of the opening. After that, he ensured that the device was indexed so that a small hole was visible on the top rear and then pointed Sheng's arms in the direction of a well-used hay target that had been tied in such a way as to imitate the shape of a man, clear marks where arrows had punctured its chest. Satisfied he was in a proper position, Scar wrapped his fingers in cloth and took hold of one of the metal rods that had been heated in the fire, the tip glowing red. "Now don't let go," he advised, touching the red-hot tip of the rod to the hole in the tube.

There was a momentary pause and then... ***BANG!***

Thick gray smoke poured from the mouth of the device as Sheng stood in both awe and panic. Scar laughed heartily at Sheng's surprised response. His young friend had reacted just as he'd expected! The moment was all the more entertaining to Scar as the people who had packed the makeshift dojo were now out in the courtyard, just as surprised and panicked as Sheng, all searching for the source of the bizarre sound.

The smoke cleared and Sheng spotted the smoldering hole left by the iron ball, dead-center in the target's head, as it had penetrated the tightly packed hay dummy. "*WHAT IS THIS THING??!!*" Sheng roared, his hands shaking as he quickly gave the device back to Scar.

"It's a hand cannon!" Scar smiled. "I procured a dozen of them."

They stood looking at the hay target, one man pleased and the other terrified. Sheng couldn't believe what he had just witnessed.

"I also learned of something called a *fa chu* in the market and had some brought back from Kyoto by messenger along with the gonnes, powder, and iron projectiles," Scar explained, holding up a small, inch-long stick infused with a strongly odorous scent for Sheng to see. "Watch what this can do!"

Scar produced a small piece of paper no larger than five inches square from a fold in his robe and laid it out on the table to their left that normally held archery supplies while the fighters trained. He then sprinkled a very small amount of the powder for the gonne into the center of the paper, readied an oil-soaked wick, and then wrapped it up into a ball, tying it securely closed with the remnant of protruding lamp wick.

"Now normally, I would have packed a handful of iron balls in with the powder," Scar said, "but for the sake of demonstration, I felt it wise to leave them out."

He touched the odd-smelling stick against the licking fire in the container and it immediately burst into a brilliant flame. Scar then used the fa chu to ignite the wick on the palm-sized paper ball. Quickly, he tossed the sphere at the man-shaped target, striking it in the would-be belly. Nothing happened as it dropped to the ground without effect; but a moment later, there was a sudden hiss followed by an even larger explosion than the gonne. So large, in fact, that the hay target caught fire!

"Imagine if that had projectiles in it!" Scar grinned. "Iron balls, sharply ground stones, even obsidian shards...they would be devastating within the area of detonation."

"Possibly too devastating," Sheng replied. "It seems a vulgar way to engage a foe. Where is the honor in *these weapons*? I would rather fight Master Hasegawa face to face than strike with magic fire."

"It is no magic, my son," Taekori said from behind them. "Believe that Hasegawa will use anything he can to his advantage. These are the tools of the future. We would be wise to learn to use them to their full potential."

"In time, perhaps," Sheng mused.

"I hate to interrupt," Tatsuo ventured, appearing seemingly out of nowhere. "But the time has come to speak with our captains and determine a course of action against Hasegawa. They wait for us in the temple."

"You three go on ahead," Scar said, turning his attention back to the burning target. "I'll make sure this fire is put out. I'll join you in a moment."

As soon as the three men had gone out of earshot, Scar looked into the shadows on the nearby bushes. A man, his eyes reflecting the firelight, stepped into view.

"How did you know I was there?" the man asked the old gardener.

"You were not that well-hidden, even for my old eyes, *spy*!"

"I'm no spy," he replied coolly.

"Come now. No lies! You didn't think I would recognize a spy when I see one?" Scar snorted. "I lived for nearly a decade as a spy in the emperor's court; and before that, a spy for Taekori in Hasegawa's own dojo. You don't walk like a villager, you don't speak like a villager…you are trained and dangerous."

"Fair enough, old man. What now? Will you kill me now that you know I am here?" he asked.

"You're unarmed," Scar replied, "so I won't be killing you, at least not yet. I'll let you live, but you have to leave. I want you to go tell your master what you have seen here, go tell him that we will be coming for him and he will pay for his atrocities!"

"Tell him yourself," the spy grinned mischievously, his eyes looking beyond the old man.

Confused, Scar quickly turned, finding himself face-to-face with a man whose identity was hidden behind a black mask, his eyes glowing eerily with supernatural power. Before Scar could react, everything went dark. Hasegawa and the spy left Scar lying unconscious on the ground in front of the target, the flames growing brighter as the dry straw crackled and burned.

The two then hurried up the stairs to the temple and pushed their way through the crowd of people as they searched for Sheng and Taekori. They did not have to look long as they found the father and son amidst a circle of very capable men and women who all appeared to be gathered for a meeting. The disturbance had been noticed as voices stopped and all eyes looked towards the intruders, uncertain of what was happening, taken aback by the appearance of a stranger in mask.

"Taekori," Hasegawa shouted as he pulled his sword from its sheath, "where are you?!"

"What is the meaning of this?" Tatsuo spat back before anyone else could reply. "Who are you?"

"I remember you, the *younger* Subaru," Hasegawa laughed. "You ran away from the Kamakura dojo when you were not yet a man. I heard you *found* your father, that must have gone well. Pity he ended up dead – he was one of my most loyal men."

"*HASEGAWA*?!" Tatsuo cried out.

"In the flesh," he replied.

There was little time to mount a defense. The people at the temple were caught unaware and unprepared. No one was armed, though racks of weapons were close by. Because of this, no one made any sudden moves, but it was obvious that their thoughts turned to fighting: Hasegawa could see it in their eyes.

"I came for Taekori and his son, that is all. No one else need die tonight."

Two brave men stepped forward, blocking Hasegawa's view of a table that was the center of the group's attention as they met, a table covered in maps and books. "If you have come for our leaders, then you will have to go through us first," one of the men threatened, his fists clenched menacingly as he took a fighting stance.

"Really?" Hasegawa laughed, amused at the show. He struck out with two quick, bloody slashes of his blade, sending both men reeling to the floor. "If you insist." Hasegawa readied to kill more men as he watched the anger in the room boil on all of their faces.

"Enough, Takeshi Hasegawa," Taekori said, stepping forth. "You needn't kill anymore. You did not come for them. Strike me down and leave the rest in peace to grieve the fallen."

"Where is your son, the traitor with the *Chinese* name...where is *Sheng*?!"

There was a commotion from behind the wall of people and then Sheng leapt from between them, a sword in hand, the blade razor sharp, "You will not take my father's life nor any others on this night, *sensei*. You will pay for what you've done to so many, for what you did to my mother!" Sheng lunged forward, swinging the mystical sword given to him by his father in great, sweeping arcs, the steel katana singing as its razor sharp blade cut through the crisp evening air.

"At last," Hasegawa sighed, delighted with the opportunity to kill his betrayer.

With a resounding clang, their swords met, Hasegawa deflecting Sheng's masterful strike. The onlookers stepped back as far as they could, allowing a space for the two adversaries to fight. "Arm yourselves, *NOW!*" Taekori ordered to his best men. Suke-chan and Tatsuo had already done so and had taken the spy by surprise, leaving him unconscious as they watched for an opportunity to jump in and overcome their foe.

Hasegawa was faster than they had ever seen him, showing no signs of slowing with age. He fought like a young man, athletic and powerful, his prowess secretly imbued by the spirits and the mask. Thankfully, Sheng too was nimble and deft, sidestepping, parrying, and striking again with articulate precision as he searched for a weakness in his enemy's form.

Again and again, their blades met, neither man gaining an advantage over the other. Sheng, though, showed signs of fatigue. However, Hasegawa never slowed. In fact he seemed to be toying with Sheng as they battled. This arrogance was the weakness that Sheng had searched for and he would use it to his advantage. Sheng used his strikes now, not as an offensive, but as a strategized movement of steps each one luring Hasegawa into the position Sheng desired.

Finally, Hasegawa was right where Sheng wanted him, his blade pointed downward after glancing Sheng's blow, his shoulders and hips aimed in opposite directions in an awkward stance. This was the time to strike! Sheng's sword never stopped moving, but sliced cleanly, slashing Hasegawa across the face. A horrid screech filled the room as the warlord stepped backwards in shock. Sheng looked at the tip of the blade, expecting blood, but finding a black, oily substance that stained the edge, the sword's blade absorbing the muck in an artfully beautiful yet unpredictable swirl like ink mixing with water. As the blade took on the blackness, so did Sheng's heart. Hate raged inside of him.

Hasegawa gasped, the blade having slashed across his mouth, cutting his cheeks, the mask gaping open at the mouth displaying the gruesome wound beneath. He could taste the blood, feel it dripping down onto his black, hooded robes. For the first time in months, ever since the spirits had entered him, he felt fear. Quickly, he pulled a throwing dagger from the sash worn around his waist and sent it whistling through the air. At the same time, he smashed a smoke pellet against the stone floor and disappeared within the gray cloud that engulfed him.

"*NO!!!*" Sheng screamed as the smoke cleared.

In the chaos, Hasegawa's dagger had found its mark. Taekori lay on the floor, the small double-edged blade lodged between his ribs. His breaths were shallow and strenuous as Sheng dropped at his side.

"Father," Sheng cried, "can you hear me?"

"I'm here, my son," Taekori wheezed laboriously, coughing on blood.

"Do not leave me, Father. You can't leave me!"

Taekori coughed again. "I will never leave you," he assured.

"I will avenge you," Sheng promised.

"Justice, not vengeance," Taekori whispered as his eyes slowly closed.

Sheng sobbed and moaned woefully as he took hold of his father's hand. He stared at the blood soaked patch on the right breast of Taekori's robe, the dagger firmly planted in his chest. A tear had gathered in the corner of his father's eye. Sheng watched as it trickled down his cheek and into his beard. Kimiko had joined Sheng, her arms wrapped tightly around him, her cheek on his shoulder as her tears wet his karate gi.

"Where is Scar?!" Sheng barked, demanding the attention of all in the dojo.

"I last saw him outside," Tatsuo said, suddenly realizing that Scar had never rejoined them. "I'll go look for him."

"Go now!" Sheng growled angrily. "Find him and prepare the army. We march for Kamakura!"

24

WOUNDS & WAR

"Fetch the physician!" Hasegawa snarled at a passing servant, his words slurred because of the wound stretching across his face. Carefully, he pulled the blood-soaked mask off of his head and angrily threw it down on his desk, small splatters splashing form the impact. The startled man quickly left, afraid that he might become an inadvertent target.

"I thought you said I was invincible?!" he spoke aloud. "But now look at this, look at my face. The boy could have killed me while I toyed with him like it was a game!"

There was no audible response in the empty room.

"But I don't understand?" Hasegawa continued. "If that mask is my protection, then how did a simple sword do this. You promised me power!"

Still, he spoke as if to no one.

"Trust you...*trust you?* How can I trust you? You ask me to do these things in your name when the glory should be mine. You want me to put my life in your hands, yet you allowed *this* to happen."

The servant returned with the physician, interrupting Hasegawa's seemingly one-sided conversation as they entered through the door into his study. Both men struggled to hide their reactions as they looked upon the gruesomeness of his wound.

"Drink this quickly," the doctor said as he handed Hasegawa a cup filled to the brim with rice wine. "It will dull your pain."

Hasegawa took the drink and sent the ceramic cup smashing against the wall. "Just fix my face," he growled.

With nervous hesitation, the physician unrolled a long strip of cloth, assorted medical tools contained within. He set about meticulously cleaning the cuts in Hasegawa's face in an effort to lower the risk of infection, applying homeopathic salves as he worked. Soon, he began suturing closed the gashes that stretched from each corner of his mouth. All the while, Hasegawa sat deathly still, as if in a trance, never once flinching in pain. Finally, the physician finished. He looked down at his shaking, bloodied hands, then up at the face he so feared. If he had done a poor job, or Hasegawa did not heal satisfactorily, then certainly he would be blamed. And, having seen many of the bodies left in the wake of the master's wrath, he knew he would certainly join them in their death.

Hasegawa's face was swollen from the horrid trauma, his cheeks bulbous and inflamed. He looked as if he was smiling, catgut sutures stitching his face together in an awkward, permanent grin – certainly a horrid sight to behold. The doctor and servant were dismissed and Hasegawa gazed upon himself in a silver handheld mirror. Tears welled in his eyes as he realized that the monster he had become on the inside was now visible outwardly for the whole world to see.

Poor Master Takeshi Hasegawa, a voice whispered in his head. *Children will cry when they see you.*

Yes, another spirit spoke from within, *now you have no choice but to wear the mask.*

"The mask is torn, damaged by Sheng's cursed blade," Hasegawa replied. "It is of no use to me now."

It can be fixed, the voice said.

Just like your face, the third yōkai mocked. *You know what to do.*

"Shut up! Get out of my head!"

247

Hasegawa finally had enough of the pain. He poured himself a cup of rice wine from the pitcher on his desk and quickly gulped it down, following that cup with another and then another until the jug was empty. Soon the room moved even when Hasegawa was standing still. However, his pain had greatly subsided as the alcohol numbed his senses. The only problem now was that the spirits' voices in his head had become incoherent, a multitudinous chorus of whispers and growls, none of which was distinguishable, just a chaotic, raucous pulsing in his mind.

He staggered into the hallway, the bloody mask clenched in his fist as he took hold of the first, startled servant he could find. The girl let out a squeal, quickly covering her mouth to muffle the sound as she looked upon the master's face.

"Didn't the physician do a lovely job?" Hasegawa chuckled in his stupor. She did not reply, only nodded as he continued, the smell of alcohol permeating from behind his lips. "Who mends the clothing at the dojo? When something is torn or in need of repair, who fixes such things? Tell me, girl."

"I...I can take you to her," the servant girl stammered. "This way, Master."

She led him through the halls and down to the service quarters beyond the kitchens. Here, the passages grew narrower and the rooms smaller. Many years had passed since Hasegawa last visited this part of the fortress. The man who had cared for all who lived inside the walls of his compound was long forgotten, terror now followed in his wake. On the left and to the right, men, women, and their children ducked into their small living spaces as they saw their master coming, all praying he would not linger long.

The girl finally stopped next to a room and peered around the doorway as they neared the end of the hall, "She is here, Master Hasegawa." The girl bowed and then hurried away as he passed her and entered the claustrophobic quarters.

One wall of the small room was lined with stout, wooden shelving, each plank holding neatly folded and stacked piles of assorted fabrics in a variety of hand-dyed colors as well as many beautiful silks and furs. Lastly was a shelf filled with the various tools required for a seamstress to practice her craft; items like shears, measuring devices, and a collection of bone and steel needles. The woman who did the work was very old, her face wrinkled and sagging, her fingers arthritic and crippled. Her apprentice sat at her side, young and hopeful, happy to learn the trade.

"It is the most esteemed master of the dojo come to visit, *hiiobaa-chan*," the young girl said addressing her *great-grandmother* and announcing his entrance.

Hasegawa stood before them, blood dried on his neck, chest, and robes, his movements slowed by the alcohol. "She is nearly blind with age, Master Hasegawa, but she does great work," the girl said with a sweet smile. "How may she help you?"

"I have come for supplies," he explained. "I wish to repair something very...*personal*."

The girl looked at his fist, the wrinkled up cloth catching her eye, "Let her take care of it for you, Master. She will do an exce..."

"No," Hasegawa said curtly. "I will do it myself. Just give me what I need and I will be off."

"Yes, Master. Then tell me what you require."

"A needle and heavy thread," he replied.

She stood from her place next to her great-grandmother and retrieved a sharp, steel needle from amongst the supplies and then found a small spool of rope-like twine that she hoped would be satisfactory. "Will this do?" she asked, handing the items to Hasegawa.

"I believe so," he said, looking at the course thread in his open palm before closing his fist. "Tell no one what was discussed here. Do not speak of why I came to your great-grandmother."

Hasegawa left them and returned through the many hallways and stairwells to his room, stopping in the kitchen and demanding another jug of rice wine on his way. He sat down at his desk and poured another full cup, drinking it straight down before starting the task of mending the mask which rested in a ball in front of him. Hasegawa straightened it out and stared at the gaping slit across the face of the mask, the cloth split from ear to ear. Another drink and he attempted to thread the twine through the slender eye of the needle. With great difficulty, he finally managed the feat and then set to task, closing the tear with a haphazard, drunken array of stitches.

Once finished, Hasegawa held the mask up to inspect his handiwork, the stitching forming an evil-looking, mischievous grin from ear-to-ear. There was something pleasing to him in the whimsical nature of the pattern-less non-uniformity of the strands that secured the mouth shut. The repair lacked the professional quality the old seamstress may have provided, but he didn't care. If anything, he decided, the hauntingly bizarre mask would terrify his enemies. That grin was the last thing he wanted Sheng to see; payback for his now-disfigured face.

Much better, one of the three yōkai spoke inside of Hasegawa's mind as it admired the unexpected upgrade to the mask.

Indeed, another spirit said. *I think it captures our essence quite nicely.*

The three spirits laughed inside of Hasegawa's head, his own thoughts hard to separate from the whispers of the yōkai. With great pride, he took the repaired mask and stretched it down over his face, the stitched smile on its façade mirroring the scarred atrociousness beneath. Hasegawa, too, joined in with the laughter of the spirits that possessed him, his sinister cackle echoing throughout the halls and carrying across the dojo grounds. Gone was his pain; and with it, the fear and doubt created by Sheng. Soon he would take revenge on his treasonous student, then all of Japan would be his.

Several hours had passed since Sheng's grief had turned to hope. As Taekori's motionless body had laid sprawled on the floor, Sheng had been so distraught that he failed to realize his father's chest still moved with life, if only just a little. His lungs, though weak and failing, still drew breath. Hayami had realized this and pointed the fact out to Sheng – his father lived!

They managed to carefully move his body to a bed and then went to work on his wound. Taekori had lost a significant amount of blood and they lacked a person formally trained in medicine, but many an injury had been dressed by the warriors who had seen bloody fields of battle. Scar in particular had much experience, but he occupied the bed next to his old friend and was of no help thanks to Hasegawa, the lump on his head throbbing where he was struck. Kimiko had dealt with many wounds sustained by the girls in the underground thieves guild of Kyoto. There, she also treated women of questionable repute whose profession had naturally put them in the company of abusive men. Stabbings were not unusual for the capital city's sordid secret side.

Kimiko had carefully removed the throwing dagger from the wound in Taekori's chest, trying not to graze his ribs as she slowly extracted it from between the bones. Thankfully the wound was clean and easily closed. The tip of the blade, she feared, may have punctured his lung, but as she listened with her ear to his chest, she heard no tell-tale indicators of fluid collecting nor irregularity in his breathing. In fact, he seemed to be breathing much easier now that the blade had been removed. Kimiko had also suspected that Hasegawa might have laced the dagger with poison, but Sheng's father wasn't fevered and seemed to rest peacefully now in spite of his injury. She carefully double checked her sutures before applying salve to the area and then covering the site with a clean linen bandage. "Sleep well," she whispered, patting him gently on the arm before standing.

"I believe your father will recover to the fullest," Kimiko said to Sheng in a hushed voice as she washed Taekori's blood from her hands in a water-filled, brass basin. "The wound was not as bad as I had expected. Clearly Hasegawa did not visit us with the intention of killing anyone. Otherwise, our losses would have certainly been greater and he would have brought along samurai to aid him."

"Thank you for caring for my father," Sheng replied, standing behind her, his hands on her hips. As he contemplated her words, he gently kissed her on her bare shoulder.

"Of course," she smiled, turning to face him, her body pressed between the stand of the washbasin and Sheng. "You are my family now. Your father has become my father. I care very deeply for both of you."

She ran her hands up his chest and then wrapped her arms around his neck, her soft lips meeting his. They stood kissing, their hearts racing as they held onto one another. If only they could stay like this forever.

"Sheng!" Daisuki shouted excitedly as he raced into the room.

Kimiko, her skin flushed, looked away from Sheng, her finger raised to her smiling mouth as she shushed their large friend, "Be mindful of the people resting in here."

"I'm sorry," he whispered in reply, still louder than Kimiko would have liked. "But the tree, Sheng, the tree is blossoming!"

"Come with me," Sheng smiled at Kimiko, taking her by the hand as he hurried out of the quiet room, leaving his father to recover.

They hurried down to the garden. Scar had done well to maintain the peaceful space, his past as a gardener a welcome reminder that even a warrior can find serenity. There, upon their return from Fuji-san, Sheng had found a small cherry sapling and carefully grafted in the delicate branch from his mother's tree that grew up within the mountain. His prayers had been answered as, with the arrival of spring, small buds sprouted on the foreign branch. He'd managed to bring a small piece of his mother back with him and seeing the successful new life grow gave him great hope.

"She is still with me," Sheng smiled, gently touching the small branch.

Kimiko squeezed his hand tightly, happy to see him smiling. "This is how she would want to see you," Kimiko said. "Your mother would not want you to be consumed with war and revenge."

"I know," Sheng replied. "She would want me to marry and start a family. I think she would be happy we're together."

"She would," Kimiko agreed, resting her head against his shoulder. "But you're also just like your father. War is in your blood. You're brave, same as Taekori. She'd also be proud of that, proud of the honorable man you've become – I know my parents would be as well. "

Daisuke, joined by Hayami, loved seeing his best friends together and couldn't be happier for them. Had he been told ten years ago that this is where life would take them, he could never have imagined such happiness. So much had changed, yet everything felt *right*, like they were exactly where they needed to be. Fate had brought them to this point and, with good fortune, Hasegawa, the Kamakura dojo – their past – could be put behind them, allowing them to live in peace.

"What will we do when this is all over?" Daisuke asked, slapping Sheng on the back with his large, meaty palm. "Will we return to Kamakura? Or maybe start anew in Kyoto?"

Sheng's gaze lingered on the hope-bringing branch. "I want to start a new village from the community that has sprung up here at the temple. There, we can work the land – harvest, survive – have children and grow old."

"Farmers, huh?" Suke-chan chuckled. "I guess I can live with that."

"When this fight is over," Sheng continued, "I never want to take up a sword again. My whole life, it seems, has been a preparation for battle. My hands have spilled enough blood in Hasegawa's name. I realize now that we – I – accepted a life that was a lie and rationalized his demands as being for the *greater good*. I may never atone for what I've done, but I can try."

"But think too of all the students you helped as they transitioned into their new lives at the dojo…small, scared boys, not unlike us when we first arrived in Kamakura. Your own experiences gave you compassion for them and you were an encouragement to them when they needed it the most," Suke-chan said as a reminder. "Not all that you did under Hasegawa's command was evil."

"But I looked the other way," Sheng frowned. "I knew full well what Master Hasegawa was doing and I never once spoke of it, never questioned his actions. I may as well have taken those boys and murdered their families myself. Inaction, at times, can be as dangerous as action."

Daisuke looked long and hard at his best friend, knowing his words, obviously carried as a burden, were true. "Hasegawa will never harm another child, never destroy another family," he said to Sheng, "not after we're done with him. Let's go find Tatsuo. The time has come to finalize our plan. We must prepare to strike.

Sheng nodded in agreement, never looking away from the budding tree, Kimiko still at his side, "Strike we will. His terror has reached its end."

Tatsuo stood leaning over a table in the armory area of the temple, his palms flat on the wooden surface, a large map stretching from one side of the table to the other. Small wooden totems had been carved and then crudely hand painted: black for Hasegawa's men, white for the resistance warriors, and red for the fighters in the outlying supportive villages. Sheng studied the positions of the figures. Their spies had reported small outposts and encampments of Hasegawa's soldiers throughout the greater region, each of these assigned one of the black markers. The positions were mostly in the open and guarded paths of transit, often times positioned so as to allow quick raids on nearby villages. The remaining black figurines stood clustered in the area of Kamakura with a focus at the city's main gate and of course the dojo itself. The greatest presence, and threat, of Hasegawa's army would be readied to defend him there. From previous discussions involving Scar and Taekori, they all agreed that the outposts should be the first to fall. This would eliminate the certain wave of reinforcements at the dojo and would ensure protection of the villages if the outposts were controlled by the resistance.

"How do you suppose we deal with the outposts?" Tatsuo asked, his friends all gathered around the table.

Hayami was first to answer. "The spies said there was no more than a dozen men at each outpost. There are eight in this area and five more on the main road to Kyoto," she explained, pointing at the map. "We needn't supply all the warriors from our own ranks. Of the liberated villages, how many have ready, fighting men?"

"Some of the villages would be more prepared than others; but even in the weakest villages, there would be close to eighteen men ready to fight," Tatsuo replied.

"Then I suggest we send only one of our warriors to each village," Hayami continued, moving a white figure into each of the clusters of red carvings on the map. "Then we are down only thirteen fighters, but they can operate as a captain and ensure that the people are organized by implementing a proper strategy. If two villages with two captains unite and strike a nearby outpost, they'll surely outnumber Hasegawa's men and can easily take the camp. From there, they can move on and join with the next group, leaving some behind to maintain the post and communicate via scouts. This allows us to then move on the dojo in Kamakura with those who have joined us here."

"That's an excellent plan, Hayami, but I fear we will need every warrior we have to take the dojo in Kamakura," Sheng said. "If we had more men, then we could put your idea into action."

Kimiko spoke up, "I wasn't sure when to tell you this, but now seems the right time. The mistress Shiroi Usagi, in Kyoto, has sworn her allegiance to our cause. She can supply the additional fighters needed. I need only tell her where and when. Her girls will do the rest."

"Girls?!" Tatsuo laughed. "What good are girls against armored samurai?"

"They make up for in speed and skill what they lack in brute strength and male-stupidity," Kimiko replied with a wink. "They are highly trained in the art of ninjutsu and fiercely loyal. They will not let us down."

"The thieves guild will work with us?" Sheng questioned, attempting to steer the conversation back on course. "What does Usagi get out of this? How does this benefit her?"

"A free Japan is her greatest concern," explained Kimiko. "If

Hasegawa is not stopped, then he will surely move against the emperor. It is not a matter of *if*, but *when*! War will come to Kyoto; and with it, death and destruction. She cares deeply for the girls – orphans – who find harbor within the underground, girls that are hopeless and lost, girls like me. Kyoto must remain as it is and Usagi knows that is worth fighting for, even dying for!"

"What do you think, Suke-chan?" Sheng asked his oldest friend.

"Well," he paused, thinking it over, "If these girls fight half as good as Hayami and Kimiko do, then it would be an honor to be in their company. Ninja from the thieves guild would be a welcome addition, at least *I* think so."

"Tatsuo. What do you say?" Sheng wondered.

"I think securing the roads and supporting the villages is not only strategically important, but it proves to the people that we are on their side. We will see only increased support against Hasegawa. If Kimiko trusts the mistress Usagi, then so do I."

Sheng nodded in agreement. "Right then," he continued. "Here's what I'm thinking...let's send a capable leader to each village as Hayami has suggested. At the same time, we send word via a messenger to the thieves guild in Kyoto. We'll tell them to meet us in Kamakura in three days. There's an abandoned warehouse near the harbor that was partially rebuilt after the earthquake: that will be our meeting place . Time is of the essence so as soon as we are done here, Kimiko, send a rider to Kyoto with a letter detailing our strategy for Usagi. We'll send our fighters on ahead in small groups. They'll leave several hours apart and travel by different paths so as not to appear like an army. They can utilize horse carts to carry weapons, armor, and supplies, while appearing as merchants to any strangers that may come upon them on the roads. The five of us will follow last. We can't risk being seen in the vicinity of the city till we are ready to strike."

"What about Scar, and your father?" Hayami asked.

"We'll leave them here to rest and recuperate," Sheng reasoned in response. "Their time for war has passed. This is our fight now. I will not risk losing my father now, especially in his weakened state. We'll leave a few people behind to care for them and maintain the daily routine of the refuge."

"And once in Kamakura," Tatsuo wondered, "what do we do then? The gate to the dojo is strong and they will surely not open it to us willingly."

"I've been thinking about that," Sheng answered. "Once we have all gathered at the old warehouse, we will eat, rest, and arm ourselves. That following night, we do three things. First, our army of samurai...we will send them out in full force against Hasegawa's unsuspecting guards. Their goal is to take the city of Kamakura and eliminate reinforcements from reaching the dojo. Second, our ninja...Hayami and Kimiko, there is a secret tunnel that leads into the dojo grounds from outside its walls. In the chaos created by the warring in the streets, you two will have easy access to the tunnel, allowing the ninja to quietly enter the garden and wait for the right moment."

"How will we know it's the right time? Will you have some sort of signal?" Kimiko asked.

"That's the third move," Sheng grinned. "You'll know it's time when you see and hear the certain confusion we'll create."

"And how will you do that?" Hayami smirked.

"Tatsuo, Daisuke, and I are going to walk right up to the front gate and surrender to Master Hasegawa."

"*WHAT?!*" Suke-chan and Tatsuo exclaimed at the same time.

"That's right," Sheng nodded. "We're going to surrender. This will attract the most attention away from Hayami and Kimiko, giving their ninja the greatest opportunity to find offensive positions. All the students and masters will be watching and the guards will all swarm to our position, leaving their posts empty. Most importantly, it draws Hasegawa directly into the open. He'll come to us. The masters all know the truth. Everyone within the walls of the dojo lives in fear of Hasegawa. With luck, they'll follow us when they see we stand against his evil and will join our side. They're just waiting for someone to free them from his insanity."

"And you think this will work?" Tatsuo mused somewhat doubtfully, rubbing his chin as he considered the boldness of the plan.

"I *know* it will work," a voice spoke from outside their circle. It was Taekori! He'd woken and managed his way, albeit painfully, to the main hall. "Takeshi Hasegawa is blinded by his pride, has been for many years. You can use that as a weapon against him. The man will not refuse your surrender. He will revel in it. The greater the spectacle, the greater his ego will grow. That is how you struck him before. Hasegawa let his guard down and took you for granted. Just know that he will be less likely to make the same mistake a second time."

"That's it then," Sheng decided, energized by the approval of his father. "Everyone make ready. Daisuke and Hayami, begin prepping the supplies and loading the carts. Tatsuo, prepare the men who will head to the villages and stress the importance of taking the outposts quickly and without detection. Kimiko, send a rider to Kyoto. After that, we eat and rest – tomorrow we move on Kamakura."

25

INTO DARKNESS

Night passed quickly. Sheng slept very little, his thoughts restless, his heart heavy with the burden of looming death that would certainly follow the coming conflict. The plan was sound and they had the numbers to put Hasegawa's army to the test; but, he knew that the faces he'd seen every day, the friendships he'd built over the last several months of intense training at the hidden temple: many of these men and women would not make the return trip from Kamakura. They would fall in battle, fighting for the future of Japan – an honor to be sure – but their names would be forgotten to time, their stories lost if ever told at all. He'd spent all night thinking over these things. When the chirping and merriment of birds, a stark contrast to his brooding and contemplative mood, announced the early arrival of dawn, Sheng surrendered to the fact that rest was out of reach and reluctantly chose to leave his bed behind. He wrapped his robe around himself and tightly tied the belt, trying to be as quiet as possible. Kimiko stirred as he left the room, but she had apparently found sleep more attainable and never woke.

Sheng headed down to the main floor of the temple. He wanted to look over the map while he could still be alone, the bustle of the day not yet underway. The pleasing smell of food wafted from the kitchen, the cooks seeming to be the only other people in the refuge awake at such an early hour. They had provisions to divvy as they prepared rations for each man and woman who would valiantly march on the road to war. From the bravest swordsman to the lowly stable boy who cleaned up after the animals, every person at the dojo was important and Sheng recognized this. He was thankful for each and every one of them who had joined in the cause.

He entered the weapons area where the map still rested flat on the table, the wooden figures outlining their planned positions and movements. But he would not be alone. Taekori sat on the floor with his legs crossed, a black cloth laid out in front of him. The katana used to slash Hasegawa rested across his lap as he intently studied the weapon. The blade was stained black at its point. No matter how hard Taekori had rubbed and cleaned the stain, the discoloration remained – a blemish in the steel. He'd never seen blood do anything like this to a sword, especially one as well-crafted as this sacred heirloom.

"What is it, father?" Sheng asked, taking a place on the floor next to Taekori. "What happened to the blade?"

"I honestly have no idea," he replied. "Fresh blood wipes clean from the most meager of swords. Rusting and pitting takes many years, especially a tainting like this. I just have no clue."

The men – father and son – studied the weapon. There was no explanation and the longer they stared at the blade, the more worrisome it became.

"Do you suppose whatever happened weakened the steel?" Sheng wondered.

"On the contrary," Taekori replied thoughtfully. "As I hold the blade, I feel a strange energy coursing through me. I feel stronger. The pain from my wound diminishes. The blade, too, seems different: lighter, faster, more...*lethal*. And oddly enough, I feel more deadly as well. I long for the battlefield as I hold this sword in my hands – it's like I'm a young again, this old man you see before you fading away."

"That's incredible!" Sheng mused.

"Indeed! I feel like I could fight Takeshi Hasegawa's entire army myself."

"Let me have a look," Sheng said, holding out his hands to receive the weapon from his father.

Taekori winced as he passed the blade to his son, the pain in his chest once again a reality and a stark reminder of what power the curious sword must possess. Sheng felt the energy his father spoke of immediately as the hair on his arms and the back of his neck tingled, standing up on end. The effect, Sheng realized, was much like gorging oneself on food to the point of bursting, yet never feeling full, always wanting more. The longer he held the sword and experienced its strange power, the more power he wanted.

Sheng's father, resigned once more to the reality of his condition and spoke, "I have never used this blade in battle. Our family has maintained its secrecy for centuries, yet I believe you may be the first of us to actually wield it against an enemy. There is certainly danger inherent in the blade and so it must not be considered lightly. Each strike of the blade bears a cost. I'm uncertain of who pays more: the one struck or the one who strikes. Please remember this as you face Hasegawa. Perhaps this blade should be your last resort?"

"I will think on this, father."

"I trust you will," Taekori smiled. "You have greatly impressed me, Sheng. As I have watched you in this short time, the way you treat all who follow your leadership with respect, the way you love Kimiko…you have made me proud. Your mother would most certainly be pleased with you too. I wish you and Kimiko all the best. She will be a wonderful daughter-in-law."

"Thank you, father," Sheng nodded. "Kimiko is definitely special and I could not imagine life without her now that we have been reunited. We plan to perform an official ceremony when we return from Kamakura. For now, my focus – *our focus* – is on defeating Hasegawa."

"Well spoken, son."

Taekori and Sheng sat together in silence till the excitement of the new day began to surround them. The temple was wide awake, organizing and finalizing preparations for the war march. The scene was impressive to be sure. Scar had finally woken from his long sleep, a result from being struck in the head on the night that Hasegawa *visited* the hidden dojo. He now stood alongside Taekori and the two old friends watched in awe at the rag-tag army that had assembled in answer to the call to fight. The men and women, all onetime farmers, peasants, refugees, and the like, readied for war, the weapon racks in the temple all but empty as they armed themselves with the tools that had been the focus of their intense training and preparation.

Sheng and Tatsuo spoke with the thirteen captains who would leave for the villages and organize strikes on Hasegawa's outposts. Tatsuo hated sending some of their best fighting men off in opposite directions, yet he knew the strategy of securing the roads. Stopping reinforcements from heading to Kamakura was of the utmost importance. The men acknowledged their orders, then mounted their horses and headed out.

Kimiko had sent word to Shiroi Usagi of the Kyoto thieves guild via messenger the night before. Her ninja would be in route to Kamakura by the day's end.

Daisuke and Hayami ensured that each group was packed, their accompanying carts filled with the necessary rations and supplies to make the journey to Kamakura. Their armor was well hidden, as were their weapons, woven tarps tied down to secure the cargo beneath. To any passerby, they appeared to be travelling merchants. Upon double checking the last cart, the rebel army set out for Kamakura, leaving minutes apart to space them out on the main road. From there, they would disperse and travel on side roads as well to better hide their numbers. Regardless, there was no turning back. Within the hour, the entire army had left the safety of the hidden refuge and were now totally exposed on the road.

The dojo was eerily quiet as only a few people had stayed behind to ensure the animals and crops were cared for, a grievous reminder of what was at stake when the battle would begin. With that in mind, the leaders gathered for one last conversation in the now empty courtyard with Taekori and Scar.

"You five have done a remarkable job recruiting and training these people to fight Hasegawa's evil," Taekori smiled. "I couldn't be prouder of what you have accomplished. For what it's worth, I would give nearly anything to fight alongside you in Kamakura. If it weren't for this injury, I would be joining you. But I know that in my present condition, I would only be a hindrance and a distraction. I have asked Scar to remain behind as well, much to his objections. He too has seen enough war and has survived more battlefields than the rest of us have endured combined. He has earned a peaceful death."

"Should the worst happen," Sheng said sternly, "know that we who die do so with great honor, fighting for what is right."

"Those who die will do so with great honor, of this I'm certain," Taekori continued, "but I do not believe that you will be lost in this battle – none of you. Last night I had a vision. I will not tell you what I saw for your destiny is your own to discover, just know that my dream has given me a hope for the future, both yours and for all of Japan. Now go! You must begin your journey to war."

Spring rains greeted Sheng and his companions as they trotted along the increasingly muddy road to Kamakura. The hoods on their robes did little to shield them in the torrent and the dampness was accompanied by the last chills of winter, the air crisp, the wind biting. Even so, they pressed on.

Along the way, the caught up with their soldiers who trudged along in the muck in small, unassuming companies. In these moments, the band of leaders shared words of encouragement to drive their army forward in steadfast resolution. But the road was surely difficult and morale was easily threatened.

Thankfully, they met no opposition on the road. Their strength could be saved for the real conflict instead of wasted on small skirmishes. The closer they came to Kamakura they began to realize that the torrential rains had been a blessing in disguise. Near the city, the roads were used as trade routes, but the merchants and guards who typically travelled them were reluctant to do so in the weather. Fewer passersby on the road meant less likelihood of being exposed and the longer the arrival of an army could remain concealed. So fortunate were they that when they arrived on horseback to the outer parts of Kamakura, a half-day ahead of their warriors, the entrances into the harbor and outer market were unguarded. Sheng and his friends slipped through the docks unnoticed and began setting up the decrepit storehouse-turned-base for the staggered arrival of their people. By late that evening, they were ready. Some of their army would certainly push through the night, but they expected the majority to camp, sleep for a time, and return to the road before daybreak. This was evident by the slow stream of their people starting around midnight.

The next morning, a third of the samurai had arrived at the makeshift base. The rest of the day was used for rest and preparation. As the hours passed, the warehouse became more and more crowded. Even so, they were collectively careful and managed to avoid drawing any attention to their staging site. By dawn of the next day, not only had all of the rebel forces arrived safely, but Usagi and her ninja warriors had come as well, just as promised and completely undetected under the cover of night.

The floor of the warehouse was a sight to behold. Sheng had hoped they would make it this far, but now, seeing all these people who pledged their lives to fight against Hasegawa, he could hardly hide his excitement.

If only father and Scar could see this! he thought.

Usagi's ninja fit right in with the samurai who marched on Kamakura. Together, they ate, laughed, sparred, and readied for war. The mood was light even under the crushing weight of what would follow that very night. And in the midst of it all, Sheng was proud of all that these people had accomplished in such a short time.

"What's on your mind?" Kimiko asked, stepping up alongside Sheng and taking hold of his hand, their fingers entwined.

"A little bit of everything," he sighed. "I have so many emotions about the coming war…my feelings all seem appropriate and yet at odds with one another. Does that make sense?"

"It does," she smiled.

"Usagi is impressive, as are her girls. I can see why you followed her all those years."

"The thieves guild – Usagi – saved my life," Kimiko replied. "She's actually a lot like you. She is fiercely loyal to the ones she loves and she is one of the most stubborn people I have ever encountered, but stubborn in a good way, you know? She would gladly die if it meant just one more orphan would survive."

Sheng nodded, "I've been very impressed by her ninja. They are honestly not what I expected."

"Really?!" Kimiko laughed. "And what were you expecting?"

"Well, they are trained thieves…"

"But I'm one of them," she reminded teasingly.

"I know. You are the only reason I gave them a chance. But I have found that her girls are honorable and respectful. I am pleased to say the least."

"They will not let you down," Kimiko assured.

"I'm certain they won't," Sheng agreed. "I wasn't expecting Usagi herself to accompany her fighters."

"Like I said, she is fiercely loyal. She would never ask any of us to risk our own lives in an endeavor such as this without also putting her life on the line. Our sacrifice is her sacrifice: that is her way. I only wish Asami could have come along as well, but the youngest girls in the guild could not be left on their own."

"That is the sign of a true leader and Usagi is a welcome addition as we face this ever-growing threat. And Asami, she is doing her duty as well. There is great honor in that."

Sheng and Kimiko, still hand-in-hand, continued watching the fellowship between the two groups as they came together. This was the beauty of hope, Sheng realized: two peoples of very different backgrounds, experiences, and beliefs united against a danger that threatens all in its path. Hope.

The hour had grown late and the sun was beginning to set. "I believe the time has come," Tatsuo said as he joined them, patting Sheng confidently on the shoulder as he spoke.

"Right," Sheng replied. "I'll address our warriors."

He squeezed Kimiko's hand tightly as he left her side and headed into the center of the large, open room. What was left of the sun's last light filtered into the warehouse through the large holes in its rotting ceiling. Soon they would need torches to see. But the light that remained was enough and a hush fell over the crowd of anxious fighters as the young man they looked to as their leader stepped forth.

"My friends," he began, "I want to thank you all for being here at this time. We gather beneath the shadow of a looming menace, a peril that threatens all of Japan yet is unspoken, unbeknownst to the people who dwell within its very presence. What we accomplish tonight may never be remembered beyond our generation, may never be recorded in history, yet we will face this evil all the same. We fight for our families. We fight for our villages. We fight for the loved ones we've lost. We fight for the future. Wear your armor proudly and ready your weapons, but fear not. Tonight we fight for Japan!"

With those words, a unified roar erupted within the abandoned storehouse. As Tatsuo had said, the time had come.

"What whispers does the night bring?" Master Hasegawa asked aloud. He stood in his study, staring out the window at the dojo grounds below. His swollen, stitched face was hidden beneath the crudely reconstructed mask, his body shrouded within a flowing, jet black robe, its hood pulled up over his head as his eyes glowed white within its shadow.

The spirits answered him, their voices carried on the wind. "Your life is in danger," they warned in sighing breaths. "The one named Sheng has returned to Kamakura."

"What?!" Hasegawa laughed loudly. "I have nothing to fear from that man. Rather, he is not much more than a boy, a nuisance at best."

"But he scarred your face?" the wind replied.

"Nothing but luck!" he growled.

"Even so, he comes for you."

Takeshi Hasegawa's white, ghostly eyes narrowed as he considered the threat. "Then let him come," he grinned in arrogance.

Sheng ordered the lanterns that glowed within the warehouse be extinguished as Kimiko and Hayami scouted the immediate area for any sign that their plan had been compromised. They returned with an assurance that the city was sleeping and the patrolling guards were few and far between.

"It's now or never," Sheng nodded, his eyes fixed on Daisuke and Tatsuo. "Start sending them out. Direct the samurai to remain as quiet as possible. Vigilance is their ally. They must sweep the city, eliminate the patrols, and take control of the prison armory. Kimiko and Hayami – as planned, the two of you as well as Usagi will head for the secret tunnel into the dojo. I have prepared this map. Take it and find the way. Once inside, wait for us to make our move. We'll surrender and when Master Hasegawa comes to face us, we'll attack. That will be your signal to strike. Eliminate his guards first, then we see where things go."

"And what about the other sensei there at the dojo?" Kimiko asked. "Suppose they don't go along with you and they side with Hasegawa; what would you have us do?"

"If they choose that path, then so be it. We fight them too," Sheng replied. "But I don't see that happening. Surely they will turn against him."

"So that's it then?" Tatsuo smirked. "We're actually going to surrender?"

"We are," Sheng confirmed. "But do not let the guards take your weapons. We must be ready to fight."

"And if the guards refuse and try to take them by force?" Suke-chan chimed in.

"We deal with them quickly and move to the courtyard ourselves," Sheng answered. "Our main objective is to get Hasegawa out of his private wing of the dojo and into the garden."

"Then that is that," Tatsuo sighed.

The doors to the warehouse were opened and the samurai dispersed in silence, marching along in their armor, swords drawn as they began the search for Hasegawa's guards throughout the city. Sheng and Daisuke wished Kimiko and Hayami luck, sending them on their way with hopeful kisses. Usagi followed along at Kimiko's side as the ninja blended into the shadows and disappeared from sight.

"Well here we are," Daisuke observed sheepishly. For a moment, Sheng's mind had wandered and he was taken back to his childhood, seeing not the stout, strong warrior Daisuke in front of him, but the young and round Suke-chan of their youth. "We've been through a lot, you and I," Sheng heard the boy say. "We're back in Kamakura, back to where this all began all those years ago. You've been my best friend since before I can remember and I'm proud to think of you as my brother. Whatever happens tonight, know that I love you, Sheng. I seriously do!"

Sheng's eyes welled up as the memory of the boy faded and the man stood once again before him. He threw his arms around Daisuke and the two friends embraced joyously, giving little concern for what might come.

In a way, they both believed that their destinies had brought them to this point, that they were meant to be in Kamakura at this precise time and for this exact purpose. Perhaps fate had not dealt them this life, but that it had guided them, molded them, so that when the time was right, their goodness could bring balance to Hasegawa's evil. Regardless, they embraced, sharing in a brotherhood that no one could fathom. Through all the adversity that had come their way, all the struggles, questions, and death, they had remembered the guidance of their parents and had grown into men of honor and integrity, even if at times compromised by a loyalty to a man who they knew little of and yet still trusted as right and true. But Hasegawa's deceit was now well known and never again would they tolerate his wickedness. Indeed the time had come.

The two men pulled Tatsuo into their embrace before they set out in defiance. After all, if it weren't for him Sheng and Daisuke may have never arrived at this junction. Their destinies were all intertwined. Now encouraged and certain, Sheng took hold of the mysterious blade and slung it across his back, his trusted katana at his side. Together, the three friends left the secrecy of the empty warehouse behind and set out into darkness.

26

DEMONS & DESTINY

The first, sudden cries of panic rang out as rebel samurai swarmed through the streets. As hoped, Hasegawa's guards were caught off guard and struck down, the samurai leaving a bloody trail in their wake. So thorough and ruthless were they that even as patrols became alerted to a disturbance, only one bell had been sounded in warning, the unfortunate man who managed to raise the alarm slaughtered shortly after. The only true opposition was at the prison where fortified guards dug in as long as they could, though greatly outnumbered. Even so, some of the rebels fell in the bloody battle, their lives given in defiance to Hasegawa's thirst for power.

The ninja had slipped through the city unnoticed and had discovered the secret entrance to the dojo just as Sheng had illustrated on the map. They traversed the darkness and found themselves inside the grounds, exiting from beneath the dojo temple. Kimiko, Hayami, and Usagi thought it best to separate and the group divided into thirds, taking up positions and spreading out across the garden, silencing any guards they happened upon.

Just as planned, Sheng, Daisuke, and Tatsuo walked right up to the main gate of the dojo where they were met by armed men, men they recognized as longtime members of Hasegawa's personal guard. The men recognized the three friends as well, knowing Sheng and Daisuke as masters there at the dojo.

"Master Yamashita, Master Suzuki," the head guard called out from above the barred gate, "Master Hasegawa has given strict orders to kill you on sight. I apologize, but that is his command."

"So you then will be the one to execute us, guardsman?" Tatsuo shouted back.

"I would prefer not to," he replied. "Please, just leave and I will not report that I saw you here."

"We can't do that," Sheng answered. "We have come for Hasegawa. Only he need answer for his crimes. Let us pass and you will be spared."

"Please, Master Yamashita," the guard pleaded, "I do not wish to disobey the master of the dojo, nor do I wish to fight you. Heed my warning and leave before I have no choice."

Daisuke countered this time, "Like Sheng said, we can't do that."

The guard looked around reluctantly as if he was deeply debating the options in his head. "What will you do with Master Hasegawa? Do you plot to kill him?"

"If I say *yes* will you let us in?" Sheng questioned.

Again, the guard clearly deliberated, this time whispering back and forth with another person who was just out of sight. With no more banter, the three friends heard the familiar sound of the bars being lifted from the gate and the heavy doors swung open to allow them entry. The path however was not clear. A dozen armed men stood inside of the corridor that led to the courtyard.

"Where is the guard who we've been speaking with?" Sheng demanded to know, the men they faced staring them down and threatening with drawn swords.

One of the aggressors tossed something their way, the bloody object hitting the floor hard before rolling to a stop at their feet. The three samurai looked down angrily, now recognizing what it was: the severed head of the guard.

"What's this all about?" Tatsuo barked. "I thought he was granting us passage?!"

"He refused a direct order from the master of the dojo," one of the guards replied. "Master Hasegawa is more powerful than you realize. We'll all gladly take our chances with you than stand against him any day!"

With that, the guards lunged forward, their swords raised to strike. Sheng and his companions quickly countered the men's attacks, leaving the walls in the hallway spattered in blood, their bodies littering the floor in red-stained heaps.

"So much for an alliance," Daisuke said as they sheathed their katana and carefully made their way past the bodies, then out into the courtyard.

The moon glowed brightly in the night sky, the gardens awash in its white light. Many students had been awoken by the commotion and could be seen peering in sleepy confusion from the windows of the dormitories. The masters, too, were awake, rushing out to the courtyard to see what was going on.

"Sheng?! Daisuke?!" a familiar voice cried. It was Master Kinshi. "And Tatsuo, my boy...is that really you? After all these years! What are you doing here? Master Hasegawa has been furious with you. Why, we don't know, but it started after you never returned from Kyoto. We had no idea what happened to you. We all feared you might even be dead!"

"Master Kinshi," Sheng replied with a bow, "we never returned because we learned the truth concerning Takeshi Hasegawa and his plot to take power for himself. Unknowingly, we went to Kyoto as ambassadors. Only upon arriving did we learn that he had other plans. He meant for us to kill the emperor! Hasegawa sent us as assassins, not peaceful emissaries!"

"That's not true," Master Kinshi said in disbelief. "Hasegawa would never ask such a thing of you."

"Oh no?" came the reply from behind them.

"Master Wong," Suke-chan grinned.

"Hello, my friends," Wong continued. "I have known Hasegawa longer than the lot of you have lived combined. Never have I seen him like this. Master Kinshi, you must see this. I know you agree. Hasegawa has become a danger to himself and to this institution."

"Is that so?!" a booming voice echoed from within the encircling crowd that had now gathered. Nearly everyone in the dojo had heard what was happening as the rumor spread quickly: Sheng and Daisuke had returned, and they had come for Master Hasegawa! Teachers, students, and servants alike; all came to witness the chaos.

"Face us, Hasegawa," Sheng shouted.

"Certainly," he replied, stepping from amongst the circle to meet his most accomplished student face-to-face. Master Hasegawa stood before them, his hood still raised, the mask upon his face. "I've been waiting for this moment for quite some time. You failed me in Kyoto. I thought you were loyal, that you wanted what was best for Japan. Instead, you sided with a defunct system enslaved to tradition. This is bigger than us, Sheng. No matter what happens this night, it doesn't end here. There is a reckoning coming and there is nothing either of us can do to stop that. All we can hope is that we can take power first and lead our people to greatness. No more emperor, no more shogunate, real freedom. And you can do this with me, Sheng. You can stand at my side. Join me, Sheng."

"I made that mistake once," Sheng growled, "and I'll never make it again. If it means my death, then so be it."

"As you wish," Hasegawa snarled. "Guards!"

There was no reply as the crowd began whispering amongst themselves, many in shock of what they were hearing. Hasegawa hadn't only lied to Sheng, he had been lying to all of them.

"*Guards!*" he shouted again.

And again, there was no answer.

"What is going on?" Hasegawa questioned, obviously perturbed. "*GUARDS!!!*"

"They're not coming to help you," Tatsuo laughed. "You have no men left to fight at your side. We have taken the city, the prison…Kamakura is no longer under your control."

"The shogun has promised me an army. They will march against you with a single word."

"But without your men, our force outnumbers the shogunate's warriors," Tatsuo taunted smugly. "Add to that the number of daimyō who support us now that we have liberated the villages you so greedily attacked

271

and you've lost all political clout. Face it, Hasegawa, you are at your end."

Master Hasegawa lowered his hood, fully revealing the stitched grin of his mask, his face beneath smiling just as wide in anticipation of the certain bloodshed that would follow. "It sounds as if you think I'm at a disadvantage. But even without an army, you two are no match for me."

"Two?" Tatsuo laughed. "Have you become so crazy that you can no longer count?"

"No, Tatsuo, your arrogance has moved my hand," Hasegawa replied, presenting his sword and swinging the glinting steel faster than any of them could react, cutting Tatsuo down in the blink of an eye.

Tatsuo lay on the ground gasping, the precision of Hasegawa's unexpected strike leaving him only breaths away from death. The blade had sliced him from throat to naval, blood spilling out in spite of his armor. A gurgle marked the end of his life, his eyes still open, staring blankly up at Sheng and Daisuke.

"What a shame," Master Hasegawa mocked, watching sticky blood drip from the blade of his sword. "Who's next?"

Sheng's anger nearly pushed him over the edge. All he wanted to do was kill this man – gut him, slash him, slice him, it didn't matter how, just so long as he died.

Kimiko took this horrific event to be her signal and the three groups of ninja emerged from their hiding places quickly surrounding the circle in a show of decisive numbers. The rebels clearly had the upper hand.

"You will pay for Tatsuo's murder," Sheng spat angrily. "You can end this without any more blood. Just surrender and do what is honorable."

"Have you really not figured this out yet," Hasegawa chided. "No matter what you do, it will never be enough. You cannot kill me. I have powers you can never comprehend. You and your pathetic band of friends can never come between me and my destiny. I will rule Japan, and if I have to kill every single one of you along the way, then so be it. This is your last chance, Sheng. Join me or die."

"Never."

"Then the blood of all these people is on your hands." Hasegawa stretched out his arms at his sides and took a deep breath, then threw his head back and screeched a terrible scream. Black wisps erupted from his mouth.

Sheng and company looked on curiously, many in the crowd terrified. The youngest students covered their ears from the shrillness of his cry. The wisps floated through the air like smoke, each swirling mist singling out a master from the dojo before forcing its way up their nostrils. Their reactions were violent, the pain causing their arms to flail as they shook viciously. Then, just as strangely as it began, it stopped, leaving the masters slack jawed and staring, their mouths hanging agape, their eyes shiny and black.

"I've never seen anything like this," Sheng admitted, fear creeping into his head. "This is impossible!"

"Is it, young Sheng?" Hasegawa laughed menacingly. "My fellow masters, *attack*."

This was it. This was the fight that Sheng had anticipated, but in no way lose to how he had imagined. What had happened was uncertain, all he could reason was that this was the realm of the supernatural, of oni and yōkai, the stories of old Master Shou from his childhood. The masters moved with speed and fury that neither Sheng nor Daisuke had ever witnessed in all their time at the dojo. Even without weapons, their unarmed attacks were brutal, their strength inhuman.

"Try not to kill them. They are innocent in this," Sheng warned.

But that was easier said than done as the masters were tireless, their attacks only growing stronger and faster as they fought. The ninja sprang into action and countered bravely, hoping to sway the odds in their favor through quick, unified strikes. Still, the masters seemed unstoppable, dodging two, three, even four attacks at once. How was this possible?!

In the midst of this, Hasegawa had begun dashing through the battle, slicing his way between the clusters of fighting. Slowly the ranks of ninja began to dwindle as his strikes killed more and more of Usagi's girls. For whatever reason, Sheng had focused on fighting off the masters and had unintentionally ignored the greater threat, falling for Hasegawa's distraction rather than facing him directly. At a glance, Sheng counted at least eight dead ninja, noting that Kimiko, Hayami, and Daisuke were all still alive...for now.

Sheng rightfully turned his attention to Hasegawa, drawing his sword from his side and going directly after the man in the mask. "Enough tricks," he derided his old sensei. "Face me!"

Hasegawa struck out, killing another of Usagi's girls. Sheng waited no longer, he realized he couldn't. Hasegawa wasn't going to fight fair. The next swipe of Hasegawa's blade was countered by Sheng's katana, sparing Usagi who never saw the strike coming. Now Sheng had Hasegawa's attention. The two faced off in the midst of the chaos that engulfed them.

Sheng would strike and Hasegawa would deflect the attack, then Hasegawa would counter and Sheng would parry. This went on and on, the two foes locked in a battle that transcended the mortal and symbolized the very essence of the moral. This was not man versus man, student versus master. This was good versus evil as the two opposites matched blows over and again. Several times, Shengs blade evaded his opponents block and cut through Hasegawa's robes, yet the attacks left no wounds. On the other hand, Sheng was bleeding from multiple cuts on his arms and thighs, though none were life-threatening. If he wasn't careful, before long, one of Hasegawa's strikes would prove fatal.

Daisuke saw that Sheng had broken off from the larger group and was now fighting Hasegawa alone. He quickly threw himself headlong into the battle and staggered their old master simply with the unexpected and devastating impact of three hundred pounds wrapped in armor. But Hasegawa righted himself and was back in the fight without missing a step. They friends now had two swords to his one. Even so, the battle never seemed to shift in their favor. As hard as they tried, Hasegawa was always just that much better.

"Is this the best you can do?" he mocked, laughing easily as the two samurai struggled to catch their breath.

With his foes weakening, Hasegawa saw an opportunity and acted quickly. He reached into a pouch hidden beneath his robe and produced a small, black and round object, then held it high and slammed it hard against the bloodied ground. In a bright explosion, a ring of fire erupted forth, encircling Sheng and Hasegawa and separating them from everyone else, the flames licking higher and higher. Sheng could hear Suke-chan's shouts from beyond the wall of fire, but the heat was too intense to cross through. Hasegawa had the advantage.

"Do you see now?" Hasegawa asked arrogantly. "Do you now understand that no matter what you do, you cannot stop me? Tell me you know this!"

"You're right," Sheng replied. " I am no match for you. Whatever has happened to you has made you stronger and faster than I will ever be. I understand that. I don't know how, but it has happened."

Hasegawa walked along the blazing wall, running his hand through the fire, the flames dancing between his fingers. He remained unburnt, even his clothing withstood the scorching heat. "I have discovered what true power is and now no one can stand in my way."

Sheng watched Hasegawa's psychotic display of inexplicable invulnerability. Reluctantly, he tossed his sword on the ground knowing full well that he was at his sensei's mercy.

"That's it then?" Hasegawa mused. "I'll give you one last chance, but this is it, no more. My grace is all but gone. Join me and I will make you the greatest warrior Japan has ever known. And you can serve at my side with all the wealth and power you can ever imagine. Join me and *really* live."

"If that is all you have to offer me, then I choose death," Sheng replied calmly. "What you offer is not life, for what is life without love, without peace?"

"With the money and power I can give you, Sheng, you can buy all the love you want!"

"That isn't love, Master, and death would be a welcome reprieve from such a life."

"Then you choose *death*?"

"I do," Sheng said.

"Then we will end this now," Hasegawa grinned sadistically, his head cocked to the side as he readied his sword.

The monster of a man let out a cry as he raced forward, his katana raised high ready to strike down the son of his former ally who had betrayed him. In his mind, Hasegawa pictured Taekori, the face only fading back to Sheng's as he felt the sudden and impossible twinge of pain; a pain that began in his chest and seared through his insides as the razor-sharp tip of the mysterious blade burst forth out his back.

In his fervor to strike Sheng down, Hasegawa's pride had become his weakness. Sheng had goaded him into attacking, only to strike before Hasegawa could. Never while dueling would Hasegawa have raised his sword so high for a certain victory blow; no, he would have protected his core. But unarmed, Sheng seemed certain to die and so Hasegawa threw caution to the wind. Sheng had used this to his advantage.

Hasegawa dropped his sword as his legs went limp beneath him, landing on his knees as he went into shock. "How can this be?" he mumbled in disbelief. "This isn't how this ends!"

Sheng removed the sword from Hasegawa's chest, the once silver blade now strangely blackened by the blood of his enemy. "Take off your mask, Hasegawa. I want to look you in the eyes."

"I...I can't," Hasegawa wheezed. "Please take it off for me."

Hesitantly, Sheng reached out and took hold of a spot of cloth on top of Hasegawa's head. As he did, Hasegawa suddenly reached out and clasped his hands tightly around Sheng's wrists. Even mortally wounded, Hasegawa was still inhumanly strong. Sheng pulled back with all is might. He broke Hasegawa's grip and tumbled backwards to the ground, the mask slipping easily from Hasegawa's head. Sheng looked upon the face of his enemy, a face he'd known since he was only a boy. He studied the stitches that stretched from each end of Hasegawa's mouth in an attempt to mend what damage the mysterious blade had done.

Now, without the power of the mask, Takeshi Hasegawa was fading fast – no supernatural power to stay his bleeding. Hasegawa's eyes were open, but barely, and his brow furrowed from the pain as Sheng noticed tears in his sensei's eyes. In a way, Sheng pitied the man.

"Please," Hasegawa gasped, the blood in his lungs gurgling with each labored breath, "end my suffering, Sheng. Show me mercy."

Sheng looked down at the mask he clutched in his left hand and the mysterious blade he gripped in his right. "Do you see what you have done?" Sheng asked softly. "All the evil that you would have caused if you succeeded? Certainly you see the madness of it now, at the end of your life. You wouldn't have saved Japan, you would have destroyed it."

Hasegawa collapsed from where he'd sat propped up on his knees, now laying on his side in the red pool that flowed from his body, his horrid face pressing into the dirt as the encircling flames reflected in his eyes. As hard as he tried, he could not muster the strength for a response, his breaths now slow and shallow. Blood trickled from the corner of his mouth as he whispered words too soft for Sheng to discern. Hasegawa coughed up more blood and sighed one last breath, his eyes never breaking from

Sheng's. The great Master Takeshi Hasegawa was dead.

Immediately, the flames subsided and the masters of the dojo became ruefully aware of their surroundings, the blackness draining from their eyes as they looked upon the bodies strewn about the courtyard. What an awful sight to behold and such a dire contrast to the beauty of the tranquil, moonlit garden.

The mood was somber in the early morning hours as those who survived Hasegawa's final onslaught lamented the fallen. Sheng sent word to the samurai spread throughout the city requesting they bring their dead brothers to the serenity within the dojo's walls. The girls tearfully unwrapped each face of their fallen thieves guild sisters, mourning each loss as they went along. Sheng knelt at Tatsuo's side, joined by Daisuke. Both men were speechless as they considered the cost of their actions on this night, knowing full well that either of them could be laying in his place. In the midst of all this sadness, there was Hasegawa, lifeless and forgotten as the world moved on without him.

EPILOGUE
THE LEGEND OF THE BLADE

"Months passed, then years. Immediately following the battle in Kamakura, Sheng and Daisuke thought it best to hand complete control of the dojo over to the masters who remained. It is believed their only caveat was that the dojo teach not only the martial arts and military science to the *bushi,* that is to say warrior class; but also, as a school, open their doors to those who could not afford a *then modern* education consisting of learned wisdoms gleaned from all throughout Asia; including Confucianism, waka poetry, and traditional art, for example. It should be of no surprise to learn that Sheng and Kimiko married. Together, they relocated along with Daisuke and Hayami to the place of Taekori's birth and the traditional territory of the Shimazu in the Satsuma Province at the southernmost tip of the island of Kyūshū. There they started new lives, raising children, who in turn had children of their own, and so on. It is from Satsuma that we trace our family lineage.

"Of course you'll never read this account in the history books. The name of Takeshi Hasegawa was forgotten, as was his evil, and overshadowed only a few decades later in the year 1333 when former emperor Go-Daigo moved to reclaim his title having been banished following the Genkō War. He was aided by the infamous samurai warrior Ashikaga Takauji who had been sent to Kyoto to kill him only two years earlier, but instead, Takauji turned his back on the shogunate and helped Go-Daigo capture Kyoto and reclaim the imperial throne. At the same time, their ally, Nitta Yoshisada, laid siege to Kamakura and successfully defeated the Hōjō clan. This marked both the end of the Kamakura period in Japan, but also the end of the Hōjō regency. The regents, along with hundreds of their samurai, committed suicide after the fall of the Kamakura Shogunate. Together, Go-Daigo, Kusunoki Masashige, Ashikaga Takauji, and Nitta Yoshisada accomplished what Takeshi Hasegawa could not, seizing total power of both the imperial and military leadership of Japan. However this was relatively short lived as war was a way of life in medieval Japan and leadership changed often through the rule of feudal law. Very fascinating stuff…"

"It's the most incredible thing I've ever heard, grandfather," a young man replied excitedly, leaning against the back of the sofa on which he sat. "Why have you never told me this story before?"

"You were never old enough before, Hiro," his grandfather laughed, round-rimmed glasses resting on the bridge of his nose. "You are now precisely the same age as your ancestor, Yamashita Sheng. His story is complicated and violent, inappropriate for a child. I believe now was the right time for you to learn this important part of your past."

"It's an unbelievable legend, grandfather," Hiro replied.

"As are all stories that begin in truth and end in myth, and Japan has no shortage of legends," the old man winked.

Hiro continued flipping through the large, leather-bound journal that his grandfather had laid out on the coffee table in front of them. The pages, many yellowed and brittle with age, bore their family's stories and history, a genealogy of sorts but with a touch of the mystical, as well as maps and historical detailings. There were also hand-drawn illustrations and etchings throughout. Hiro paused a while on one image in particular: a sketch imagining both Taekori and Sheng in full samurai armor, a Shimazu clan circled-cross banner draped behind them.

"Is this what Sheng and his father actually looked like," he asked.

"Perhaps," the grandfather smirked. "That illustration is hundreds of years old, yet its subjects lived still hundreds of years before the portrait was made."

"I wish I knew for sure," Hiro laughed. "It's funny, but doesn't Sheng kind of look like me?!"

"The resemblance is certainly there," the old man smiled, joining in his grandson's laughter.

"If only the legend were true," Hiro lamented as he closed the heavy book and took a sip of hot tea from his mug.

"You still don't believe?" his grandfather asked.

"I don't know. It's just too fantastic; I mean...yōkai aren't real, oni aren't real, right? Ghosts and demons are just stories told to scare little children and plot devices in bad horror movies, aren't they?"

The senior Yamashita turned his attention away from their conversation, his gaze falling somewhere beyond. He seemed to ignore the very walls of his home, his thoughts searching far beyond the restraining structure of logic. "You must close your eyes and open your mind, young Hiro. Come with me. I'd like to show you something."

Slowly and with great effort, the thin, frail grandfather stood, using a cane as he hobbled across the modernly furnished living room and out through a glass-paned door that led to his patio. Hiro followed, stepping out into the beauty of the warm, sunny summer day. They stood together in the narrow, quant garden, all the space that a dwelling in Tokyo could afford. The sounds of the city roared all around them, yet this small oasis in the midst of steel and brick offered peace all the same. In the very center of the garden was a delicate cherry blossom tree, its branches thin and fragile-looking, its trunk crooked and twisted, yet its flowers were full and aromatic. The tree was a certain sight to behold, stretching up towards the light even as the surrounding buildings towered high above.

"I have always marveled at this tree, grandfather," Hiro mused. "The fact that it grows is a legend all its own."

"I'm glad you like it," Grandfather replied. "It's time I formally introduced the two of you. Hiro, I'd like you to meet your ancestor – *Amikori*."

"No way!"

"Indeed," the old man laughed. "When I was about your age, my father told me this same story and, just like you, I didn't believe at first. This was shortly after the Second World War mind you and I was still living in the United States. My father and mother had moved to Los Angeles from Kagoshima when I was just an infant and had started a grocery store. As soon has the political stresses of the war had settled, I decided to travel. I hand copied notes and places from the journal. I charted Sheng's movements as best as I could based on the included maps. When I returned to Japan, my plan was to debunk the legend. But what I truly found was only more questions that needed answered. I began in Kamakura, searching for the dojo, but there were no records of such a place and no ruins left to explore. Perhaps the dojo was destroyed in 1333 when the shogunate fell? Perhaps it never existed at all? From there, I travelled to Kyoto. The court and temples are somewhat different now from their descriptions in the journal, yet that should be expected with the passing of time, I suppose. The last part of quest took me to the woods between Kyoto and Fuji-san. I backpacked along old roads. Eventually, with a little direction from locals and an immense amount of luck, I discovered the overgrown ruins of a long-forgotten temple buried deep in the forest. From what I could reconstruct in my mind, the layout was very much as described in the journal. And what's more, call it luck or fate or destiny, I found a solitary cherry tree in full blossom, though the trees around it had long-since withered. A shrine marker stood next to it. I could hardly believe what I was seeing, and what's more, what I was reading. Though the stone marker was well-weathered, amongst the illegible words, a single name could be recognized: *Amikori*. I harvested some blossoms, one of which you saw dried in the pages of the journal. I also gathered seeds from the ancient *sakura*. It shouldn't have been there, no scientific explanation for that tree to still grow. After all, it is why the cherry blossom has become a tradition for our people, a reminder that all life is fleeting – here for a time and then gone. I ended my journey by searching Fuji-san for any sign of the cave where Taekori had made his home, but there was no evidence to be found, perhaps the mountain itself chose to hide the secret forever, the cave disappearing after Fuji-san's last major eruption over three hundred years ago. Regardless, I returned to Los Angeles in 1955 with a pocketful of seeds and a head full of questions. Much like you must feel at the present, Hiro."

"It's just so much to try and understand all at once, grandfather. This tree in and of itself is a miracle!"

"A miracle indeed," the old man winked. "Most sakura only blossom for a few weeks at best, and usually in April or May, but Amikori blooms for most of the spring and even now, in July."

"If you found the temple and Amikori's tree, what happened to the mysterious sword that Taekori entrusted to Sheng? And the mask worn by Takeshi Hasegawa, what happened to the mask?"

"I'm glad you asked, Hiro. The sword is actually the reason I decided that the time had come to tell you the legend in the first place. During the Second World War, my family was forced into an internment camp in the spring of 1942. My father told me it was because we were considered *issei* – first generation immigrants born in Japan and ineligible for U.S. citizenship under the laws in that day. We weren't allowed to return to Los Angeles till '46; and when we did, our home had been ransacked and vandalized."

"That's ridiculous!"

"That's the politics of fear," his grandfather continued. "To that point, our family still guarded the secret of the mysterious blade. My father had hidden the black-bladed sword extremely well within a secret panel in our living room wall, in front of which stood a heavy bookshelf. We returned to find the books strewn about the floor and the shelf toppled. The plaster had been torn down off the wall, the slats splintered, broken, and marred with axe marks. The sword itself was gone."

"And the mask of Takeshi Hasegawa?" Hiro worried.

"The mask was hidden along with the sword, both items carefully wrapped together in a black, satin shroud."

"So what happened to the sword after that, grandfather? Where did it go? Did you ever try to find it?"

"I wanted to search for it, yes. In my youthful anger, I wished to tear the whole city apart if I had to just to find the blade, but no one would listen to us. The police didn't care that our home had been ransacked. Why would they then care that we had been robbed as well? After all, Americans never understood the significance of our swords. Look at how many were confiscated or surrendered during the war and then kept by the soldiers as prizes – or worse – destroyed?"

Hiro shook his head sadly, fully aware of the disrespect the Japanese people, *his people*, endured during such a confusing time. "War makes men do terrible things," he replied solemnly.

"A few years ago, a friend of mine…a *business associate* you might say…told me a story about a fantastic, ancient katana he saw on display in the private collection of a man in America," Hiro's grandfather continued. "He told me that he attended a meeting with this *collector* in the office of his towering building in New York City. The man's office itself held relics worthy of the finest museum, artifacts spanning a millennia of history. He said there was pottery from ancient Greece and armor dating to the Roman Empire. There was centuries-old Ming china and relics of the Han dynasty. My friend even claimed to have seen cuneiform tablets and ancient papyrus scrolls. I cannot stress the uniqueness of this collection. And there, amongst the artifacts, was a curious katana blade, its blade as black as night though its craftsmanship appeared simple with little ornamentation. The sword seemed out of place considering how impressive the rest of the collection. Why not a sword from a well-known master like Masamune? He asked the business man who gave no reply."

"Why are you telling me this, grandfather?"

"Because, Hiro my boy, I want you to go find the sword and bring it back to me," he explained. "I am too old to attempt such a thing now and I want nothing more than to see the katana one last time. My last wish is to have the blade returned to its rightful place: in the stewardship of the Yamashita family."

"And where do you suggest I begin?"

"Go to New York City. Seek the collector. He goes by the name of *Triton*."

The End

It is with the utmost respect for Japan, her people, and their culture that I framed The Legend of the Blade. My hope is that this book inspires you to further discover the richness of Japan's history during the Kamakura period – a complicated time rife with both war and beauty. Japanese terms and language are used throughout the book. I encourage you to look up these words and further your knowledge.

As with any story set within a historical period, much study was required to understand the practices and customs of that age as well as the context in which the characters would live and interact. Countless hours were spent reading, discovering, and comparing the records relating to the Kamakura period, samurai, and Japanese history. I'd like to thank the editors of the following Wikipedia pages regarding the history of Japan:

(https://en.wikipedia.org/wiki/History_of_Japan)

(https://en.wikipedia.org/wiki/Kamakura_period)

(https://en.wikipedia.org/wiki/Kamakura_shogunate), and the associated links.

The following are also good links if you want to learn more about samurai and their role in Japanese history:

http://www.history.com/topics/samurai-and-bushido

http://www.japan-guide.com/e/e2127.html

http://afe.easia.columbia.edu/special/japan_1000ce_samurai.htm,

https://www.tofugu.com/japan/ancient-japanese-weapons/

http://www.pbs.org/wgbh/nova/ancient/history-of-the-samurai.html

http://www.ushistory.org/civ/10c.asp

Thank you for exploring the beauty, mystery, and intrigue of feudal Japan along with me. I truly hope you enjoyed reading my novel, *The Legend of the Blade.*